"Charles Sheffield has produced another outstanding novel—vivid characterization, realistic high-tech background, and rapidly moving action. Opening a Sheffield book is like switching on a mind link." —Robert L. Forward, author of *Dragon's Egg*

"Charles is one of those SF writers who makes the rest of us think seriously about a career in retail sales. In fact the only reason we allow him to live is that we are all SF *readers* too. He has the scientific grounding of a Clarke, the storytelling skills of a Heinlein, the dry wit of a Pohl or a Kornbluth, and the universe-building prowess of a Niven—and he may have a better take on the psychology of space-born humans than anyone else in the field."—Spider Robinson

# THE NIMROD HUNT

# CHARLES SHEFFIELD

BAEN
SCIENCE FICTION
BOOKS

THE NIMROD HUNT

Copyright © 1986 by Charles Sheffield

A Baen Books Original

Baen Publishing Enterprises
260 Fifth Avenue
New York, N.Y. 10001

First printing, August 1986

ISBN: 0-671-65582-5

Cover art by Melo

Printed in the United States of America

Distributed by
SIMON & SCHUSTER
TRADE PUBLISHING GROUP
1230 Avenue of the Americas
New York, N.Y. 10020

To John, Judy, and Jessica

# Prolog

# DEATH ON COBWEB STATION

The first warning was nothing more than a glimmer of light. In the array of twenty-two thousand monitors that showed the energy balance of the solar system, one miniature bulb had flicked on to register a demand overload.

To say that the signal was neglected by the crew at Vulcan Nexus would be a gross overstatement. It was never seen. The whole display array had been installed in the main control room of the Nexus mainly for visiting dignitaries and media: "There!"—with a wave of the hand—"The power equation for the whole System at one glance. The left side shows energy supply. Each light displays the energy collection from a solar panel. And there on the right are the demands."

A moment or two to examine the array of gently winking lamps, and the tour would go on. The most impressive part was still to come: the powered swoop past four hundred million square kilometers of collectors, each sucking in its share of Sol's radiance. With the arrays orbiting only two million kilometers above the solar photosphere, Sol's flaming disk filled thirty degrees of the sky. It was an unusual visitor who gave the display room a second thought— not after the roller-coaster ride past the solar furnace, skimming over vast hydrogen flares and the Earth-swallowing whirlpools of sunspots.

So the overload signal was not seen by the crew. But human neglect of minor energy fluctuations was no cause for concern. Supply and demand had long been monitored by an agent far more efficient and conscientious than unreliable homo sapiens. The distributed computing network of Dominus at once noted the source of the energy drain: Cobweb Station, twelve billion kilometers from the Sun. Station demand had increased by a factor of a hundred over normal use. Even as that information came back through the computer network, a second light went on in the display panel, then three more. Each light indicated a demand growth by a factor of ten. Dominus switched power supply from the solar arrays to the orbiting fusion plants out near Persephone. Reserve supply was more than adequate. There was still no fear of emergency, no thought of disaster.

And there was no reply from Cobweb Station. The inquiry was elevated in priority, and Dominus brought new data online. A communications silence from Cobweb Station for the last seven hours was noted, and correlated in turn with the pattern of energy use and the signal showing that the Mattin Link system had been activated (though not yet used for either matter or signal transmission).

Dominus flashed an alert to the control display at Ceres headquarters and scanned all probes beyond Neptune. The nearest high-acceleration needle was thirty million kilometers from Cobweb Station: twenty-two hours at a steady hundred gee.

Dominus dispatched the probe seconds before the problem first came to human attention. The technician on duty at Ceres checked the status flags, noted the time, and approved the probe use. But she did not call for a report on energy use from Cobweb Station; her mind was elsewhere, contemplating an after-work date. She was looking forward to the skirmishings that went with a new partner—always exciting, never quite predictable. Overtime to examine power fluctuation in the Outer System formed no part of her evening plans.

She knew the scope of her duties and responsibilities. Her action was consistent with them. That she would later become the first scapegoat was merely evidence of the need for scapegoats.

Meanwhile, there had come a demand for more energy. That surging rise by two orders of magnitude, plus the simultaneous multiple use of the Mattin Link transportation system, finally moved the problem to high-priority levels. Dominus signalled for an increase to maximum probe acceleration.

Probe T was less than two years old. It contained the new pan inorganica logic circuits and a full array of sensors. It had picked up Cobweb Station's image on active microwave while two hundred thousand kilometers out. The massive station showed as a scintillating grainy globe, pocked by entry ports and knobby with communications equipment. Although Probe T's data regarding its target included nothing as to station purpose or contents, it was smart enough to try all-channel signalling as soon as it was within range.

Cobweb Station held its silence. Probe T was puzzled now to see that the station's entry ports were all open to space. It shot a Mattin Link message back to Dominus, reporting the peculiarity, and approached to thirty kilometers. The high-resolution sensors were now able to pick up images of small, irregular objects floating close to the station. Probe T launched two bristle explorers, one to inspect the flotsam, the other to examine the interior of the station.

The second bristle explorer's report was made, but never sent. It did go inside Cobweb Station, as instructed, but by that time every message circuit on Probe T was occupied to capacity. A blast of emergency signals deluged Dominus through the Link, *and rarely-used indicators sprang to life on every control board from Vulcan Nexus to the Oort Harvester. The first bristle had met the debris outside Cobweb Station. Its imager revealed the bloated, frozen bodies of station guards. Still in their uniforms, weapons unsheathed, they floated gutted and stifflimbed in the endless sarcophagus of open space.*

*Throughout the solar system, alarm bells were sounding their requiem.*

# Chapter One

# MORGAN CONSTRUCTS

"LINK NETWORK COMPLETE. STAND BY FOR CONFERENCE CONNECT."

The ringing, disembodied voice sounded from all sides. In the few seconds before final Link connections were made, the Ambassador to the Stellar Group turned to the two men standing by his side in the domed hall.

"I want you to understand this situation very clearly," he said. "Although the hearing is taking place in the Star Chamber, there is currently no criminal charge at issue. This is strictly a briefing for the ambassadors. Your testimony must be as accurate and complete as possible. Understood?"

Ambassador Dougal Macdougal was a tall, imposing figure, on whom the traditional and ancient robes of office, handed down from one ambassador to the next, sat as if they had been made for him alone. His brow was noble, his chin almost too firm.

The other two men exchanged the briefest of glances, then nodded.

"Don't just bob your heads!" said Dougal Macdougal. "Say it. We need your explicit commitment, on record. We are in enough trouble already. I do not want to add to it."

"I understand perfectly," said Luther Brachis. He was a match for Macdougal in height, but massively broader. Even in the low gravity of Ceres, his booted tread shook the gold and white floor of the Star Chamber. On the left breast of his combat uniform sat a gaudy phalanx of military decorations, and the swirling Starburst of Solar Security was blazoned across his right sleeve. Eyes of washed-out blue-grey looked steadily at Dougal Macdougal. There was a momentary tightening of lips on the wide mouth, a millimeter jut to the jaw. For Luther Brachis it was equivalent to a furious outburst. "I will describe everything, and conceal nothing," he said at last.

The ambassador turned at once to the other man. "And you, Mondrian? Come on, man—say it now. The Link may be complete in a few more seconds."

Esro Mondrian looked up. He was slightly below average height. The ambassador and Luther Brachis towered over him by a full head, and in contrast to the other two men Mondrian's build was frail and angular. Unlike them, he wore the plainest of costumes. The severe black uniform of Boundary Survey, precisely tailored and meticulously clean, stood unadorned by medals or insignia of office. A single fire opal at his left collar served as identification badge—and hid its multiple functions of communicator, computer, and weapon.

Finally, Mondrian shrugged. "Steady on, Dougal. You know I'm not in the habit of concealing data from anyone who legitimately has access to them. Once we have full identification for the parties tapping into this Link I'll give them all the information that I have."

His voice was pleasant and low in volume. But Dougal Macdougal did not respond to the conciliatory tone. He was about to reply when the lights for full Mattin Link operation began to blink. He shot one annoyed glance at Esro Mondrian and turned to the sunken well of the room. In front of them, in the hemisphere of the Star Chamber's fifty-meter central atrium, three oval patterns of light were flickering into existence. Within them formed the three-dimensional images of the ambassadors.

At the far left hung a shrouded, pulsating mass of dark purple. As that image steadied, Brachis and Mondrian recognized the swarming aggregate of a Tinker Composite, imaged in from Mercantor in the Fomalhaut system. The Tinker had clustered to form a symmetrical ovoid with appendages of roughly human proportions. Next to the Tinker (but fifty-eight lightyears away from it in real space, halfway across the Stellar Group) loomed the dark green bulk of an Angel. And far to the right, still showing a margin of rainbow fringes as the signal transients were damped, hovered the great tubular assembly of a Pipe-Rilla, linked in from its home planet around Eta Cassiopeiae, eighteen lightyears away.

"MATTIN LINK NETWORK COMPLETE," said the ringing voice. "CONFERENCE MAY PROCEED."

It was an historic moment. All four representatives of the Stellar Group were in simultaneous full audio and visual contact for the first time in twenty-two Earth-years. Dougal Macdougal, conscious that the event would be part of Stellar Group history, turned his attention away from Luther Brachis and Esro Mondrian.

"Greetings. I am Dougal Macdougal, Solar Ambassador to the Stellar Group. Can you all see and hear me, and each other?"

The question was a piece of diplomatic formality. The Link computer would have confirmed full audio and visual before permitting any of the participants to enter the link. "Yes," said the Pipe-Rilla, in a fair approximation to human speech. "Yes," echoed the Tinker and the computer-generated response of the Angel ambassador.

"We have called this special Congress to discuss a . . . difficult situation," continued Macdougal. "A recent event here in the Sol system is a cause for concern, and could be a major problem affecting the whole Stellar Group. We may have to propose unusual—perhaps unprecedented—control measures. Naturally, any decision on such measures will be made by the whole Stellar Group. To describe the background to the problem, I have arranged for special briefings from two of the principals who have been involved from the beginning . . ."

Mondrian and Brachis exchanged bitter looks. "He's waffling," said Mondrian, under his breath.

"Of course he is." Brachis glared at the Solar ambassador. "He won't put the problem out on the table, he'll leave it to us to do that. The bastard! And I'll bet he's already decided where he's going to put the blame."

"First, a statement from Commander Luther Brachis," said Macdougal, almost as though he had heard that last remark. "He is the Chief of Solar System Security, and is responsible for the monitoring of all anomalous events within one lightyear of Sol." He stepped forward and took up a position next to the Pipe-Rilla, so that all the ambassadors appeared to be in line facing the witnesses. Hidden lamps framed Brachis in an oval crossfire of illuminations. "You may begin," said Macdougal.

Brachis nodded to the four shapes in their cocoons of light. His blunt lion's face was dour and angry. "The ambassador correctly stated my duties. Security is my job; from Apollo Station and the Vulcan Nexus, all the way to the Dry Tortugas

past the edge of the Oort Cloud." There was a gruff
pride in his deep voice. "I have held my position
for five standard years. Two years ago, I received a
request for a security development project on Cobweb Station. That is a research facility twelve billion kilometers from the Sun—in the ecliptic,
roughly midway between the orbits of Neptune
and Persephone. It has served as a research center
for Security activities for more than seventy standard years. The project that began there two years
ago was a secret one. It was given the code name
'Operation Morgan.' I approved the project request.
With your permission, I will defer description of
that project's objectives for Commander Mondrian's
later testimony."

Brachis smiled grimly. "Let me only say this:
Operation Morgan was conducted with tightest security. Forty of my department's most experienced
and reliable guards were assigned to the project,
and they took up residence on Cobweb Station.
Power supply came from the Solar System's general grid, controlled from the Vulcan Nexus and
from the main center here on Ceres. In two years,
no anomaly of any kind was ever noted. Progress
reports on Operation Morgan suggested excellent
results and no difficulties. Until twenty days ago.
Then an anomalous energy demand triggered a
flag in our monitoring system."

Luther Brachis paused. "That is the first part of
my testimony. Any questions?"

The four figures facing him were silent. There
was the usual faint hiss from the Mattin Link connection. The Angel was restlessly moving its upper
lobes, while Dougal Macdougal looked from side
to side. No support for Brachis would come from
the Solar ambassador. "Continue," he said at last.

"Very well. The energy requirement I referred to
came from Cobweb Station. It came at a quiet
period, near a change of shift. I am afraid that the

increased load was not noticed at first by my staff."
He spoke the words as though his mouth were full
of grit. "Even when the Link system was prepared
for action, we did not react at once. I take full
responsibility for that. When we *did* respond and
an investigating probe finally reached Cobweb Station, it was too late. The Station was deserted. The
Mattin Link had been operated—seventeen times.
All my staff were dead." He turned to look accus-
ingly at Esro Mondrian. "And I learned something
I should have explored for myself long ago: the
true nature of Operation Morgan."

He halted. His attitude said clearly that his testimony was finished, but now there was a stir
from the ranks of the ambassadors. "You . . . said
the Link was . . . activated." It was the Pipe-Rilla
ambassador, thorax plates gently vibrating. "To
what destinations?"

"We do not yet know. But the energy drain said
that it was many lightyears."

As Brachis had given his testimony, new individual components had flown silently in to add to
the Tinker Composite. Now it bulked much larger
than a human. There was a fluttering of tiny purple-
black wings, and a sibilant facsimile of human
speech came through the Link. "The records, if
you please. We would like to attempt our own
analysis of possible destinations. And to do that
we must know more about the nature of the
project."

Brachis bowed his head. "For that, I must refer
you to Commander Mondrian. My own records
will be sent to you at once. I will be available to
answer any further questions." He stepped backwards. His look at Esro Mondrian was an odd
mixture of old antagonism and new shared problems.

Mondrian had been performing his own close
inspection of the ambassadors. He knew he had no

hope of recognizing any particular assembly of a Tinker Composite; but the Angels and Pipe-Rillas both had stability of structure, and it was possible that he had met one of them before on their home worlds. In any case, he had to talk right past Dougal Macdougal and try for some kind of sympathetic response from the other ambassadors.

"I am Esro Mondrian," he began, "Chief of the Boundary Survey security forces. I have worked in the past with each of your local monitoring groups, and visited your home systems. We are all fortunate, in that we live in stable, civilized regions, where there are few unknown dangers. But most of my work lies out near the Perimeter, in the Boundary Region, fifty lightyears and more from Sol."

Mondrian heard a sound from the sunken atrium in front of him—Dougal Macdougal clearing his throat. The ambassador was already getting impatient. Mondrian swore to himself. The fact that Mondrian needed *time* to explain the reason for his recent actions meant nothing to the ambassador.

He hurried on. "On the Perimeter, distances are enormous, our resources are limited, and the operating uncertainties are large. A few years ago I decided that we needed a new type of security instrument out there. One that could function with minimal support from our home bases, and one that was tougher and more flexible in operation than the *pan inorganica* brains could provide. While we were still looking at alternatives, I was approached by a scientist, Livia Morgan. She had an intriguing proposition. She claimed she could develop symbiotic forms combining organic and inorganic components, perfect for our needs." He smiled grimly and nodded at the figures in front of him. "I knew of at least one natural example to prove to me that such a thing was possible."

The Angel in the Mattin Link connection swayed

slowly back and forwards, blue-green fronds waving. It was itself a symbiotic life-form, discovered one and a half centuries earlier when the expanding wave-front of the Perimeter had reached Capella. The visible part of the Angel was the Chasselrose, a slow-moving and mindless vegetable form. Shielded in its bulbous central section lived the sentient crystalline Singer, relying upon the Chasselrose for habitat, transportation, and communication with the external world. "*Imitation is . . . the sincerest form of flattery,*" said the computerized voice of the Angel.

"The Morgan Constructs would be designed to patrol the Perimeter," went on Mondrian, after a hard look at the Angel. (The Angels had that disconcerting habit of employing human clichés and proverbs. No one was ever sure whether it represented the symbiotes' perverse form of racial politeness, or some strange sense of humor.) "We had the Construct specifications drawn quite precisely. The individual units would be mobile, tough, and highly intelligent. Livia Morgan had said they would be 'indestructible.' We have reason now to hope that she was exaggerating. They would cruise the unexplored areas of the Perimeter and seek out life forms inimical to intelligences of the Stellar Group. However, no matter what they found they would serve a reporting function only. They would *not*—under any circumstances—be able to harm an intelligent life-form, or any life form possibly having intelligence.

"I was present during the initial demonstrations of Livia Morgan's Constructs. They were exposed to each of our four species, to the seven other possibly intelligent organisms known within the Perimeter, and to a variety of simulacra of differing degrees of apparent intelligence. The Morgan Constructs recognized each known form and responded to each in a friendly and harmless manner. They treated the new simulacra with appropriate caution and respect. I authorized the development to proceed, raising the Constructs to the next level of sophistication. Livia Morgan began the work. But somewhere out on Cobweb Station, a crucial design blunder must have been made." He turned to face Dougal Macdougal. "May I show the imagery obtained by our probe?"

"Carry on." The ambassador nodded. "And I hope that it's short. We can't hold the Link all day."

Mondrian did not reply. Behind him a sphere of darkness began to form. Within it glowed the rough-textured ovoid of Cobweb Station as it had appeared to one of the bristle probes. At first the whole station was visible. Then the field of view narrowed steadily, increasing in resolution. Soon the twisted and flattened objects outside the airlocks were recognizable; they were the space-suited remains of human beings. The cameras closed remorselessly. If those suited bodies had been alive when they were expelled from the locks, they would not have survived long. The images showed missing limbs, disembowelled trunks, and headless torsos. The cameras closed in on one figure, a turning, eyeless corpse lacking feet and hands.

"That is the mortal remains of Dr. Livia Morgan," said Mondrian expressionlessly. "Although neither she nor the guards were able to send any distress signals from Cobweb Station, the monitors preserved a complete record of their last hours of life. They had no warning. The Constructs suddenly ran wild. They hounded the guards remorselessly through the station interior. Livia Morgan attempted to negotiate with two of them. She was seized and systematically dismembered. Unless you insist, I do not propose to show you details of those scenes. Take my word for it: the Morgan Constructs are cunning, and deadly, and seem utterly inimical to human life. We are obliged to assume that they are no more friendly to any others of the Stellar Group."

The images behind Mondrian faded. "But even that is not the worst news," he continued. "The Morgan Constructs have disappeared. After the events that you have seen, they somehow managed to operate the Mattin Link—something that they should have found impossible to do. That is further proof of their extraordinary intelligence. All seventeen of them transmitted through the Link to unknown destinations. We are doing our best to trace them, but for the moment our working assumption is a grim one. Somewhere within the fifty-eight lightyear radius of the Known Sphere— we hope it is out close to the Perimeter, and not near one of our home worlds—we now have seventeen formidable threats, of unknown magnitude. I should say that I do not think we are, any of us, in *immediate* danger. Since the Constructs were designed and trained to work near the Perimeter, it is highly likely that they chose to flee there. But we have no idea how long they will choose to stay in that region. The purpose of today's meeting is to inform you of the facts, and to consider ways of dealing with the situation." He lifted his head, and stared steadily at the four beings before him. They looked back at him blankly. The Tinker, Angel, and Pipe-Rilla were too alien for Mondrian to be able to read their feelings, and Dougal Macdougal merely seemed irritable and slightly bored.

Esro Mondrian took a deep breath. Whatever was decided in the next few hours, it was unlikely that he would like it. He stepped backward, to line himself with Luther Brachis.

"Honored Ambassadors," he said, "that is the end of my official statement." And, he thought, it is probably the end of the easy part. Already there was a premonitory buzz from the Pipe-Rilla's circuit.

The fourteen-foot figure was standing on its pipe-stem legs, forelimbs clutching the tubular trunk and long antennae waving. "Questions?" it said. "Questions, if you please."

"Of course."

"Tell us more about the ... *capability* of the Morgan Constructs. Seventeen creatures out of your control certainly sounds unpleasant, but not a ... cosmic issue. You designed these creatures without major means of aggression. Correct?"

"I am afraid not." Esro Mondrian turned to offer Luther Brachis the floor, but the other man seemed more than ready to let him answer. "We designed the Constructs to have considerable powers of self-defense. Remember, they had to operate alone, far from any support, against unknown dangers. Unfortunately, the same capabilities can also be used offensively: their power plant can produce small fusion weapons; and they contain power lasers and shearing cones—enough to destroy any ship. By design, they contain the latest detection equipment we could produce, since we wanted them to be able to detect other lifeforms at the longest possible range. I could provide full details, but perhaps a summary example is more informative: any single Morgan Construct can destroy a city or lay waste a fair-sized planetoid. In combination—something that luckily we never expect to encounter—they could put a whole security fleet out of action."

Throughout Mondrian's reply there had been a slow stirring within the Tinker Composite. As he ended there came a burst of speech, almost too fast to be deciphered.

"Why?" gabbled the Tinker. "Why, why *why*? In the name of Security, you humans have produced a danger to yourself and to all other species of the Stellar Group. Why did anyone *need* a Morgan Construct? Look at yourselves. You have been exploring the region around your Sun for over six hundred of your years. We have watched that exploration for more than three centuries, ever since humans discovered our world. Now the Perimeter covers a sphere one hundred and sixteen lightyears in diameter—more than two thousand star systems, with a hundred and forty three planets that can support life. And *nowhere*, at any place within that sphere, has any species been found that is dangerous or aggressive . . . except yours. You are lifting a mirror to the Universe, and seeing only your own faces. We Tinkers say two things: first, that until you *created* this danger there was no danger. And second, tell us why you continue this insane rush to expand the Perimeter. It is now fifty-eight lightyears from Sol. Will you humans be satisfied when it has reached eighty lightyears? Or one hundred lightyears? Or one thousand? *When will you stop?*"

Mondrian looked at Macdougal. "Ambassador, I can if you wish attempt an answer to that question. But I should point out that I have long suggested that the Perimeter be frozen, or the expansion slowed. The human outward move should be suspended until we know what is along the Perimeter—because the region outside our known area may contain any number of terrible dangers. To us, and to all the Stellar Group. So with all respect, I agree completely with the Tinker Ambassador on that point. I also know such a decision is made at levels far above mine. But so long as expansion *does* proceed, something like the Constructs is essential. We must take measures to protect ourselves against whatever we find—"

"That's enough!" Dougal Macdougal had lifted his hands in protest. "Commander, you are well beyond your area of authority and competence. You came here to present a statement of situation, not to offer your own unsound views on human development." He turned to face the other three ambassadors. "I agree with you: both these men"—he gestured sharply at Mondrian and Brachis—"are at fault in permitting this problem to arise. They have created a present danger to the Stellar Group. And when this meeting is over, I will move at once to have them removed from office and stripped of all their powers. They will not be permitted—"

"No-o-o." The single word came from the Angel, delivered slowly and heavily through its computer link. "We will not permit such an action."

Macdougal had been caught slightly off balance. "You mean—you won't dismiss Mondrian and Brachis?"

"Exactly." The topmost frond of the Angel went into slow but wide-ranging oscillation. "It cannot be. *The punishment must fit the crime.* We, the Angels of Sellora, now request a move to Closed Hearing—full closure, closed from everyone except for the four ambassadors now present."

"But there should be a record—"

"With no record. It is necessary to discuss a question so serious that it can only be permitted in full Closed Hearing; a question of the highest significance. For this, we invoke ambassadorial privilege."

Even as the Angel spoke, an opaque canopy was sliding into position around the atrium. The lighted areas around the four ambassadors were visible for a few moments longer; then there was nothing in the center of the Star Chamber but a ball of scintillating darkness.

Luther Brachis looked at Esro Mondrian and shook his head. The two men were standing alone outside the dark sphere. It was the first audio and visual meeting of the four ambassadors of the Stellar Group in twenty-two years. And the first Closed Hearing in more than a century.

# Chapter Two

# THE FORMATION OF
# THE ANABASIS

"What do you think they're doing in there?" said Brachis. His face was gloomy, and he was biting his fingernails. The two men were standing outside the darkened atrium. The ambassadors had been in closed session for more than two hours.

Mondrian shook his head. "Who knows? Relax, Luther. You're not behaving like yourself. Didn't you come here all set to cut me to ribbons?"

"I sure as hell did." Brachis smoothed the row of decorations on his left breast. "I'm no different from you. You'd like to have my group working for your department—don't give me any nonsense, now, you know you would. And I'd like to control your area. But hell, that has nothing to do with *this* deal. You and I have a lot more in common with each other than we do with those three characters—I realized it when I was talking to them. They're all less human than a goddamned *jellyfish*."

Mondrian smiled, a little grin of inward satisfaction. "Good thing your job responsibility stops a lightyear out. Those happen to be our *friends* that you're talking about. And why do you exclude Macdougal? I happen to *like* the Pipe-Rillas—at least they are amusing, which is more than you can say

19

for him. I'd rather spend time with a Pipe-Rilla, or even with a Tinker, than I would with our friend the ambassador."

"Don't even *mention* that bastard. Did you hear what he said about stripping us of our positions?" Brachis ran his fingers again across his beloved decorations. "What about the Angels? How will they react to this thing?"

"That's another matter. I don't feel too comfortable with them. That's why I wonder what the Angel is saying in that Closed Hearing." He was toying unconsciously with the fire opal at his collar, where his own decorations for service and valor, an obligatory part of the uniform of Boundary Survey, had been reduced to miniaturized points of gold light, flashing and gleaming in the depths of the gemstone. Brachis saw him doing it and grinned. "You're a fraud, Esro. You're as proud of those as I am of mine—but you're too proud to admit it."

Mondrian sighed. "I certainly worked for them— the same as you did for yours. Maybe I only value what I am about to lose."

The two men fell silent. Their questions, spoken and unspoken, would not be answered for another hour. When the opaque screen finally shivered away, Esro Mondrian and Luther Brachis found that the atrium now had only two occupied places. The Pipe-Rilla and Dougal Macdougal were still in position, but the Angel and the Tinker had disappeared. And Macdougal had the face of a man who has seen ghosts.

The Pipe-Rilla gestured to Mondrian and Brachis to come forward. "We have reached agreement." The high-pitched voice still sounded cheerful, but that was an accident of its voice-producing mechanism. The Pipe-Rillas always sounded cheerful. The nervous rubbing of the forelimbs told a different story. "And since your own ambassador appears to be ... indisposed, it becomes my duty to tell you the result of our discussions." The Pipe-Rilla gestured around him at the two empty places, and then at the muttering, miserable figure of Dougal Macdougal.

"What happened?" said Brachis.

"A point of dispute arose between your ambassador and the ambassador for the Angels. The Angel has ... forceful means of persuasion, even from a distance of many lightyears. Ambassador Macdougal should recover ... in just a few of your hours." The Pipe-Rilla waved a forelimb to dismiss the subject. "Commander Brachis and Commander Mondrian: attention. Please be silent while I summarize our deliberations and conclusions. First, on the subject of your own blame."

There was a long pause. Mondrian and Brachis froze.

"We decided that you are both responsible in this matter," went on the Pipe-Rilla. "Esro Mondrian for initiating and approving a project with enormous potential for danger; Luther Brachis for failing to ensure that monitoring under his responsibility was suitably carried out, and so permitting the escape of the Morgan Constructs. You are both culpable in high degree; but Mondrian much more than Brachis. Your ambassador urged that you should both be relieved of all your duties, dismissed from security service, and stripped of privileges."

Again Brachis put his hand to his left breast. "If I could make one statement on our behalf—"

"Not yet." The Pipe-Rilla was finding it hard to remain self-controlled. Its vocal modulator began to stammer and shake. "Of course, as the Angel ambassador ... p-pointed out to us, we could not consider such a course of action. It would be preposterous. In any civilized society, it is the individual or group who *creates* a problem that should naturally have . . . responsibility for s-solving the problem. The cause must become the cure. The creation of the Morgan Constructs and their subsequent escape came from your actions and inaction. Livia Morgan is . . . d-dead. And therefore the seeking out and disposal of the Morgan Constructs must also be in your hands. We know that humans have codes of behavior quite different from the rest of the Stellar Group, but in this case there was little to discuss. We were . . . adamant." There was another shift in the Pipe-Rilla's posture. When it spoke again its voice was jerky and no longer employed human speech. *Dominus* was forced to cut in at once and provide computer translation.

"Beginning today," said the Pipe-Rilla, "there will be created a new group within your department of System Security. It will be of a form peculiar to human history . . . a 'military expedition' . . . what your species knows as"—there was an infinitesimal pause, while *Dominus* sought the suitable word—"an *Anabasis*."

"A *what*?" grunted Brachis.

"Anabasis. Not a promising omen," said Mondrian softly. "As I recall it, the original Anabasis was all defeat and retreat. Better check our translation box."

The Pipe-Rilla took no notice. It was in some kind of trouble, with limbs moving spastically and with fluttering thorax. "The Anabasis," it went on, "will be headed by Esro Mondrian, who has principal responsibility for the problem we now face. He will be assisted by Luther Brachis. Your task will be simple: you will train . . . Pursuit Teams to find the location of the Morgan Constructs, and . . . follow them to their . . . hiding-places." Now even the computer could not help. The speech pattern of the Pipe-Rilla was becoming more and more fragmented and disorganized. The voice rose in pitch, and the giant figure began to shiver and shake. "Each pursuit team of the Anabasis will contain . . . one trained member of each intelligent species . . . of the Stellar Group—Tinker . . . Angel . . . Human . . . and—Pipe-Rilla. The pursuit teams . . . will find the Morgan Constructs and—if necessary"—the voice rose to a shriek—"destroy them. *Destroy—*"

And suddenly the Pipe-Rilla had gone. The Link had been broken. Brachis turned to Mondrian in perplexity. "What the hell's going on there?"

Mondrian was rubbing at his chin, fingering the narrow line of beard. "The Pipe-Rilla couldn't stand it. Of course not! I should have guessed it, none of them can. No wonder they had to have a Closed Session, and a secret vote."

"But why?" Brachis was scowling. It had just got through to him that he would now be reporting to his rival Esro Mondrian.

"Think, Luther! You know the rules of the Stellar Group as well as I do. Prime Rule: Intelligent life must be preserved, and never, for any reason, destroyed. That is true at the individual level, and even more true at the species level. And yet they are directing us to find the Morgan Constructs and *destroy* them!—the only creatures of their kind in all the Universe. It must have been agony for the alien ambassadors to make that ruling. Didn't you see how upset they became when they saw the images from the Cobweb Station probe? They told us today, we're the most aggressive species they know—but they must be afraid we're less bloodthirsty than the Morgan Constructs."

"But if they can't stand violence, why did they insist that there should be a member of each of the Stellar Group on every Pursuit Team? What will happen when a Pursuit Team tracks down a Morgan Construct, and has to wipe it out? The other species will just fall apart."

"They will. But that's consistent, too, with their

way of thinking. Remember the legend of the old firing squads, where one man would be given a blank instead of a live bullet? It's the same principle. Each species won't know *for sure* if it was the one responsible for the death of a particular Morgan Construct."

Luther Brachis shrugged. "They don't understand us too well, either," he growled. "We care about intelligent species, but I'd blow a hundred Morgan Constructs to bits and not think twice about it, for the sake of Solar System security. Now I don't know if I'll get the chance. Damn it, Mondrian. Do you realize what you've got out of this? What you've been looking for all along—you screw up *more* than me—so you're put *in charge* of me! Did you ever hear of a more ass-backwards logic in your life? You ought to be sitting there in deep trouble, instead of ready to grin all over your face. Though I must say, you don't seem to be smiling much."

"You know me, Luther. I could be smiling inside, and you would never know it."

*And but for one factor,* thought Mondrian, *I might be laughing. The ambassadors are just too frightened of the Morgan Constructs. They say, find them, and destroy them! That's no good to me. I must have the Morgan Constructs alive.*

*To:* The Anabasis (Office of the Director).
*From:* Office of the Solar Ambassador.
*Subject:* Instructions for Pursuit Team selection and assembly.

*Item one: Pursuit Teams.* As agreed in the ambassadorial meeting of 6/7/38, a total of up to twenty-five Pursuit Teams will be established. The final selection of each team will be determined by the Anabasis in consultation with the ambassadors.

*Item two: Composition of Pursuit Teams.* As agreed in the recent ambassadorial meeting, each Pursuit Team will contain four members: one human, one

Tinker Composite, one Angel, and one Pipe-Rilla. Team members from each species will be proposed by that species. The Anabasis will have the right to reject candidate team members on the grounds of incompatibility with other team members. Any such rejections by the Anabasis must, however, be confirmed and approved through the Solar Ambassador's office.

Captain Kubo Flammarion frowned, scratched his left ear with a grubby fingernail, grunted, and laid down the written document. He underlined the last sentence he had read. There was Dougal Macdougal, trying to push himself into the middle of things again. Why should rejections have to go through the ambassador's office?

He sniffed, poked absently at his still-itching left ear with the writing stylus, and read on.

*Item three: Selection of Solar Pursuit Team candidates.* Human candidates must be volunteers, less than twenty-four standard years of age, in good physical condition, and unbound by contract commitment or marriage.

*Item four: Species.* Human candidates must be unaltered *homo sapiens*, male or female. Synthetic forms, *pan sapiens*, *delphinus sapiens*, and Capman modulations are excluded.

*Item five: Qualifications.* Pursuit Team members must have at least a Class Four education (which may be achieved during training). Candidates will be excluded if they have previous military training, or fail standard psych profiles for interaction with aliens.

*Item six: Training—*

Flammarion did a double-take, and his eyes flashed back to the previous item. *Impossible.* What the hell was Macdougal trying to do? He jammed his cap onto his bald head and headed next door to Esro Mondrian's office. He gave a flat-palmed bang on the open door and went in without waiting for a response.

"Did you see this?" He slapped the sheet on the desk in front of his superior with the assurance of long familiarity. "It came through less than an hour ago. I'm supposed to recruit pursuit team candidates, am I? Take a look at that. Macdougal has slapped so many conditions on it, I don't think we'll find one acceptable candidate in the whole System."

His wizened face was scowling. A long stint of security service out near the Perimeter had produced three permanent results: premature aging, total lack of interest in personal hygiene, and a permanent rage against bureaucratic procedures. For four years he had been Esro Mondrian's principal assistant. Others wondered why Mondrian tolerated the scruffy appearance, disrespectful attitude, and periodic outbursts. Mondrian had two good reasons: Kubo Flammarion was totally dedicated to his work and, even better, knew where the bodies were buried. He kept no written records, but when Mondrian needed a lever to drag a special permit from Transportation or a fast response from Quarantine, Flammarion could deliver the dirt. Some deputy administrator or under-secretary would receive a quiet, damning call, and the permit magically appeared. Mondrian sometimes wondered what odd facts about him Kubo Flammarion had tucked away inside that scurfy, straggle-haired skull. He was too wise to ask.

"I saw this document," he said calmly. "And Commander Brachis already ran a check. For a change, it's not Macdougal's fault. Those conditions came from the other Stellar Group members."

"Yeah—but how hard did Macdougal protest?" Flammarion jabbed at the page. "There's the killer.

We're supposed to find pursuit team candidates with no security training. That excludes *everybody*! Everybody in the Solar Federation, man or woman, does the standard service."

"Everybody over sixteen years old, Captain," said Mondrian.

"Yeah. But *before* they're sixteen, they're protected by the parental statute." Flammarion was bobbing up and down on his toes, angrier by the minute. "We can't touch 'em before they're sixteen, and that's when they go straight to security reserve. These instructions make the whole damn thing impossible."

"Not quite. We will find the candidates." Mondrian was leaning back in his desk, staring thoughtfully across the room at a three-dimensional model of the Sphere. The scale model showed the location and identification of every star within it, color-coded as to spectral type. Colonies were magenta, and stations of the security network were highlighted as bright points of blue.

The Sphere was now nearly fifty-eight lightyears in radius, centered on Sol. It marked the domain in which instantaneous transmission of messages or materials could be accomplished. The main outbound probes contained their own Mattin Links. Through them more equipment—including other Links—could be transferred. Every century the probes extended the Perimeter by almost ten lightyears. And somewhere out near that Perimeter, in the three-lightyear spherical shell that comprised the little-explored Boundary Layer, now lurked the Morgan Constructs.

"Where, for Shannon's sake?" blurted Flammarion. "You mean we'll find 'em *out there*?" He had followed Mondrian's look and misinterpreted it. "You think we can find candidates in the Colo-

nies? I don't believe it. They need every hand they
can get for their own projects."

"Quite right, Captain. I don't look to the Colonies."

"No?" Flammarion scratched at his stubbly chin.
"Then it sounds impossible!"

Mondrian had turned to face another wall of his
office, where a display screen showed the view
from Ceres, looking inwards towards Sol. "Not
impossible—just very difficult. Don't forget that
one planet of the solar system still refuses to be
part of the Federation. And the people there seem
more than ready to trade their offspring . . . if the
price is right." He pressed a control on his desk,
and the display went into a high-speed search and
zoom.

"*Earth!*" In the low gravity, Kubo Flammarion
was almost floating away with quivering incredulity. "You don't mean Earth? You can't be serious."

"Have you ever been there, Captain?"

"Sure, twice—but a long time ago, before I went
out with the service. And it's supposed to be even
worse now than it was then. You know what Luther Brachis calls Earth? The world of madmen!"

Mondrian gave Flammarion a long, strange look.
"Does he, indeed?" He did not raise his voice, but
it took on a cold, bitter tone that brought a sudden
total attention from the other man. "The world of
madmen. Am I to assume that you agree with
him? I see that you do. Very well, Captain. Let me
put it to you in this way. You are now free to meet
with Commander Brachis to discuss the require-
ments from the ambassador's office. If you can
bring me within twenty-four hours a proposal guar-
anteed to provide the human pursuit team candidates that we need, I will consider it. But *unless*
that happens, you will make arrangements—*immediate* arrangements—for you, me, and Com-

mander Brachis to visit his 'mad world.' I will accept no excuses or delays."

He turned away, in a dismissal so sharp and unequivocal that Flammarion felt as though Mondrian's presence had vanished from the room.

"Very good, sir." Kubo Flammarion rubbed his sleeve across his nose, and almost tiptoed from the room. At the door he took a long look at the glowing display screen, now filled by the cloudy blue-white ball of Earth.

"Madworld!" he muttered unhappily. "We're going to Madworld. Shannon help us all, has it come to that?"

# Chapter Three

# ON THE BIG MARBLE

Earth was served by a single Link exit point. Travellers stepped into the Link Chamber at the center of Ceres, and were at once spat out by the transfer system at a point close to Earth's equator. Mondrian, Brachis, and Flammarion found themselves at the foot of a gigantic dilapidated tower, reaching up to the sullen overcast of a tropical afternoon.

Brachis craned his head back, following the silver-gray column upwards. "What the devil is it?"

"Don't you recognize it?" Mondrian was for some reason in excellent spirits. "We're at the foot of the old Beanstalk. Everything to space and back went up and down that for nearly two hundred years."

Luther Brachis stared at the beetle-backed cars, nestling in their cradles along the hundred-meter lower perimeter. "Up *that*? People rode those things to geosynch? I guess they had guts in those days. Why do they still leave it around here on Earth? It must be a billion tons of dead weight."

"It is—but don't even suggest getting rid of it, not to people down here. They think it's a historic relic, one of their most valued ancient monuments." Mondrian spoke casually. He was looking off to

31

the west, with an experienced eye and an air of anticipation. There were woods there, and he was watching the fronded crowns of individual trees. It was coming . . . it was coming . . . *Now*!

The blustery equatorial breeze ruffled their hair. Brachis and Flammarion gave a simultaneous and uncontrollable gasp of horror. Flammarion glared wildly around him. "Lock failure!" he shouted. "Lock failure! Emergency. Where—where's—" He slowly subsided.

Esro Mondrian watched with malicious satisfaction. "Relax, both of you. Kubo, I'm ashamed of you. I thought you told me you'd been on Earth before? It's not a pressure failure, or a collapsed lock. It's wind—natural air movements! They occur all the time here on Earth, every day. So you'd better get used to them before the natives die laughing at you."

"Winds! Damn it, of course there are winds." Luther Brachis's broad face turned rosy with anger. The big man had recovered himself quicker than Flammarion, who was still breathing hard and staring all around him. "Damn you, Mondrian. You *planned* that, didn't you? You could have warned us both—but you wanted your fun!"

Mondrian affected to ignore him. He was stepping forward, away from the Link platform towards an odd-looking throng of a couple of hundred people clustered by the exit. The other two hesitantly followed him, towards a long covered ramp that led below ground. As they approached the crowd there was an immediate babble of voices. "Hottest little nippers on Earth" . . . "Need a Freudhopper? The best, for a good price" . . . "Trade crystals for you, high rate and no questions" . . . "Want to see a coronation?—genuine royal family, forty-second generation" . . . "Visit a Needler lab factory tonight? Top line products." They spoke standard solar, poorly pronounced.

Most of the crowd, men and women, were half a head shorter even than Flammarion. Mondrian strode through them confidently. They wore brightly colored clothes, their purples, scarlets, and pinks in striking contrast to the quiet black of Security uniform. Mondrian brushed aside the grasping hands. He paid no attention to anyone until a skeleton-thin man in a patchwork jacket of green and gold fell into step beside him.

"You a busker?" he said.

The skinny man grinned. "That's me, squire, at your service. And welcome to The Big Marble. You want it, we got it—and I know where. Tobacco, roley-poley, lulu juice, you name it and I'll take you to it."

"Cut it, shut it. You know Tatty Snipes?" Mondrian's question in low earth-tongue interrupted the sales pitch.

"Certainly do." The busker faltered for a moment, taken aback by Mondrian's use of his own argot, then half-heartedly began again. "Paradox, slither, velocil—you can get them all from me. Like a guided tour of the Shambles? Never you mind what the rule book says, I'll find you—"

"Slot the chops. You bring the Tatty to me—at once. All right?" Mondrian reached out and touched the busker's hand. There was the dull glow of a crystal, then the dirty fingers closed on it firmly. The man looked at Mondrian respectfully.

"Yessir. Right away, squire." The skinny figure started to dive off into the crowd, then checked himself and turned back. "Name's Bester, sir—King Bester. I'll be back with Tatty in half an hour. She's just a couple of Links from here."

Mondrian nodded, and sauntered across to sit on a solid bench planted a hundred meters away beneath a Sun-simulator. After a look at each other, the other two men uneasily followed him.

"He's right at home here," whispered Flammarion. "Did you hear him chit-chat in their own lingo? What is it, earth-gobble? I couldn't understand half of it."

Brachis nodded. He had recovered his composure, and was beginning to look around him with real interest. "I should have anticipated this," he said grimly. "It's my own fault. I had all the information—just didn't use it."

"You *knew* he spoke earth-tongue? How could you?"

"Not exactly that." Brachis brushed away the admiring hand that was trying to touch his glittering decorations. "But I should have guessed he might. Use your common sense, Kubo. Don't you know I've tracked Esro Mondrian's movements for the past four years?—just the way you must have traced mine. That's what a Security department is for. And Mondrian's records show that he has been coming here to Earth an average of five times a year, ever since we started tracking. He knows the place well."

"But what's he *do* down here?"

Brachis shook his massive head. "That's still a mystery. We couldn't trail him when he was on the surface. Maybe this time I'll find out."

When they came up to Mondrian he was sitting quietly on the bench, staring thoughtfully at the surrounding group of Madworlders. Once King Bester had been picked out by Mondrian, the rest of them had given up their importuning. Now they stood a few yards away, watching the three visitors with frank curiosity, grinning and nudging each other and whispering comments in the old Earth languages.

Flammarion sat down on the bench next to Mondrian. He looked suspiciously at the wooden seat, and at the flat surface beneath his feet. It was old, weathered brick, closely laid. Tiny ants were hurrying out of the open cracks to explore the side of

the men's boots. They showed most interest in
Kubo Flammarion, perhaps drawn by the interesting smell of long-unwashed flesh. He shuffled his
feet from side to side, keeping a wary eye on the
energetic insects.

Luther Brachis remained standing, his attention
on the crowd. "This is all quite futile, Esro," he
said after a while. His voice was flatly contemptu-
ous. "Just look at them. Can you see any one of
those cretins being accepted into a Stellar pursuit
team? You're wasting all our time."

It was another skirmish. The two men had not
yet settled into a new relationship. So far as the
ambassadors were concerned, it was all decided:
Luther Brachis now reported to Mondrian for everything connected with the Anabasis. But Brachis
was still responsible for Solar Security, and he
had retained that department intact. He found the
present situation intolerable. For years the two
had been equals and rivals, with a mutual understanding that one day there would be a final piece
of infighting, and one or the other would gain
overall authority. Brachis had accepted that idea.
What he could not accept was Mondrian's victory
by arbitrary fiat—unrelated (or *inversely* related)
to performance. And he owed Mondrian something
for that episode with the surface wind.

"Would you take responsibility for training one
of those idiots?" he went on. "They're dirty. And
ignorant. And unhealthy."

He was deliberately needling Mondrian. The visit
to Earth had been forced on him at short notice,
shortcutting the usual quarantine of his own department. Now there was a chance for revenge,
even if it meant overstating the situation.

Mondrian slowly turned his head to stare up at
Brachis. "You underestimate the potentials of Earth.
This was the stock of your own ancestors."

"Sure it was—half a millennium ago. But we're

seeing the dregs. That's what you have left when the top tenth of each generation is skimmed off for seven hundred years to go into space. It's a flawed gene pool now. Look back over the past century, and you won't find any worthwhile talent has come from Earth."

"Have you attempted that exercise?"

Brachis laughed. "I don't need to. Just look at them. I tell you, we're wasting our time. Let's get out of here."

Now his goading was more obvious—but harder to ignore. Mondrian's mouth took on a tight, angry look. "I disagree. You overestimate the demands of the pursuit team, and you underestimate the potential of the people of Earth; not to mention the effectiveness of the training programs that I have developed over the past decade. I could take any one of those"— he pointed out at the crowd— "*any one* of them, and I could train them to be a successful pursuit team candidate."

Brachis saw his opening. "Would you wager on it?"

"Certainly I will. Name the amount."

"I would." Brachis snorted. "But you know you're not risking anything. Not one of those people is eligible for training—they're too old, or they're probably bonded by some sort of contract, or they'd never pass the physicals. Look at their teeth and hair. Wait until we see somebody in the right age group, and healthy, and *then* tell me if you're willing to make a wager."

"I'll do it—damned if I won't."

The argument was interrupted by the sudden return of King Bester. The thin man called out to them from the edge of the crowd and began pushing his way rapidly towards them, closely followed by a tall woman. They arrived at the bench, and Bester gave a grinning nod and held out his hand.

Mondrian ignored him. He stood up. "Hello, Tatty," he said quietly. "How's business?"

"Good. Or it was, until you interrupted me. I was in the middle of a deal, up in Delmarva. I told the King to go to hell, but he wouldn't take no from me for an answer."

Mondrian took the hint, and another packet of crystals quietly went into King Bester's open hand. Then he patted the bench, indicating that she should sit down next to him.

She remained standing, examining the other two Security men. After a moment she nodded to them. "Hello," she said, in excellent standard solar. "I don't think we've met. I'm Tatty Snipes."

She was tall, slim, and spectacular. She towered over Mondrian by at least twenty centimeters and stood eye to eye with Luther Brachis, who openly gawped at her. She stared back at him. Her look was direct and bold, with glowing brown eyes. But there were tired smudges of purple darkness underneath them, and the grey tone of Paradox addiction in her complexion. The skin of her face and neck was clear and unblemished, but it was the skin of someone who never saw sunlight. Her sleeveless dress of dark green revealed an array of tiny purple-black dots along her long, thin arms. In contrast to King Bester and the rest of the crowd, Tatty was spotlessly clean, with neat attire, carefully groomed dark hair, and well-kept fingernails.

"First time here for some of you?" she said. "What's the deal, Esro?"

He squinted up at her in the strong Sun-simulator light. After a few moments he reached up to touch her arm. "Sit down, Princess, and I'll tell you."

"I'll sit down all right, but not here. Too much light—it would fry me. Let's link back north, to my place, and I'll give you some genuine Earth food." She smiled at the uncertain look on Kubo

Flammarion's face. "Don't worry, soldier, I'll make sure it's not too rich for commoners."

*R.H.I.P.—Rank Has Its Privileges.* That had never been more true than in the first days of space development. One odd, predictable, but unexpected consequence of automation and excess productive capacity had been the re-emergence of a class system. The old aristocracies, diminished (but never quite destroyed) during the days of world-wide poverty and experimental social programs, had returned; with some curious additions to their ranks.

It had been surprising, but inevitable. When all of Earth's manufacturing moved to the computer-controlled assembly lines, efficiency went up and employment needs went down. In the fuzzy area of "management" and government, most business and development decisions were also routinely (and better) handled by computer. At the same time, boredom with academic studies had squeezed the education system to a few years of mandatory schooling. Living accommodations were passed on across the generations; old family possessions, the older the better, defined one of the few forms of property that could not easily and cheaply be duplicated in the robot factories.

The unemployment rate was ninety percent. The available jobs on Earth called for no special skills—so who would get them?

Naturally, those with well-placed friends and relatives. There had been a wonderful blossoming of nepotism, on a scale not seen since the seventeenth century. Education was most available to those with titles and influence; so the best jobs *specifically* called for education.

Meanwhile, away from Earth there was a real need for people. The solar system was waiting for development. It offered an environment that was demanding, dangerous, and filled with unbounded opportunities. And it had a nasty habit of cancelling any man-made advantage owed to birth, degrees, or spurious qualifications—cancelling *permanently*. The rich and royal were not without their own shrewdness. After a quick look at space, they stayed home on Earth, where safety, superiority, and status were assured. It was the lowborn, seeing no upward mobility on Earth, who took the other direction—outwards.

The result was too effective to have been designed by human planners. The tough, desperate commoners fought their way out, generation after generation. The introduction of the Mattin Link quadrupled the rate of exodus. The society that was left on Earth became more and more titled and title-conscious. It was well protected from material want and free from external pressures. Naturally it developed an ever-increasing disdain for the emigrants—"vulgar commoners"—who were spreading their low-born and classless fecundity through the rest of the solar system and out to the stars. Earth was the place to be for the aristocrats. The Big Marble, the *only* place to be. And the only place to live for anyone who despised crudity, esteemed culture, and wanted a certain sophistication in life.

King Bester *was* a king, a real king who traced his line across thirty-two generations to the house of Saxe-Coburg. He was one of seventeen thousand reigning monarchs on and under Earth's surface. He regarded Tatty Snipes, who was Princess Tatiana Sinai-Peres of the Cabot-Khashoggis, as rather an upstart. She had only six centuries and twenty-two generations in her lineage. He did not say it, of course, in her presence—or Tatty would have knocked the side of his royal head in with one blow of her carefully-manicured and aristocratic fist. But he certainly thought it.

And King Bester, like Tatty, was no fool. He knew quite well that the real power had moved away from Earth—the Quarantine operated by Solar Security was only for people moving *outwards* from Earth. He could sense the brawling, raw strength that ran through the off-planet culture. But he was also afraid of it. It was easier to stay with the familiar rituals of the Big Marble—and take a little from the visitors like Mondrian and his colleagues. They were more numerous than System government liked to admit, and they came down to Earth for reasons rarely shown on their travel permits.

King had quietly tagged along with Tatty and the visitors, hanging at the back of the little group and studying the three men, while Mondrian explained the reason for the trip to Earth.

Tatty had apparently heard of the Morgan Constructs and the "accident" on Cobweb Station, but the whole thing was news to King Bester until he deduced it from Esro Mondrian's words. He was not much interested. It was much more fascinating to examine Mondrian, Brachis, and Flammarion, and ask in which categories of pleasure-seeking their interests would lie. Bester had his own ideas of Earth visitors. No matter how the official agenda read, there would always be a hidden one. And that was where the profit lay.

He thought that Brachis would be easy. Big, powerfully-built, lusty, still in early middle age, he could be offered things unheard of through most of the Solar System. Flammarion was easy, too. He already had the poached-egg look to his eyes that suggested the habitual use of alcohol. One shot of Paradox, and Flammarion wouldn't look elsewhere for entertainment while he was down on Earth.

The problem was Mondrian. His eyes had frightened King Bester on first look, with their cold depths. But on the other hand, Mondrian wasn't much of a prospect, anyway. He was no stranger to Earth. He had probably developed his own needs already, and from the way she looked at him, Tatty Snipes had in the past helped to serve them.

Once they reached Tatty's underground apartment, Bester stopped any pretense of listening to Mondrian. He quietly helped himself to the free food and drink—Princess Tatiana had decidedly royal tastes—and moved a little closer to Kubo Flammarion, ready to begin a more private conversation. The scruffy man's pleasures could probably be guessed, but that had to be confirmed before his pockets could be emptied.

"How would you like to witness a public beheading?" Bester said quietly. "Full staging—steel axe, authentic block, and hooded executioner. It's an absolutely top-quality simulacrum on the block, and the spurt from the neck looks exactly like real blood."

"Bleagh!" Flammarion looked at him in disgust, and shook his head. He put down the slice of underdone beef he was holding. "You trying to make me throw up?"

"No? How about him, then." The King gestured at Mondrian, deep in conversation with Tatty. "Think he'd be interested?"

Kubo Flammarion scratched his head. "Nah. To get him hooked, it would have to be a real victim and real blood." He pointedly took a couple of steps away from Bester, who turned to Luther Brachis.

"How about you? How would you like to know about some of our entertainments—I mean the Big Marble specials, the ones not in the catalog."

Luther Brachis looked at him pleasantly. "And how would you like a big fistful of knuckles," he said, in poorly pronounced but quite passable Earth-argot, "right up your royal nose?"

King Bester suddenly decided that his glass needed refilling at the sideboard across the room.

"I didn't know you spoke their lingo, too," said Kubo Flammarion admiringly, watching Bester's departure.

They looked at each other. Luther Brachis wondered about the possibility of a switch in Flammarion's loyalties. "It's good to have a few cards you don't show," he said quietly. "I'll bet there are a few other things about me you don't know—and a few about your boss, too. Just keep watching."

# Chapter Four

# IN THE GALLIMAUFRIES

Tatty shook her head when she learned what Esro Mondrian was looking for. "Not here, in the areas where I have most clout," she said. "There's a local ordinance forbidding the off-Earth sale of anyone with more than four degrees of consanguinity with my imperial clan—and that includes *everybody*. They all claim the relationship, even if they don't really have it."

"So what can we do?" asked Mondrian.

"Try over in BigSyd, or old Tea-run?" she mused. "Maybe. I don't know the dealers there, though. And in Ree-o-dee you need to pay off so many people. The other drawback is that they're all a few Links away. Better if we had somebody locally."

"How 'bout Bozzie?" chipped in King Bester. "Top bod for that line of business. And nearby."

"Could be. Worth a shot. I don't know what he has, though." Tatty turned to Mondrian. "I'll have to find him first—but he'll be in the Gallimaufries, so it shouldn't be hard."

Kubo Flammarion had been struggling to make an intelligible record of the conversation. That last exchange was too much. "Bozzie?" he said. "In the Garry-what's?"

43

"Bozzie. The Duke of Bosny," explained Tatty. "He's also Viscount Roosevelt, Count Mellon, Baron Rockwell, *and* the Earl of Potomac. Upstart houses, every one. But he prefers plain Bosny, or just Bozzie. He hasn't lived in Bosny City for years, but he claims to have been born there. He certainly shows consanguinity with every major royal line in the Northeast, and he's a big mover and shaker down in the Gallimaufries"— Flammarion raised his eyebrows—"the basement warrens, two hundred levels below us." She looked at Bester. "Think we can do it today?"

"You'd have to hurry. We'd never find Bozzie after dark—he'll be up topside with his Scavvies, scouting the surface."

"But it must be dark already up on the surface," protested Mondrian. Then he paused and shook his head. "I ought to keep quiet. I know it was late afternoon when we landed—but I've no idea how far west we came through the Links."

"You landed in Africa," said Tatty. "We picked up six hours coming here. Local time is two in the afternoon. But we're in the northern hemisphere, and it's winter. So it will be dark early—something else you're not used to out there." She paused for a moment, calculating. "I think we can do it in time," she said at last, "provided we take the fastest routes. Hold onto your hats, and let's go."

Tatty Snipes lived on the sixteenth level. It was prime real estate, minutes from the surface and within easy reach of a Link entrance. But it had no direct drop connection to the poorer levels of the Gallimaufries. They had to travel north, then double back. Led by Tatty, the group travelled a hundred kilometers horizontally to descend two hundred levels and five thousand meters. They did it in thirty minutes. It was a race along confused networks of high-speed slideways, a plunge along the vertiginous corkscrews of spiral staircases, and finally a series of long dives through the black depths of vertical drop-shafts.

"First time I've felt comfortable in days," said Flammarion, savoring the long moments of zero-g.

The last drop was a long one, down a curving chute that expelled them into a vaulted chamber, hundreds of meters across. The rocky roof was studded with powerful sun-simulators that lit the whole enclosure. The space was crammed full. The three Security men stared around them at a baffling jumble of stalls, corridors, partitions, tents, and guy-ropes. Slender support columns ran from floor to roof at thirty meter intervals. Their steel pylons held up shish-kebabs of ramshackle multi-level platforms, many of them open-sided, with rope ladders hanging to the ground beneath. The floor of the chamber was not rock, but rich black earth. Bright-blossomed flowers had been planted everywhere, growing profusely along the zigzagging walkways and festooning every wall and column.

"Bozzie's Imperial Court," said Tatty. "He likes flowers. Stick close to the King, now. If you get lost here I don't know how you'd find your way back."

The human population of the Gallimaufries was as numerous as the plants and no less colorful. Gaudy jackets and robes of saffron, purple, and vermilion were favored, trimmed with sequin brilliants and piped with blue, silver, and gold. The clothes were all dirty, and the smell appalling. King Bester's costume, garish and grubby when they had first seen it, now appeared clean, modest and conservative.

And then the first impression of the Gallimaufries faded. A second element emerged, a quieter counterpoint to the vivid brawl. It was the bright clothes and bustling movement that caught the eye and drew the visitor's attention. But mingled with those, almost invisible among them, were others. Like lilies among orchids, these people sat in small groups on benches by the walkways, or walked slowly along the alleys. Their stillness and silence merged them with the background. Their clothes were simple, monochrome tunics of grey or white.

"Commoners," said Tatty, following Luther Brachis's look at a group of three women, each dressed in a plain ivory tunic. "There's the raw material for your pursuit teams. Bozzie has contract rights over almost anybody in grey or white. They can't say no. Stay here and take a look—maybe even make an offer if you see what you need. Some of them might want to get out of here, no matter how bad your deal sounds. I'll go find Bozzie and bring him back to you."

She ducked under a guy rope, rounded a tent, and headed for the edge of the chamber. Her height allowed them to follow her progress for the first thirty meters, then she was lost in the tangle of people and buildings.

Brachis turned to Esro Mondrian.

"Ready to change your tune now?" he asked. "If not, I'm prepared to go ahead with that bet. I tell you again, *nothing* good has come out of Madworld in three hundred years. Earthers are losers. They're too decadent and spineless to do anything. They'd never be acceptable as Pursuit Team members, no matter how much you trained them."

His tone was mild, but some nuance in it turned Esro Mondrian's lips white. "I'll make the bet," he said. "Name your terms."

Brachis had an irritating smile on his face. "Certainly. Let me make it easy for you, and keep it simple. You select any pair of candidates that you like down here—today, if you can. Train them any way you want to. And you will have a reasonable time—shall we say two years?—to bring them to the point of acceptability by the Stellar Group as pursuit team members. Do that, and you win."

Mondrian paused. "And the stakes?" he said at last.

"How about my personnel monitoring system against yours? Don't pretend that you haven't got one. You've known for years where all my people travel, just the same as we've tracked yours."

"Accepted," said Mondrian at once. He took a deep breath. "I will select two people. Here, today. And when their training is completed, I wager that both will be accepted for the pursuit teams." He turned to Bester and Flammarion. "You are witnesses. There is my hand on it."

Brachis took Mondrian's hand for only a split-second, then dropped it. He turned to look at the bustling court around him, and pretended to hold his nose. "There they are. Take your pick. White or grey uniforms, Princess Tatiana said. I'm glad you will be doing the training, not me, because I'm not sure I could stand the smell."

The brightly-clad courtiers were all grubby energy and extravagance. By contrast, the commoners were listless and subdued. A team of three was passing as Brachis spoke, leading an odd-looking beast on a chain. Its muzzle was blunt and the forehead low, but the animal looked around with sparkling brown eyes and showed more interest in the scene than its keeper. It paused by Flammarion, who looked horrified, and sniffed at him inquiringly.

"No danger," said King Bester, when Kubo Flammarion seemed ready to dive off into the crowd. "Quite harmless. Seen things like it a hundred times."

"What is it?" said Flammarion, as the creature turned its head up towards him, opened a mouth full of needle teeth, and offered him a spiky smile.

Bester shrugged and snapped his fingers. "No

name, squire. Just an Artefact—something from a Needler lab. Like to visit one?—arrange it easy."

Although Flammarion shook his head, Bester was too experienced a salesman to miss the sudden and strong interest shown by Luther Brachis. But before he could follow up on it, he was interrupted. Running along the path, dodging in and out of the bustling courtiers, came a young man. He was perhaps twenty years old, carrying a garland of flowers. He was followed closely by a laughing girl. "Not fair, Chan," she cried. "No fair. That was cheating. Give it back."

The man paused close to Mondrian, shaking the flower posy at her teasingly. She was slight, thin, olive-skinned and moderately attractive; but he was an Adonis: golden blond hair, tall, with a loose, agile build and sculptured good looks. If the people he ran among were aristocrats, his face and bearing pronounced him their emperor. Both man and woman were dressed in the plain ivory tunics of commoners.

Unperturbed by the appearance of the Security men in their dark uniforms, he dodged behind them to escape. Mondrian took one long, probing look, then moved forward to grasp the man by the arm. The youth stared back at him, mouth open. The woman moved to their side, and put her hand in turn on Mondrian's. Several courtiers stopped their promenade to watch what was happening.

"You." Mondrian moved forward, tightening his grip. "Both of you. Are you under contract?"

The man stared back impassively. But the woman thrust herself between him and Mondrian. "What business of yours? Let go."

"There might be a position for you. Let me talk to Bozzie. I'll make you a good offer—"

She wrenched free, screamed at the man, "Chan! Follow me! Now!" and threw herself into the crowd. The youth gave one astonished look at Mondrian, then went after her. In a couple of seconds they were twenty yards away, heading for the safety of a covered arcade.

"Those two," cried Mondrian. "Stop them."

The courtiers did not move. Flammarion began a half-hearted pursuit, though they were moving at a speed he had not even attempted in a quarter of a century. The couple were making the last turning into the arcade when Luther Brachis acted. He pulled a palm-sized cylinder from a holder at his waist and pointed it at them.

"Don't shoot!" screamed King Bester.

A green spiral of light flashed from the cylinder, corkscrewing a tight helical path through the air. It touched the escaping pair one after the other in the middle of their backs and threw off a shower of sparks there. They ran on, and were out of sight in a second behind a long curtain of golden beads.

Brachis looked at Mondrian and smiled grimly. "You're going to lose your bet anyway, Esro. So I'll give you a look at the monitor system you won't get." He pulled a flat disk from his belt. "I've had this a month, but it's my first chance for a real test. Look."

He held the disk horizontal. At its center, a double arrow of light moved and turned. While they watched, it lengthened perceptibly and changed direction.

"A Tracker?" said Mondrian.

Brachis nodded. "Direction and distance. As soon as they've been tagged with the beam we can follow them for at least twenty-four hours. This is designed to track up to five people at once. It gets very confusing if they all go separate ways—five arrows to deal with—but with two it's fairly easy. See the arrows, they're keeping close together." He handed it to Mondrian, who at once held it out in turn to Flammarion.

"Go and follow them. Bring them back here."

Kubo Flammarion stared at him pop-eyed, then at the Tracker.

"Not by yourself, man," went on Mondrian impatiently. "You don't know the place. He'll help you." He pointed at King Bester, who was pointedly looking elsewhere. "And he'll be very well rewarded," he added.

Bester nodded. "Now you're talking, squire." He banged the palms of his hands together, and took the Tracker from Flammarion. "Arrow not moving. They must have stopped. Be back with 'em in a jiffy-jo. Come on."

With Kubo Flammarion a distant second he set out along the line defined by the arrow. Mondrian looked mildly at Brachis, and shook his head. "I'm going to win the bet. With those handsome two you kindly tagged for me. Unless you want to concede?"

"The bet stands. Nothing good comes out of Earth." Brachis led the way to a seat, his face thoughtful.

*Nothing good, eh?* said Mondrian softly to himself. *But some things on Earth are enough to interest you mightily. So you'd like to visit a Needler lab, would you? I caught that look at King Bester.*

He went to sit beside Brachis. Both men were quiet for many minutes with their own thoughts.

Tatiana came back into the dimly-lit room and sat down opposite Mondrian. "All done," she said. "They've transferred title. The two of them are yours."

Mondrian nodded, but he did not look up. In front of him on the table was an open bottle of ancient brandy, and next to it a balloon glass holding a quarter of an inch of the amber liquid.

"Do you have any idea how I had to work to find that for you?" went on Tatiana. "I started looking right after the last visit. And you haven't even sniffed it."

Mondrian roused himself to give her a grave half-smile. "Not your fault, Princess. You know me. Most of the time I'd kill for brandy like this."

"So what's wrong?"

"I wish I knew. Something's wrong with the deal we made. For one thing, your friend Bozzie didn't ask enough money for those two."

"But you told me yourself you had no idea how much they should cost."

"True enough. I didn't. But King Bester knew, and I was watching his face when Bozzie accepted our offer. He positively gawped." He picked up the glass, and breathed in the delicate centuries-old bouquet. "Well, we're committed now, even if I'm not comfortable with it. I told Flammarion to ship them up the lift system and get them off Earth as soon as he could, before Quarantine could change their minds. Now I wish I hadn't. I wish I'd taken a look at the two of them myself."

"You did see them."

"Only for a second or two, when we first met them. Luther Brachis took charge of their exit permits—and *he* seems much too pleased with himself. I'm telling you, Tatty, something's not right."

"Where's Brachis now?"

"He slipped away with King Bester, and they didn't say where they were going. But I think I know. They've gone to a needler lab. I'm sure Brachis has heard of them often enough, but I doubt if he's ever been to one."

"What does he want there?"

Mondrian shook his head again, and at last took a tiny sip of liquid. "He didn't tell me." He smiled, but it was more like a rueful grimace. "Tatiana, my dear, if anyone knows that people sneak down here to Earth for their own secret reasons, you surely do. Can you make an arrangement for me—for tonight? I have to see Rattafee again."

"Rattafee! Didn't you know?" Tatty looked shocked. "Rattafee's dead. I'm sorry, Esro, I assumed you would have heard about it. She overdosed on Paradox, nearly a month ago."

He closed his eyes. "That is . . . not good news," he said at last. "She was the best I've ever had. I thought I might even be making some progress with her. Now . . . I don't know where to turn. Where can I go?" His voice was bleak.

"I heard talk just a few days ago about a new Freudhopper, living somewhere down in the deep basement levels. I can find out more about that if you want me to. Maybe get an appointment for you in a week or so. You know it takes time if the Fr'opper's any good." She hesitated. "I can check it for you tomorrow if you want. Tonight, I was hoping you'd stay here with me. For just the one night." She leaned across the table to put her hands on his shoulders. "Esro, I'm not asking much. You don't have to fake it for me any more—none of the same old promises, how you'll find a place for me up there, and take me with you away from Earth. You don't need to tell me all that. Just stay for tonight. That's all I'm asking."

He put his hands gently on hers. "Princess, you don't understand. Or maybe you understand better than I do. When I come down here to Earth, I *always* want to see you. But I have to be honest with you. Most of all, I come to Earth to meet the Fr'oppers, to see if they can help me. I'll stay here tonight, of course I will. But can you make an appointment *now* for the Fr'opper meeting, as soon as I can be fitted into this new one's schedule? That way I'll have some hope of a few hours' sleep tonight."

Tatty leaned forward and kissed Mondrian quickly

on the lips. "Of course I will. My poor, poor Esro. Is it still as bad as ever?"

"Worse. Every year, it tightens and tightens on me." He sat up straight and drew in a long breath. "One other thing, Tatty. I have to know what Luther Brachis is doing while he's here on Earth. I'm sure he's up to something. I'm trying to put King Bester on my payroll, but I'm not sure he stays bought and we need an honest thief. Could you contact The Godiva Bird and put her onto Brachis?"

"That will cost you a fortune. Do you know how much Godiva charges for her favors?"

"Budgets are not the problem. Go ahead and do it. I don't think he'll be able to resist her; women are one of his weaknesses."

"Pity they're not one of yours." She smiled bitterly at him. "Poor Esro. You're so driven. I'll make the arrangements. You sit and rest. If only you could just relax sometime—for even one night."

"We're all driven, Princess—every one of us." He looked at the tiny glass spheres, each filled with purple liquid, that sat within easy reach. There was a row of them in every room in the apartment. "Maybe I'll learn to relax—and maybe that's when you'll stop being a Paradox addict."

She had been moving to the door, to the communicator in the next room. Now she paused. "I can't argue with that," she said slowly. "For God's sake, I wish I could. Just try to rest, Esro. I'll be back as soon as I can."

# Chapter Five

# NEEDLER

"Don't be crazy," said King Bester. "Nobody in their right mind lives on the surface."

A "surface apartment" of Delmarva Town was defined by convention as anything less than one kilometer underground. The final outer layer, where roof met open sky, was reserved for automated agriculture and land management. *Humans, keep out!* Anyone with a strange urge to taste the "natural" life could gratify it easily enough by travelling to central Africa or South America. There the surface reservations, complete with protected wild species, still stretched across thousands of square miles.

The surface of Delmarva Town was a fine place for agriculture. And it was the perfect place for an illegal Needler lab—for those who could stand the idea. Luther Brachis and King Bester tried to hide their discomfort from each other as they left the final ascent tube and walked up a ringing steel staircase out onto the cultivated soil of the city. Brachis hated those unpredictable breezes. They still carried to him their message of air failure and hard vacuum. And King Bester, comfortable in the cramped warrens of the cities, trembled under the star-filled night sky, with its cold brilliance.

Walking closer together than either realized, they hurried across three fields of dark-green mutated sedge. King Bester knew their destination exactly. After only a few minutes under open sky he was ducking thankfully into a roofed enclosure. They descended a short flight of steps to an unlocked door and a darkened room. Standing within was a tall, stooped man with a domed bald head, jutting red nose, and long straggling beard.

"The Margrave of Fujitsu," said Bester formally. "Commander Luther Brachis."

The Margrave stared at them gloomily, closed the door, turned, and pressed a light switch. At the other side of the room sat a bulbous plant, about five feet high and two feet across. When the light hit it the leaves of the swollen upper end began to open. In less than thirty seconds a single vast flower was revealed. The central portion resembled a human face, with pink cheeks, curved red mouth, and blind blue eyes. After a few moments, the mouth opened and a thin, beautiful tone came forth. It was a crystalline, pure soprano, singing a wordless lament. There was steady development, from a simple theme through to its complex coloratura embroidery.

"One of my most successful creations," said the Margrave, in excellent standard solar. "I call this *Sorudan*—the spirit of song. The melody never repeats unless I so desire. I will be sorry if I am ever obliged to sell." He turned the level of the light down. The voice slowly faded, and the theme passed through sublime downward ripples of semitones to a final cadence. The sightless eyes closed. Moments later the petals began to curve in around the silent face.

The Margrave led the way into the next room. Luther Brachis followed slowly. Even if the display of Sorundan had been laid on just for his benefit, it made no difference. The ugly artist had created a work of astonishing beauty.

The walls of the next room were lined with cages, drawings, photographs, and models. Brachis saw to his satisfaction that the range of Needler output was diverse and seemingly unlimited in form. Aquaforms, peering out from their tanks of green-tinged water, sat next to the crouching raptor shape of gryphons. In one holograph a skeletally thin kangaroo stood next to—and loomed over—a giraffe. In another, an inch-long bear-like creature ambled along the flat pad of a water-lily. And everywhere, mobile plants quivered and snaked among the cages, following a moving source of overhead light.

The Margrave of Fujitsu waved his arm across the display. "The King tells me you're not interested in a simple art product," he said gruffly. "Why don't you outline your requirement to me? Then I'll tell you if I think it can be done, and how much it ought to cost."

Luther Brachis nodded. "I have a special need, one I'm willing to pay for very well. But the King will have to wait outside while I explain it. This has to be for your ears only."

King Bester looked startled, began to object, and then shrugged. "Fine idea," he said unconvincingly. "Get paid either way, so I don't care."

He went sulkily to the outer room, and watched while Luther Brachis carefully closed the door. Bester put his ear close against it, but he could hear nothing. He waited impatiently for fifteen minutes, even standing on a stool in case he could see anything over the top of the door. It was useless. By the time the door opened again and the other two men came out, he was hopping up and down with inquisitive frustration.

"I'll send all the specifications as soon as I get back to Ceres," said Brachis.

The Margrave nodded solemnly and opened the outside door. "Give me two weeks after that before you look for results. By that time I will be able to tell you if I can make what you want. And you will need a suitable intermediary. I dare not meet with just anyone."

"I understand. I will make arrangements." The heavy door closed. The light vanished, and Brachis and Bester were in the darkness of a moonless Earth-night.

"Why are they called 'Needlers'?" said Brachis, as they went up the stairs to the open surface. "I looked at the Margrave's whole lab, and I didn't see one place where they prick anything."

"Don't prick," said King Bester, in awkward standard solar. "Least, not any more. Did when technique started, ages back. Early days, they were all biologists. Playing around with female animals, produced offspring, no poppa."

"You mean parthenogenesis? Lots of organisms propagate like that."

"Yeah. Partho-that. Knew was fancy long word. Biologists heat eggs, put eggs in acid, give electric shock, poke with needles—and egg develops. Then later started a new game: if use *hollow* needle, real fine, can inject stuff into cell middle. Can put new DNA into nucleus."

"King, when they taught you standard solar, didn't they ever mention pronouns? Why don't we just talk earth-tongue?—you're making my head ache."

King Bester wiggled his eyebrows, grinned, and shrugged. "All right, squire. Not many foreigners understand it, so I tend not to use it. I'll be glad to switch. After they learned the DNA injection and splicing techniques, the Needlers never looked back. They learned how to put duck DNA in an eagle, spider DNA in a mosquito—anything in anything. Tricky technology, of course—you or me try it, and the egg would die. But some of 'em got hot-shot good at it—like old Fujitsu there. You want it, he'll make it." The King stared at Luther Brachis with vast curiosity. "Did he say what he'd do for you?"

Brachis did not answer at once. They were standing at the top of the flight of stairs, waiting for their eyes to adjust to the darkness. King Bester took Brachis by the arm. "Don't rush it, squire. There might be Scavvies around. They come up out of the warrens at night, see what they can find. If you ever meet Bozzie's Scavengers up here, run for it. They're tough and they're mean, and they'll cut you to pieces for your clothes—or just for the fun of it."

They stood there for a couple of minutes. Both men were reluctant to step up onto the surface again. Finally Brachis took a few paces forward and forced himself to stand and look around. If he was going to be visiting Earth again, he had better learn to be comfortable there.

He looked and listened. The steady breeze on his face was already less disconcerting. The smell of decay—it must be dead plants and animals, crumbling to unplanned and uncontrolled dissolution—made him wrinkle his nose in disgust. The sedge around them rustled in the wind as leaf moved over leaf. He looked up. There was a broken layer of cloud overhead. In the open patches of sky he could see stars, strangely soft-edged and subdued. They seemed to move and flicker while he watched.

He began to walk to the entry point to the lower levels. "The work the Margrave is doing for me is none of your business," he said, finally answering Bester's question. The hook had been set back in the lab. Now it was time to strike. If King Bester could be caught with anything, it would be his enormous curiosity. "Mind you," he went on, "things would be quite different if I were sure you were on my side. I could tell you a lot of things then about my plans—and you could be involved in them, too. There could be jobs for you, down here and off Earth."

Bester started to snap his fingers in excitement. "Try me—just try me." They were moving across the surface to return to the underground levels.

Luther Brachis shook his head. "Too risky. First, I'd have to be sure you were working for me, not for Esro Mondrian."

"I don't work for him—swear I don't. Never met him before."

"We'll see. But we have to work slowly, and carefully. I may say a lot about Esro Mondrian, but I'll never say he's not smart."

"He frightens me," said Bester. "I don't like to look at his eyes."

"Stay that way. It's safest. You think you're ready to do a job for me, then?"

"You name it, squire." King Bester was almost too eager. "I'll do it."

"Very well. As a beginning, I'll want you to keep a close eye on the product that the Margrave of Fujitsu will be developing for me back there." Brachis smiled. "You wanted to know what I ordered. You'll have that. I'll send you the specification to hand-deliver to the Margrave in the next few days. Don't tell anybody about it. And I want you to keep an eye on it as it's being develped."

"You think he can make it for you?"

"I feel sure he'll try. His pride won't give him any way to refuse. You'll see the result and know how well he did even before I do."

They were almost back to the level where Tatty Snipes lived. She had arranged sleeping accommodation for both of them in large, luxurious apartments. King Bester rolled his eyes when he saw them, and gave thanks aloud that he didn't have to pay for them.

"But I still don't understand why a Needler is not a legally permitted trade," went on Brachis, when they were finally standing at his apartment door. "The products are wonderful. You could export them all over the Stellar Group."

King Bester fidgeted in his patchwork clothes, and shook his head. "Uh-uh. They have a problem. The Needler labs make all kinds of Artefacts—but all the good ones have one thing in common: their DNA is mostly human. It's not permitted, but they all do it—or they can't compete with the others. Remember Sorudan? That was more human than the smart chimps in the transportation system. Same's true for everything else you saw in Fujitsu's laboratory."

Luther Brachis did not reply. But from the expression on his face, Bester had the odd idea that he could not have given the big Security Commander better news.

An hour before dawn, Esro Mondrian was fully awake. He had slept for perhaps three hours after midnight, then awakened shivering and perspiring. Tatiana lay by his side. When it came, the soft buzz of his communicator did not waken her.

She was lying with one arm and leg across his body. He moved slowly and carefully to free himself, then tiptoed in the darkness to the next room. Once the door was closed he turned on a low-powered light and switched to voice mode.

"Commander Mondrian?" As he had expected, it was Kubo Flammarion. The wizened little man drank too much, but he ate little and slept less. The two men were both awake twenty hours out of twenty-four.

"This is Mondrian. You're calling early, Kubo. Where are you?"

"At the lift facility." Flammarion's voice was nervous. "Getting ready to take the two we found in the Gallimaufries away to Ceres. But we have a real problem, and I thought I ought to call you before I did anything else."

"Report."

"The woman is fine. Her name is Leah Buckingham Rainbow. Her title is free and clear, she's twenty-two years old, and she's in first-rate physical and mental condition. Prime training material. It's the man." He paused. "He's . . . mm . . ."

"*Report!*"

"His name is Chancellor Vercingetorix Dalton," said Flammarion hurriedly. "He's a wonderful physical specimen, twenty years old, and *his* title is clear, too." He cleared his throat. "Only trouble is, he's a —er—a moron."

"What!" Mondrian did not raise his voice, because he did not want to waken Tatiana. But its intensity seared along the communication link.

"A moron. Remember when we first saw them, the woman seemed to lead the action? Well, when we caught them she did all the talking. He seemed to be listening, and he kept nodding. But he didn't say anything much, just gave his name when we asked for it. When you see the result of the psychological tests you'll see why. That's just about the only thing he *can* say, with any understanding. He takes all his cues from her."

"*That's* why Bozzie was so happy to make the deal." Mondrian sat hunched by the communicator, his head in his hands. "Damn the man, he knew it! The fat fraud. Kubo, how bad is Dalton? Did you get a profile?"

"Pretty hopeless. Mental age of maybe a two-year-old. Him and the girl were raised together, and she's always looked after him. That hasn't helped him at all."

"Who knows about this?"

"Right now? No one. But the reports will go to

Security. I suppose that means that it will go . . ."
Flammarion hesitated.

"To Luther Brachis? Of course it will. We can't
stop it." The fury had gone from Esro Mondrian's
voice. Now it sounded as though it was trickling
through cracked ice. "He'll think he's won the wager. But I'm not ready to admit it. Kubo, look at
that profile carefully, and try to answer this question. Do we have a situation where we could hook
Dalton into a Tolkov Stimulator?"

There was a silence at the other end.

"Kubo?"

"Yes . . . uh, I'm sorry. I guess . . ." There was
another silence. "I guess so. The profile looks right.
There ought to be a decent chance. But, Commander, the Stimulator . . . it's top security use.
It's not—I mean it's supposed to be—"

"Don't gibber at me, Kubo. When I want a mon-
key on the staff I can find one down here on Earth.
I know better than you do the restrictions on Stimulator use. But I think I can handle them. The
training of the pursuit teams *is* a top security
issue. The Anabasis has special powers."

"I know. But Commander, it's not just approv-
als. It's the Stimulator. It only works one time out
of ten."

"So we're playing a long shot. I'll accept that.
Don't forget, when the Tolkov Stimulator *is* successful, there's a switch from subnormal to super-
normal. The subject becomes extremely intelligent."

"But Commander, if it *doesn't* work—then it kills
the subject."

"Right. And then the wager with Brachis would
be off. Kubo, don't waste time telling me how the
Stimulator works. Get on with the job."

"Yessir." Flammarion stood to attention. "As you
say, sir. Except that . . . Commander, we'd need to
find somebody who'll lock themselves away and
work with Chancellor Dalton for a long time—

months, maybe even a year. And from what I've heard, it's absolute hell on both of 'em. It's like torturing the person it's used on. After a few tries applying the Stimulator to somebody, the person doing it will usually up and quit. You'd never get anybody willing to use it on Dalton. It would be torture for *them* as well as him. Unless you mean that I'll—"

Flammarion realized where his logic was taking him, and his tongue froze in horror.

"Relax, Kubo. You're not a candidate. I know the problems of using a Tolkov Stimulator as well as you do. But I'll get somebody." Mondrian leaned back, calculating. "All right. Do this—immediately. Take both of them, the man and the woman, along to the confinement facility on Horus. Maximum security environment. Set up there for education and pursuit team training. And make sure a Stimulator is available, too. Clear?"

"I'll do it, sir."

"Thanks, Kubo. I know I can trust you. Now, one more thing. Have living quarters prepared on Horus for somebody who will work with Dalton."

"Yes, sir. Who will it be, sir?"

"Don't worry about it. I'll find someone."

"Yes, sir. But, er, sir—"

Mondrian was poised to cut the connection. "What else, Kubo?"

"The living quarters. Will they be for a man or a woman?"

Mondrian paused for a few seconds. "Assume it will be a woman," he said softly. He pressed the disconnect and moved silently back into the bedroom.

Tatiana had turned to lie flat on her back. She was still sleeping soundly. Mondrian moved to her side and set out to rouse her, caressing her infinitely slowly and gently. She pulled him close before she was more than half-awake, and muttered with pleasure at what he was doing.

They made love for a long time, quietly and in total darkness. Afterwards she held him locked tight, rocked him up and down, and whispered in his ear. "That was different. Usually you pull away when it's over, but this time you stayed with me. Esro, it was wonderful."

"It was fantastic," he said softly. "Tatiana, you're very dear to me. I know you told me not to make you the same old promises, and I won't do that. But I'll make you a new one. Princess, I need your help. I have an important job that needs doing. It's away from Earth, and it may take a long time, but I must have somebody I trust totally. If you'll agree to help me, I promise you we'll leave Earth— together."

She jerked beneath him, as though trying to sit up under his weight. "Esro, are you serious? I mean, after all this time, then you ask me to go with you, just like that. I can hardly believe it."

"I'm quite serious. We'll go—if you want to."

She began to rock him again, and tightened her arms about him as hard as she could. "Of course I want to!"

"Think twice. I'm not sure you'll get Paradox easily once you're away from Earth. That's one of Quarantine's strongest prohibitions."

She paused, licking her lips. There was fear and hunger in the brown eyes. "I still want to," she said at last. She laughed nervously. "The stuff's killing me anyway; I've known that for years. When would we go?"

"Very soon. I'll need to get special permission from Quarantine, and an exit permit, but Flammarion can start working on that in the morning. I'd expect to be leaving Earth in three or four days. Can you be ready?"

Tatty was suddenly crying. "Ready? *Ready?* Esro, if you want me there, I'm ready this minute. I'll go right now."

Fortunately, she could not see his face.

# Chapter Six

# AT THE HORUS
# CONFINEMENT CENTER

The asteroids of the Egyptian Cluster are a solar system anomaly. The orbits of the cluster members share a common inclination and a perihelion distance of about three hundred million kilometers, supporting the idea that they *are* a cluster, although one now far dispersed spatially. They also share the common material composition of the smaller silicaceous bodies of the solar system. And yet they are, every one, anomalous. Instead of moving in the ecliptic like all well-behaved planetoids, their common orbital plane is inclined at an angle of nearly fifty-nine degrees to it.

The physical data for the Egyptian Cluster are given in the Appendix to the General Ephemerides of the solar system—a fair measure of their importance in the big scheme of things. But even with a minor group there is a natural pecking order. Horus, twenty kilometers across, is an asteroid low on that order, very much an undistinguished specimen. No more than a bleak wedge of dark rock, it lacks atmosphere, regular form, useful minerals, easily accessible orbit, or any other interesting property.

It is the perfect place for a maximum security

facility. Mindful of this, generations of excavators have turned Horus into a worm-riddled cheese of black silicate, hollow and tunneled and chambered. The echoing inner cavities, with their entrance corridors paradoxically reflex and convoluted, are an ideal location for assured privacy and security.

Or for incarceration.

In one of the central chambers of Horus, comfortably appointed as ample living quarters, sat two men and two women: Kubo Flammarion, Chancellor Dalton, Tatiana Snipes, and Leah Rainbow.

Flammarion had been talking steadily for a long time, while the other three listened with varying degrees of attention. Chancellor Dalton fidgeted and played with the plate and fork sitting in front of him. Tatty Snipes stared ahead with a dull, lifeless face the color of dirty chalk, while her hands trembled whenever she lifted them from the table. Alone of the three, Leah was following every word that Flammarion had said.

"But you *can't*," she said again. Her face was frowning and furious, and she spoke standard solar so badly and so angrily that Flammarion could only just understand her. "You absolutely can't. Don't you understand? I've looked after Chan ever since he was four years old, when his mother sold him down in the Gallimaufries. If I'm not with him, he'll be lost. Totally lost."

"At first." Kubo Flammarion looked enormously uncomfortable, and he was not enjoying his job at all. "But he'll be all right. Princess Tatiana will look after him."

"Chan like Tatty," said Dalton proudly. It was the most complex statement Flammarion had heard him make since they arrived on Horus.

"How can she look after him?" exploded Leah. "Just look at her. She can hardly look after herself."

That finally roused Tatty to a response. She straightened in her chair. "Do you think I *want* to be out here? Do you think I'm happy about the idea of baby-sitting that overgrown lump—that—that *moron*? I don't want any of it. I want to go home—back to Earth, away from this god-awful, god-damned, god-gone place." She leaned forward and buried her face in her trembling hands. After a few moments she began to groan deep in her throat.

"Moron!" shouted Leah. "What do you mean, *moron*—"

Flammarion waved his hand across her face and interrupted her. "Don't hassle Tatty just now. She's not herself. Can't you see she's in Paradox withdrawal? Go easy on her. All she can think about is that she needs a shot."

"Shot for Tatty," said Chan Dalton. "Tatty my friend." And he went across to her, and hugged her happily.

Flammarion offered him an uncertain look. The tests that assigned Chan Dalton the intelligence of a two-year-old were imprecise in many ways, and their conclusion was just an average of many factors. Sometimes Chan seemed to understand nothing that was said to him. At other times he would fix his gaze on the speaker and nod intelligently, as though listening hard and following every word. Leah had assured Flammarion that this was no more than a protective coloration, something she had painstakingly taught Chan to let him operate in the tough environment of the Gallimaufries. But it was difficult to believe that someone who *seemed* to listen intelligently was not doing so. Her explanation had only halfway persuaded Flammarion.

"I won't leave Chan, and you can't make me," said Leah at last, standing up from the table. "You say you want me to become a candidate for one of your stupid pursuit teams? Just you try and force me. If you make me leave here I won't cooperate at all, on *anything*."

Flammarion wriggled his shoulders uncomfortably in his tunic. He had been coached in the next part very carefully by Esro Mondrian, but he was not sure how well he could carry it off.

"How much do you care for Chan?" he began.

Leah went around to stand by the blond youth's side. "More than anything or anyone," she said fiercely. "He's *all* I care about. More than anyone on Earth, or anyone in the Stellar Group. Can't you tell that's a stupid question?" She put her arms possessively around Chan's waist.

"I thought so," said Flammarion. "In all those years of caring for him and loving him, didn't it ever make you sad to know that Chan would not develop as a normal human? I'm not talking about the physical side, I mean his mental maturity. Didn't you grieve, to think that he'd always be like this, and never know the world that we know?"

Flammarion had been very uncomfortable at first, referring to Chancellor Dalton in his presence like this, as though he were not even there. But after a while he realized that his discomfort was inappropriate. Chan was not aware of most of the references to him. In some ways, Chan was quite unconscious of his own self.

Flammarion's questions were having a visible effect on Leah Rainbow. She was looking sad and angry, and her eyes were blinking. "Of course I've grieved, you silly old man. I've wept more for Chan than for myself. I've often thought I would give anything I have, sell my body to slavery, bond to a Pipe-Rilla, anything, if it would give Chan adult intelligence. I still feel that way—I would do *anything*. But now I know it's a hopeless wish."

"Then listen to me now." Flammarion leaned forward and lowered his voice confidentially, ignoring the fact that there was no other person within seventy million kilometers of the four of them. "A few years ago, a gadget was invented on Oberon Station. It was designed for use in working with alien forms scattered around the Known Sphere—forms who might be intelligent, but were borderline cases. That invention is called a Tolkov Stimulator. Only a few of them have been made, and their use is prohibited on humans except in cases of Stellar Group emergency. A Stimulator *heightens the level of mental activity*—and when it works it produces a *permanent* change on the subject. You understand me?"

"You mean it makes people smarter?"

"Sometimes. Some people. It makes others insane—that's why it's prohibited for general use. Anyway, Esro Mondrian, my boss, has access to a Stimulator, one we can use for the Anabasis. Under the right circumstances, he might make it available." Flammarion leaned towards Leah. "*Available for Chan.*"

"For Chan," echoed Dalton happily. He was still standing with his arms around Tatty Snipes. "For Chan."

"See?" said Flammarion. "He knows. But I'm quite sure that Commander Mondrian *won't* make it available to Chan if you refuse to cooperate with us and won't carry on with pursuit team training. That's why I asked: how important is Chan to you?"

Flammarion paused. He had reached the end of Mondrian's prepared speech. Now all he could do was sit and wait for Leah's reaction. He advanced to Chan's side, and stood there uncertainly.

When her response came it was a surprise to Flammarion. Leah burst into tears, and hugged Chan Dalton to her. "Chan, did you hear him? Oh, Chan, you're going to grow up—read, and write, and know the animals and flowers and days of the week, and dress yourself, and know the names of all your friends. Won't that be wonderful?"

"You mean you'll do it?" said Flammarion, standing bolt upright and stretching the creases in his wrinkled uniform.

She rounded on him, her tears giving way to fury. "Of course I'll do it, you great fool. You know your pressure points, don't you? You know just where to probe and twist, to make me do what you want. I'll do it—I'll go away, and train, and study, and do my best to be a pursuit team member. But it will be on these conditions: you have to promise me that Chan will get a *full* treatment here, the best that can be given; and you must let me know as soon as he becomes normal."

"*If* he becomes normal," said Flammarion. "The Stimulator isn't a sure thing. There's a good chance it will fail. Even if it works we won't know for a while. It's a funny process, slow at first, but then at the end the understanding all comes at one rush. What I'm saying is, there's no guarantee that final understanding will *ever* come. Chan may stay a moron for all his life." *And that won't be very long, but I can't tell them.*

"But if he does, he'll be no worse off than he is now." Leah said. "Will I be able to visit him while you're giving the treatment?"

"Maybe just a couple of times." Flammarion cleared his throat, as though the next fact was sticking there. "The period when the Stimulator is being applied is very . . . intense. It's a tough time, for the person being treated, and also for the one giving the treatment. For Chan's own sake, he has to interact with just one person until the course is finished. And that person will be Tatty."

"For how long?"

"I don't know. Maybe a few months, maybe more. By that time I expect your training will be over, and you'll have pursuit team assignment. Look, Leah, how much of all this do you think you can get across to Chan? It would make Tatty's job a lot easier if he knew what was going on."

"I don't know." Leah had recovered her self-control. "It's a bit abstract for him. But I can try." She turned to Chan. "Channy, why don't we go away and play, just us, in the swim-room? We can leave Tatiana and the Captain here."

Chan nodded. "Captain smell bad," he said agreeably. "We go."

"There," said Leah fiercely to Flammarion. "Chan may not be smart, but he's telling you something you should have been told a long time ago. I wish I'd said that. You smell, Captain. To be more precise, you *stink*. Come on, Chan, let's get out of here."

She headed for the door before Flammarion could reply, dragging Chan along by the hand. Kubo Flammarion gave a perplexed look at her, then shrugged, scratched his head, rubbed his sleeve across his nose, and went over to Tatty Snipes. He took a purple globe from his pocket and pressed it firmly against her arm. "Only half a dose, Tatty, but better than nothing. Wait a minute or two, and you'll start to feel better."

She groaned as she felt the injection, but after a few seconds she raised her head, and color began to seep back into the livid cheeks. "Thanks, Kubo. I thought I'd die when Esro told me there'd be no more shots—that I'd be on my own. Are you disobeying his orders?"

"I suppose I am." Flammarion sat down next to her at the table. "You see, Tatty, I know Esro Mondrian. He doesn't behave like a normal human. I sometimes think he's tough enough himself to stand anything, and he assumes you must be the same. But not me. I've got my own problems, and I know what a hard time you're going through now. But if we can just *ease* you off Paradox, little by little, you have a chance of making it all the way."

Tatty held up her arm, showing the regular line of blue-black dots from elbow to shoulder. "You're an optimist, Kubo. Eight hundred shots say you're wrong. *I hate him*," she said suddenly, "bringing me away from Earth, sending me here like that, not telling me when he'll be coming out himself ..." She bowed forward again, making little sounds of misery in her private grief.

"He'll be here in a few days." Flammarion reached out a hand, as though to touch Tatty's hair, then withdrew it. "He's unbelievably busy, trying to get the whole pursuit program training going. And we're still having a terrible time with the ambassador's office. Macdougal wants to be in the middle of everything. And the only person who can deal with that is Commander Mondrian."

"Don't make excuses for him; that's not part of your job." Tatty looked up wearily. "Kubo, you think you know Esro. Believe me, I know him a lot better—probably better than anyone who just works for him. If he had to do it for his own reasons, Esro would sell to the devil you and me and everyone he knows, and not think twice about it. But that's not the thing that has me most upset. The shameful thing is that *I knew it*—knew it years ago, and still I'm here, out in the middle of nowhere, still doing what he wants me to do. I shouldn't be blaming him, I should be blaming *myself*." She stood up slowly, leaning back to stretch her tired muscles. "No more pity, Kubo. Give me the rest of the bad news. You told Leah Rainbow that the Stimulator is hard on the person being treated *and* on the person who does the treating. Esro never mentioned that. What's the problem going to be for me?"

Flammarion sighed and sat down. He felt an increasing resentment. It was happening again— Mondrian making the mess, and leaving the explanations to Kubo Flammarion.

"Let me explain about the Tolkov Stimulator," he said. As he spoke he kept his gaze on the table in front of him; that way he could pretend to himself that he was unaware of Tatty Snipes, and of her growing expression of horror at what she was hearing.

# Chapter Seven

# THE FR'OPPER

Esro Mondrian had puzzled over the careful directions long before he tried to follow them. They meandered through an endless series of descent shafts, to the deepest basement levels of the Gallimaufries; far down into Earth's crust, where continuous cooling was needed to make the levels even marginally habitable, and only the power maintenance crews visited on a regular basis. It seemed inconceivable that a Fr'opper would have an office down in those smoking warrens. But the instructions had been quite specific.

The final hundred yards of his journey were in near-total darkness, stepping carefully along a steadily descending shallow ramp. At the foot, Mondrian paused and took a miniature flashlight from his belt.

"No light, please," said a soft voice a few yards away from him. "Take hold, Commander Mondrian, and follow me."

"You are Skrynol?"

"I am." A warm, fleshy flipper touched Mondrian's fingers. He walked, step by slow step, led by the Fr'opper in front of him. Finally he was

77

guided to a seat covered by warm velvety material, and told to sit back and relax.

"You're an optimist," he said. "Could *you* relax, when you don't know what the devil is going on? I've been to Fr'oppers before, but I've never had to put up with anything like this. Why do you want to be in pitch darkness? I'd like a little light."

"That is understandable," said the soft voice, "but it is not a good idea. With light here, you might feel much *less* relaxed. Not every product of the Needler labs is a work of art in esthetic terms."

Mondrian sat forward in his seat. "Are you telling me you're an *Artefact*?"

"I do seem to be saying that, don't I? Does it give you a problem?" There was a trill of laughter from the blackness in front of Mondrian. "Does it make you doubt my capabilities? If so, I can refer you to others who will provide excellent testimonials. And from my assessment of your mental condition, the Fr'oppers you have visited in the past have done little for you. Could an Artefact do worse?"

Mondrian grunted and leaned back again on the seat. "That's a logic I can't argue with. But how can you say you've assessed my mental condition, when I've been here only two minutes?"

"You're asking for trade secrets. I do not reveal them. But if you want proof that I can do what I say, you shall have an example. Sit there quietly, relax, and let your thoughts wander where you wish. I am about to attach a few electrodes." Cold touches came on forehead, hands, and neck.

The temperature in the room was far too hot for comfort. Mondrian sat in silence, sweating heavily, and tried to follow the Fr'opper's order to relax. He was wondering what form could be so horrible that the sight of it would be worse than the oppressive and stifling darkness. He leaned forward, eyes wide, and tried to see something of the being in front of him. It was useless. Was he wasting his time here, on yet another unproductive visit to a Fr'opper?

"I have enough," said Skrynol suddenly. "Remember, I cannot read your thoughts, and will never claim to do so. But I can read your body, and through that your emotions, and they tell me more about your thoughts than you may be prepared to believe. For example, let me read back to you a few of the more obvious and familiar indicators. Your pupils are somewhat dilated—yes, before you ask, I can see you very well, even though you cannot see me—and there is a slight eye flicker. Your body temperature is elevated perhaps half a degree over what I estimate to be its usual value. Your muscles are tense, but in tight control—you are now making a conscious effort to relax your back and shoulders. Your pulse is elevated, ten or so counts a minute above normal. Palms wet, perspiration high in acids and low in potassium ions. Mouth tight, lips a little dry. Nasal mucus membranes dry also, and probably a fraction of a degree cooler than expected. Frequent swallowing, and tight sphincters. In summary, you are hugely excited, and tremendously controlled. Now, those are mere physical variables. A med machine could tell you as much. But I can integrate all the factors and place them in context. And I can *guess*—nothing more than a guess—at the mental state that produced them. And I conclude this: at the conscious level, Commander Mondrian, you are pondering me, and my probable appearance. That is perfectly natural. But below that, in the center of your real attention, are two other worries. You have lost something, and it is enormously important that you find it. And that concern takes us deeper yet, to the reason that you are here in the first place. The thing that is lost is important to

you, only because it *protects* you from the thing
that you fear most. The hidden thing."

Mondrian was sitting bolt upright in the darkness. He had been thinking about the Morgan Constructs, and where they might be—but until the
Fr'opper mentioned the "lost something," that
thought had been no more than a nagging background worry.

"The hidden thing," he said grimly. "Is it the
source of my nightmares—the reason why I wake
up terrified every night?"

"Of course it is.'" Skrynol's voice was calm. "You
did not need me to answer that question, did you?
—you could answer it for yourself. So now, shall
we begin the search for the hidden thing? We must
find it, before we can hope to get rid of it."

Mondrian leaned back. "I am in your hands."
He suddenly seemed more nervous, turning and
twisting the fire-opal at his collar. He had noticed
a faint smell in the air, a trace of odor like over-
ripe peaches. "What do you want me to do?"

"Sit completely still. I am about to attach a few
more electrodes." Again the cold touches, this time
on Mondrian's chest and abdomen. "Very good.
Now we are going to explore *below* the conscious
levels. Today, just the first stratum. I will speak
certain key words, and you will answer however
you choose."

It was standard Fr'opper technique, outlawed
off Earth for centuries, and with an uncertain and
unsavory reputation even on the planet. Mondrian
nodded to signify his assent. The question-and-
answer period began. And suddenly, it was no
longer the standard session. He had drifted into a
dazed semi-conscious state, aware that he was talking, but not sure of the content. It went on for a
long time. Finally Mondrian realized that he was
again being addressed directly.

"*Mondrian*! Do you know what you have been

saying to me? If necessary, I can repeat the important points for you."

· He came back to full wakefulness, realizing that he could remember all he had said—even though it had been taken without his control, from levels within that he did not know existed. He nodded. "I know. I said . . ."

The memory came spinning back in, with terrifying detail. Skrynol had somehow coaxed him to build a series of mental pictures, little by little. They were still bright in his mind.

. . . *He had taken on a form like a giant spider, and was sitting quietly at the center of a great web. The strands shone with their own light, each one visible, running off in all directions. But there was a point beyond which their luminescence faded. He could see a well-defined region of web, with himself in the middle. Beyond that all was darkness. While he watched and waited, he felt a trembling in the glowing strands of the web. He looked out along the lines to see what prey was there, but the disturbing object was too far away. It lay in the dark region. He knew from the delicate vibrations along the gossamer strands that the prey was approaching.*

*And suddenly it was no longer prey. It was a danger, a force that he could not control, creeping in towards him along the luminous threads. And he was not waiting at the center of the web until the moment arrived when he would set off to seek his victim. He was bound at the web center, unable to flee from whatever approached him out of the distant darkness . . .*

"*Excellent!*" said Skrynol's voice. Mondrian found that suddenly he was shivering and hot all over, wanting to run away as fast as he could.

"We have penetrated much farther in one session than I had dared to hope," went on Skrynol. "Have you ever retrieved that set of images before?"

"Never." Mondrian was recovering self-control,

but he was still fiddling nervously with the fire-opal at his collar. "What are those thoughts? Are they the 'hidden thing' that you talked about?"

Skrynol laughed again, with that high-pitched trill of amusement. "If it were that simple, then you would not need the services of a good Fr'opper. No, what we found today is the mind's first level of defense. The images you built are a second-level reference. They are no more than an analogy to your real fears, and *those* fears stem from a much deeper and earlier hidden experience. We have a long way to go. Let us meet again in one week."

Mondrian felt the electrodes being removed from his body. "What do I owe you?" he said huskily.

"For today, nothing." There was a pause. "To give a more honest answer, you have already provided my payment for today. When the electrodes were attached, two of them included small cathe-ters. While you were building your protective mem-ories, I drew blood from you. Just a little. Don't worry, you have plenty left—I took less than a quarter of a liter, only five percent of your total body supply. It will be replenished in a very short time."

Mondrian took a deep breath. "Nice of you to tell me about it. Why did you want my blood?"

"For the best, simplest, and most honest of rea-sons: to drink. My metabolism is not suited to the digestion of most forms of food."

Mondrian stood up from the velvet seat. "I sup-pose I ought to be thankful that your needs are so modest," he said coldly. "Will that be your stan-dard charge for services—or do you increase the price as the treatment continues?"

"You know I wouldn't do that." Skrynol was laughing again as they wound their way back to the exit. "I want you as a regular customer. If I drained you, that would be the end of it." There was a sly note of humor in Skrynol's voice as

Mondrian again set foot on the ramp. "You're safe enough with me, Commander Mondrian . . . as long as you're still in treatment. The time to watch out will be the day you feel you're cured. Because then you will not expect to return here, and I will have no incentive to hold back my appetite. For the moment, do not worry . . ."

Mondrian made the return journey to the upper levels almost in a trance. He could not get the spider-web images out of his mind. They made him horribly uncomfortable, even though he was absolutely convinced that Skrynol had made more progress in one session than anyone else in dozens.

Back at the Link Entrance level, he transferred to the appropriate exit point and wearily walked the rest of the way to the apartment. Without Tatiana's presence, the living quarters felt cold and desolate. Mondrian went through to the inner room, reached up to his collar, and carefully removed the fire-opal. Then he went across to the communicator and called for a private circuit up from Earth. Within a few seconds he had been connected with Border Security's principal laboratory on Pallas.

"Hasselblad?" he said. "This is Esro Mondrian. I have a special job for you. I just made a multiple medium recording, all wavelengths, of something down here on Earth." He looked at the fire-opal for a few moments, weighing it in his hand. "I didn't know what screening might be operating, so I tried every setting. I want to know what images you can get out of it. It will be on its way up to you within an hour or two. Give it top priority, will you? I need the answers within a week."

# Chapter Eight

# STIMULATOR AND NEEDLER LAB

"No!" The scream resonated through the rocky chambers, incredibly loud and violent. "No, no, no, no, no."

"Chan! Chan! don't run away. Wait for me." Tatiana was chasing hopelessly in pursuit. The screams ahead of her were fading. Somehow he had escaped again, running blindly and tearfully off through the maze of interior tunnels. He could not get away from her for long, not with the Tracker to reveal his distance and direction, but the complexity of the interior of Horus made the search a long and tedious business. Ten generations of burrowing and excavating had left a staggering legacy of debris: old synthesizers, broken tools, obsolete communications equipment, mounds of supply containers—few things were worth hauling back from the Egyptian Cluster to re-use elsewhere in the system. Now the whole mess had to be climbed over, moved aside, and burrowed through.

Tatiana continued the pursuit. She felt close to tears herself, and the hardest part was still to come. When she caught Chan Dalton, she would have to give him medication and use the Tolkov

Stimulator. More and more, it all seemed a point-less exercise.

She went on, grimy and tired. Even before Flammarion had left Horus, Chan had been difficult to handle. He was bigger, stronger, and much faster than Tatty. She could often manage him only by using the stun field, slowing and weakening him enough for her to overpower him.

"Cha-an?" she cried, her voice breaking. "Chan, come back to Tatty." Silence. Had he found a new hiding-place? Maybe he *was* becoming more intelligent, just a little; or maybe it was all her wishful thinking. Every day she looked into the bright blue eyes, willing him to show more understanding; and every day she was disappointed. The innocence of a two-year-old stared back at her, always unable to comprehend why the woman who fed him, dressed him, hugged him, and put him to bed at night was also torturing him.

Most of the tunnels inside Horus terminated in dead ends. After a while, no matter how Chan tried to escape, he would finish in one of them. Usually the same ones. He simply lacked the memory and intelligence needed to learn the pattern of the paths. Tatty peered at the Tracker and went wearily forward. She was not more than twenty or thirty yards away from him now. He had to be hiding in the next chamber. She saw a rough pile of plastic sheets draped over powdered rock. Chan must be behind that, cowering brainlessly with his face pressed to the dirt. Tatty lifted the stunner and miserably went the last few yards. He was there. Weeping.

It broke her heart to take him back to the training center. She knew she would not need the stunner. Once she had hold of him his resistance disappeared. He let himself be led along by the hand, passive and hopeless. But when he saw the Stimulator he began to cry again, silently. She sat

him in the padded seat, grimly fitted the headset
and the arm attachments, and turned away as she
increased the power. The screams of pain when
full intensity was reached were bad, but she could
stand those. It was when the treatment was over,
and she released Chan and gave him food, that
Tatty always felt ready to faint. He would crouch
in the chair, sweaty and panting and looking up at
her pleadingly. His face was not that of a human.
It belonged to a tormented animal, dull, resigned,
uncomprehending. She was torturing a helpless
beast, punishing it again and again for a reason it
could not understand.

Kubo Flammarion had instructed her in the use
of the Stimulator before he left. He had told her
that Mondrian would give her more detailed advice when he came to Horus; but Mondrian never
came. Not even a message. Day after day, she
patiently did her best to follow Flammarion's suggestions. The three-fold way, of Machine, Medication, Motivation. It had to be followed with scrup-
ulous care. "The Stimulator won't work unless
you back it with two other things," he had said.
"You have to follow the drug protocol that we've
set out for you, night and morning, without fail.
But even more important than that, you somehow
have to make Chan Dalton *want* to learn."

"*How*, for Shannon's sake? He doesn't seem to
understand even the *idea* of learning."

Flammarion shrugged and scratched his head.
"Damned if I know, Tatty. All I can tell you is
what they told me. If he doesn't have motivation,
he'll never develop. And where there *is* motivation, nine times out of ten the Stimulator will
work a miracle. Here, how about using Leah's picture?" Flammarion produced a grimy image from
his uniform, a copy of Leah's official identification
when she was inducted into training for the pursuit team program. "Chan loves her more than

anything in the world. Show him this every time you use the Stimulator—tell him that when the treatments are over he'll be able to go and see Leah again."

Tatty took the picture. Every day, after the injections and after the Stimulator sessions, she made her speech. "Chan, see the nice picture. Come on, Chan. *Get smarter!* You've got to *want* to be more intelligent, just a little bit more every day. Then you'll be able to see Leah again—look, here she is. She'll come and see you."

Chan stared at the image. He smiled, and seemed to know who it was, but that was the only level of response. The days wore on. Tatty was finally ready to give up the effort. It was hopeless. Chan would never learn.

She was also feeling more and more desperate about her own situation. No visit from Mondrian. No calls. No messages. He had tricked her into leaving Earth, duped her into doing what he wanted, as he always did—and then forgotten about her. She tried to call him. She could not reach him. Finally, after many attempts, she managed to send a signal from Horus that got past the shielding layers of guards and assistants, right through to Mondrian's private office on Ceres.

"I'm sorry." One of Mondrian's personal assistants took the call. "Captain Flammarion is busy in a meeting, and Commander Mondrian himself is not here."

"Then where the devil is he?" snapped Tatty. She had run out of patience.

There was a brief pause. "According to the itinerary here at the office, Commander Mondrian is visiting Earth. He will be there for two days."

"He's *what!*"

Tatty disconnected the communicator in a cold, clean rage. To drag her to Horus to do his dirty work was bad enough. But to use her, then neglect her and go back to Earth himself, without even telling her . . . Tatty felt the bitterness filling her body, burning in her stomach. She went on into the other room, where Chan Dalton was connected to the Stimulator. The session was almost over. He was sweating prodigiously, rocking his head from side to side in the neck brace and headset. Tatty went to his side.

"Chan! Can you hear me?"

The eyes came open a slit. They were bloodshot and bulging slightly. There was still meningeal inflammation and some excess pressure inside the skull case, but he was listening. She put her arms around him.

"He's using us, Chan. Both of us." Tears were running down Tatty's cheeks. "Oh, Channy, I'd have done anything for him, anything in the world. I thought he was wonderful. I could even stand it when I found I'd be marooned out here, because I thought I'd be helping him. Even do without Paradox, if I had to. But it's no use. He doesn't care about us—about anything except himself. Chan, he's crazy and heartless. He's a devil. He'll destroy you, if he has to, the way he destroyed me. Don't let him do it, Chan."

Tatty fumbled in the small overall pocket above her left breast. She took out a thin wallet, and from it a miniature holograph. She held the image out in front of Chan Dalton's face.

"Look, Chan. Look at this. This is the person who brought us away from home. This is the person who took Leah away from you. Look at him, Chan. This is the person who makes you go into the Stimulator. Do you see him, Chan? You must get away from here, and find him. Look carefully, Chan. If you finish here, I can let you go and find him."

There was a long pause. The bloodshot eyes opened a fraction farther. Chan Dalton took a deep, shuddering breath. He stared at the hologram, and at the smiling face of Esro Mondrian. And at last a faint spark of understanding and feral cunning seemed to glow for a moment behind those innocent eyes.

The Margrave of Fujitsu paused for a moment, lifting his ugly head from the tiny screen. "And what did you expect to see?" he said. His voice was puzzled.

Luther Brachis grunted, and shrugged his shoulders. "Well, that's a hard question. But more than this." A sweeping gesture of one arm took in the whole room, from the grimy skylight window that looked up and out onto Earth's surface, to the monstrous computer entry and display system that covered a whole wall. "Apart from the microscopes, almost everything here could be part of a standard computer lab. If you hadn't told me, I wouldn't know this is a Needler lab at all."

"Ah. I see." The Margrave bent again to the Casimir Effect microscope, and made a minute adjustment to the settings. He laughed harshly without looking up. "Of course. You expected to see Needlers, did you?—men in white coats, perhaps, sticking pins in cells? Sorry, but you are seven hundred years too late." He finally straightened up, and lifted a foot-high pile of computer listings from the desk by his side. "In the earliest days, yes. A strange set of methods was used at one time to stimulate parthenogenetic egg development. Ultraviolet radiation, acid and alkaline solutions, heat, cold, needle puncture, radioactivity—almost everything was tried, and a surprising number of them worked. After a fashion. But those methods produce only exact copies of a parent organism, not interesting variations. And even when mutations arise as a side effect of stimulation, they are quite random. As a way of producing an art form it would be hopeless—like dropping a block of marble off a cliff, and hoping to find a masterpiece of sculpture when you got to the bottom. Today, everything is planned. Look at this listing."

Brachis took the stack of sheets and stared blankly at the top one. "They don't mean a thing to me, Margrave—"

"Not Margrave. I am simply Fujitsu. Mine was an imperial line when most of your under-level braggarts were wearing animal skins and eating their food raw."

"Sorry, Fujitsu. Anyway, I don't see much here. Just page after page of repeated random letters."

"Ah, yes. Random." The Margrave stabbed at the top page with a long index finger. "Quite so. This is random in very much the same way as *we* are random, you and I. What you are holding there is the complete DNA sequence for a living organism, in its correct order. This output simply indicates the nucleotides in each of the chromosomes, letter-coded for convenience: T for thymine, G for guanine, C for cytosine, and A for adenine. The whole listing is built—as are we—from those four letters. Taken together, they constitute the exact blueprint for production of a . . . an animal." He looked at Luther Brachis. "I am sorry. You are no innocent, and I will not insult you by treating you as such. I will be more specific. The blueprint for production of a human being."

"But DNA has a coiled spiral structure. There's no spiral shown here. And anyway, we don't *want* to produce a human being."

"A coiled spiral is topologically equivalent to a straight line—and a straight line presentation of data is far easier to comprehend and analyze. Don't worry that this is currently a human encoding. It is only my starting point. It is, if you will, the theme from which we will construct our sublime variations. Any one of these nucleotides can be changed to any other of the four. We have full chemical control of the sequence. The chain can be split, lengthened, shortened, and modified in any way that we wish." He tapped the stack, with its endless jumble of letters. "You asked me earlier, what is my job? Since I am merely evaluating the possible effects of inserting different DNA fractional chains into this coding, what can I do that cannot be done better and faster by a computer? I have been asked that many times. I can only give you an answer by analogy. Do you play chess?"

"Somewhat. It is still required training for Level Six education." Luther Brachis saw no reason to mention that he was a Grand Master. It was hard to see how withholding that information could have future value, but the habit of concealment was ingrained.

"Then you probably know that, despite many centuries of work, the best computer chess-playing programs still fail to beat the best human players. Now, how can that be? The computer can store a million times as many games in its memory. It can evaluate all possible moves, far ahead, to see which is the best. It is tireless, and does not make foolish errors. And yet the humans win. How? Because they can somehow grasp within the quirky, slow, organic computer of the brain the *overall* board position, in a holistic way that goes beyond individual moves. The computers play better every year—but so do the humans! The greatest chess players *feel* the board, in its entirety, and can extrapolate its potentials for more levels than any computer." The Margrave turned to the screen, where a long sequence of the coded letters was displayed. "That same ability is possessed by the best Needlers. In a string of a hundred billion nucleotide bases, random substitution, exchange, or deletions would prove totally disastrous. No viable animal or plant can result. But it is my special talent—and I assure you, Commander, that in my field I admit no peers—to sense the final and total impact of changes in the sequences. To grasp the pattern, whole. More than that, I can estimate how different changes will *interact* with each other. For instance, suppose I were to invert the order of the section on the middle of the screen, and make no other change of any kind. What would it do? I am not absolutely sure—which is why what I do is an art and not a science—but I believe that it would produce a perfectly formed individual, just a little more hirsute than the norm. Really, very little change. We are all of amazingly robust genetic design. There is much redundancy in the DNA chain, and it stabilizes us against minor copying errors in the genetic codes."

"Just *who* is that on the screen, Fujitsu?" said Brachis abruptly. He was feeling more uncomfortable than he expected with the Margrave, largely because the other man treated his profession with the cold, clear-eyed enthusiasm of a true fanatic. To the Margrave of Fujitsu, Luther Brachis suspected that he was just another section of interesting genetic code.

The Margrave smiled directly at Brachis for the first time, showing crooked teeth. "It is no one you know, Commander. And don't worry, when I am finished you will see only your Artefact, and nothing of what lies behind it. The listing you have in front of you already has within it part of my general design for your project. King Bester delivered your specifications to me a week ago. It is such an intriguing challenge that since then I have worked on nothing else."

"You mean that you are almost finished?"

"Not yet. As I said, it is a challenge. And also a mystery, which makes me ask a question. If you do not wish to answer, that is your business. But I cannot help wondering about the form that you provided to me. May I?" He flashed onto the screen a colored high-resolution image of a life form. "There are elements of your specification, here, and here"—he touched the lower part of the screen—"that I found enormously difficult to mimic using organic components. Is this perhaps some kind of cyborg, inorganically enhanced?"

The screen showed a four-meter oblong shape, with well-defined head, compound eyes, and a small mouth. The body was silver-blue, terminating in a tripod of stubby legs. Regular indentations ran along the whole length of the shining sides, and lattice-like wing structures were held close to the body.

Brachis thought for a moment, before finally nodding. "I see no reason you should not know. It is partly inorganic."

"Then you know I cannot actually *copy* this with organic components. The best I will be able to do is make the exterior appearance very similar, and match the psych profile you gave me. That will be close enough to fool anyone except an absolute expert."

"That will be excellent. Remember, it is the mental performance that matters, more than the actual physical appearance."

"That is the easier part."

"So when do you expect to have all the Artefacts ready?" For the first time, Luther Brachis was betraying impatience. He had stood up and was looking at his chronometer.

"Another two weeks." Fujitsu stroked his straggly beard, and turned his pale look on Luther Brachis. "Is that satisfactory?"

"For all twenty-five copies?"

"Unless you tell me differently. After the first, the rest are easy. I will require the remainder of my payment, in trade crystals, hand-delivered as soon as the Artefacts leave Earth."

"Delivery before payment? You are a trusting person."

"Find someone on Earth who will agree with that, Commander, and I will deliver your order free." The Margrave smiled his snaggle-toothed smile. "I would never threaten you, but as we say in my family, I have a long arm. It reaches far out, and it brings my full dues to me through time and space. My clients all pay—in one way or another." Fujitsu was walking with Brachis to the massive door. "One final question. This project is the most challenging that I have had for many years. No one before has ever asked me to replicate an organism—and such a strange one! Can you tell me who made them? I would much like to meet their creator."

"I can give you a name, if that is what you want." Brachis paused, ready to close the outer door. "The artefacts you are building for me are called Morgan Constructs. They were created by a woman, Livia Morgan. Unfortunately, she is now dead."

It was raining on the surface, a heavy downpour under black clouds. Brachis strode rapidly back towards the tunnel entry point. Would Fujitsu now explore the nature of the Morgan Constructs? He thought not. And it was worth the risk of giving their name, to see if King Bester stayed bought. The King would certainly pry the information out of the Margrave. The real question was, would anyone else then hear about it?

Brachis was hurrying, showing less than his usual caution. He realized his mistake when his feet were abruptly pulled away from under him, and he went skidding flat on his back down a steep slope. At the bottom he tried to stand up. He found a loop of rope tight around his ankles.

"Got him," said a soft voice. A shielded lamp shone in his eyes.

Brachis stood up slowly and carefully. There were five of them. Four were dressed in dark, mottled clothes that blended into the vegetation patterns of the surface. The fifth man, obscenely fat, wore a sequined robe and carried an ornate mace. Knives and grinning teeth flashed in the lamplight. They stood in a small circle around Luther Brachis. (He recalled King Bester's words. "Never forget: the surface is *dangerous*. There's the Scavvies. as well as the local patrols.")

"Scavengers, is it?" growled Brachis, in low earth-tongue. "What you want, then? Money, trade crystals? I got."

"A bit more than that, squire." It was the fat man, smiling in the circle of light.

"Do a deal, then? I got friends."

"I know that." The fat man lifted a huge arm and pointed the mace at Brachis. "See, I know you. There's people topside who'd pay to have you back—specially when I send 'em a few fingers or toes, to prove I'm serious."

Brachis thought he recognized the shape, and the gloating voice confirmed it. "Bozzie?" he said rapidly. "Listen, squire, we can do a deal. I can get you—"

"Not Bozzie to you," said the other man viciously. "And not squire, either. Off-Earth trash like you call me *Your Majesty*. All right, lads, *do him!*"

The four came diving at him from sides and back. Luther Brachis switched to Commando mode. He smashed the larynx of the man on his left with the outer edge of his hand, at the same time back-heeling another in the testicles. He pivoted right, and stabbed a third in the eyes with the stiff outstretched fingers of his right hand. He spun through a three-hundred-sixty degree turn. His right arm

swept onwards like a flail. The sleeve of his combat uniform, hardened by rapid acceleration, shat-
tered the jaw of the fourth man. Then all were
down, grovelling on the dark earth.

The Duke of Bosny had seen the instant demoli-
tion of his Scavenger group. He dropped the lamp
and went waddling towards the dark fields. Brachis
caught him in a dozen strides, hurled him face-
downwards to the ground, and knelt on his back.
He took a grip on Bozzie's neck, forearms locked.

"Now, *Your Majesty*. Time for some honest answers. And if you lie, you'll think that your Scavvies
got off easy."

"Anything! Anything." The Duke of Bosny was
trembling, quivering on the ground like a monstrous jelly. "Don't hurt me. Please! Take what
you want."

"I want an answer. You were lying in wait for
me. Did you know it was me, or was it a set-up for
anyone who came along? Remember, now, I have
to have the truth."

Bozzie hesitated. Luther Brachis tightened his
grip, flattening the windpipe.

"No!" Bozzie gave a whistling scream. "I'll tell
you. We saw you when you first came up onto the
surface. I recognized you then. We all watched you
go into the Margrave's lab, and decided to wait for
you."

"That the truth?"

"It is, it is. For God's sake, don't hurt me. It's
the truth."

Brachis nodded. "I believe you. Sorry, Bozzie.
That was the wrong answer."

He shifted his grip, moved his hands to lock on
his own arms, and twisted hard. Bozzie's neck
cracked sharply. He jerked, shivered, and lay silent. Luther Brachis did not give him a second
look. He went to each of the other four in turn,

breaking their necks cleanly and effortlessly. The whole episode had taken only a couple of minutes.

He thought of rolling the bodies down towards an irrigation ditch, then decided against it. Scavvie fights on the surface were common enough, this would look like just another one—perhaps a bit more notable than usual, because the Duke of Bosny had been one of the victims.

Brachis brushed himself down and hurried on towards the tunnel entrance. Already he had begun the self-discipline needed to put the incident temporarily out of his mind. He did not want it to interfere with what came next.

He could tell himself, with a kind of mocking self-awareness, that he knew very well he was behaving illogically. He should worry more about the possibility that he had somehow left clues on one of the bodies. But it seemed unimportant now. He had to get to a certain apartment on the fifty-fifth level.

After only two meetings, he was rushing to his tryst with Godiva Lomberd, just as though she were an innocent virgin, as though this were his first romance. There was no questionable outcome for this rendezvous, no uncertainty, no doubt what they were going to do, no danger of rejection. It would be a wholly commercial transaction, a meeting controlled by lust, the sordid temporary purchase of a woman's body.

Brachis could tell himself all that, and it made no difference. He was going to meet Godiva Lomberd again, and for the moment nothing else was important.

# Chapter Nine

# CHAN; A DEAL WITH SKRYNOL

The rings were all of different sizes and colors; the cylinder tapered from a blunt point at the top down to a thick base. And the rings would all fit onto it only if they were placed in the correct sequence, largest to smallest.

Chan Dalton was sitting on the floor, hunched over the toy. His handsome face was wrinkled with effort. He picked up the rings one after another, studying each, then putting it down between his splayed legs. The whole chamber was cheerfully decorated in pinks and blues, with paintings and drawings around the wall and a thick soft carpet on the floor.

Chan had carefully positioned himself in the exact center of the room. After long deliberation he picked up the red ring and placed it on the cylinder. A few moments more, and he did the same thing with the orange one. Then the yellow.

"He's getting it right!" Tatty was whispering, although there was no chance that Chan could hear her. They were watching him through the one-way glass set into the nursery wall. "Could he ever do that when he was with you?"

Leah Rainbow shook her head. "Never—he

wouldn't have had the slightest idea!" Her voice showed her excitement. When she first arrived at Horus she and Tatty found it difficult to talk. They had finally and simultaneously realized why. They were like mothers to Chan—and both the old and the new mother felt jealous of the other. Tatty resented it when Chan ran to hug Leah as soon as he saw her, with a great yell of pleasure and excitement; Leah hated the proprietary way that Tatty organized Chan's day, telling him what to do next, where his clothes must go, and what he had to eat. Leah thought of that as *her* prerogative.

The daily session with the Tolkov Stimulator had been another cause of tension between them. Leah took for heartlessness Tatty's firm insistence that Chan had to have daily treatment, whether there was a visitor or not. She would not help Tatty to catch him or to strap him in. And the presence of her own picture and Esro Mondrian's, where Chan could see them both when he was in the Stimulator, had perplexed her. What was Tatty doing?

But when the treatment began, she could not ignore Tatty's anguish and misery as Chan writhed in the padded seat. The thing that had finally won Leah over was the bedroom and nursery that Tatty had made for Chan. They were so thoughtfully done, and showed so much evidence of love and caring.

She remembered Horus very well from her brief stay before she went off for training. It had been horrible; gloomy, dirty, depressing—more like a barracks than any place to bring a child (and Chan *was* a child to Leah, in spite of his physical age and appearance). Now it was transformed.

"How did you possibly manage all this?" she said, after Tatty had shown her around room after room, elegantly decorated and furnished, and each one designed to take advantage of the natural and manmade features of the interior of Horus.

Tatty laughed. It was wonderful to have somebody appreciate her efforts. Chan took it all for granted, and Kubo Flammarion seemed more comfortable with the old dirt and mess.

"I got tired of living in a pit," she said. "Nobody would tell me how long I might be here. But all the old excavation and service robots are still around, because nobody thought it worthwhile hauling them away. I found out how to re-program them—it took time, but I had plenty of that—and set them in to clear out the trash and make this place livable. One of them could even produce pretty good carpets and wall hangings. So once I started, I guess I became a bit compulsive. Poor old Kubo Flammarion." She smiled at the memory. "He came out here a couple of weeks ago, and I wouldn't let him into Chan's quarters until he took a bath and cleaned his uniform. He did it, but he was devastated. And Chan made it worse. 'Kubo change,' he said. 'Not stinky any more. Except hat.' And he stole Kubo's cap and threw it into the garbage disposal—Kubo hadn't bothered to clean it, I suppose he thought we'd never notice. But Chan noticed. He *is* improving, isn't he?" Her voice was full of relief. "I wondered if I was imagining the change, just because I was wishing it so hard. But you see it, too. He's a bit smarter, I'm sure of it."

"He certainly is," said Leah. "Look at him now."

Chan had carefully and slowly assembled the complete stack of rings. Now he was just as painstakingly taking them off again. They watched until he had finished, then both applauded. Next he picked up a set of red plastic blocks. They were of complex individual shapes, but could fit together to make a perfect cube. He fiddled with them aimlessly for a while, then threw them down in a heap on the floor.

"That's still too hard for him," said Leah. "He's progressing, but it's terribly slow. At this rate it will take years."

"It's not linear," said Tatty. "According to Kubo, if it works at all we can expect to see slow progress at first. Then it will all come in one big rush, maybe in one session on the Stimulator. We don't know when it might happen, and we don't know how far Chan will go, because we're not sure what was wrong with his brain in the first place. He could finish up slow, or average—or even supersmart, I suppose, though the chance of that is pretty small. All we can do is wait and see." She looked down at Chan. "Well, that's just theory. We've got more practical things to worry about first. I have to get his dinner ready. If you want to, you can help feed him—though there's not so much need for that now. He's still a bit messy. But he's no worse than Kubo. You should have seen the two of them—it was disgusting. Want to come with me to the kitchen? You still haven't told me just what you've been doing in your training program."

"I'll get to it," said Leah. "You know, when Bozzie sold us back on Earth I thought it was the worst thing that could ever happen. I was terrified. And now I'm in the middle of the training— and I love it! We just finished the end of the first phase, that's why I have a short break. But I'll have to leave Horus again the day after tomorrow, and go back to Cobweb Station. We'll be meeting some of the alien partners, and starting to form a real team. I already met a Tinker. They're not as weird as people say. Ours even made jokes—in standard solar! And none of us has been able to make any headway at all with *their* language. It doesn't have verbs or nouns or adjectives or anything—just buzzing sounds. And the language of the Angels is supposed to be far *harder* than Tinker talk! We have to rely on computers for our translation—though apparently *they* understand *us*. It's disturbing. I was told in training that humans are the smartest species, but I'm beginning to have lots of doubts . . .'

The performance with the rings had put both women into a good mood. They were chatting happily as they walked through into the dining area. Chan was left playing on his own in the nursery. For five minutes after they left he sat on the floor, not moving. Then he stood up, ran rapidly across to the door, and up the narrow ramp that led to the one-way mirror. He made sure no one was behind it, then hurried back to the nursery.

First he went across to the smiling photograph of Esro Mondrian that Tatty had pinned on his wall, in among all the colorful drawings of animals, plants, people, and planets. He stared at it hard. Then he went back to the middle of the nursery floor and the pile of red plastic blocks. He picked up four of them and quickly and economically began to put them together. In less than thirty seconds he had assembled the whole cube. He stared at it for a few moments, then just as quickly took it apart and placed the pieces on the carpeted floor. Finally he lifted his eyes, and stared again at Mondrian's picture.

He smiled. And it was a perfect copy of the smile on the face of Esro Mondrian.

Four hundred million kilometers away, that face was beaded with perspiration. Mondrian lay in darkness on a hard couch, gritting his teeth and breathing in short, fast gasps.

He could see nothing, smell nothing, feel nothing—even the electrodes on his body no longer produced sensation. After a while the total darkness drained all volition. He felt that he was alone, that there was nothing else in the universe. The endless series of questions did not help. They seemed to come from *within*, from inside the deep hiding places of his brain. He struggled to give answers that would end the questioning. The effort was agony, tearing at the lining of his skull. He groaned aloud.

"You are resisting again," said the soft voice of Skrynol. "Every time we approach this area, evasion begins. I think we must stop for today."

There was a gentle touch on Mondrian's sweating body. The electrodes were being removed. "We're getting nowhere," he said hoarsely. "I'm wasting your time and mine."

"On the contrary, we are progressing. As we define the area that you will not allow me to enter, I will be able to infer its nature more and more accurately. Already we have certain facts. For example, I know you are hiding the result of a very early experience—something that happened before you were three years old. You have spent all your life since then building mental walls around it. That is why they are hard to break down. Second, your recurring dreams are all related to that same experience. There is a pattern. They are always either a re-creation of your trauma, or a flight from it. The vision is always the same: you as a central figure, surrounded by the warm, light, safe region."

"That is not a new insight. Other Fr'oppers have told me the same thing. They said the safe region is symbolic of the womb."

"Of course they say that." Skyrnol's voice sharpened. "It is a simple-minded conclusion. And it is a wrong one. I can recognize womb symbolism, and this is something quite different. Let me continue. You feel that you control everything within the safe region—but the region is shrinking. Every day, the dark has approached a little closer. You sense devils in that dark. But there is no place to hide, for you are always at the *center* of the lighted region. If you run away—in *any* direction—the danger will be closer yet. So you cannot flee, and you dare not stay. That is the source of your nightmares."

"Even if you are right, how can it help me?"

"We must go back—farther, deeper. And you must help me to do it."

Mondrian remained silent.

"You are afraid," went on Skrynol at last. "I understand that. Our secret fears are always sacred. You can be helped. But only if you really want to. You must trust me more, tell me your secrets, let me feel with you and for you." There was a laugh in the darkness. "You are horrified at that idea. I know. But our secrets are never as well-kept as we would like to imagine. Let me tell you one of your secrets, because until it is out of the way we will never reach back far enough."

Mondrian became totally still. "You think I have secrets?"

"You have at least one. According to your official record, you were born on Oberon, the son of a mining engineer who was pregnant when she went out there. Correct?"

"That is right."

"So tell me about your mother. What sort of a woman was she?"

"I have told you several times. I have no memory of my mother. She was killed in an accident soon after I was born."

"You have told me that. And you have been lying." Skrynol's fleshy hand came out to grip Mondrian by the shoulder. "Your mother is dead, true enough. But you remember what she looked like. And you were not born on Oberon. *You were born on Earth*. As a child, you were *sold* on Earth.

Do not try to deny it. *I know.* You lived on Earth for the first eighteen years of your life, a commoner, in poverty and misery until you made a chance to escape. Today you are an educated, sophisticated man. You have refined tastes. You appreciate beauty, ideas, good literature, great music, great art, fine food and drink. And yet you were *shaped* on Earth. Part of you is still locked into the dirt, ignorance, and stupidity where you began. Your nightmare begins *here*, on this planet."

Mondrian writhed in Skrynol's grip, reacting more to the words than to the pressure on his shoulder. "Damn you, Skrynol. You could search the solar system, and never find that in any record. Only *one person* knew. How for Shannon's sake did you make Tatiana tell you?"

"She did not tell me, Mondrian. I deduced it. Your self control is phenomenal, but it cannot be perfect. Every time the subject of Earth, and of people born on Earth, came up, half a dozen physical variables in your system varied a point or two. A small thing, but enough. I added other questions, and integrated their answers. The conclusion was clear."

"Damn you. Who will you tell?"

"I do not know. Perhaps nobody."

Mondrian was fumbling in the darkness at the shirt pocket of his uniform. He pulled out a thin packet, and thrust it blindly in front of him. "Then let this give you an incentive for silence. Look inside."

The packet was removed from his hands. There was a long silence, then a soft clicking noise. Light slowly brightened the chamber. "Darkness is essential during questioning," said Skrynol. "But it is no longer serving a useful purpose."

Mondrian sat upright. Crouched before him was a giant tubular shape. The pale lemon of the body bifurcation showed that Skrynol was a female Pipe-

Rilla. She was not of the usual form. There were changes to the long thorax, and one pair of fore-limbs had been augmented by fleshy appendages resembling human hands and arms. Skrynol held out the package that Mondrian had given her.

"To satisfy my curiosity," she said, "where and how did you manage to obtain these pictures?"

"On my first visit." Mondrian touched the fire opal at his collar. "This holds a multiple-wavelength imaging device. I tried many spectral regions; thermal infrared and microwave were both satisfactory."

"Ah." Skrynol was crouched quietly on long, orange-black hind legs, nodding her head. "A failure on my part. I observed your apparent nervous manipulation of that gemstone. I noticed it was oddly at variance with your general control; but I failed to draw a conclusion. Mondrian, your power of deception is amazing. Will you tell me why you thought it necessary to make images?"

"I wanted to learn the shape of someone who claimed to be too hideous to be seen. Perhaps you were not too strange to be seen, but too *familiar*. I thought you might be hiding something—I had no idea what."

"And when you saw the result?" Skrynol stood upright, towering towards the roof. Her dark compound eyes peered down at Mondrian. "Surely it would have been more in keeping with your job to report your findings, rather than bring the pictures here."

"Report to whom? Myself, as head of Security?" Mondrian shook his head. "There were too many unanswered questions. I could have made a fuss, and then looked like a fool. You resembled a Pipe-Rilla, but there were differences. You had said you were an Artefact, a clever product of a Needler lab. That could have been true."

"*Could* have been?" Skrynol tilted her dark head. "You reject that hypothesis?"

"Yes. I am now convinced that you are not an Artefact. You are a Pipe-Rilla, surgically modified for Earth environment and for efficient human speech. And that eliminated my second possibility—that you were some kind of renegade Pipe-Rilla, hiding here from her fellows."

There was a hissing laugh eight feet above Mondrian's head. "You mean a 'criminal,' as you call it, taking refuge on this world? Come now, Mondrian. What crime could I commit, with punishment worse than banishment to this planet, and endurance of these surgical disfigurements?" Skrynol held out the fleshy forelimbs. "As your people say, 'Why this is Hell, nor am I out of it.' You have a third conjecture?"

"Yes. The one that must be correct. You were modified and sent here *with the knowledge and approval of your government*. Earth is the only planet of the solar system where such concealment is possible. You are a spy and observer for the Pipe-Rillas."

Skrynol slowly lowered herself, with a cantilevering of long, multi-jointed limbs, until once more she was face to face with Esro Mondrian. "All the members of the Stellar Group feel a need to observe humans. You are too violent, too unpredictable. But if I admit that you are right, then are you not now in danger? I must protect my secret."

Mondrian shook his head. "You have been physically modified, but you are still mentally a Pipe-Rilla. You are not capable of violence. Whereas I . . ."

"A shrewd observation, and one that I cannot dispute. But I am not without other means of persuasion. You have your own needs. You could announce my presence here, true; but if you did, your treatment here with me would cease. And we are making progress, approaching the heart of your problem. You admit it?"

"I am sure of it." Mondrian laughed without humor. "Why else would I dread these sessions with you?"

"So you must make your own evaluation: am I a danger to humans so great that you must reveal my existence now, or does your *personal* need dominate the situation?" Skrynol leaned back on her hind joints and chittered with amusement. "Your human term for this is unique to your species, but it is appropriate. You call it a 'conflict of interest' —always, you see, you think in terms of conflict, war, battle, fighting."

"What would a Pipe-Rilla call it?"

"It would not arise. To us, the good of the many always takes priority over the need of the individual. We do not claim credit for this. It is built into us from first meiosis. It is the reason that I am here, alone and deformed, many lightyears from home and mates. But humans are often dominated by individual needs. And so, Esro Mondrian, you must make a decision. Exposure for me, or treatment for you. Which will it be?"

Mondrian was silent for a moment. "What is your name?" he said at last. "Your Pipe-Rilla name?"

"I could tell it to you. It is not a secret. But you will not be able to say it—unless you propose to learn to stridulate." The Pipe-Rilla laughed. "You must still call me Skrynol. That is similar to a word in our speech which means 'the insane one.' A mad Pipe-Rilla, living on Madworld—it is appropriate. I say again, we have a stalemate. I know your secret. You know mine. What will we do now?"

Esro Mondrian gestured to Skrynol to come closer. He carefully straightened the tunic of his uniform. "What I already intended when I came here today. Why do you think that I brought the packet of pictures? We agree, we both have needs. And once we acknowledge that, we can negotiate."

# Chapter Ten

# LUTHER BRACHIS
# MAKES HIS BID

The offices of Dougal Macdougal, Solar High Ambassador to the Stellar Group, formed a huge and perfect dodecahedron. Five hundred meters on a side, it sat deep beneath the surface of Ceres. Access to it was provided by a dozen entrances on every one of its twelve faces.

The magnificent private office of Dougal Macdougal was at the very center of the dodecahedron. It had just one entrance, approached down a long corridor. Halfway along the corridor and opening onto it was a tiny office, barely big enough for one person. In that office, seemingly for twenty-four hours a day, sat Lotos Sheldrake. A diminutive doll-like woman with the unlined face of a child, she guarded access to the spacious inner sanctum like a soldier ant protecting the queen's chamber. Macdougal saw no one until she had approved the visit; nothing entered that office, not even cleaning robots, unless she had inspected it.

Luther Brachis walked slowly down the approach corridor. He entered Sheldrake's cramped office and sat down uninvited on the single visitor's chair.

Lotos Sheldrake was reviewing a list of supplicant names, crossing off about half of them. She did not look up until her analysis was complete. "A surprise visit, Commander," she said at last. She raised her pencil-thin eyebrows. "You want an audience with the ambassador? We are honored—I believe this is the first such request."

"Don't give me that, Lotos." Brachis smiled grimly. "When you see me come in here and try to meet with old numbnuts, you'll know it's time to cart me off to the recycling yards."

"That is no way to refer to His Excellency, the ambassador." Sheldrake did not look in the least upset. She leaned back in her seat. "So what's your business?"

"You know about the Morgan Constructs, and the decision made by the Stellar Group ambassadors?"

An imperceptible nod, and the hint of a smile on the doll's face. "I know. Poor Luther. After all your efforts, you were told to report to Esro Mondrian. My heart bled for you."

"I'm sure of it," said Brachis drily. "Bled liquid nitrogen, if I know you. But let me get right to business. Do you know what actions it would take to reverse that decision—to get me back to at least an equality of rank with Mondrian?"

"Suppose I do know. Why should I tell you?"

"Still the same sweet Lotos." Luther Brachis pulled an object about two inches long from his pocket. "Take a look at this, then let's continue the conversation."

Lotos Sheldrake warily pointed the viewer across to the wall, and pressed the control on its side. A three-dimensional color image appeared. At its center moved a silver-blue cylinder with a tripod of stubby legs and a lattice of shining wing-like panels.

Sheldrake hissed, and jerked back from the display. "Luther Brachis, I hope for your sake this is an old holograph. If you have located a Morgan Construct and not revealed the fact to us, you will have earned the death penalty. Remember, we do not share the rest of the Stellar ambassadors' softness of heart. It *is* an old holograph, is it not? Or a simulation?"

Brachis shook his head. "It is less than one week old. And it is not a simulation." He watched, as her hand went out towards a button set into the smooth top of her desk. "Listen a little longer before you call the guards, Lotos. You don't want to make a fool of yourself. What you are looking at is not a Morgan Construct, I promise you that. It is an Artefact. But examine it as closely as you want to, and I feel sure you will be unable to detect the difference."

Lotos Sheldrake hesitated, then pulled back her hand from the button. "There was recent talk on Vesta of Artefacts being made to resemble mixtures of organic and inorganic systems, but I dismissed it as wild rumor. What's your game, Luther? I will give you two more minutes."

"I'm here to help you, Lotos." Brachis reached for the display unit and put it back in his pocket. "Mondrian and I have the responsibility for training the pursuit teams. If we do poorly, and team members are killed by the Morgan Constructs, then we humans will be blamed by the others of the Stellar Group. Now, you and I know that the training responsibility will not be yours, or Ambassador Macdougal's. You will have nothing to do with it. But we also know that if things go wrong, it will be considered your fault. He'll be the first person to take the heat. And you'll be the second. Do you want that?"

"You're as sneaky as Mondrian." There was grudging respect in Sheldrake's voice. "Keep talking, Luther."

"The big problem is this: how do you train a group to seek out and destroy a Morgan Construct, *when they have never seen anything like one*? Build more, to use for training? That would be vetoed by the ambassadors before you could even finish the suggestion. Use some other creation, maybe, a safe one that resembles a Morgan Construct? That sounds good—but we know of nothing remotely like the Constructs."

"Your point, Luther? Two minutes are up."

"Suppose that you, Lotos Sheldrake, were in possession of something that looked like a Morgan Construct, and acted like one—but was perfectly safe? Suppose this being was an Artefact, created unable to harm a human or other intelligent life-form?"

Lotos Sheldrake smiled, showing an even array of pearly teeth. "Sounds familiar. That's what Livia Morgan said about her Constructs."

"And she was wrong. I know. But the rules governing the manufacture of such Artefacts are well-established. And this time there would be every opportunity for controlled checking—you could run these creatures through their paces in every environment you like, for as long as you like, until you are convinced that they are perfectly safe. Now, suppose there was a limited number of these Artefacts, and they were all available *to you alone*. You could go to Ambassador Macdougal, and tell him that you—you alone—had the answer to all the problems of practical training. In everything except their ability to harm us, these creatures will look and behave like Morgan Constructs—they were designed and built that way." Luther Brachis leaned back in his seat. "Interested? There are exactly twenty-five of them, available now, packed away in suspended storage."

"Where?"

"I didn't hear that, Lotos. But if you could arrange for me to be reinstated at a level equal to Mondrian, my hearing might improve fast."

"Do you realize what you're asking? You want

Macdougal to persuade the other three species of the Stellar Group to change their minds. How for Shannon's sake is he supposed to do that?"

"It will be simple. All he has to do is tell them that I had a bigger hand in the original fiasco. According to their insane logic, if I'm as guilty as Mondrian, we will share responsibility for clearing up the mess we made."

Lotos Sheldrake raised her eyebrows. "That may just be stupid enough to work. But how do I know that I'll get credit for all this? What about Esro Mondrian?"

"Are you afraid of him?"

"Of course I am. I'm not a fool, Luther. You and Mondrian are both dangerous men." She smiled beatifically. "But you're a comparatively simple soul. When you don't like somebody, you'll do your best to kill them on the spot. Now with Esro, people who get in his way tend to die and never feel the wound. He always has at least six different agendas going, and I feel I can never guess more than four or five of them. And when he wants to, he can charm the pants off anybody he meets— anybody at all. He manipulates me, he manipulates you, he uses everybody." She looked admiringly at Brachis's powerful body. "You, now, you're dangerous like a bear. He's like a snake. You are ambitious; he is *driven*. Yes, Luther, I am afraid of Esro Mondrian. And so is any rational man or woman. End of speech."

"You're afraid enough to kill the deal? So what kind of animal are *you*?"

"Need you ask, Luther?" Lotos Sheldrake opened her innocent eyes wide. "I'm a sweet little honeybee. All I desire is a little nectar from each flower, with harm to no one. And when did you hear me say the deal was off? I am merely taking routine precautions. What's to prevent Mondrian from arranging a supply of these same Artefacts, once he knows they exist? For that matter, what's to stop *you* doing the double-cross? You know their source, and I do not."

"I have a way to reassure you fully on that question." Luther Brachis sat scowling in his seat, arms crossed on his broad chest. "We can talk about this in detail—when every other issue is resolved."

"Then with that understanding, you have my cooperation. I will explore this with Ambassador Macdougal as soon as possible." She was looking at her watch. "And I will be back in touch with you before the end of the day."

"One thing more." Luther Brachis remained sitting. "As part of this deal, I want one additional favor—a small one."

"Thirty seconds."

"I want Solar citizenship arranged for someone—fast."

"From one of the colonies?" Lotos Sheldrake began to shake her head. "I can't—"

"From Earth."

"*Earth*! Who is he?"

"She. It is a woman, Godiva Lomberd."

"But why *citizenship*? Why not just a long-term visitor's agreement?"

"I want to engage in a contract with her."

"Ah." Lotos Sheldrake stared curiously at Brachis. She laughed. "A contract! Can this be? Luther Brachis, the invincible, considering a contract with an Earth-woman. You have told me fifty times that nothing good ever comes from Earth. You had me persuaded of it. My opinion of you goes down. Maybe you are a blind mole, and not a bear."

"But you will arrange for her citizenship?"

"If the Artefacts are as good as you claim." Lotos Sheldrake looked briefly at a notebook on the desk in front of her. "Let us assume that all is as you say. Then I believe everything can be arranged here within five days." She stood up and began to shepherd Brachis towards the door. "And when all is ready, and you transfer Godiva Lomberd up from Earth, bring her here to see me. I am curious to meet the woman who made Commander Luther Brachis go soft in the head."

"You have it with you?" asked the Margrave.

King Bester nodded and patted the bag he was carrying. "Every last crystal of it."

"Then come in." The heavy outer door closed firmly, shutting out the sky of Earth, and the Margrave led the way to his private study. It was a room that had been decorated with immense care, somehow blending to one harmonious whole the Qin dynasty terracotta horsemen, Beardsley prints, original Vermeers and van Meegerens, and the computer-enhanced images of Earth from space. In one corner, shielded from all direct light, stood Sorudan. It was Fujitsu's masterpiece, the prize creation that he would never consider selling.

The Margrave waved Bester to a comfortable-looking armchair. "I think that a small celebration would not be out of order," he said. He scrutinized Bester closely, assessing the level of sophistication of the other man's palate, frowned, and disappeared into a closet in the corner of the study. He emerged carrying a bottle of pale amber liquid and two small glasses.

"Despite all our progress," he said, "one cannot improve on perfection." He carefully poured an ounce or two of fluid into each glass, and handed one to Bester.

The other man sniffed it, wrinkled his nose, leaned his head back, and drained the glass in one long swallow. He rolled his eyes. "Mm. Bit of all right, Fujitsu. What is it?"

The Margrave glared at him. His opinion of Bester had been confirmed. "It *was* one of the finest distilled liquors ever produced on Earth. Santory scotch whiskey, cask-aged in the Hokkaido deep vaults, single malt, two hundred and fifty years old. When I hear of the ambrosia of the Gods, I wonder how it differed from this." He shook his massive bald head, and took a first delicate sip. "Superb. Ah, well, I suppose we may as well get down to business. Did Brachis say anything regarding the delivery?"

"Not a thing." King Bester lifted the bag and prepared to stack its contents on the table that sat between them. "I've counted these, and you might want to do the same." He saw the Margrave's look. "Not because of anything I've done," he said hastily. "This is just the way they were given to me."

The bag was full of virgin trade crystals, their unused surfaces gleaming a dull rust-red in the subdued light of the study. King Bester lifted the crystals out one at a time, carefully examining each one and gloating over its quality before placing it on the table in front of the Margrave.

"Best I've ever seen. Wait a minute, though, what's this one doing in here?" Bester drew out a flat, plate-like crystal, round in shape and a couple of inches across. Unlike the others, it had a smooth surface and no inner glow to it. "I don't remember this one going in there."

As he spoke, the blue-grey surface came alive. There was a swirl of colors, and then suddenly a picture. The likeness of Luther Brachis had formed in miniature on the face of the plate and was peering out at them.

The tiny image spoke, in a metallic voice. "Remember what you told me, King? That any information you got from Fujitsu would come back to me alone. What happened to your promise, King?"

Bester stared down at the image, eyes bulging. He was still holding half a dozen crystals in his hand. The Margrave had jerked nervously to his feet.

"But you didn't keep your word, did you, King?" went on the tinny voice. "You found out from the Margrave about the deal for the Artefacts—and you found another buyer for the information." The light from the small plate was steadily increasing. Now the face of Luther Brachis had almost disappeared, swamped by the intensity of the glowing crystal. "That was a very bad mistake, King," said Brachis, in distorted tones.

"Bester! Look out!" As the Margrave shouted the words, he started towards the door of the study. "Don't touch the crystals."

His cry was too late. King Bester had tried to drop the crystals he was holding, but they stuck to his palm. He shook his hand wildly, trying unsuccessfully to dislodge them. They had begun to glow brighter, together with all the ones on the table.

"As for you, Fujitsu," went on Brachis, "I don't know how much you were in the deal. If you are innocent, you have my deepest apologies. But that is all I can give you."

The Margrave was at the door. He paused for a moment, and pointed back. His face was distorted with fury. "I will receive my due, Brachis. *My full due.* That I promise you."

He did not attempt to say more, because King Bester began a hideous high-pitched screaming and a mad capering dance around the study. The crystals in his hand were now incandescent. Lines of fire from each one were spreading up his arm, running in blue-white sprays of sparks to his shoulder, and then out onto his chest. The flames spread further. At the Margrave's last sight of him, King Bester had become a brilliant living torch, a faceless apparition of fire that still screamed and leaped in impossible agony.

The Margrave ran through the laboratory, slammed the heavy door behind him, and dashed up the stairs that led to the surface. At the top he halted. A new voice, inhumanly high and pure, had been added to Bester's screams.

"*Sorudan*! The light!" The Margrave hesitated and looked back towards the closed door. Then he groaned, shook his head as though to banish the sound from his ears, and fled away from the laboratory. Blind to any danger from Scavengers, he ran headlong through the cultivated fields. Behind him the windows of his laboratory shone brighter and brighter, and the unworldly melody rose ever higher and more beautiful.

He was fifty yards away and just beginning to feel safe when the explosion came.

In his compulsion to be sure of destroying the laboratory, Luther Brachis had indulged in massive overkill. Everything within a quarter of a mile of the laboratory was vaporized. A vast crater formed in the outer layers of Delmarva Town.

The Margrave's religion taught that the reward for a life well lived was the separation of body and soul. Upon his death, it was Fujitsu's desire to be released from all corporeal bonds. His component atoms would then be free to ride the swirling winds of Earth, as they moved endlessly around the turning globe.

In his miscalculation of the size of explosive needed, Luther Brachis had granted the Margrave his heart's desire.

# Chapter Eleven

# THE BREAKTHROUGH

On the good days, Tatty could not resist reaching out to Chan and hugging him. He was a grown man, big and agile and powerful, but he was also a little boy. And like a little boy, he was proud of any new thing he could do, and eager to show off to Tatty.

On the bad days, the simple and lovable child just vanished. Chan would say nothing, cooperate in nothing; was interested in nothing. She wanted to reach out and shake him until he took notice.

And *this* was a bad day. One of the worst. Tatty told herself to keep calm and not lose self-control. With another Stimulator session due in an hour, she had to be available to comfort Chan and ease him through the agony and misery. But for the moment . . .

"Chan! Come on now, look at the display. See, that's *Earth*. You were born on Earth, and so was I. These are pictures of parts of Earth. Chan! You—you—*look at the display!*"

Chan stared vacantly at the three-dimensional display for a second, then again began to study the fine hair along his forearm and wrist. Tatty swore, and slammed down the button to advance the presentation. Useful or not, she had to run through the whole program.

*Not one word of it going into his head*, she said to herself. *Too abstract for him—far too abstract. Whose stupid idea was it to give astronomy lessons, when he can't even pick out the letters of the alphabet? He's supposed to absorb at an unconscious level, is he? Sure. Some hopes. He never remembers the lessons ... and he doesn't seem one bit interested in them. Waste of his time. Waste of my time, too ... but what else is there for me to do here? ... I should be on Earth ... if only I could get away from this awful place. Earth. Oh God, look at those gorgeous pictures. Seas and skies and rivers and forests and cities. I wish I were there now, back in my apartment, just me and ... if Esro Mondrian were here now I would kill him ... heartless, passionless, treacherous, monstrous, ruthless ...*

While her thoughts consumed her, the lesson continued. Chan toured the whole solar system, bit by bit, in gorgeous, three-dimensional images. The training center on Horus was an expensive one. The trainees were moved *into* the display, seeing, hearing, and sensing everything as though they were present at each location. Chan and Tatty floated together down to the surface of Venus, where the atmosphere corroded and burned, and every boulder and jutting rock shimmered in the eternal heat. Somehow, the closed surface domes supported four hundred million people. Then inward, inside the orbit of Mercury, on all the way to the Vulcan Nexus, where the solar photosphere flamed and erupted in savage storms of light. The surface seemed close enough to touch. Tatty shrank back in real terror, even though she knew it was just a display. Chan stared at it impassively, with no trace of emotion.

They moved out, on past Earth to the thriving Mars colonies. There was a sense of enormous excitement here. Zero hour was only a few years away—the magic moment when sufficient volatiles would have been shipped in through the outsized Mattin Link system, and a human could survive on the surface with no breathing equipment. Already the atmosphere was almost as dense as on the top of Earth's highest mountains. Defying basic biology, daredevil young people were venturing out on the surface every day, without oxygen masks. The lucky ones were found in time and brought back suffering from extreme anoxia.

Chan and Tatty were carried farther from the Sun, out to the hive of the Asteroid Belt where a hundred busy minor planets made up the commercial and political power center of the solar system. From there it was outward again, to the huge industrial bases on Europa, Titan, and Oberon. Wearing Monitor headsets, Chan and Tatty were plunged deep into the icy slush below the deep atmosphere of Uranus, where the Ergatandromorph Constructs tirelessly built their fusion plants and the Uranian Link system. That work was still three centuries from completion. Chan, interested in nothing, stared woodenly at the Ergas.

When the survey of the old solar system was at last complete, Tatty looked at Chan. Still no reaction. Sighing, she signalled for the lesson to continue. Together they leaped four hundred billion kilometers, into the outer darkness. They watched the world-sized bulk of the Oort Harvester at work, a gigantic cylinder lumbering along through the hundred billion members of the cometary cloud. Slow and tireless, a quarter of a lightyear from the Sun, it hunted down bodies rich in simple organic molecules, converted them by the billions of tons to sugars, fats, and proteins, and sent the products back through Links to the inner system.

Finally Chan and Tatty leaped again, and reached the quiet outpost of the solar system. Over a lightyear out, they drifted among the Dry Tortugas; these arid, volatile-free shards of rock marked the boundary of Sol's domain. Beyond this point, any matter was gravitationally shared with other stars. The Sun was a chilly pinprick of light, less bright than Venus seen from Earth. Temperatures hovered a few degrees above absolute zero. Together, Chan and Tatty looked at billion-year-old metal tetrahedra, enigmatic relics left by a race that was old before Man was young.

So far the lesson had been a general one, designed to show Chan the structure, economy, and infrastructure of the solar system. Now it became specific to pursuit-team training. The display changed scale again. It moved out beyond the solar system, to consider the geometry of the Stellar Group. The region of accessible space was a vast sphere, fifty-eight lightyears across and centered on Sol. The Perimeter marked its outer boundary. The probe ships, limited to a tenth of light speed, expanded the sphere by at most ten lightyears a century. Humans had encountered no other species possessing the Mattin Link, so the Perimeter remained centered on Sol. And communication with anything or anyone *outside* the Perimeter was impracticable . . . unless and until (people had talked of it for centuries) the expanding spherical bubble of the Perimeter met a second bubble . . . blown by another species, who had also learned the secret of the Mattin Link.

(Humans had written thousands of papers and millions of words, attempting to analyze the implications of such a meeting. Just as, in an earlier era, writers had endlessly discussed the first contact with extraterrestrial intelligent beings. Like those analyses, many of the new papers were well-argued and persuasive—and contradicted each other.)

In the final segment of the lesson, the home

stars of the other three known intelligent species were shown within the sphere. The Pipe-Rillas had been found first, in the binary star system of Eta Cassiopeiae, eighteen lightyears from Sol. Next the Perimeter had reached the Tinkers, twenty-three lightyears out. Their home world was Mercantor, circling the star Fomalhaut. And finally there were the newcomers to the Stellar Group, the Angels. They lived on a planet that orbited Capella, forty-five lightyears from Earth. They had been discovered by the probes only a century and a half ago. The Angel language, civilization, and thought processes still offered major mysteries for humans.

In the last half-minute of the lesson, images of each species were added to the displays. They had been provided by Kubo Flammarion, in an optimistic attempt to make Chan feel comfortable in advance with alien forms. The screen first showed the quivering purple-black mass of a Tinker Composite, then an enlarged view of the individual components from which the Tinker was made. They were fast-flying legless creatures of minimal intelligence, each about the size of a hummingbird and massing only fifty grams. The individuals possessed just enough nerve tissue to permit independent locomotion, sensation, feeding, breeding, and clustering. Each had a ring of eyes on its blunt head, and long antennae to allow coupling into the Composite. The components were purple-black, with shiny, sticky-looking bodies. Tatty stared at them in fascination. She was sorry when the display moved on to show the arthropod cylinder segments of a Pipe-Rilla, and finally the dull green fronds of an Angel. She looked at Chan to see how he had reacted to the sight of the aliens. He was not looking at the display at all. He was staring at *her*.

"Chan," she began in annoyance. Then she saw his grimace of discomfort. He grunted, and reached up to place his hands on the sides of his head. "Chan, what's wrong?"

"Head bad." He mumbled. He was rubbing at his temples, then his eyes. "Picture—make head bad."

Was he at one of the critical points? Flammarion had told her to be specially watchful for headaches. They could lead to fever, nervous degeneration, and rapid death. Tatty went across, knelt by his side, and took his head between her hands. "Let me look."

He sat there quietly, not protesting as she lifted his eyelid and shone a light to look at the eyeball. So far, so good. There was none of the reddening of inflammation that she associated with Stimulator after-effects. His temperature was normal, too. So now came the step she was dreading—the daily ritual of forcing Chan into that terrible machine. It was a little early, but they might as well get it over with.

Tatty sighed, and stood up. "Come on, Chan." She took him by the hand and led him through to the other chamber. Amazingly, today he was not screaming in anticipation, or struggling to escape and run away. Was he *really* sick?

"Chan, do you hurt?"

He looked at her, then slowly shook his head. "Not hurt." At her urging, he sat down quietly in the Stimulator chair and allowed himself to be strapped in. She hesitated before she connected the headset. Kubo Flammarion had provided no instructions for a case like this. The protocol demanded daily treatment. But if Chan had something seriously wrong with him, what would exposure to the Stimulator do?

Tatty finally turned on the power. Usually she could not bear to watch, but now she felt compelled to do so.

For a few minutes Chan sat quiet, eyes closed.

There were frown lines on his smooth forehead, and he was gripping the armrests so hard that the tendons in the backs of his hands stood up white and prominent.

Suddenly he began to moan, a long, breathless sound high in his throat. Tatty knew it well, the sound that Chan made when the power build-up was approaching its peak rate. At first there was nothing to see, but inside Chan's skull a complex series of fields was being generated through both cerebral hemispheres. Natural patterns of electrical activity within the brain were sensed by the Stimulator, modulated, and fed back at vastly increased intensity. At the same time, the body's motor control was inhibited. That damping was necessary to prevent Chan from tearing himself to pieces with uncontrolled muscular response. The spasmodic jerks, writhing and twitching that the body still went through were sometimes spectacular, but Flammarion had made it clear to Tatty that they were unrelated to what Chan was actually feeling. The agonies that Chan felt were real enough, though. They arose within the brain itself, a pain far more intense than anything of physical origin.

A crisis was approaching. Chan had begun to throw himself about madly in the chair. His face was blood-red, and the veins in his neck and forehead stood out as purple cords. Suffused by blood, the medication injection points on his bare arms showed as bright patterns of stigmata. At this point in each treatment, Tatty always feared that Chan would die of heart failure or apoplexy. When the Stimulator monitor chattered to a final burst of activity, a despairing high-pitched scream filled the chamber. It cut off abruptly. Chan suddenly sagged forward against the restraining bonds, and slumped motionless in the chair.

Terrified, Tatty ran to his side. This had never

happened before. She looked at the monitors, and was relieved to see that Chan's pulse was still strong. But it was very fast, and his blood pressure was disturbingly high. She put her hand on his shoulder and shook him. The Stimulator activity registered as zero. The treatment should be over. Usually at this point Chan was awake and weeping; she would take him in her arms, help him from the chair, hold him close to her, and comfort him. According to Flammarion, that psychological support was supremely important to prevent catatonic withdrawal. But now . . .

"Chan! Can you hear me?"

There was a flickering of eyelashes. The eyes were opening. At first only the whites were visible, then blue irises slowly rolled downward into view. Chan sighed, and licked his lips. Suddenly he was staring at Tatty, frowning as though he had never seen her before.

"Tatty?" he said hesitatingly.

"Ohh-hh." Tatty let out her breath in a long, heartfelt sigh. She placed the palms of her hands on Chan's cheeks and drew his head forward to rest on her shoulder. "There, my Chan, my baby." Her voice was gentle and soothing. "Rest on, Tatty, let it pass. You'll be all right in a few minutes."

"No!" Suddenly he wrenched away from her and stared around him. Then with a wild cry of anguish he was running from the chamber and down the outside corridor, staggering in his step and bouncing crazily off the smooth walls.

Tatty was filled with an awful sense of foreboding. Something was different—and terribly wrong. After a Stimulator treatment Chan *always* needed soothing, and then he would sleep.

She snatched up the Tracker and her case of anesthetic drugs, and started after him through the tunnels of Horus.

In a few minutes she realized that he was not

following his usual paths. Chan was normally perfectly predictable, fleeing again and again from the Stimulator over the same familiar routes. This time he was off in a new direction, doubling back, changing course, avoiding blind alleys, and moving always farther away from her.

She hurried on. There was no possibility that he could actually escape—Horus was a maximum security facility, and Tatty had hopelessly explored all the possible ways of escape often enough herself. There were none. All he could do was delay his discovery and capture—and he was certainly doing that.

Even with the help of the Tracker it took almost half an hour to find him. He was at the farthest end point of the tunnels. When she finally approached him he was sitting quietly on an old excavating machine, staring blankly at its molecular decomposition nozzles. Tatty approached him warily. If necessary, she could shoot the tranquilizer into him from ten yards away.

"Chan," she said softly.

"Here, Tatty."

"Are you all right?" She saw that he had been weeping, and the tears were still bright on his cheeks.

"No. I mean . . . don't know. If was all right before, then not all right now."

Tatty felt her skin quiver into gooseflesh. The articulation of the words was awkward, still with the baby-talk overtone that Chan always used. But their cadence and meaning had changed totally. It was a stranger talking to her.

"Chan, you're talking differently. How do you feel?"

He paused for a long moment. But it was not the usual silence of indifference; he seemed to be pondering her words, finding it difficult to speak. Twice he began, and twice halted before a word was out.

"Feel . . . strange," he said at last. "Just the same, and not same. All things are . . . mixed. I don't *know more*, all same things there in my head. But now . . ." he frowned. "Same things, but things not same. Now can *see* them; before, didn't notice." He paused, and swayed where he stood. He put one arm out blindly to the side, to support himself against the wall. "I feel . . . like . . ."

He slipped slowly to the floor in a faint. Tatty stepped forward to catch him. For a change, she blessed the weak gravity maintained on Horus. She would be able to carry Chan back to his bedroom with fair ease, and lay him out on the bed for the electronic doctor to perform an examination. Holding Chan, she hurried to the living quarters.

Back in his room, Chan remained unconscious. But all his vital signs were strong, and all indicators showed normal. Tatty sat down on the bed next to him. She wanted to send a signal off to Ceres, but at the same time she was reluctant to leave her charge. He *seemed* stable enough; but suppose he suffered some kind of fit while she was away? She was the only person who might save him. More than that, if this were the breakthrough point for the Stimulator treatment she *had* to be there when he awoke. Flammarion had emphasized it to her often enough. Chan would need her help for the next few hours.

Tatty finally ran through into the next room, grabbed a container of drink and a couple of packs of supplies, and rushed back in to sit beside Chan. He remained unconscious while she ate a makeshift meal; but he was beginning to mutter and whimper in his sleep. Tatty looked at her watch. Soon it would be time for his regular sleeping hours. She went across and dimmed the chamber lights, then quietly lay down at his side.

Her vigil was no novelty. She had often sat with

him after the Stimulator session, and told him stories until he went to sleep. Soon after their arrival on Horus she had changed his bed for a much broader one, on which she could stretch out in comfort beside him and tell him simple tales of Earth and life in the Gallimaufries, until finally the tears stopped and exhaustion took over.

Now Chan groaned and shook his head, then sighed and snuggled up close to her. His forehead was filmed with sweat, but he was not feverish. Tatty closed her own eyes, and let her mind drift away in speculation. The implications of the day's events were just coming home to her. If Chan had made the crucial breakthrough, he might be on the road to normal intelligence. That was wonderful news—she had grown as fond of Chan as she had ever been of anyone. And she must call Leah. But it had other implications—great implications . . .

*If his treatment is ready to end, I'll be free! Out of prison. Free to leave Horus, free to return to my own life on Earth. It's only two months—but I feel as though I've been away forever. Can I go back there, now?—and what will I do about Esro?*

"Tatty!" said Chan suddenly. He jerked around and gripped her hand so hard that she cried out in pain.

"I'm here." Tatty put her arms around him. "You're all right. Everything's all right, Chan."

"No." Chan put his head on her breast. "It's not all right. Tatty, you knew me—you knew what I was. And now, everything is . . . *hard*. Everything is . . . what is the word? . . . compli-cated? And it was all simple."

"That's the real world, Chan."

"But it's so . . . so—Tatty, I don't like this. I'm *frightened*."

"It's all right. Hold on to me, Chan. You are

right, it is not easy. Not easy to be human. But you have good friends. We will all help you."

He nodded, his head still on her chest. But he began to cry again, dry deep-chested sobs that went on for minute after minute. Tatty felt tears welling from her own eyes. It had seemed so obvious that Chan would be better if the Stimulator worked. Now, she sorrowed for the loss of the innocent child.

She cradled him to her, stroking his head and patting his shoulders. After a few more minutes, she became aware of another change in him. It was one that filled her with foreboding, mingled with a dreadful anticipation. Chan was becoming physically aroused, groaning and moving his body against hers.

Kubo Flammarion had told her in her first briefing that this might happen if the Stimulator treatment were a success. He had warned her that rejection of Chan might make him regress, or do permanent psychological damage. But at the time it had seemed too improbable an event to worry about.

"Tatty!" Chan's voice was terrified. Handsome and beautifully formed, and long past puberty, he had been blissfully unaware of his own sexuality. Now uncontrollable urges were possessing him, and he had no idea what was happening.

It was the puzzled fear in his voice that made Tatty think less about her own worries. "It's all right, Chan. It's not something bad. Let me help." She leaned over him, helping his inexperienced fingers with snaps and fasteners. Gently, she guided him along another critical segment of his rite of passage, from child to full manhood.

And while she did so, Tatty despised herself. She hated her inability to remain aloof. Two months was a long time—too long. Her own response was something she could try to banish, but it would not be denied. She shivered, hesitated, resisted, and finally groaned and clutched Chan to her.

During their lovemaking he began to weep again, and at his climax cried out Leah's name.

At the height of her own passion, Tatty wept also. Her tears were silent. But she thought of Esro Mondrian, and at last whispered his name beneath her breath.

# Chapter Twelve

# WITH LOTOS SHELDRAKE

Twenty thousand years ago Man had hunted the sabertooth tiger and woolly rhinoceros. Five thousand years ago the quarry was wild boar and bears. One thousand years ago, out on the great plains of Africa and India, the prize kills had been lions, tigers, and elephants.

Now on the great game preserves in Earth's equatorial regions, hunting was strictly forbidden. Blood lust had to find other outlets. *Adestis* was one of the most recent, and perhaps the best ever.

Dougal Macdougal loved Adestis. Lotos Sheldrake had never tried it until today, but she hated the very idea of it. She had insisted on being included in Macdougal's party only for her own unspoken purposes. Now she clung to her bright-sided weapon, and struggled across the spongy ground after the ambassador's group. The air was thick and humid, filled with large, drifting spores that floated along easily in the seemingly light gravity. Their destination was visible ahead now. No more than a few minutes' walk away, it was an enormous brown mound reaching far up towards the grey sky. Already Lotos could see the first file of pale-bodied warriors moving nervously at the entrance holes. They were tasting the air, feeling the approach of danger with their sensitive antennae.

Dougal Macdougal strode confidently on in front, heading directly for the giant round-topped tower. The forty other members of the party followed him, with Lotos Sheldrake bringing up the far rear.

Lotos suspected she had too much imagination for this sort of game. She could already imagine the curved jaws of the defending soldiers tight around her waist, or the sticky and madly irritant spray enveloping her. The projectile weapon she was carrying would kill a warrior outright—*if* she aimed true, and hit in the head or the even more vulnerable neck. A body shot would not do. The soldier would die eventually, but before it did so the creature's dying reflexes would make it fight on, to kill anything that did not smell and taste right. And the soldiers were only the first line of defense. Beyond them lay the dark interior tunnels, swarming with their own inhabitants.

For the attacking party to succeed, they would have to penetrate to the central chamber of the tower and kill its giant occupant. Dougal Macdougal had led the way to the base of the structure. Avoiding the main entrances, he fired a thread-thin grapnel line high above ground level. Then he attached a running pulley and hauled himself up, to many times his own height. In a few seconds he was braced against the side of the mound. The others followed, helping each other. There was little risk at this stage—even a direct fall would not be fatal.

Clinging to the pulley lines, the attacking group lifted sharp picks. They steadily hacked their way into the hard cement side of the mound until they had an opening big enough to crawl through.

Below them, the defending soldiers were in total confusion. They ran here and there, touching each other with their antennae and criss-crossing the approach routes to the tunnel entrances. None of them thought to crawl up the side of the tower.

"Quick now," said Macdougal at last. "Everybody, inside." He was panting and excited—far more enthusiastic for this than for any of his official duties.

Lotos scrambled through, nearly last of the group. She found herself in a spiral tunnel that wound steeply down toward the middle of the fortress. There was an overpowering smell of animal secretions and fungal growth, and the curving wall was smooth and as hard as cement. The tunnel was deserted. They ran along it at top speed, until after a hundred paces the leaders skidded to a halt. Scores of workers were emerging from side passages, blocking their way.

"Shoot your way through them," said Macdougal. He was waving his weapon around, as much of a menace to his companions as to their enemies. "They're no real danger—but keep your eyes open for the soldiers. They'll have learned by now that we're inside, and they'll be after us."

The projectile weapons were powerful enough to blow asunder the soft body of the workers and render them harmless. But there were hundreds of the creatures. Progress became slower and slower, through a carnage of dying tower-dwellers. Lotos found that she was skidding her way over layers of pallid flesh and greasy body fluids, losing her footing every few seconds. In a couple of minutes she was last of the group again, at least ten paces behind the rest. But the big central chamber was in sight ahead.

She paused to catch her breath. And from behind her came a scrabble of hard claws on the tunnel wall.

Lotos turned, filled with alarm. Less than ten paces from her were seven soldiers, approaching fast. She screamed a warning, lifted her weapon, and fired on automatic. A stream of projectiles cut into the warriors. Four curled up into death spasms, knotting their bodies on the hard floor of the tunnel.

But the other three were still coming. Lotos blew the head off one of them, and cut another in half with a hail of fire. The last one was too close. Before she could change the position of her weapon, mandibles as long as her arm had reached forward to grip her around the chest. Their inner edges were sharp and as hard as steel.

Lotos had her arms pinned to her side. She could not free the gun, or fire it at the soldier. The others of the party were shouting, but they could not get a shot at her attacker without hitting Lotos. The pressure on her chest increased steadily, from discomfort to impossible pain. Lotos felt her arms break, her ribs cave in, her heart burst. She could not breathe. She bit down hard on the switch between her rear molars. As everything turned dark around her, she felt a gush of blood into her throat, spouting from her open mouth . . .

Lotos was sweating and shivering in the balcony seat. THAT IS THE END OF ADESTIS FOR YOU, said a harsh voice in her ear. REMAIN SEATED IF YOU WISH, BUT FURTHER PARTICIPATION IS NOW PROHIBITED.

She ripped off the Monitor headset, threw it aside, and leaned over to look at the sandy arena below. The attack on the termite mound was still going on. With the termination of sensory contact, her own five-millimeter simulacrum had automatically "died" down there. And just in time! She was still in agony, still feeling the pressure of breaking ribs and cracking spine—Adestis did not let losers off easily. If she had failed to activate the Monitor switch, the chance of death from heart failure would have been better than thirty percent. In any case, the *pain* was real enough! It would continue for hours. That realism was one perverse reason for the popularity of Adestis.

Lotos drew in a long breath and looked around her. Over half the forty participants had already been returned. They were all alive, clutching eyes, heads, or ribs—the soldier termites had their preferred points of attack. The other twenty still wore the headsets and crouched blindly in their places.

There was a sudden gasp from Dougal Macdougal's cowled figure on her right. It was followed by a boil of activity near the bottom of the ten-foot mound just below. Either the intruders had managed to kill the queen and were fighting their way out, or the number of defenders had been too much for them and the attack was abandoned. Tiny human-shaped figures—less than a dozen of them now—came racing out of one of the tunnels at the base of the mound onto the sandy plain. But they were still far from safe. Dozens of maddened termite soldiers hurtled at them from all sides. The projectile weapons fired continuously. And uselessly. In less than thirty seconds, all the figures had been buried by defenders. Every player in the circle around Lotos shuddered back to body consciousness.

THE QUEEN IS STILL ALIVE, said the harsh voice. YOU HAVE BEEN DEFEATED. THAT IS THE END OF ADESTIS FOR YOUR EXPEDITION. THE ADVENTURE IS OVER.

Dougal Macdougal was groaning in his seat and clutching at his hips. A soldier must have gripped him below the waist. But he was grinning madly. He looked quickly around him.

"Everybody got back," he said. "Good—no casualties. That was *close!* We were within *twenty seconds* of the queen when the rest of those soldiers arrived. Talk about damned bad luck!"

"Talk about what you like, Dougal," said a small plump man in the uniform of a liner captain. He was whey-faced, leaning far forward and nursing his genitals. "I'll tell you one thing, you'll never talk me into another of these. It *hurts!* Do you realize where that soldier grabbed my simulacrum?"

"It's nothing, Danny." Macdougal was still grinning. "You'll be back to normal in an hour—and we'll be ready to tackle another one tomorrow."

"Without me, then."

"Without me, too," chimed in a tall, dark-haired woman, who was rubbing tenderly at her neck. "When they tell you it will be full sensories, they're not joking. I couldn't move my jaw—couldn't work the switch until the last possible second. I thought I was dead."

As the argument spread, Lotos wiped the sweat from her forehead, combed her hair carefully, and quietly slipped away. She had seen all of Adestis that she needed to; and more than she wanted to.

When Lotos got back to her tiny office, Esro Mondrian was waiting. He was sitting in the visitor's chair, staring impassively at her Appointments calendar. He didn't look up as she came in.

"Is it the end of the universe, Lotos?" he said quietly. "It must be. I think you have three hairs out of place."

She shook her head. "Adestis."

That startled Mondrian, enough for him to drop the pose of casual indifference. He stared at Lotos Sheldrake. "You amaze me. *You* played Adestis? I must revise my opinion of you."

"Cut it out, Esro." Lotos slid behind her desk, and relaxed into her chair with a sigh of relief. "I didn't do it for pleasure, you know that. And it *wasn't* pleasure. It was revolting. I did it for information."

"About the game?"

"About the ambassador." She tapped a file on her desk. "I got your coded report."

"But you didn't believe it? Then it serves you right."

"I wasn't sure. So I decided to see for myself."

"And?"

"Your report is accurate. As you said, Dougal Macdougal is a latent masochist. Maybe not so latent, either. You should have seen him when Adestis was complete—grinning all over his face, even when he was hurting like hell. But it means he could be dangerous when he's dealing with the Stellar Group. Sol doesn't need a masochist in that position."

"I agree. But we can't change it."

"Not now. He has to be handled with even more care than I thought."

"You know how to do that, if anyone does." Mondrian studied her expression closely. The experience Lotos Sheldrake had been through seemed to have made her unusually open and indiscreet—or was it a new pose that she was carefully cultivating? "You can make Macdougal do what you want."

"Maybe." She nodded absently. "All right, Esro. That's enough flattery. What's going on? According to my schedules, you're supposed to be out on Oberon. What are you doing here?"

"I want to give you some information."

"Give, Esro? You never gave anything away in your whole life." Lotos smiled. What she had just said was the truth, but it did not affect her feelings. She had always liked Mondrian. She was the daughter of a hard-rock miner, raised in the dust-tunnels of Iapetus, and every step out had been a fight. By the time she has ten years old she was as tough as a drill bit. She had evaluated her only assets there, and when she was thirteen—the optimum time—she carefully bargained away youth, innocence and virginity for an escape from Iapetus. She was never going back there. Never, *never*. Lotos could read signs of the same struggle and determination behind Esro Mondrian's refined tastes and formal manners.

"Not *give*," she went on. "You mean *trade* information."

"All right, I mean trade." Mondrian paused for a moment, wanting to choose his words exactly. "Let me give you the context. This is something you'll know anyway in another twenty-four hours. It will be coming in over the Mattin Link communications system. I am giving you—or trading—one day. But you alone will have that day. No one else in the solar system knows anything about this yet."

"So how do *you* know?" Lotos did not expect an answer, and Mondrian showed no sign of giving one. After a moment she shrugged, dialled for two cups of sugared tea, and nodded at Mondrian. "All right, I'll bite. Tell me all."

There was a pause. (For effect? With Esro Mondrian, she was never sure.)

"We've tracked down a Morgan Construct," said Mondrian at last. "The first one."

"Ahhh-h." Lotos drew in a long breath. "Damn it, Mondrian, you are quite right. I've had not even a hint of this."

"I know. You should fire your information chief—she's not as good as she used to be. Are you recording?"

She nodded. "Personal system."

"Keep it on. I'm only going to say this once. Out near the Perimeter there is a star named Talitha—*Iota Ursae Majoris*, when you check the catalogs. It's a three-star system, a bit more than fifty lightyears away from us. The main star is type A7 V, and it's about ten times as bright as Sol. The others are a close binary pair of red dwarfs—very dim, maybe a thousandth as bright as the primary. We've known about all that for quite a while. What we *didn't* know about, until the probes got there seventy years ago, was the planetary system around the primary. It's substantial—three gas giants, and six smaller metal-rich ones. The probes reported evidence of life on the innermost planet. It was named *Travancore*. It's small, less than half of Earth's mass, and it has flourishing native life-forms—vegetation, at least, and probably animals. But the first probe didn't detect any signs of intelligent life, so we didn't show great interest in exploration. As a result, we don't know much about the place. Now the Angels—don't waste my time asking me how—have managed to trace one of the Morgan Constructs to Travancore. It is still alive, down there on the surface of Travancore, under some sort of canopy of vegetation."

He stopped.

"What's it doing there?" asked Lotos.

"You tell me. You now know all that I know, except for one other thing. The Angels sent one of our smart probes down to the planet. It stopped signalling when it reached the surface and that was the last they heard of it. We have to assume that the Construct destroyed it. So it knows it has been discovered, and it will be ready for anything that comes after it."

Lotos Sheldrake sat back in her chair, quietly sipping tea from a porcelain cup that looked as delicate and fragile as she did. "Are you asking for any action from me?"

"Not on this. You'll need to decide what line Dougal Macdougal ought to take when he discusses it with the Stellar Group ambassadors. But I must get ready for action. I already have the first pursuit team assembled and waiting, out on Dembricot: one human woman, a Tinker ten-thousand composite, a sterile female Pipe-Rilla, and their preferred form of Angel—an experienced Singer carried by a new-grown Chassel-Rose. They are all in training now, using the pseudo-Construct that you provided."

"How is that working out?"

"It is perfect." Mondrian smiled. "If you will not mention that it is an illegal Artefact, from Shannon-knows-where on Earth, then neither will I. It's the perfect training tool. You did it for your own purposes, I know, but I still owe you an action-favor."

"And now I owe you an information favor. Let me try to pay that at once." She picked up a slender blue cylinder from the front of her desk. "You will hear about this officially in three days. And you won't like it. But according to a new ruling from the four Stellar ambassadors, you no longer out-rank Luther Brachis in the Anabasis. Henceforth you two will have equal powers."

"What!" Mondrian lost his calm manner and jerked up rigid in his seat. "That's crazy—and impossible. There's no way it could work with two people running things. Why would the ambassadors make a mad change like that?"

Lotos shrugged indifferently. "Do you understand ambassador logic? When you do, explain it to me. They make a rule, I just pass it on to you—sooner than you would normally hear it. You will have time to make your own plans."

"Plans be damned." Mondrian bit his lip, and stared hard at nothing for a few seconds. "When will this new ruling be effective?"

"In three days. That's when you would normally have heard about it—with no time to maneuver."

"Three days." Mondrian took a deep breath. "All right. I want you to do something else for me—and if you do, you'll have a big piece of equity with me, to trade in whenever you want to. I must remain in absolute control of just two things: the approach to Travancore, and the management of the operation to destroy the first Morgan Construct. After that, I don't mind what Brachis controls. Can you arrange it?"

"Why not throw in the Galaxy, too?"

"Don't play around, Lotos. Can you do it?"

"Maybe." The doll's face was still inscrutable, but there was the hint of a new look creeping into the eyes. "I can surely try. And I will try very hard, if you will do me one other favor."

"Name it."

"It's not *it*—it's *her*. Do you know a woman called Godiva Lomberd?"

Mondrian frowned. "No. Should I?"

"You should." Lotos smiled. "And according to my information sources—who are not *always* wrong—you do. You're caught, Esro. Don't tell me lies just for practice—you don't *need* practice."

"All right. So I know her. Or I did, back on Earth. What about her?"

"Luther Brachis has entered into a contract with her." For the first time, Lotos Sheldrake allowed emotion to show on her face. "Esro, I want to meet her. I want to know who she is, where she came from, what she wants. I want to know her better than she knows herself. I don't expect you to deliver all that. Just arrange for me to meet her—and leave the rest to me."

Esro Mondrian stared at her. He wondered how much Lotos knew—did she suspect that *he* had been the one who first arranged for Brachis to meet Godiva? It seemed impossible for Lotos to have come by that knowledge—unless Tatiana had told her.

Mondrian shook his head. "Luther Brachis has had five hundred women since I've known him. They come and go. Godiva Lomberd is just another one. You don't dabble in my business, Lotos, and I don't dabble in yours. Otherwise, I would ask you *why*—what makes you think Godiva Lomberd is different from all the others?"

"I don't know. But she *is* different—I've seen the change in Luther. And damn it, and damn her, I'm going to find out what's going on." Lotos Sheldrake shook her head, then somehow forced a formal smile onto her face. She had revealed too much. She lifted her cup. "Would you care for more tea, Esro? Otherwise, I think we must both get on to other business."

The storage facilities on Earth were not the best in the system. Far from it. For high-quality cold storage of living organisms, the wise buyer went to Phoebe, or possibly Hyperion, where the ambient disturbances were less and the maintenance personnel incorruptible.

But from the purchaser's point of view, Earth storage offered one unarguable advantage: anonymity. Provided that the rental was paid on time, which meant one full year in advance, no one questioned the contents of the pallet. According to the rumors, more than three thousand rightful Earth monarchs slept their dreamless storage sleep in the Antarctic warehouses. No one could ever accuse the usurpers of murder; but it would be a long, long time before the real kings and queens would be recalled from slumber.

The warehouses were kept only a few degrees above freezing. The two people searching the long files wore heavy clothing, thick gloves, and boots. They cursed the layer of frost that made every identification tag difficult to read.

" 'ere we are." The short, red-haired man bent over the long box, scrubbed again at the tag to take a second look, then nodded to his companion to grab the other end. "Ready?"

The fat blond woman with him nodded. "Let's do it. Just this one, and we're done for the day. Up's-a-daisy."

The container slid easily onto the moving rollway. The man and woman stood at each end, making sure that the ride out was smooth. They finally emerged into a long, white-walled room, filled with medical equipment and banks of monitors. Working as a team, they efficiently dumped the container onto one of the long tables, broke the seals, and hooked in the pumps and catheters. The woman checked the inner identification against the work order she was carrying.

"Look at that." she said. "An A-label! That's interesting. It's been a long time since I've seen an Artefact come out of the cooler. Any idea what we got here?"

The man sniffed, pulled off his thick white gloves, and shook his head. "Nah. Last time we did an A-label, it was one of them four-wing dragon-fliers. Gor, we 'ad a good laugh with that one—all over the lab, it was, an nearly 'ad a leg off Jesco Siemens before we could tie it. We'd better keep a good watch on this 'un."

The top and side of the long box had been removed, and the pumps and wipers were slowly removing the thick layers of semi-solid jelly, warming it as they worked. A shape began to emerge. The two stared at it.

"Uurgh. Don't care for the look of that," said the man. "It's 'ideous."

They were staring at a pair of long, bony feet, still with thick black gunk between the knobbly toes. While they watched, the rest of the figure slowly came into view. It was a male; naked, tall, angular, hollow-chested and skinny.

"Gor. How'd you like to find one of them under your bed?" said the fat woman. "Are you *sure* we got the right one?"

"Think so." The man peered at the form he was holding, and rubbed his nose with a stubby finger.

"Well, I don't see nobody in their right mind making an Artefact what looks like that—never mind waking 'im up." She took a step closer and looked again at the naked body on the bench. "This looks more like one of the bloody royals, somethin' the family stuck down in the vaults and never wanted to see again. Check it. An' check that the payment was made, too—if not, it's gettin' a bit late to stick it back in there. It'll be spoiled."

The man frowned and bent again over the label. He scratched his head. "It's this one, all right. See the chit? Paid in full, in advance. An automatic bank draft, from somebody's final estate. What's it say 'ere? Fu-jit-su—see, same as the I.D. mark on the container, Fu-jit-su. We've done our bit, an' if there's anythin' wrong it's nothin' to do with us."

The protective layer of jelly had almost gone. The catheters were going in while the last layers were being removed, and the deep-heat batteries increased in intensity. There was finally a horrible spluttering cough from the body, and a choking grunt as lungs filled with thin oil labored to expel it. With another cough, a spray of brown liquid went out onto the floor. Suddenly the figure sneezed and shook its head from side to side.

While the workers looked on it painfully levered itself upright. Claw-like hands scooped at the thick jelly that still filled the eye cavities. The head was massive, with a bald, domed skull. A full beard grew beneath a thin mouth, and was shadowed by a prominent red beak of a nose.

The mouth spoke: "Hh-hmm. Thank you."

There was another violent cough. Then the tall figure stood up straight, still naked and splotched with the black coating. In spite of its bizarre appearance, it was strangely dignified. It looked at the two workers.

"Thank you," it said again. It took in a long, lung-expanding breath. "I appreciate your services. But now I must go. Time is short, and I have important work to do."

The Artefact jerked into motion, and headed towards the door of the chamber. The man and woman looked at each other, then ran after it.

"You can't go yet," cried the man. "You've forgot your bath—an' your clothes. You 'ave to 'ave a bath, it's the rules. Don't you worry about the price, everythin's been paid for."

But the tall Artefact was not listening. It was already out of the door, striding purposefully towards the surface elevators.

# Chapter Thirteen

# CHAN AND LEAH

Chan Dalton had been on Ceres before; briefly, in transit from Earth to Horus. Kubo Flammarion had taken him to his office there, showed him the big solar system displays, and let him play with the buttons and switches that selected the real-time displays from every planet and moon known to the Stellar Group.

Now Chan was there again, sitting at the same console. Tatty was on one side of him, Kubo on the other. Tatty had become used to the change, but Kubo Flammarion still found it hard to accept—for instead of playing idly with the controls, Chan was *studying* them, and asking endless questions.

"And this one?" he said, flicking through a series of images and pausing at one of them. It was a low-orbit satellite view of a dreary grey landscape.

Flammarion nodded. "That's one you'll need to know—if you pass the entrance examination. It's where your first training courses with the other team members will be held. *Barchan*, it's called. It's a desert world, Eta Cass system. Barchan is two planets sunward from S'kat'lan, the home world of the Pipe-Rillas. You'll be able to breathe the air there—just—but it's so hot you'll probably

151

prefer to wear a suit on the surface. Want to take a look from ground level?"

Chan shook his head. His eyes were already skipping on to another image, while his fingers danced their way across the board.

Flammarion caught Tatty's eye, and he frowned. When Chan had possessed no more than an infant's mentality, there had been nothing wrong with his coordination. Now he was operating the control board far faster than Flammarion would ever do it. But there was mainly affection in the older man's scowl and rueful look. He could not conceal his pride whenever Chan did something unusually clever. Kubo Flammarion had no children, and never expected to. But there was parental approval in his expression when he looked from Chan to Tatty.

"How about this one?" said Chan. The screen showed a verdant world, where even the oceans were covered with a thick carpet of vegetation.

"That's Dembricot," said Flammarion. "In the Tinker system. Move out of the way for a minute, and I'll show you something interesting on that planet." He leaned over and linked in to a surface camera, then zoomed across to take a close-up view of a building that nestled in among tall spiky ferns. "See that? You're looking at the main training center for Team Alpha, before they headed out."

"Team Alpha?" Chan's bright blue eyes were fierce in their attention and concentration.

"That's the name we gave to the first Morgan Construct pursuit team. Your friend Leah, she's in it, along with the three aliens. She hates that name, Team Alpha—says she's going to call it something *she* likes, as soon as she can."

"You mean Leah is *there*? Can we talk to her— use your, what is the word, comm-unic-ator, with her?"

"We could have, through the Mattin communication link. Trouble is, she's no longer on Dembricot." Flammarion again leaned over the controls. "You see, Chan, they're finished with their training. Leah came through it in fine shape—just the way you will when the time comes. But now they're going on to the real thing: Travancore. Let me see if I can link us *there*—maybe we can get at least the one-way visuals."

He juggled the controls with black-nailed fingers, sniffing occasionally and cursing noisily while a mystifying succession of imperfect images fled across the screen. "There," he said at last, "that's probably as good as we'll get. It's a very limited band-width for the signal—no problem with voice-grade, but we'll get nothing more than a rotten picture."

They were looking again at the surface of a planet from a low orbit, sweeping along only a couple of hundred kilometers up. At first sight it was a repeat of Dembricot, with a dense, wall-to-wall covering of vegetation. A closer look showed major differences in the grainy image. Instead of being flat and uniform, the green of Travancore pushed up into millions of small hillocks and hummocks, each one only a few hundred meters across.

"Take a good look," said Kubo Flammarion. His voice sounded very serious. "According to all our reports, Travancore is a pretty odd place. Those hills are solid plant life—surface gravity is low, and the vegetation grows six kilometers deep. Vertical jungle, says the radar analyses, layer after layer of it."

"How can a ship land there?" asked Chan.

"It can't—not in the usual way. There's no solid surface to put a ship down on, and no way it could stay in one place. It would sink down and down, I don't know how far. So a ship has to *hover*, and drop off people and cargo, and then lift again.

That's one reason Travancore makes such a hell of a hiding place—we can't do a space survey, and we can't do a mechanized ground survey. But *somewhere* under all that mess, if you believe the Angels, we've got one of the Morgan Constructs. It's the job of Leah and the rest of Team Alpha to go down there, find the Construct, and destroy it. And if you pass the training, you'll be doing the same thing—destroying some other Construct, somewhere else.''

There was a series of clicks from the communicator, and a small red pattern appeared in the upper left corner of the display.

"Hey, we're in luck," said Flammarion. "I put in the tracer signal, but I didn't really expect a success. That's the signal I.D. for Team Alpha. They are in orbit around Travancore. With any luck we'll be able to talk to Leah now."

He began to set up a new control key.

"Wait a minute," said Chan. He stood up, staring at the screen. He was suddenly breathing heavily.

"And here she is," said Flammarion happily, ignoring Chan's comment. Then he spun around in his seat, and found he was looking at a rapidly retreating back. "Hey, where are you going? I've got her here on the link for you!"

Leah's dark countenance was looking out of the screen at them. "Chan?" they heard her voice say. "Chan, is it really you? This is wonderful!" Then she looked puzzled, and her eyes scanned across the room. "Chan, where are you? I've been longing to talk to you ever since I got the news."

Tatty Snipes came forward and stood in front of the screen. "I'm sorry, Leah. I ought to have guessed that this might happen. Chan's here, and he's doing fine. But he's finding it hard to talk to you."

Leah looked bewildered. "Hard to talk to *me*? Tatty, I've known Chan since he was four years old—so don't give me that line. What have you two done to him? For your sake, he'd better be all right. If he's not, I'll come back from Travancore and tear your heads off—both of you."

"Calm down." Tatty grinned. "Training hasn't done much to make you all sweetness and light, has it? I'm telling you, Chan is all right—better than all right, he's so smart it frightens us. But I'll tell you exactly what's wrong with him just now. It's *you*—he finds it hard to talk to you. You see, he's *embarrassed*."

"Space-fluff!" Leah shook her dark hair clear of her eyes. "You're crazy. Get your head screwed on right, Tatty Snipes. Do you know how long Chan and I have known each other? Since I was six and he was four. We ate together, cried together, slept together, bathed together—*everything*, from the first day we met down in the Gallimaufries." She paused. "He was my baby," she said at last. "He was like a sweet little angel-boy."

"I'm sure he was," said Tatty heavily. She was having her own problems with this conversation. "But now he's not your baby, and he's not an angel-boy. He's a *man*."

It took Leah a couple of seconds to catch the implication of Tatty's words. Then she looked horrified. "Chan? Did somebody— did you and he—"

"Yes." Tatty turned to Flammarion, who had listened to the last exchange with total incomprehension. "Hey, Kubo, would you go and bring Chan back here? Leah really wants to talk to him."

As soon as Flammarion was out of the room, Tatty looked again at the screen. "Yes. Somebody did. It was right after the successful Stimulator treatment, the one that made the big breakthrough. And I was the somebody. And I won't lie to you, I'm glad I was the one. But Leah, it honestly wouldn't have mattered *who* it was. Chan spoke your name all the time we were doing it. He wanted you. God, maybe he even thought I *was* you."

The other woman stared stonily at the screen. Finally, she sighed. "All right, I guess I understand."

"I know, Leah. I know how you must be feeling."

"No." Leah shook her head. "You sure as hell *don't* know how I'm feeling. You can't know. Tatty, for all those years, ever since we were little children, I looked after both of us. And I had my own secret hope. I dreamed that Chan would somehow become intelligent, and he'd grow up, and we'd become lovers. Just a fantasy, and by the time I was twelve I knew the truth. He was the little boy who would *never* grow up. I would have to look somewhere else for that kind of love." Her dark eyes were wistful. "You know, there was no trouble finding sex. There never is. But that wasn't that I wanted. And now you tell me my dream came true. But it was *you* and Chan—why am I telling you all this?"

Kubo Flammarion came back into the room, trailing Chan along behind him. As they arrived in camera range, Leah was suddenly gone from the screen.

"Here he is," said Flammarion. Then his eyes widened and he stared at the display. "Well, blast it. Now where did *she* go?"

Tatty swiveled quickly around in her seat. "Leah had to go. Her pursuit team had a meeting. Let's forget it, Kubo, it just won't work today." She looked up at Chan. "I spoke to Leah. She sends you all her love, and she can't wait until she has a chance to see you."

Chan blushed with pleasure, a flood of pink across his fair cheeks. "She did?" he said seriously. "Thank you, Tatty. I wish I could have said the same thing to her."

"I told her, on your behalf," said Tatty. "But she

had to go. They're on a strict training program out there."

"You can say that again," agreed Flammarion. "A few more days, and Team Alpha will be down there on the surface of Travancore—if you can call it a surface. We shouldn't bother with that place now, Chan—better if you concentrate on Barchan; that'll be *your* next stop."

He winked at Tatty. He didn't know quite what had happened, but he sensed that somehow she had carried them through an awkward situation. Now they needed to change the subject and get Chan thinking about something else. Flammarion keyed in the sequence to take them back to the first image. "Barchan," he began. "Take a good look at it." Then as the scene changed he leaned back in confusion. Instead of the heated dust-ball that would be Chan's next training site, the screen was displaying the face of Esro Mondrian.

He looked out at them and nodded casually. "Sorry, Kubo. I just ran an override on your display unit. I need to talk to Tatty." He smiled at her pleasantly, with no trace of embarrassment. "My congratulations, Princess. You did it. I knew you would. And as for you, young man"—he inclined his head to Chan—"welcome to Ceres. From everything I hear, you're going to be an outstanding addition to the next pursuit team."

"And you'll win your bet," said Tatty bitterly. "I guess that's all you care about."

Mondrian looked at her with a hurt expression. "You know that's not true, Tatty. Anyway, we can talk about that later. I mainly called to say that I've arranged for us to have dinner together tonight, and you'll have a chance to meet an old friend."

"I have no friends on Ceres." Tatty shook her head. "Not one, unless it's Kubo here."

"Yes, you do. More than you know." Mondrian

smiled at her. "I'll come over and pick you up at seven. Dinner will be just the four of us: you, me, Luther Brachis—and Godiva Lomberd."

"Godiva!" Before she could do more than say the name, Mondrian had vanished from the screen. In his place were the swirling sand-clouds of Barchan. Tatty stared at them, her fists clenched.

"Damn you, Esro Mondrian. Damn you, damn you! Ignore me for months, then think you can call up and suggest dinner, as though nothing had happened. No way!" She swivelled to face the others. "I'll see him in hell before I'll see him at dinner."

She paused. She had just seen Chan's face. It was white, with a glassy, staring look in his eyes. "Chan! Are you all right?"

"Who—was—that?" he whispered. "That . . ."

"Him?" Flammarion shrugged. He had not noticed Chan's expression. "He's my boss, that's who. Commander Mondrian, the head of the whole security operation. You want to meet him? You will, soon as your training program gets going."

Chan was nodding. "Yes," he said softly, almost too quietly to hear. His hands were clasped tightly together, and he shivered as he spoke. "I want to meet Commander Mondrian—very much." He gave a quick glance at Tatty's face. "He wants you to go to dinner. Will you go?"

"Never!"

Chan's look became more intense, reading Tatty's facial expressions with a total concentration. He had regained his own self-control phenomenally quickly. "I think you will," he said at last. He nodded. "Yes, I think you will."

# Chapter Fourteen

## ON CERES

These are the Seven Wonders of the Solar System:
- The Vulcan Nexus
  - The Oort Harvester
    - The Sea-farms of Europa
      - The Uranian Lift System
- The Mattin Link
  - The Venus Domes
    - The Tortuga Tetrahedra
      - The Persephone Fusion Network
- The Vault of Hyperion
  - Oberon Station
    - The Jupiter Bubble
      - Marslake

There are a dozen items on the list. That is not an error. For although everyone agrees on the first four, all the rest are a source of violent argument. Is the Hyperion Vault more impressive than Oberon Station, merely because it is bigger? Is the Jupiter bubble more deserving of inclusion than the Venus Domes, because it is more difficult to maintain? How does technical sophistication trade-off against beauty and elegance—or, for that matter, against importance to the human race? Why are visiting aliens all so taken with the Harvester, and so bored by the Sea-farms? And is it at all fair to include the metal tetrahedra of the Dry Tortugas on such a list, since they are not the result of human efforts?

For some reason, no one ever puts the reconstruction of Ceres anywhere in their catalog of marvels. A minor planet, less than one thousand kilometers in diameter, has become the most populous and influential body in the solar system. Should not that be regarded as a major miracle?

Ah, but the work was done long ago, using the same ages-old technology that built the Earth-warrens and the Gallimaufries; and whatever the technology, the results are too familiar. Ceres is on no one's list.

It should be. After centuries of steady work, modern Ceres possesses less than half the mass of the original. Instead of a body of solid rock with minor intrusions of organic material, Ceres is now a sculptured set of concentric spherical shells. One within another, varying in roof height from less than ten meters to nearly a kilometer, the internal chambers extend from the center of the planetoid all the way out to the surface. The original body offered less than two million square kilometers of available surface area; the honeycomb of modern Ceres provides close to two *billion*—more than ten times the original land area of Earth.

And if Ceres itself does not qualify as a major wonder, then surely that term applies to its transportation system. It was designed to move people and goods efficiently through the three-dimensional spherical labyrinth of tunnels and chambers. It is a topological nightmare: a complex interlocking set of high-speed railcars, walkways, drop-shafts, escalators, elevators, and pressure chutes. The trip from one point to any other can be made in less than one hour—with the help of a computer route guide. And no one would even attempt it without that assistance; an unguided journey, if it could be done at all, would take days.

After a few sessions of Kubo Flammarion's coaching, Tatty had reached the point where she could handle the route instructions provided by the transit computer. She did it cautiously, checking each interchange that she had to make on the way. On her first visit, before their stay on Horus, she had been obliged to lead Chan everywhere. But this time he took one look at the overall plan, listened impatiently to Flammarion's lecture on route selection, and promptly disappeared. He was gone for many hours. When he came back he seemed to have been all over the planetoid, and he knew the internal layout of Ceres in complete detail.

Lately Chan had seemed to be avoiding Tatty, but before she went off for dinner with Esro Mondrian he came wandering into her living quarters. She looked at him warily. On Horus, before Chan's change, her behavior had been quite casual. She had allowed him to see her in random stages of undress. Now she closed the bedroom door firmly as she went in and locked it behind her. Uncharacteristically, Chan stayed. He lounged and fidgeted in her kitchen for two hours, while she bathed and dressed in the bedroom; and he was still there when she came out. He examined her appearance closely, standing behind her as she looked at herself in a full-length mirror. She was wearing a white dress, sleeveless and off the shoulder, with pale mauve accessories. The purple marks of Paradox shots were slowly fading from her arms, providing a curiously apt match to the clothes that she wore.

Chan caught her eye as she studied her hairstyle. "Very . . . el-e-gant?" he said. "Is that the right word to use?"

"It is. Thank you."

"You look very beautiful. But I thought you would rather go to hell than have dinner with Mondrian."

She turned and looked at him. Her face was pale. "All right, Chan, that does it. What do you want? I've got enough on my mind, without you adding to my worries."

He shrugged, and said nothing in reply. But shortly before the time that Mondrian was due to arrive, Chan left the apartment.

Tatty continued her careful application of make-up. At one minute to seven she went to the apartment door and opened it. She smiled in satisfaction. As she had expected, Mondrian was there. He was precisely punctual, as always. And just as though they had planned it together, he was dressed in formal uniform, a plain black trimmed with just the same pale mauve that she was wearing. He looked full of suppressed energy and an odd nervousness. He bowed formally, and kissed her hand.

"You look magnificent," he said. "The Godiva Bird will be envious."

Tatty shook her head. "Godiva Lomberd is never envious of anyone. She never needs to be."

She stepped outside quickly and closed the door, making it clear that she did not propose to invite Mondrian into her living-quarters. He stood there looking at her for another moment, then shrugged, took her arm, and led her away along the walkway.

"You seem to be upset, Princess," he said softly. "I hope this evening will relax you."

Tatty did not reply for a moment. She thought she noticed the figure of Chan, dodging away along the walkway in front of them.

"What do you think I am?" she said at last. "Some sort of Artefact, or slave? Something that you can put into cold storage when you don't need it, and pull out when you do?"

"You know I don't think that way."

"Do I? When you leave me to rot on Horus, and never visit, or call, or send a message? This evening is supposed to relax me—when I never know what to expect from you? You treated me *worse* than putting me in storage. At least if that happened I would be unconscious. I wouldn't be watching my life tick away, wasting months and months just waiting."

She tried to shake her arm free of his hold. Mondrian would not release her. He sighed. "Wasted months. I know, a month on Horus can seem like a year. But were they *wasted*? Chan is a full person now, instead of a baby. That isn't a waste of anyone's time." He stopped walking, still holding her arm tightly so that she had to swing to face him. She was at least six inches taller, and she stared angrily down at his calm eyes. After a few silent moments he shook his head sadly. "Princess, if you think that badly of me, then why did you agree to come to dinner? I knew exactly what you were going through, those past few months. I told you at the beginning, I needed somebody I trusted completely—because I wasn't sure if I would be able to keep an eye on things. Do you know why I didn't come to Horus? Because I couldn't. I wasn't off having fun. I was *busy*—busier than I've ever been in my life."

"You found time to go galloping off to Earth. What were you doing there?"

She had expected almost any reply, but not the one she got. Mondrian merely shook his head again. "I can't say. You'll have to take my word for it, Tatiana—it was business, not pleasure, but I can't tell you what it was."

Tatty was starting to feel the guilt that only Esro Mondrian could create within her. She began to think that *she* was the unreasonable one, the cruel one, the woman who carped and whined at a desperately busy man. She knew how hard he worked. How many times had she awakened in the early morning, to find Mondrian gone from her side? Too many to count. But he was not being unfaithful to her. He would be in the next room, pacing up and down, writing, dictating, making calls, worrying. Her only rival was his work. And she had known that for years.

Mondrian reached up, and lightly touched her cheek. He looked very upset. "Don't be sad, Princess. I thought tonight would be a happy occasion—the chance to see Godiva again, just like old times. Can't we try to enjoy ourselves?"

Tatty put her hand on his. They turned, and began to walk again, side by side. "I'll try, Esro. But everything is so strange to me here. It's not like Earth. I could hardly believe it when I heard that Godiva had left Earth, and come out here with Luther Brachis."

Mondrian slipped his arm through hers. "I suppose I must take responsibility for that—I put Godiva onto Luther in the first place, so she could bring me information." He laughed. "Not such a good idea, was it? After the first few weeks she said she wouldn't tell me any more, and the *next* thing I knew she was up here with him." He gave Tatty a quick sideways look. "Did I misjudge the Godiva Bird? You know her a lot better than I do. I thought I understood what she wanted, what she is really like. Now I'm not so sure."

"She's a private person—hard to know. I first met her four years ago, at Winter Solstice. We both attended the Gilravage, the big party down on the lower levels. She gave a performance. She danced as Aphrodite. She created a sensation. After that we met fairly often."

"Where did she come from?"

"Nowhere special. Somewhere down in the Gallimaufries. I suppose she must be a commoner. If she's not, she never talks about her family. The first few times we met I hated her—all woman do, instinctively. We feel as though she'll take what she wants, and we have no defenses. But after a while I realized that she is a nice person."

"The whore with the heart of gold?"

"Close to that. You see, I don't think that Godiva is *bright*, like me or you." Tatty spoke quite unself-consciously. "She just does what she can with what she has. She happened to be born with certain unique assets, and she uses them. Sex for money, I can't see that as a big sin. People who went with her had a wonderful time. Godiva never had a man under false pretenses, and she never hurt anyone."

"Not even when she was spying on them?" They were now approaching the restaurant, and Mondrian had slowed his steps. "Don't you think her actions might have hurt Luther Brachis?"

"Sure they might. But that was *your* action, really, not hers—and even when she was watching Brachis for you, she certainly didn't mean to harm him."

"What happened when a man fell in love with her?"

"It's a funny thing, but no one ever did. She handled everything on a commercial basis—she must have made a fortune. But she would never accept a permanent relationship. Until Luther Brachis." Tatty turned to look at Mondrian. They had halted, and were standing outside the restaurant door. Over his shoulder she caught another disquieting glimpse of a tall figure, ducking back into the shadow at the side of the corridor. Was Chan still following?

She took another swift glance around them. "Look," she said, "if you want to interrogate me about Godiva, do it after dinner. I'm hungry, and you've done nothing but plague me with questions. Let's go inside."

Mondrian smiled. "Sorry, You're quite right. I was just being nosy." He moved forward, and the frosted glass doors opened before them. "You know me, I've got too much curiosity for my own good. But I promise you, not another question about Godiva."

"There's no need for any." Tatty inclined her head off to the left as they entered the foyer. "Now you've got the real thing."

They were exactly on time, but Luther Brachis and Godiva Lomberd must have arrived early. Stepping out of a communication booth and heading back to the table area was a full-figured blond woman. She was in half-profile to Tatty and Mondrian, and they could see that she had a dreamy and absent-minded smile on her face.

"Look at that walk," said Tatty. "It shouldn't be allowed. It's totally natural, and Godiva never thinks twice about it—but ten billion other women would kill to have it."

Godiva Lomberd was dressed in a gown of palest lemon. It was high-necked, full-length, and full-sleeved. When she walked, the material undulated with its own rhythm. An observer could not ignore the exotic body within, the warm and pliant flesh that rippled beneath the decorous clothing.

Mondrian was nodding, a bemused look on his face. "You may find this hard to believe, Tatty, but I had honestly forgotten about that phenomenon. She's in a quarter-g field, and yet she looks and moves just the same."

"And she probably always will. She hasn't aged a day since I first saw her. Remember what I told you, before you ever met?"

"You said that nobody could watch the Godiva Bird walk without realizing that she was naked underneath her clothes. I laughed at you. But you were right."

They did not call out to Godiva, but simply

followed her back to the table. It was located in a dimly-lit area at the rear of the restaurant, a quiet location intended for small, intimate parties who wanted discreet service and no public attention. No other tables were occupied, and Luther Brachis was sitting alone, looking at a menu. When they arrived at the table, he at once stood up and greeted Tatty cordially.

She had not seen him since they were all on Earth together. She was astonished by the change in him. He was still in superb physical condition, but now his face was more cheerful and animated. He had lost five to ten kilos, and his eyes glowed with health and well-being.

He nodded to Mondrian, then turned to stare hard at Tatty. "I don't know if I ought to have dinner with you, even though Commander Mondrian particularly requested it. I understand that it is mainly thanks to you that I will be losing a surveillance system." He turned to Godiva. "What should I do about that, dear? It was Tatiana's success with Chancellor Dalton that made me lose the wager."

Godiva slowly smiled, a broad and dreamy smile. "I could never be annoyed with Tatty, or with Commander Mondrian. They are the people who introduced me to you."

She looked up lovingly at Brachis. Her mouth was wide and full-lipped in a face that was slightly too plump, with full, red cheeks. The wide-set eyes, pale blue in color, held their usual trusting and contented expression. Her chin was a little too long, her nose slightly bobbed and asymmetrical, her forehead a shade too high. Any analysis of individual features would always add up to something of no exceptional beauty. But the whole was much greater than the sum of the parts. The totality of Godiva was stunning. She arrested the eye, so that in a crowded room she was inevitably the center of attention.

Brachis shrugged and turned to Mondrian. "You see my problem. If I am annoyed with Princess Tatiana, Godiva will interpret it as a lack of esteem for her." He laughed, and gestured for everyone to sit down. Mondrian ignored the wave of the hand indicating that he should sit opposite Godiva, and placed himself opposite Brachis. As he did so he nodded apologetically to Tatty and Godiva. "Will you give the two of us a few minutes for private security business? Then I promise that will be the last business talk of this evening."

Godiva merely smiled, and said nothing, but Tatty at once stood up. "Come on, Goddy-Bird. We don't want to hear their boring business. You can show me around this place—I don't know where we are."

She sounded cheerful enough, but Brachis was frowning when Mondrian sat down. "What's the game, Esro? You told me Tatiana just wanted to have dinner with Godiva tonight—there was to be no work. I agreed only on that basis."

"I know." Mondrian leaned forward, and spoke softly and rapidly. "This is new, it's urgent, and we can handle it in two minutes if you'll give me a straight answer to one question: Have you been getting a lot of interference from Dougal Macdougal?"

Brachis scowled and suddenly looked murderous. "Aye. Constant interference. I can't do one damned thing without him sticking his big nose in. And he's the Stellar ambassador, so I can't tell him to go away. The man's a complete bonehead."

"He is. And we've not reached the hard part yet—that comes when the Anabasis tangles with the Morgan Constructs."

"True enough. We can't possibly handle that

Construct on Travancore unless we get Macdougal out of the way."

Mondrian nodded. "So we have to get him out of the way. We can't afford to have him second-guessing us."

Brachis was biting his lip and looking sceptically at Mondrian. "Easy enough for you to say that. But how do we do it? He's immune to hints. You'd have to kill him to be rid of him, and I've not quite come to that yet."

"I know a better way. Dougal Macdougal would keep out of our way *if the other ambassadors told him to*. You know he grovels to them."

"He does. But they'll not tell him to get out of our hair."

"They might." Mondrian lowered his voice still further. "I can get the Pipe-Rillas to suggest it to the Angels and the Tinkers—to push for our complete independence in operating the Anabasis. But it wouldn't work unless the two of us make a truce. A *real* truce. No more sabotage, no more tricks, no more doing each other down." Mondrian smiled grimly. "Until the Anabasis is over, I mean. Naturally, after that it can be business as usual."

"Sabotage?" Brachis laughed. "From me? Ah, you've just got a suspicious nature." He leaned back, whistled softly to himself, and stared up at the ceiling. "Interesting," he said at last. He gave Mondrian a quick and calculating glance. "That's quite a proposal you're making. I hope to hell you're not expecting a decision from me without a lot more information and discussion."

"We must have that—but not tonight. I just wanted to start your thoughts going."

"You've done that. They're going. I'd give a lot to get rid of Dougal Macdougal—he's been nothing but a pain and a damned nuisance to me." Brachis looked around him. There was still no sign of Tatty and Godiva. "But you've given me only half the story, haven't you? Now you have to tell me what the Pipe-Rillas want in return. I don't believe in something for nothing. Neither do they—or you."

Mondrian nodded. "That's why a truce between us is *essential*. The Pipe-Rillas want something from us, all right. Something very explicit. They want the secret plans for human expansion beyond the Stellar Group."

"The *what*?" Brachis gave a hoot of incredulity. "Secret expansion plans? There's no such thing— everything we intend to do on the Perimeter is spelled out, and they have it."

"I know. But the Pipe-Rillas don't believe it's all. They are convinced that we have other intentions, ones we have not told them about. You have to remember the way they think of humans. In their eyes we're madmen; aggressive, rash, and dangerous."

"And they're not far off the truth, for some of us." Brachis gave a bark of laughter. "We're dangerous enough. But how can we give them secret expansion plans, when we don't have any?"

"We make them up—secretly, just you and me. And then we drop word in a few places, saying they exist. For a start, you could hint it to Macdougal's office. Except for Lotos Sheldrake, that whole place leaks information like a sieve. The rumor will get back to the Pipe-Rillas, and confirm their ideas. And then we finally give them the plans themselves."

"How?"

"Leave that to me. I have a delivery system."

"You mean the Pipe-Rillas already think you're a traitor?"

"That concept is not in their vocabulary. In their view, you and I would be allowing the better side of our natures to triumph over human wickedness. They don't seem to understand cheating."

"Well, I sure as hell do." Brachis gripped the

edge of the table, and leaned forward. "And so do you. How do I know this isn't all some game of *yours*, setting me up for something?"

Mondrian shrugged. "I realize that I'm going to have to prove that to you. And I'm willing to do so." He motioned slightly with his head. "But we'll discuss that later. Here come Tatiana and Godiva."

The two women had appeared in the doorway, a dozen tables away. A tall waiter was walking ahead of them, carrying a broad covered dish. He came forward, placed the silver tureen between Mondrian and Brachis, and straightened up.

"With the compliments of the management," he said stiffly. "Enjoy this. I will be back shortly to take your order." He hurried away, bowing his head deferentially to Tatty and Godiva as he passed them.

"That's peculiar," said Brachis. "I've been here a dozen times before, but I don't remember them bringing free appetizers."

He reached out and took hold of the cover, lifting it from the dish. As he did so the fire opal at Mondrian's collar suddenly changed color. It began to pulse with a vivid green light. A high-pitched whine came from it.

"Drop that!" Mondrian leaped to his feet, took a lightning glance around him, and grabbed the tureen away from Brachis. In the same motion he hurled it away towards the side of the room. "Get down, all of you!"

He grabbed the end of the table and tilted it upwards, so that it served as a shield. At the same moment Luther Brachis dived at Tatty and Godiva, grabbing one in each arm and knocking them off their feet. He dropped on top of them.

There was a hollow, deep *whomp*, and a bright flash of white light. The table that Mondrian was holding flew violently backwards, throwing him on top of Brachis. A sound like violent hail rattled on the other side of the table. Then there was a sudden and total silence.

Tatty found herself lying on the floor, her ears ringing. Sharp pains tingled and stung all the way along her left arm. Brachis and Mondrian were both lying on top of her, making it impossible for her to move. As she tried to wriggle out from under them, she heard a curse and a pained grunt from above.

"Agghh. Esro, for God's sake get your head out of my guts. Esro? Esro!"

The weight on top of her shifted. Tatty could move to one side, and finally crawl free. She stood up, aware of the dull, stunned feeling inside her head. Their table, upside down, showed a cracked, splintered surface. The plastic was pocked and cratered, with metal splinters embedded in its surface. Off to her right, the wall showed a similar pattern of shrapnel impact. Godiva stood at the other side of the table. She looked stunned, but otherwise unharmed.

"Help me," said Tatty. She nodded at Godiva to take hold of the overturned table, and between them they lifted it off the two men. Mondrian was clearly unconscious. Tatty dropped to her knees and leaned down, looking first at his face, then feeling for his pulse. It was slow and steady. She noticed, in an abstracted sort of way, that her own left arm was punctured and bleeding, marked by scores of metal fragments.

Luther Brachis was now on his feet, holding his hands to his head and staring vacantly around him. His right shoulder was riddled with metal pellets. The restaurant staff had appeared and stood helplessly looking on.

"Medical care," said Brachis gruffly. "Did any of you send for it?"

One of the waiters nodded.

"All right, then." Brachis motioned to Esro Mondrian. "Take him outside. He'll live, but we have to get him to a hospital—fast. And then"—he suddenly shivered, and put his arms around Godiva. His voice dropped to a whisper. "And *then* I'll catch the bastard who did this."

He shook his head again, reached for his shoulder, tilted, straightened, and started a slow crumpling. Tatty and Godiva both reached out for him. They lowered him gently to the floor. Their hands came away from his uniform covered with bright fresh blood.

Tatty wiped her palms absently on the front and side of her clean white dress. As she did so, she suddenly thought of Chan Dalton. Where was he, what had he been doing? That picture of Mondrian, back on Horus—it had been the spur that drove Chan towards intelligence. She had done it *deliberately*, with hatred. Was this the terrible result?

*No. Please God, no!*

But Tatty felt sure that she was right. She had *caused* this carnage. She dropped to her knees, cradled Esro Mondrian in her arms, and hid her face against his tunic.

There had been that sudden, terrible period when the whole world rushed in on him. It had created nausea, staggering pain, and total disorientation. At the time, Chan would have said that nothing could ever be worse than those final few minutes in the Tolkov Stimulator; it was the moment when his innocence ended.

But there are degrees of torture, refinements of pain beyond the simple or the immediate. A more complex animal admits more subtle agonies.

Those agonies came later, and more gradually.

Chan could not put his sufferings easily into words. He felt as though the illumination level of the world around him had been slowly increasing, hour by hour and day by day. When the lighting had been very dim, back in the happy days on Earth, he had seen almost nothing of the world. The Tolkov Stimulator had produced the first flood of light. And ever after that the radiance level had risen, little by little, so that detail was gradually added—to the point of discomfort, and beyond.

Occasionally a single event would produce a flare, a quantum change in the brightness around him. The sight of Esro Mondrian, earlier in the day, had done just that. It brought in a torrent of new sensation. He *knew* Mondrian—but how, and from where, did he know him?

Chan brooded on that question for a long time. Mondrian's weary, aristocratic features were utterly familiar, more familiar to Chan than his own face. But he could not say *why*. The memory was there in his brain—and he was denied access. Thinking about it made his mind devolve along an endless loop.

Finally Chan had wandered disconsolately over to Tatty's apartment. He had no particular reason for going there, no explicit goal in mind. But maybe she could help him; or if not help him, comfort him.

He had found her cold, remote and unsympathetic. She was making her own mental journey, and it was one that did not admit companions. When she went into her bedroom, he had hung around in the apartment. He should have left, but he felt that he had nowhere to go. Finally she came out again, dressed for her dinner appointment. And it was then, looking over her shoulder at their reflection in the full-length mirror that hung on the living-room wall, that Chan had become disoriented and faint. For the first time in his life he experienced a complete sense of self-awareness. That tall, blond figure, staring back from the mirror with bright blue eyes, was *him*— Chancellor Vercingetorix Dalton, the unique composite of thoughts, emotions and memories, housed in the familiar frame. There he was. There was his own identity.

Chan felt like screaming. Instead, he left the apartment; quickly, so that the opportunity to explore the flood of thoughts would not be lost or diverted by conversation with others. In the corridor he saw the approaching figure of Esro Mondrian. That merely added to his internal storm of feelings.

Chan did not want to speak. He hid until Mondrian had passed by and gone on to Tatty's door. Chan watched from the shadows, and followed the pair along the walkway. He had no objective, beyond an unarticulated urge to keep Mondrian within his sight.

At the restaurant Chan was greeted by a waiter, who politely barred his way. Did Chan have a reservation? If not, what was the size of his party? Chan shook his head without speaking, and retreated in confusion. He wandered blindly away along the corridor. His head was throbbing. At each intersection he made a random choice of direction and was carried up, down, east, west, north, and south through the convoluted interior paths of Ceres. At last he found he had travelled all the way to the surface chambers. Great transparent viewports looked out on the jumble of ships, gantries, landing towers and antennae that covered the periphery of the planetoid. The surface was a bustle of activity, twenty-four hours a day.

Beyond the surface stood the silent stars. Chan settled down to look at them, and to worry.

What was he? A month ago, he had been a moron. A misfit, with the brain of an infant and the body of a grown man. Only a few days ago Chan had asked Kubo Flammarion for more details: before the Stimulator his brain had not developed. He understood that—but *why* had it not developed? Was the cause chemical, physiological, psychological, or what?

Flammarion had just shaken his head. They did not know the answers. Chan had always possessed what appeared to be a perfectly normal brain; and now, after the treatment, Chan *had* a normal brain—a better-than-normal one, according to all the recent tests.

Kubo Flammarion seemed content with that answer. He did not realize how totally unsatisfying it was to Chan. If no one could explain the source of abnormality, what assurance was there that Chan would not regress? And in how many other ways, less easy to measure, might he be abnormal? How would he even *know* he was abnormal? Maybe he was still a total misfit, but merely a smarter one.

Without realizing it, Chan was performing an exploration of his own sanity and normality. The process was natural for maturing humans. But Chan was doing it on an accelerated time scale, trying to make in weeks the adjustments that would normally take years. He had no time to examine the libraries, to cull from millions of pages and five thousand years of common human experience the reassurance he needed.

Chan stared at the stars, pondered, and could find no acceptable answers. He felt confused, overwhelmed by uncertainty and sorrow and pain.

The easiest way to avoid that pain was to retreat from it, to hide in sleep and mindlessness. He gazed far out, looking beyond the starscape for the edge of the universe. He felt dreadfully tired. And after a few more minutes his eyes closed.

Seven hours later he awoke on the bed of his own apartment, exhausted and empty-headed. He could not say where he had been, what he had done. His last memory was of him and Tatty, examining the reflection of her evening dress in the mirror. Seven hours of his life had disappeared.

Chan did not have the energy and resolve to rise from his bed. When Tatty came to him, wearing that same white dress now stained with Luther Brachis's dried blood, Chan was still there. He looked at and listened to her with horror. He was quite prepared to believe her worst worries and suspicions.

As he had feared, he was a monster. Before she had even finished talking, Chan had decided what he must do.

# Chapter Fifteen

# ESCAPE TO BARCHAN

"And who *dared* to give such an instruction?" Mondrian's voice was weak in volume, but crackling with authority. "Were you insane enough to do it yourself, without realizing the consequences?"

The technician recoiled from the front of the bed and looked beseechingly at Tatty Snipes. She stepped forward.

"I gave the instruction," she said. "These people were only following orders."

Mondrian looked staggered. "*You*? You have no authority here. How could your word carry weight?"

"Very easily. I gave the instruction in writing, and I used the seal of your own office." She sat on the edge of the bed. "And if you expect me to say I'm sorry, I won't do it. I'll send you back for more X-rays of your head."

The medical technician looked at her in horror, then up to the ceiling as though expecting a lightning bolt.

"Don't fret and fume, and don't be a fool, Esro," went on Tatty calmly. "The medical opinions were unanimous: you would increase your chances of full recovery if you were under full sedation for a week. That week is up. And you are doing well."

Mondrian shook his head, then gritted his teeth at the pain it produced. "A week! You make me unconscious for a whole week, and act as though it is unimportant. My God, Tatty, in a week the whole system could go to hell."

"It could. But it didn't. Luther Brachis has taken care of everything in your absence."

"Brachis! Is that supposed to make me more at ease?" Mondrian struggled to sit upright. "He had a free hand to do what he liked with my operations and staff, and you *encouraged it*?"

"He knew you would be worried. He told me to give you a message. He accepts the arrangement that you talked about before the attempt to kill you, and he will try to gain the ear of Ambassador Macdougal, as you suggested. His main worry was whether you would remember anything about your conversation. The doctors warned of amnesia."

"I remember everything." Mondrian put his left hand to his forehead, which was still coated with synthetic skin. "How did *he* escape injury? I know he was shielding you and Godiva."

"He was injured, too, but his wounds could be treated with local anesthetics. In fact, he refused all sedatives—he must be made of iron."

"He is. Iron and ice. Except maybe when it comes to Godiva. He's besotted with her. How is she doing?"

"Calm as ever. I don't know how she escaped, but she wasn't even touched." Tatty shook her head. "You know Godiva Bird, she just floats over everything and never seems to notice."

Mondrian leaned back on his pillow. "You didn't detect any changes in her, then ... before the bombing?"

"*Before* the bombing?" Tatty frowned at him in perplexity.

"Yes." Mondrian waved his hand in a vague circle. "You knew her well down on Earth. And you said you were very surprised when she came up here with Luther Brachis. So I wondered, when you were with her before dinner and I was talking to Brachis, if she seemed . . . well, *different* at all."

Tatty sat thoughtful for a moment, while Mondrian lay back and looked at her through half-open eyes. "I think I know what you mean," she said at last. "She looks the same, and mostly she acts the same. But now you mention it, there *is* a difference. Whenever I met Godiva down on Earth, she was always very conscious of money. I don't mean she was stingy, exactly, but she *talked* a lot about her need to earn more. I always had the feeling she must be stashing away a fortune somewhere. She was the highest-priced escort on the planet, yet she always lived cheaply—simple food, simple clothes. There was no way she could have been spending anything near her income, but she always wanted *more.* Now she never seems to think of money for a moment. And *that's* a change. Is that what you mean?"

"I'm not sure what I mean. But here's something to think about. According to Luther Brachis, Godiva didn't have a cent when he brought her up from earth—no money, and no possessions other than her clothes." Mondrian sat deep in thought for a moment, then turned to the medical technician, who had been listening with interest. "How soon can I get out of this place?"

"Another two days. And visitors will be restricted to one hour a day."

"They will not." Mondrian pushed back the covers and swung his legs over the edge of the bed. "That answer is unacceptable. I have work to do. Bring me my uniform—at once."

The technician looked hopelessly at Tatty, found no encouragement there, and shook his head feebly. "I'm sorry, sir. I lack that authority."

"Then go and find someone who has it."

The technician scurried away, snatching one nervous look behind him from the door of the room.

Mondrian turned back to Tatty. "I suppose I'm going to have another fight with you, too."

"Not at all." Tatty smiled coldly. "You're well enough to make your own decisions now, Esro. You can go to hell in your own fashion. I came here to tell you that I'm leaving Ceres, and I already have the exit approval."

"Where are you going?"

"Home. Back to Earth. I've had my fill of Horus and Ceres." She stood up. "I suppose I should thank you for saving my life, but maybe it's not appropriate. It was my fault in the first place. That's the other reason I came here—to tell you that I was responsible for the attempt to assassinate you."

Mondrian laughed harshly. "If you go to Earth, I'll come with you. I have to make a visit as soon as they'll let me out of here. For the rest of it, you're talking nonsense. You didn't cause the bombing, and I don't know why you think you did. You were injured, too—look at your arm."

"I didn't *do* the bombing—but I caused it to be done."

Mondrian reached out to take Tatty's hand, pulling her back to sit on the bedside. His grip was much firmer than she had expected. Maybe it would be all right for him to leave at once.

"You can't make a wild statement like that and say nothing more," he said. "*Who* tried to kill us?"

"Chan Dalton. He wasn't trying to kill *us*—he was after *you*. The rest of us happened to be there."

"Tatty, you're gibbering. What are you getting at?"

Tatty hesitated and dissimulated. Finally, under prodding from Mondrian, she told the whole story: of the long days on Horus, of her growing despair of progress with Chan, of her loneliness; of her rage at Mondrian—and of her final use of his picture as an object for Chan to hate.

He listened carefully and sympathetically, and at the conclusion leaned back again on the pillows and shook his head.

"I can't prove you are wrong," he said. "But I'll wager on it. Look at a few proven facts. First, Chan must have bribed the waiter. What does that waiter say?"

"He wasn't a real waiter. After the bombing he disappeared."

"Well, maybe he wasn't a waiter but he certainly wasn't Chan Dalton. Did Chan know beforehand where we were to have dinner?"

"He says he didn't—he just followed us there."

"Very well. So how could he arrange for someone to deliver a bomb, on the spur of the moment? That bombing required careful preparation and planning. Where would Chan *find* a bomb? He is a recent arrival on Ceres, and he doesn't have contacts anywhere else. Remember, Chan may look like a twenty-year-old, and Kubo says that he's a super-fast learner. But in terms of adult contact with the world he's only a couple of months old. And that's the most conclusive point: Chan is a *newcomer* here. No matter how intelligent he is now, he couldn't obtain the materials and knowledge he would need in such a short time. If he doesn't remember what he was doing when the bombing happened, I'll accept that. But amnesia is not a crime, and I don't believe for a second that he had anything to do with the explosion." Mondrian sighed and touched his fingers gently to his forehead. "Bring him to me. Give me ten minutes to talk to him, and I guarantee that I'll prove he had nothing to do with the attempt to kill us. Prove it to *your* satisfaction, as well as mine. All right?"

Tatty looked stricken. "I can't bring him to you."

Her voice was dry and husky. "He's not here any more. Esro, do you know what I did? Chan trailed us to the restaurant, then he says he had a black-out and doesn't know what happened. I told him *he* had done the bombing—nearly killed us all. He was horrified, but he believed me. He didn't know what to do. So I helped him—helped him to *escape*."

"From Ceres? Nonsense. He couldn't possibly escape from here—for one thing, he'd need a travel permit."

"Esro, you don't understand. He already *has* a travel permit."

"Then who was insane enough to issue one to him? I'll have their carcass."

"*You* did it. Remember, you issued it in advance, so it would be ready when he went off for pursuit-team training? I asked Kubo Flammarion to give Chan all the rest of his preliminary tests as soon as possible. And Chan passed them, easily. So he could go on to the next phase, training with the aliens. He's not on Ceres now—he's on *Barchan*. In pursuit-team training."

Tatty's statement was almost correct. Chan was certainly in pursuit-team training; but he was not actually *on* Barchan. When Tatty spoke those words, he was flying four thousand meters above the planet's surface in a security aircar, receiving his final lesson on its operation and handling.

"Remember now," the pilot said cheerfully. "After you drop me off, you'll be on your own. No pick-ups, no deliveries, do your own laundry. Don't send us a message unless you've destroyed the Simmie Construct . . . or given up trying."

She laughed, as though her last suggestion was out of the question. The woman was small and tubby, with sleepy-looking brown eyes. When she was the pilot the car seemed to glide effortlessly through the buffeting winds of Barchan. Only when

Chan was given the chance to take the controls himself did he find that Barchan's air currents were strong and unpredictable. Level flight called for constant attention, and landing and take-off on the desert planet was always dangerous.

Chan dipped the car's nose and started to drop off altitude. At a thousand meters he began to circle, making his visual search for their landing target. The updrafts were stronger here, and it took all his efforts to maintain a constant altitude. "Has anyone ever done that?" he said. "Just given up trying to destroy the Simulacrum Construct, and asked to be taken back?"

"Not exactly the way you might be thinking." The pilot laughed easily, but her look missed nothing. Her hands were never more than an inch or two away from the duplicate set of controls. Chan was pleased that she had never actually touched them while he was flying.

"You'll be the fifth training group we've had in here," she went on. "And so far we've had *one* that graduated."

"What happened to the others?"

"Well, first group in was dead smooth. I dropped the four of 'em off at the training camp. One at a time—Human, Tinker, Angel, and Pipe-Rilla. All four of 'em found they could work well together. They organized a search for the Simmie, found it in three days, destroyed it. End of story. No problem. We linked them off to Dembricot for their final preparations; now they should be on Travancore, tackling the real thing."

"That was Leah Rainbow's team?" asked Chan eagerly. He had spotted the landing area, and was lining up for final approach.

"Sure was. Know her, do you? Smart woman, that. Anyway, the first one went so smooth we thought the whole thing would slide by like Angel sap. We were dead wrong. Second team came in, I dropped 'em off. Week later, the Pipe-Rilla called out, asked to be taken off the team. No explanation. That team's still waiting for another Pipe-Rilla to take the first one's place. Team Three—Your alignment's fine, but you'll land us smoother if you drop speed a couple of percent. That's right. Spot on. Hold it there. Where was I? Team Three. Right. It arrived, they got on well with each other, searched for their Simmie. Found it. But *it* got *them*."

"Killed them?"

"Hell, no." The pilot leaned back and closed her eyes all the way as soon as the car had touched down, light as a feather. "The Simmies won't actually *kill* a team—they're designed not to. But a Simmie will give you a bad time. This Simmie roughed 'em up so much, they'd had it with being a pursuit team. They split up. I picked 'em up from Barchan, and they all went home. So there we were, one out of three." She looked out of the window, and nodded approvingly. They had come to rest at the exact center of the landing circle. "I guess you'll do. Team Four, that was worst of all. They got organized, searched for the Simmie, found it, were all ready to blow it to hell. And then the Pipe-Rilla wouldn't go through with it. Even though it was only a Simmie Artefact. So *then* the human on the team—a big fat blond feller, looked like he'd not harm a fly—he got so mad with that Pipe-Rilla, he wanted to blow *her* full of holes. Might have done it, too, if the Tinker hadn't swarmed him. But it convinced all the Stellar Group—again—that us humans are crazy killers. And if you think *that* didn't cause an interstellar incident, and make life here hard . . ."

She shrugged, and opened the door of the car. A wave of dry heat like dragon's breath blew into the cabin. "That's all from me. The car's yours now—until you get your Simmie. Good luck."

Chan leaned out after her. "You've seen all the other teams. What do you think this one's chances are?"

The pilot paused with the door half-closed. "Well, if you believe it's a random process, past history says your odds are one in four. But maybe it's not so random. Let me ask *you* a question. I've looked at you pretty hard this past week. You don't fit this job. With your face and body, you're an entertainment natural—public, or one-on-one. There's five billion women would like a piece of you. So how come you land on a pursuit team, out here at the ass-end of the Universe?"

Chan hesitated. He wondered if Leah had told her about him, and if she was just prodding for more details. The waves of arid heat coming in through the open door produced floods of sweat on his face and neck that dried the moment they appeared, but the pilot seemed oblivious to the outside conditions. She waited, and her face gave him no clues. "I was born on Earth," he said at last. "A Commoner, with a contract. This just gave me a way out. And when it's over I'll be free to do what I like."

The pilot nodded sympathetically. "Ah. I've heard about Earth. Maybe after that, old Barchan don't seem to you like the ass-end of the Universe. I know Leah Rainbow seemed glad enough to be here. Did you get recruited the same way as she did?"

"Yes. We were both picked out by Commander Mondrian."

"Good enough. So I'll answer your question. I'll up your odds from one in four to fifty-fifty. Mondrian's as hard as tinker-shit and cold as Angelheart—but he's one sharp son of a bitch. And he don't pick losers." She swung the door shut and grinned at him through the window. *"Usually,"* she shouted. "But there's exceptions to everything. So good luck again."

She gave him a wave, and set off for the cluster of service buildings. Chan sat quietly in the car, inspecting the landscape around him. They were in Barchan's high polar regions, where winter temperatures would allow a human to survive without a suit except near noon. The vegetation was deep-rooted, with waxy blue-green foliage. At the pole itself it would grow in Barchan's half-gee surface gravity to fifty meters or more; here it sat low to the ground, tight-wrapped to conserve moisture. The soil beneath the plants was dry, dark and basaltic, rising in slow, brooding folds away from the landing area. Gusty surface winds lifted the top layer up and about the parked aircar in twisting dust-devils of dark grey. Near the equator that sand layer was hundreds of feet deep, and the winds blew it into the miles-long crescent-shaped *barchan* dunes that gave the planet its name. Eta Cassiopeiae's twin suns hung close to the horizon. They lit the scene with orange dust-filtered light. And this dour landscape, according to the briefings, was the most attractive part of the planet.

Chan wondered where the Simmie might be hiding. According to those same briefings, it could survive anywhere on Barchan—even in the scorching equatorial regions where only micro-organisms thrived.

The three service buildings stood about a kilometer away from the landed aircar. As Chan watched, he saw a swirling veil of dark purple emerge from one of the buildings. It blew like a rolling cloud of dust towards the car. When it was less than a hundred meters away, Chan opened the door again. The individual components of the cloud could now be resolved. They were purple-black winged creatures, each the size of a hummingbird. Within thirty seconds every one of them had entered the aircar door and settled all over the rear of the main cabin.

Chan closed the door and turned to watch. Although he had seen it on briefing displays, this was the first time he had ever watched the formation of a Tinker Composite.

It began with one component—an apparently arbitrary one—hovering in mid-air with its purple-black body vertical. The ring of pale green eyes at the head end looked all around, as though assessing the situation, while the wings fluttered too fast to see. After a moment another component flew in to attach at the head end, and a third one settled into position beneath. Thin, whiplike antennae reached out and made connection between them all. A fourth and fifth element flew over to the nucleus of the group.

After that the aggregation grew too fast for Chan to see any individual actions. As new components were added, the Composite extended outwards and downwards, to make contact with the cabin floor. In less than a minute the main body was complete. To Chan's surprise—this was something that had not been shown in his briefings—most of the individual components still remained unattached. Of the total who had entered the cabin, perhaps a fifth were now connected to form a single compact mass; the remainder stood tail-first on the cabin floor, or hung singly from the walls using the small claws on the front of their shiny leather-like wings.

The mass of the Tinker Composite had a funnel-like opening in its topmost extremity. From that aperture came an experimental hollow wheeze. "Ohhh-ahhh-gggghh. Hharr-ehh-looo," it said. Then, in an oddly accented variety of Solar: "Har-e-loo. Hal-loo."

Kubo Flammarion had warned Chan. "Imagine," he had said, "that somebody took *you* apart every night and put you back together every morning.

Don't you think it would take you a little while to get your act together? Well, make allowances for the Tinkers."

Chan found it hard to imagine. But he suspected that Kubo, a long-time alcoholic and a recent Paradox addict, knew the morning-after feeling quite well. "Hello," he said, in response to the Tinker's greeting; and he waited.

"We-ee arre-eh"—there was a substantial pause— "We are *Shikari*."

"Hello, Shikari," said Chan. "Call me *Chan*."

The Tinker paused again for a long moment. "Shikari is an old Earth word," it said at last, "for a Hunter. We think it would be appropriate. And perhaps also amusing?"

"I am sorry. I did not know that."

There was another pause. "Ahhh. We also suggested to us that we might be called Shakespeare— that 'myriad-minded man', which we also thought amusing—but we are not sure that you would be comfortable with it." The funnel buzzed briefly. "We are making a joke," it explained.

Chan wondered if the Tinker could see him—the individual components had many thousands of eyes, but could they be used by the Composite? He waved his arm at the thousands of components scattered around the cabin, still unattached to the main body. "Are *all* of you Shikari? Or only the ones of you who are now connected?"

There was again a brief pause. "We are not sure we can answer your question. We all in future time *will* be Shikari; and we all in now-time *can* be Shikari. But in now-time we *are* not *all* Shikari."

"Why not? Don't you think better when you are all connected?"

The Tinker had taken on a roughly human outline, with arms, legs, and head. But when it moved forward in the cabin it did so as a whole, through the movement of thousands of component wings.

"Chan, you ask many questions in one," said the breathy voice from the funnel. "Listen carefully. If we wish, we can all join together at one time."

"Then why not do it? Wouldn't you have more brainpower if you did that?"

"Yes—and no. If we do that, then we have more thinking material—which you may call *brainpower*. But we are also less efficient. We are *slower*. We have a much longer . . . integration time—the time it takes for us to think, and to reach a decision. That time grows . . . exponentially . . . with the number of components. When there is much, much time available, we can consider more units in us. More can join to make one body. But then the integration time becomes long . . . so long that individual components begin to starve. We must leave, to find food—or die. What you see now is the most effective form; our preferred compromise . . . between *speed* of thought and *depth* of thought. The free components that you see here will eat, rest, and mate. When the right time comes there will be exchange: rested-of-us will take the place of tired-of-us."

"But . . ." began Chan. Then he realized that they were already late for take-off. He had scores more questions—how did a Composite decide when and how to form? Was it adopting a roughly human shape mainly for his convenience? How intelligent were the individual components? (He had a feeling that question had been answered in his early days on Horus, but it had happened before the Tolkov Stimulator had worked its miracle). How did a component know when it was *needed* by the Tinker Composite? Most important of all, if a Tinker was varying its composition all the time, how could there be a single self-awareness, and a specific *personality*? Shikari certainly seemed to have not only a personality, but a sense of humor.

Chan made a great effort and concentrated again

on the car's controls. All his questions must wait until they were heading for their rendezvous with the other team members. And if what he had heard of the Pipe-Rillas and Angels were in any way correct, when *that* meeting came he would have even more questions!

He prepared to take off, then turned back to the Tinker. "Shikari, we're ready to go. If you want to take a look at the landscape, maybe you ought to come and sit—*do* you sit?—in the seat next to me. And we can start to know each other better."

"Yes," said the Tinker. "That will be very good. We have innumerable questions that we wish to ask you about you—as soon as there is opportunity."

# Chapter Sixteen

# SKRYNOL AND MONDRIAN

Mondrian awoke in a fetid, red-lit gloom, to the sound of a low and ominous humming. He gasped, tensed for a moment as a tall figure loomed high overhead, then slowly relaxed.

He knew where he was. He had been dreaming again—ghastly, terrifying, dreams, but only to be expected; the figure hovering over him was Skrynol. The nightmare visions had been carefully designed, under strict Fr'opper control. And even the noise now had an explanation: Skrynol was *singing*.

The Pipe-Rilla bent over Mondrian's sweat-coated body, peered at him with huge compound eyes, and hummed a three-toned phrase. The lights in the chamber increased.

"For your benefit," said Skrynol. She chittered strangely. "So that you can admire my beauty."

Mondrian took a handkerchief from his trouser pocket and wiped sweat from his forehead and bare chest. He had stripped to the waist at the beginning of the session. Skrynol was not fully comfortable at a temperature below human blood heat, and in the last few meetings the chamber had been hotter and hotter.

"You are in an exuberant mood," Mondrian said. "May I assume that we have made progress?"

"That is indeed true." The Pipe-Rilla bobbed her head back and forward in the gesture of assent she had learned from Mondrian. "Excellent progress. Oh, yes, excellent-excellent progress."

"Enough to sing about?"

"Ahhh." Skrynol raised her forelimbs and placed them on top of her head. "Yes. A word on my singing. Because we were doing so well, I extended the length of our session somewhat, to pinpoint a result. And as a result I took more of your blood than usual."

"How much more?"

"Some more. Rather a lot more. But I gave you replacement fluids. Mm-mm . . ." She bent over him, like an enormous and deformed praying mantis inspecting its victim. There was a flutter of olfactory cilia, and a whistling sigh. "Mm-mm. Esro Mondrian, it is fortunate that we Pipe-Rillas can so well control our emotions and our actions. I had been told before I came to Earth that human blood was a powerful stimulant and intoxicant to our metabolism—but no one could ever describe this feeling of *exhilaration*."

She reached down with one soft flipper, and drew it lovingly along Mondrian's neck and naked chest. As she did so, long flexible needles peeped involuntarily out of their sheaths on each side of her third tarsal segment. They glistened orange in the dim light. Fully extended, they would reach their hollow length more than nine feet in any direction. The official propaganda on the Pipe-Rillas described the aliens as "peaceable sap-sucking beings, unable to eat solid food despite their formidable mandibles."

Esro Mondrian gazed uneasily at the needles. *Sap-sucking*? Perhaps—but only if the word could apply to the body juices of plants *and* animals.

The urge to flinch away from her touch was strong. He resisted it, and sat upright on the velvet couch. "I know how you must feel. Some humans also experience exhilaration from blood. I draw my own excitement from other sources. Can we discuss the session now? Do you feel controlled enough to tell me what you have found?"

"Of course." Skrynol swayed back, rearing her jointed body upwards another six feet. "We do not yet have a solution for your difficulties. But I think I can fairly say that at last we have defined the *problem*. I will begin with a question. You are Chief of Boundary Survey Security. How did you come to that position?"

"Through the usual route." Mondrian was puzzled. "After I first left Earth I studied the other civilizations in the Stellar Group, and then took a job in commercial liaison with them. After that, it was a simple matter of hard work and steady promotion."

"That is the way it may appear to you. But your physical response when certain subjects are mentioned makes one fact obvious: the rise to your present position was less circumstantial than you believe. You were *driven* to seek it. As I told you in our first meeting, your nightmares are no more than analogies. But for what?"

Skrynol turned to a screen that sat behind her, and drew a circle in the middle with her left forelimb. She placed a small dot in the center, and drew a set of radii to connect it with the circumference. "It is time for a little lecture from me. This is you"—she tapped the central dot—"in the middle of a safe region. Like most members of your species, you are dominated by self-concern, and you see yourself as the center of the universe." She pointed to the radiating spokes. "You also dream of a web. And indeed, you sit in the middle of such a web—a web of information, provided to you through the Mattin Link. In your dreams there is a dark region beyond the web. And sure enough, in your working world there is also a dark region. It is this: *everything that lies beyond the Perimeter*. And it is terrifying to you. Maybe you can control everything within the Known Sphere—but how can you possibly control what is *outside* it? How can you even *know* what is there?" Skrynol tapped the screen. "In your dreams, the safe, lighted region is *shrinking*; the dark and dangerous zone always comes closer. In the real world, the Perimeter *grows*—and because of the Mattin Link, new parts of space are steadily made accessible to you. *And you to them.* You do not know what may lie beyond today's Perimeter—but you are terribly afraid of it. The safe region seems to be shrinking, but that is only because the unsafe region steadily becomes more accessible. New space is being added all the time. So. How can you minimize the danger? Simple. You look for *control*. You seek the position which permits you to have the maximum possible knowledge and control of the Perimeter: the position as Chief of Boundary Survey Security. You cannot banish the dangers—they are caused by the Solar Group's expansionist policy, and that is beyond your control. But at least you will learn of any danger as early as possible, and be in a position to combat it. You were *driven* to become Chief of Boundary Security. And you will do anything to protect the Perimeter—anything at all."

The Pipe-Rilla leaned forward until her broad, heart-shaped face was only a foot from Mondrian's. "Your nightmare is *real*, Esro Mondrian. You are afraid of the rest of the Universe—everything that lies beyond the Perimeter." She gazed into his eyes, with a dark, unblinking stare. "Do you accept my analysis?"

Mondrian gave an imperceptible nod. "I accept it," he said softly. "But I do not know where it leads. Are you telling me that the nightmares must continue as long as I hold my present position?"

"Still you do not understand. I repeat, you sought that position in an attempt to control the situation—to banish your nightmares. Your dreams are not the *result* of your position. They stem from a much deeper cause."

"But what is it?"

Skrynol shook her head. "I do not know. Not yet. I know only that it is deep-buried, far back in your childhood past. And still I cannot reach it. I need help. That is why you must do something more."

"Name it." Mondrian's face looked pale, lined and weary.

"Stay here. Travel the earth. This planet was the scene of your earliest and most hidden experiences. You may not recognize the original source of your fears, even when you encounter it; but *I* will know it, through your unconscious responses. And *then*, perhaps, we can at last help you."

"I am too busy to spend more time here on Earth."

"Until you do so, your problem will not be solved." Skrynol again swayed away from Mondrian, upward and backwards. "For today, that must be the end of this session. I can read your weariness and your distress. Put on your shirt, and I will lead you back."

Mondrian sighed, and picked up his jacket from the couch. In spite of the fatigue, his jaw was set "Not yet. We have one other item of business."

"You are exhausted. For your own sake, make it a brief one."

"I cannot promise that." Mondrian reached into his jacket pocket, and took out a black wafer the size of his thumbnail. "This is a summary of human expansion plans. It gives only a broad outline. Before you receive more, I must hear through official channels that full control of the Travancore operation will belong to the Anabasis—without interference from our Stellar ambassador, or from anyone else. I want it agreed that the Anabasis will be allowed to quarantine that planet."

Skrynol reached out and took the wafer delicately from his hand. She bobbed her head from side to side, examining the small black square. "I am doing all that I can."

"Why is it taking so long?"

There was again the chittering that Mondrian had come to recognize as the Pipe-Rilla's laughter. "Mondrian, do not make the common error of your species. Like Humans, Pipe-Rillas are all *individuals*, with their own preferences and agendas. There is as much variety of thought and desire among us as there is among your people. I must seek a consensus. And my species does not trust yours. But this"—she waved the black wafer—"will make my task easier. Do not worry. The Anabasis will have control of Travancore."

"Don't look for detail in those plans. What you have there is no more than an outline—the rest should be available in ten days or so."

"This is enough for the moment." The Fr'opper placed the wafer carefully in a body pouch. "Even if the plans you have given me are wrong in some details—in *every* detail—they are important. Someone of your species went through the mental process that creates such plans. We want to understand the mental process, the broad concepts, as much as we want the plans themselves. To my species, it is inconceivable that such ideas could ever be *imagined*, still less that the actions they describe might be carried out. But we have read of human history. When it comes to war and fighting, the human species may not—I give you the benefit of the doubt—be *wholly* aggressive. But you are certainly aggressive. And you have a saying, that where all are blind a creature with a single eye will prevail. In matters of conquest and destruction, my species is blind—and so are the Tinkers and the Angels."

"It sounds as though the rest of the Stellar Group all think of humans in the same way."

"I am afraid we do. Why else would I be here on Earth, alone? In the case of the Tinkers, their feelings are partly because of your appearance. The human form resembles a small carnivore on their home world of Mercantor. It is not dangerous to them, but it is mindless, ferocious, and annoying. Such associations are irrelevant in a creature of perfect intellect, but to most of us—I would say all of us, but I am not sure about the Angels—those factors carry large weight. Small points can be very important. For example, I am told that to a human a Pipe-Rilla's natural voice always sounds cheerful—even when it lacks the surgical modification that I underwent to ease the production of human speech."

"That is true. You all sound happy."

Skrynol bowed her head, and again placed her forelimbs high on top of it. "And this gesture, which for us indicates shame and suffering, looks amusing to you. I know. So to humans our worries and sorrows must always sound and look comical."

Mondrian hesitated. "They do," he said. "But I do not think of you as comical."

"I am relieved to hear it—and will be more relieved if you will tell me how Humans *do* think of us."

"As you have pointed out, neither Humans nor Pipe-Rillas all share the same opinions. But the popular view of Pipe-Rillas is that you are conscientious, self-deprecating—and a little dull. In human terms, you also lack initiative."

"For the warfare that you find so popular?"

"For more than that. There is an old story that

illustrates the general human view of the other species of the Stellar Group."

"A true story?"

"I am sure it is not true. But it shows the human perspective. According to the story, a ship carrying a Human, a Pipe-Rilla, a Tinker, and an Angel made an emergency landing on Dembricot. They did not have time to send out a distress signal, and no one had reason to search for them. The four of them sat down and reviewed the situation. Their food supplies were low. Their communication equipment was damaged beyond repair. They could perhaps expect a rescue eventually, but not for years. So what should they do?

"The Human asked for suggestions. The Pipe-Rilla said that she was sorry about the situation, but a mere Pipe-Rilla would not be able to solve the problem where another species had already failed. She left the group and went off into the wilderness alone. The Human asked the Tinker for ideas. The Tinker said there was no problem. Dembricot had abundant winged insect life. All one had to do was resolve into individual components, fly off, and catch as much as one wanted. The Human turned to the Angel. The Angel agreed with the Tinker, there was no problem. The soil of Dembricot was very fertile; all one had to do was put down a root system."

"And the Human suggestion?"

"The Human made no suggestion. After hearing the others, the Human repaired the ship. What you others see as aggression, we see as human initiative."

"You have a poor opinion of your fellow-members of the Stellar Group."

"Not as bad as the story would suggest. Stories like that always exaggerate to make their points. Humans like Tinkers. They enjoy their sense of humor, though they find them—if you will pardon a human joke—'flighty' and 'scatter-brained.' Angels are accurate, precise, and almost totally incomprehensible. And Pipe-Rillas look terrifying, take their responsibilities seriously, and all worry too much."

Skrynol had settled far back on her hind limbs, and was rocking gently from side to side. "It is good to have these perspectives. Did you know that we have a very similar story of shipwreck, with the same actions for the Tinker and the Angel? But in our version the Human wants to hunt, kill, and eat the native animals—and it is the Pipe-Rilla who repairs the ship and makes escape possible."

Mondrian stood up and buttoned his jacket. "Would you like to guess what story the Tinkers and Angels tell? But we've talked too long. I must go now."

Skrynol nodded, and moved in front of Mondrian. The Pipe-Rilla insisted on changing the meeting-place every time, escorting Mondrian to and from it through a maze of tunnels.

"Some day we ought to discuss just what we mean by *intelligence*," she said thoughtfully, as they went forward into total darkness. "I suspect that we might find surprises there. I think we will agree that, whatever our differences, Humans, Tinkers, Angels, and Pipe-Rillas are all intelligent—perhaps of comparable intelligence. But does this mean that we are all somehow much the same? It does not, for this important reason: *We did not follow the same road to intelligence.* Humans evolved from a rather small and weak animal, on a planet with powerful predators. You had to be clever, inventive, *and aggressive*, or you would have died out. That is why you made tools, why you changed the face of Earth, why you went to space. But compare that with the rest of the Group, who never thought of leaving their home worlds until you Humans arrived. We Pipe-Rillas are twice the size of any other life form on our planet. We are strong. We have no natural competition for living space or food. We did not need intelligence to fight enemies. But a few million years ago our planet S'kat'lan went through major changes in climate. Our intelligence developed in response to that need—and only through drastic changes in our life-style and habitat were we able to survive. But the forces we faced were all *impersonal* ones, of winds and weather. We learned early to control our population. We never fought each other, nor were we ever threatened by another species on the planet."

Skrynol extended a tough, whiskery palp behind her for Mondrian to hold on to, and headed up a forty-five-degree sloping ramp. "As for the Tinkers," she continued, "at the level of *individual components* they know aggression, and they will fight over food, space, and mates. But a Tinker Composite has no such needs—it does not eat, drink, or mate. It is in some sense immortal, and in another sense it has no permanent existence at all. It has no sense of danger at the Composite level, because at the first threat it can simply disperse. Resolved to separate elements, the Composite no longer exists. Mercantor is a cold world, and to a Tinker 'intelligence' means 'closeness and warmth.' And as for the Angels, their form of intelligence remains as much a mystery to us as it apparently does to you. The Chassel-rose will live, die, and yearn for light and fertile soil. But the Singers live a long, long time, and no one knows how they come to be intelligent, or what purpose their intelligence may serve. Perhaps in another few hundred years . . ."

While Skrynol had been rambling on in the darkness, Mondrian had listened with only half an ear. He had a new problem to worry about. The Pipe-

Rilla wanted him to roam Earth, looking for his early childhood. Where was he supposed to begin the search? In the Gallimaufries, up in the polar resorts, on the open ocean, out in the great equatorial nature preserves?—the experience Skrynol was seeking could be anywhere. He had vague childhood memories of all of those areas. But how could he spare time for any of that, when the pursuit team operation on Travancore was ready to begin?

Before Mondrian reached a lighted part of the deep basement warren, he had also arrived at a conclusion: the Anabasis had first priority. No matter how bad the nightmares, he would live with them for a while longer.

As for exploring Earth, he could make a fairly detailed list of the places that he wanted to see. And *then* what he needed was someone to go there— someone who would make full sound and vision recordings and bring them back for his review. They might provide the mental key that would unlock his memory.

Mondrian thought hard. He had to have a lot of help. By the time that he reached Tatty's apartment he knew exactly what he must say and do.

# Chapter Seventeen

# DEATH AND ADESTIS

The room had been set up as a briefing facility and battle station, complete with conference table, projection equipment, terminals and interactive map displays. The Adestis battlefield was at the rear, overlooked by a spectators' gallery. Twenty-five men and women sat at the desks serried across the body of the room. In front of them, dressed in a close-fitting black uniform that closely resembled the formal attire of a Security Force commander, stood Dougal Macdougal. His expression was totally serious as he presented a sequence of graphics. Luther Brachis had never seen the ambassador so deeply involved with anything.

"This is the enemy," Macdougal said. "In case any of you are inclined to underestimate it, let me remind you that there has never so far been a successful attack on this type of stronghold using an attack force with fewer than forty members; and even in those cases, there was substantial loss of simulacra and several human deaths."

The three-dimensional image system showed a dark, walled pit, descending to unknown depths in fibrous black soil. Above the whole system, in large glowing letters, stood a sign: ADESTIS—YOU ARE HERE.

Luther Brachis was sitting in the audience, about halfway back. He had had his private word with Dougal Macdougal, hinting at the Pipe-Rilla concern over human expansion plans. And now he was stuck. He could not easily leave without going through with the whole Adestis exercise. He was watching Ambassador MacDougal closely, irritated and skeptical. A morning of Adestis was not his idea of time well spent, but Lotos Sheldrake had been very explicit: "If you want the chance for an informal word in the ambassador's ear sometime in the next week and a half, this isn't just your best chance of it—it's your *only* chance. He'll be part of the time on Titan, with a new industrial plant, and the rest of the time he'll be away in the Procyon colony. It's Adestis, and it's tomorrow, or it's nothing. Take it or leave it."

Luther Brachis had taken it—grudgingly. When the briefing began, he had been cynically amused to see that Macdougal conducted affairs with complete seriousness, just as though it were some major military operation. After a few minutes Dougal Macdougal gave them their first look at their adversary for the day. And that was when Brachis lost his bored look and became the most attentive member of the audience.

"Remember the scale here," said Macdougal. He moved the light pointer from one side of the display to the other. "This distance is roughly three and a half centimeters. Your simulacrum will be half a centimeter in height. As you see, the quarry is a little more than one and a half centimeters across the body, and the extended legs are maybe twice that. This is a full-grown specimen of the family *Ctenizidae*; sub-order *Mygalomorphae*, order *Araneae*, class *Arachnida*—in short, a trapdoor spider. A female. One of Earth's most deadly creatures. She won't be afraid of you, but you'd better be scared of her. Let me show you some of the danger points."

The screen displayed a dark brown form crouched ominously at the bottom of the smooth-sided pit. The length of the body was divided into two main sections, connected by a narrow bridge. Eight bristly legs grew from the front body section, and near the mouth were another two pairs of shorter appendages. Eight pearly eyes were distributed along the dark back of the upper body.

Dougal Macdougal shone his pointer at the head section. "This is the place to hit her, in the cephalothorax. Most of the nervous system is here, so that's the best place to shoot. It's also the most *dangerous* place, because her jaws and poison glands are here, too. Don't forget that your simulacrum will be completely disabled if there is an injection of poison, even a small one. So watch out for those fangs, and stay well clear of them." He moved the pointer further to the rear. "This is the pedicel, where the cephalothorax joins the abdomen. If you can get an accurate hit here, do it. The body is very narrow at this point, and you may be able to blow the two pieces apart. But you'll have to be very accurate—and the exoskeleton is tough as hell there. What else? Well, you can see for yourself what the legs are like. Four pairs, each one seven-jointed. A hit where a leg attaches to the cephalothorax might do some damage; otherwise, forget them. The breathing spiracles and lung slits are all on the abdomen, on the second and third segments. Two pairs of lungs, but you may as well ignore them—even if you get a hit there the spider can still breathe for a while through its tracheal tubes. The heart is in the abdomen, here. See the four spinnerets, on the fourth and fifth segments of the abdomen? Keep your eye on those, too. You'll never break free of the silk if once you've been wrapped in it—and it dries instantly, as soon as it's in contact with air. The spider can *squirt* the silk at you, so you're not safe unless you stay at least your body length away from her."

Macdougal turned to look at the audience. "That's all I plan to say about the spider. Any questions before we put on the headsets and go down there to look at the trap? Better ask them now; we won't have time for it once we've started."

"I've got one." A skinny man two seats in front of Brachis nodded at the screen. "Those eyes look as though they ought to be vulnerable. Should we be shooting at them?"

"Good question." Macdougal shone the pointer on one of the eyes. "See their locations? They're all on the carapace—that's like a thick shield, protecting the top of the cephalothorax. And that raises another point: the carapace is *tough*. Don't try to penetrate it; save your shots for the underside or the maw and joints. The eyes are a weak point, but it won't be easy to get a good shot at more than one eye at a time. They all tend to have different fields of view—apparently spiders don't have binocular vision. So I don't particularly recommend eyes as a target. This type of spider doesn't rely much on eyesight—it goes largely by *touch*. Don't assume it doesn't know where you are, simply because the eyes aren't looking at you. The legs are terrifically sensitive to vibration patterns. If you get in trouble, but you've not actually been seized, lie perfectly still. The spider usually ignores anything that doesn't move. Anything else?"

A woman sitting near the front stood up abruptly. "Yes. Count me out, Dougal. I'm leaving. I won't fight that thing."

"The Adestis group won't refund your payment."

"Least of my worries." The woman turned to stare at the others. "You're all crazy. That's nothing but a god-damned *bug* in there. Anyone in their right mind would be content to swat it."

She left rapidly. Dougal Macdougal watched her leave, a fixed smile on his face. "Lost her nerve," he said, as soon as the door had closed. "Anyone else? Or any more questions? If not, let's get on with it."

The audience looked around uneasily. There was a slow shaking of heads, but one man rose and followed the woman from the room. He would not meet anyone's eye as he went. Finally, at a signal from Macdougal, those remaining picked up their Monitor sets and placed the light structures over their heads.

Luther Brachis waited for correlator field transients to settle and the disturbing moments of double sensation to fade. The briefings had told him what was happening. Telemetry couplers in the headset translated sensory inputs from the tiny simulacrum to direct electrical current feeds in his brain. At the same time, his brain's intention signals—the ones that normally stimulated activity in his body's motor control system—were intercepted and translated into cyber-signals in the body of an Adestis simulacrum. As Macdougal had explained it, "Your *brain* can't see—it's blind. And it can't hear, smell, taste or touch, either. All it gets from your senses are streams of electrical inputs, and it *interprets* them as sensations. Now those electrical inputs will be coming from your simulacrum."

The sensory hold tightened. Brachis grunted in surprise. He had expected the simulations to be plausible—the makers of Adestis admitted they had *imitators*, but denied that they had *competition*. Still he was staggered by the uncanny quality of the sensory inputs. They were like life itself. He had lost all sense of his own body. The simulacrum *was* his body.

He looked down, and saw his own legs, standing on a damp, pebble-strewn plain. Tiny wormlike animals wriggled away from him as he moved his feet. Fifty paces away a gigantic fly skimmed past on iridescent wings. Brachis stared all around him. Two dozen people stood in a rough circle, all experimentally raising arms, moving feet, or watching each other. The only exception was Dougal Macdougal, recognizable by his ease of movement and confident manner.

"As soon as you're ready," he said. "Get the feel of the environment, get to know who you all are—your suits here are color-coded just the way you were told before we began, so you ought to recognize each other. Then practice the feel of your weapon. And we'll get on with it. Look over there." He pointed away to the left, through air that seemed dusty, thick, and smoke-filled. "It's hard to spot, but there's the trap. The spider will be sitting at the bottom of the pit. She already knows that we are here—she will be feeling the vibrations through the ground. So walk lightly. Remember now, you're only half a centimeter tall, and you only weigh about one five-hundredth of a gram. At this size, gravity isn't too important—we can all tolerate a fall of many times our height, with no injury. But we're attacking something with a body twice our height, legs six times as long as we are, and a mass that outweighs the lot of us, easily. Don't get *over*-confident."

There was a gasp from a green simulacrum next to Brachis. "Is he joking?"

Brachis shook his head experimentally. It felt perfectly natural, as though it were his own head. "He's not joking. He's just giving what he thinks is good advice. Maybe he's right—some people may come here with the idea that the trapdoor spider is just another bug."

"Not me." Green tried a shake of his head, too. "If that's just a bug, the Hyperion Vault is just a hole in the ground. I'm telling you, if I didn't work in his office, and if he hadn't put pressure on me to come along on this . . ."

The party was slowly becoming more organized. Four of them had taken part in Adestis on other occasions, and they naturally assumed the lead. Everyone was permitted two practice shots from the projectile weapons, aiming them at head-high moss growths fifty paces off to their left. Brachis unconsciously noted that even with recoil compensation the gun he was holding delivered quite a jolt to his arm. That was a good sign. He had been wondering if the organizers of Adestis were expecting them to knock off the spider with weapons like peashooters. His gun pulled a little to the left. He took careful aim and put his second shot exactly through the fluffy pink ball of a head of moss-flower.

Halfway to the trap door the group halted again. Macdougal, who had been walking a pace or two ahead, turned to them. "Last word. After this, each of you is on your own. *Don't go down into the trap.* Not even if you think the spider is dead. This species has been known to sham dead, and the floor of that trap is her home territory. Let her come to you—and don't be afraid to run for it if things get too hot for you. The rest of us will try to draw her away from anyone who seems to be in real trouble. And another thing: *Don't shoot at the carapace.* You won't penetrate it, the ricochet could go anywhere, and you'll be a damned sight more dangerous to us than you will to her."

His final words were interrupted by a shout from the black-clad simulacrum who had been detailed to keep a close watch on the trap. The thick hinged lid was swinging open. The great body of the spider heaved itself rapidly out onto the open ground. It had apparently listened to the ground vibrations, sized up the adversary, and decided to go on the offensive.

"Scatter!" shouted Macdougal. His advice was unnecessary. The simulacra were already spilling panic-stricken in all directions.

Luther Brachis took a quick look around him. He had already noted that their approach to the trapdoor spider's lair had paid too little attention to good ground cover. The only place to hide was twenty paces off to the right, where a stand of grey-green moss grew hip high. He ran that way, dived for cover, and rolled up to a kneeling position with his weapon at the ready.

The difference between the spider's image in the briefing room and the arachnid herself was terrifying. The beast towered three times as high as his head, a gigantic armored tank that could move, turn, and attack with unbelievable speed. Against that mass, the weapon in his hands seemed useless. He could pump a hundred projectiles into that vast, glistening side, and they would have no effect at all.

The spider turned. He had a perfect side view of its broad abdomen and splayed legs as the cephalothorax swooped down on a magenta simulacrum and jerked it aloft. The simulacrum was helpless in the grip of the *chelicerae*, the pointed crushing appendages at the front of the spider's maw. A projectile weapon dropped uselessly to the ground.

Two others had run for temporary shelter directly beneath the spider's great body. Now they were firing upwards, pumping shots into the soft areas of the genitals and the exposed ovipositor. The spider jerked and shuddered as the projectiles penetrated its body, and the two attackers cheered at each spasm and shouted encouragement to each other. They moved to take more shots at point-blank range. But they had forgotten Dougal Macdougal's warning. A spout of gossamer suddenly jetted from the spinnerets, enveloping both simulacra at once in an unbreakable net of fast-drying silk.

Then the spider took a rapid shuffle backwards, ducked its cephalothorax low to the ground, and hoisted both attackers to grind them in its maw.

Brachis scanned the spider rapidly from chelicerae to ovipositor. From where he was kneeling he had a choice of three targets. He could aim at a leg, or at the pedicel that connected the abdomen and cephalothorax, or at one of the chelicerae. The legs were the easiest target. They were also the least effective. The pedicel was a vital area, but it looked heavily armored, and it would take an exceptionally lucky shot to do any good. Brachis made up his mind. He sighted briefly on the left chelicera. The weapon bucked in his grip and the organ, severed near its base, dropped to the ground in front of the spider.

Brachis moved to sight on the second chelicera, but there was no time for a shot. The spider had swivelled rapidly to face its new attacker and was now scuttling toward him across the pebbled ground. The maw was open, gaping wide enough to swallow him whole. Brachis recalled Macdougal's dry comment, that no spider ate solid food—they pre-digested their victims by injecting enzymes, then sucked them dry. But there was little comfort in that. The fangs looming up on him were more than strong enough to crush him flat.

He dropped behind the low stand of moss and huddled motionless to the ground. There was a buzzing and a hissing overhead, and a monstrous shape blocked out the light above him. Brachis turned his head to look upwards. The vast abdomen was directly over him. He could see every detail—a dozen projectile wounds leaking blood and body fluids, the oozing nozzles of four spinnerets, and colonies of tiny mite and tick parasites clinging to the coarse body bristles. Then the spider charged on. The air was filled with a sickly-sweet stench of decay.

He rolled over, sat up, and looked around. With one part of his mind he wondered how the makers of the Adestis simulacra were able to capture and transmit olfactory stimuli. But that question could wait for another occasion.

Brachis took a quick look to his immediate right and left. There had been two others diving for cover at the same moment, and the spider must have passed right over them, too. He saw that they were both still lying motionless. Still playing dead? If so, they were taking Macdougal's advice a bit too seriously.

He leaned over and tapped one of them on the shoulder. "Come on. Let's get on with it, or we'll be here all day."

There was no reply. The figure remained totally immobile. Brachis leaned closer, looking for the small green light between the shoulders that showed the simulacrum was occupied and in working order. The light was still on. He looked at the other motionless figure; *that* light was on, too.

Brachis squatted back on his heels, oblivious to the frantic battle still surging all around. The whole thing was crazy. He was *sure* that the spider had missed all three of them. He had actually seen a blurred image of the huge legs scrambling by, a good three paces away from all of them. So why were the other two still lying here, just as though they had somehow been put out of action . . . ?

He gave a startled growl of comprehension. With his weapon set to automatic he fired a blind volley of shots at the spider's belly, and at the same moment bit down hard on his rear molar control.

There was a dizzying moment of disorientation; then he again felt the Monitor headset covering his face.

THAT IS THE END OF ADESTIS FOR YOU, said a metallic voice in his ear. REMAIN SEATED IF YOU WISH, BUT—

With one movement Brachis ripped the Monitor set off his head and looked around him.

He was still sitting in the same place in the Adestis battle chamber. Of the two dozen people who had embarked on the exercise, a half were now lolling in their seats, headsets off. Their simulacra had already been killed by the spider, and now they were experiencing the vicarious agony of their own deaths. Another dozen still wore the Monitor headsets—and three of those slumped forward in their restraining harnesses, their clothes drenched with blood. Brachis saw that their throats had been cut so deeply that the heads were almost severed.

He slapped at his harness release. Before he could rise to his feet, a tall figure was looming over him. It looked familiar. At the same time as his mind rejected recognition of that tall, cadaverous figure, a skinny arm was swinging in towards his unprotected neck. A bright ceremonial sword whistled through the air.

Brachis jerked his right arm upwards. There was a clean, meaty crunch. His hand, severed below the base of the thumb, flew out and fell on the floor in front of him.

His combat uniform reacted before he had time to feel shock or pain. The shirt sensors recorded the sudden drop in blood pressure and activated a web of fibers in the right sleeve. The knit material on the right forearm at once tightened to form a tourniquet.

The sword was swinging again at his neck and head. Brachis swayed forward, in under the swing, and reached out and around with his left arm. He grasped the back of the narrow neck. The thin body was against his face. He closed his eyes, made a total, reflexive effort, and felt vertebrae snap under his twisting fingers. The dropped sword passed over his back and touched him lightly on the legs. Still entwined, Brachis and his assailant tumbled together to the hard floor of the chamber. Brachis landed underneath, grunting at the impact.

He opened his eyes. His first, incredulous impression had been correct. He was staring into the lifeless features of the Margrave of Fujitsu.

Even though Luther Brachis had done his best to persuade her, Godiva Lomberd refused to sit in the room where the Adestis attack would take place. She had listened to him quietly, smiled, and shaken her gorgeous blond head. "Luther, Nature designed some people for one thing, and some for others. Your life is Security—weapons, sabotage, skirmishes and violence. Mine has been Art—music, and dancing, and poetry. I'm not saying my life has been better than yours. But I am saying that I won't come and watch while you and Dougal Macdougal try to kill a poor harmless animal that is only doing what *its* nature programmed it to do." She placed the tips of her fingers gently on his lips. "No argument, Luther. I'm not coming—not even to the spectators' gallery."

Eventually she had relented far enough to accompany Luther Brachis to the Adestis facility. She allowed him to settle her in the neighboring lounge and order refreshments for her; and she seemed delighted to see Esro Mondrian when he arrived at the lounge a few minutes later.

"What are you doing here, Esro? I thought you didn't like Adestis."

"I don't." He nodded his head. He had with him a tiny, dark-haired woman, who was staring curiously at Godiva. "Adestis isn't for me. We came here because we heard Luther is here, and we have to see him."

"You can't do it now—he'll be right in the middle of it."

"That's all right. We'll wait." He turned to the woman with him. "Lotos, this is Godiva Lomberd. Godiva, Lotos Sheldrake. If you two don't mind, I'm going to leave you here for a few minutes. If Luther comes out, don't let him get away. Make him wait until I get back."

"Where's Tatty?"

"Still down on Earth." Mondrian hesitated for a moment. "She's . . . helping me. I needed images and recordings of some places. I guess she'll be back in a week or two."

Godiva looked faintly puzzled, but said nothing as Mondrian left and Lotos settled down to sit opposite her. They stared at each other in silence for a few seconds.

"You know Adestis?" said Lotos Sheldrake at last.

The other woman smiled and shook her head slowly. "Not really. Just enough to convince me I don't want anything to do with it. How about you?"

"Once—and never again." Lotos related the details of her own experience at the termite nest. She underplayed the danger, but emphasized her own terror and discomfort. She did her best to sound humorous and self-deprecating, and tried to create a good rapport with Godiva. While she spoke, she continued her own assessment. Since hearing of the contract with Luther Brachis, Lotos had put her own information services to work. The results were unsatisfying. Godiva Lomberd had first come to attention on Earth a few years ago, as a stage performer and courtesan—"The Godiva Bird: Model, Consort, and Exotic Dancer." All the digging that Lotos had been able to do since then had provided a simple picture: Godiva was a woman whom men found irresistible, and she had exploited that fact for money.

Looking at her now, it was easy to see why she had been so successful. She moved like a dancer, with every gesture natural, easy and flowing. She had the clear eyes and skin of perfect health; she laughed easily; and she listened to Lotos with total attention, as though what she was hearing was the most interesting thing in the world.

Still, Lotos was very uneasy. According to reports, Godiva had never formed more than a temporary and strictly business relationship with any man ... and now she had formed a *permanent* contract with Luther Brachis.

True love? Lotos Sheldrake didn't consider that for more than a second. She had a deep intuition, and it was consistent with what Esro Mondrian had reported. There was something strange going on between Godiva Lomberd and Luther Brachis. Lotos lacked Mondrian's previous acquaintance with Godiva, but she thoroughly trusted his instincts. "She's changed," he had said, as they whipped through the Ceres transportation system on their way to the Adestis Headquarters. "She wasn't like that when she was on Earth."

"Changed *how*?"

Mondrian looked angry—but only with himself. Lotos knew how much he prided himself on his accurate reading of others' motivations and secret desires. "She's ... *focused*," he said at last. "You would have to know the old Godiva to see what I mean. It used to be that Godiva paid attention to the man of the moment, the one who was buying her time ... but she remained aware of other men, and somehow she made them all aware of *her*. It was like a field she gave out. You knew, without a word being said, that she was busy *now*; but at some time in the future she could be yours, too, if you wanted her—and if you were willing to pay royally for the pleasure. Now . . ." He shrugged. "Now she pays attention to Luther. The other men around her are not even there. She's *different*."

"Maybe it's love?" suggested Lotos, giving Esro Mondrian a quick and skeptical sideways look from her dark eyes.

He did not even bother to reply. Mondrian's opinion of love as an agent for profound change of personality was perhaps even more cynical than Lotos Sheldrake's.

Now Lotos watched as other men and women wandered through the lounge. Mondrian had been exactly right. Godiva would look up casually, as though to check that each new arrival was not Luther Brachis, and then at once she returned her attention to Lotos. Even when Mondrian reappeared, Godiva gave him no more than a smile and a friendly nod. Earth's most famous and most expensive courtesan should have been much more *aware* of men. Even if she no longer thought of them as possible customers, the habit of speculative evaluation should be built in.

Mondrian sat down next to Lotos Sheldrake and looked at his watch. He had promised her half an hour alone with Godiva. If Lotos wanted to cultivate her beyond that point, she would have to take the initiative herself.

On the way back to the lounge he had stopped in for a few moments at the spectator's gallery and looked down on the battle area. Luther Brachis and Dougal Macdougal were both still there, hidden by Monitor headsets and recognizable to Mondrian only by their clothing. The actual field of encounter was a small hemispherical chamber about six feet across. A combination microscope-telescope set in the domed roof revealed all the action to any interested observer. The usual audience would be prospective players, following the procedure with avid interest. When Mondrian en-

tered, the assault on the trapdoor spider's lair was
still in preparation, and the gallery was almost
empty. There was one young woman, wearing the
blue workers' uniform of the Pentecost colony, and
a tall, thin man with a full beard. He seemed more
interested in the helmeted players in the battle
chamber than in the simulacra or the battle itself.

The close-up of the spider was daunting. It sat
motionless at the bottom of its trap, holding in its
front limbs the drained husk of a millipede. It was
easy to imagine that the rows of eyes along its
curved back were aware of the watchers above.

Mondrian looked at the spider thoughtfully. If
his arrangement with Skrynol for the Anabasis did
not work out, and Dougal Macdougal became an
impossible problem—could Adestis provide a con-
venient solution? Had it been used in the past, to
dispose of a troublesome official?

That new thought intrigued Mondrian. He went
back to Lotos Sheldrake and Godiva Lomberd and
sat down to puzzle out its potential. He had been
there for only a few minutes when the uproar
began in the adjoining battle chamber.

Godiva jerked instantly to her feet. "In there,"
she screamed, and dashed to the chamber door. By
the time Mondrian and Sheldrake had followed
her inside, she was already at Luther Brachis' side.
She was supporting him and looking in horror at
the scene around her.

Brachis was standing, white-faced but erect. His
right forearm ended in a bloody stump.

Mondrian glanced at the bodies surrounding
Brachis, then went across to him. He lifted the
arm, checked the tourniquet, and nodded. "No
blood loss now. Take it easy. We'll get you over to
the hospital."

"Thanks. Sorry about the mess in here." Brachis
nodded at the wounded arm. "Injuries getting to
be a habit."

"We'll grow it back."

"Yeah. Stop me biting my nails." Brachis looked at Godiva and gave her a death's-head smile. "Don't worry, Goddy. I'll be fine. Just have to sign my name left-handed for a while."

MEMORANDUM FROM: Luther Brachis, Commander Solar System Security

TO: All security posts

SUBJECT: Countermeasures for terrorist activities.

Effective immediately, the following special security measures will go into effect throughout the Inner System:

1) All travellers leaving Earth will be required to travel via Link Exit facilities. All other transfers will be temporarily prohibited.

2) All travellers leaving Earth will be subject to chromosome ID checks. ID's will be compared with reference ID (attached). In the event of a correlation exceeding 0.95, the traveller must be detained for questioning by Central Security.

3) All awakenings from storage facilities will be subject to direct supervision. Wakers will be subject to chromosome ID checks and checked against reference ID. In the event of a correlation exceeding 0.95, the waker must be detained for questioning by Central Security.

4) Any traveller using Link facilities whose appearance resembles the MARGRAVE OF FUJITSU (image attached) must be detained for questioning by Central Security.

5) Any off-Earth disposition of assets from the estate of the Margrave of Fujitsu must be reported to Central Security.

Luther Brachis stared at the stump of his hand,

where the nubs of new fingers were already beginning to bulge under synthetic skin. He wiggled them experimentally. "Itches like blazes." He tapped the sheet in front of him with his left hand. "Think this will do it? Will we catch him?"

Esro Mondrian shook his head. "Not if he was as smart as you think. He must have made plans for this kind of checks when he first created his own Artefact. The next one could look like anything."

"I know." Brachis looked up. "And I'm worried."

"You'll be all right. Stay well-armed, and we'll give you plenty of protection."

"You don't understand." Brachis placed his hand on the gun that sat on the table in front of him. "I'm not worried about myself. I'm afraid that the bastard might have a shot at *Godiva*."

# Chapter Eighteen

# TRAVANCORE AND BARCHAN

*Dear Chan,*

This is a letter I never expected to write, a message I never dreamed I would send. But it's our first night down on Travancore—and I'm flat-out *scared*. I wish I were with you in the Gallimaufries, watching Bozzie preach self-denial and gobble down cakes and honey. You and I can't be together now, but maybe you'll let me babble at you for a while.

We weren't allowed to bring a Mattin Link down to Travancore. Whatever happens, Mondrian won't risk the Morgan Construct having access to a Link again. So I'm firing this off to our ship, and hoping everything works out right so you'll get it before you leave Barchan. Last word I had from there said you had the hottest group they've seen since the pursuit team training began. I hope so—and I hope you won't have to visit Travancore. If you do, it will mean that we have failed.

I said we are "down on Travancore" but that's only a figure of speech. I don't know where the true surface of the planet begins—no one does. We're hanging now in a sort of half-balloon tent with a flat, flexible base, about a hundred feet down from the topmost growths of vegetation. There's another five-kilometers-plus of plant life underneath us. Animal life, too—we saw signs of that when we did our low-altitude ship survey. The whole planet is riddled with holes, circular shafts about five meters across, that dive down from the top layers. At first we thought they might be natural rain channels—it rains every day over most of Travancore. But now we're not so sure. S'glya—she's the Pipe-Rilla on the team—saw something big wriggling away down one of the tunnels when we flew overhead. Scary. But I was mainly happy that it wasn't the Morgan Construct—we were a sitting target. I tried to hide my panicky feeling, but it didn't work. S'glya has this absolutely uncanny ability to read my emotions, and she told the others.

It's an unpleasant thought, the idea that soon we'll be heading down one of the tunnels, but the Tinker has a different attitude. It argues that the tunnels are a boon—*without* them it would be just impossible to explore the vertical forest on Travancore. Maybe it's impossible anyway. We'll know in a day or two.

Even before we started the final descent here we decided that the training program we'd been through had missed the point. We were sent to Dembricot for the final sessions, because it's a vegetation world like Travancore so it ought to be good experience for this place.

Nice idea, but totally wrong. You've seen the training films of Dembricot. Flat, watery, plains of plant growth—and no more like Travancore than Barchan is. The planet is rolling, tangled hillocks of jungle, boiling up like one of earth's oceans in a bad storm.

One good thing: I can breathe the air with just a compressor. I'll even be able to manage without that when we get to a lower level. We're all doing well. S'glya needs a heating unit, and Angel had to do some mysterious interior modification before the atmosphere was acceptable, but that's all. (I wish I could understand Angel's mental processes better. The others seem to have no problem—or at least they don't admit it.)

The view from the top layer of vegetation is spectacular at the moment. Talitha is close to setting. It's low on the horizon, so it shines horizontally through mile after mile of ferns and leaves and vines. No flowers, I'm afraid—Travancore wouldn't do for old Bozzie. Everything in sight is greener than green, except for the Top Creepers. They're purple, gigantic, lateral creepers that snake away across the top of everything else as far as you can see. And I mean *gigantic*. They're only maybe two meters across, but many kilometers long. In spite of their size they're not at all dense and heavy. I tried to take a sample from one, because I couldn't see how the rest of the vegetation could possibly support their weight. When I cut into it, there was a hissing sound and a horrible smell, and the level of the vegetation around the Top Creeper actually went *down* a fraction. The whole thing must be nothing more than a wafer-thin shell stretched out over a hollow center full of light gases. Now I wonder if they are actually holding the other plants *up*.

(I'm babbling, but I tell myself it's justifiable. If by some chance you do have to come here, the more you know about the place ahead of time, the better. We were trained as well as we could be, but it wasn't enough. No one ever looked closely at Travancore before. With no defined surface and no open water, no one thought it was worth it. So we have more questions than answers.)

More about those holes—they keep preying on my mind. The Angel imaging organs (can't call them eyes) can be tuned to the thermal infra-red.

Our Angel had a heat-wavelength look down one of the shafts, and claims that it isn't vertical. It spirals down in a helix, which rules out the rain-channel idea. We'll have a better idea in the future, because I suspect we'll be going down one. I hope I'm around after that to send a description to you. Whatever happens to us, our ship should have a full record of it.

More about Travancore, too. Naturally, we've thought about nothing else since we got here. There are plenty of mysteries not covered in the briefing documents. For example: gravity and air. The surface gravity is only a little over a quarter of Earth's. So how can it hold onto a substantial atmosphere, and support this massive cover of vegetation? The air should have escaped into space long ago. Well, according to S'glya, Travancore has its atmosphere *because* it has its strange vegetative layer. The canopy of plant life is so dense, continuous, and ubiquitous that it can trap air molecules within it and beneath it. There is something close to a pressure discontinuity near the top here. And of course, it's a chicken-and-egg situation, because the atmosphere is absolutely necessary for the vegetation to exist! The plant cover must have developed very early in Travancore's history. And if S'glya is right, the shafts we saw can't go down uninterrupted towards the solid surface, otherwise they would act as escape vents for the air. So we may have to cut through barriers. And that adds one more element of difficulty. Just to increase the confusion, the Angel says that S'glya's idea about the relationship of the atmosphere and the vegetation must be wrong—for six reasons still to be specified!

Well, what's the *good* news? The team is the good news. We're an odd group. We have a Tinker who says its name in Kaliam, but who asks me to call it Ishmael. Its big thrill in life seems to be to snuggle up to the rest of us. Then there's an Angel who won't stop using human proverbs and clichés, and who says that Angels don't *have* names; and S'glya, the Pipe-Rilla, who seems to know what I'm thinking and feeling without being told, and who insists that she be called S'glya, even though that is not her *real* name. Weird. But it all *works*! Once we started to know each other, we've been achieving an absolutely unbelievable level of communication and team-work. It seems as though anything that one of us can't do, another one can. We noticed it at first back on Barchan, and since then it has just gone on getting better and better.

Better and better—but God knows if it will be good enough!

Full night here now. Time to sleep.

Keep your fingers crossed for me, Chan, wherever you are. I love you, and I've always loved you. I can't forgive myself for running away and refusing to speak to you when you were on Ceres with Tatty and Kubo Flammarion. But it was such an effort, admitting to myself that I don't control you any more. I hope you will forgive me. And I hope some day I can make up for what I did then.

*Yours, Leah.*

Chan had read it through again and again. After the third time he could have repeated it word for word.

But he kept going back to the last few paragraphs. Leah's words of love bowled him over—and her remarks about the level of communication being achieved by Team Alpha baffled him completely. Over the past couple of days he had become convinced that his own team would *never* work well together. They had too much trouble understanding each other. Well, maybe Shikari, the Tinker, was all right, and even the Pipe-Rilla usually made some sense, though neither one of those creatures seemed to have the equivalent of facial expressions. They must presumably have some sort of body language for their own kind, though he had no idea how to read it. But as for the Angel, it was mystery personified. The creature had no face, no mouth, no method of communication except through a computer. And even *that* output was often incomprehensible to him, though the Tinker and the Pipe-Rilla understood (or pretended to).

And this mismatched assembly was supposed to track down and destroy the most dangerous being in the Stellar System! They would be lucky if they were able to handle the Simmie Artefact here on Barchan.

They had established their camp down near the planet's south pole. Until they knew the location of the Morgan Construct's simulacrum, there was no point in enduring the dreadful summer heat of the equator and northern hemisphere. As evening came on and the dark sands of Barchan gradually cooled, the pursuit team settled down to its first strategy session.

The Tinker Composite had increased noticeably in size as the sun set and the air was less scorchingly hot. It was now using almost twice as many components as when Chan had first met it in the car, and its response time was painfully slow. The other three had to wait each time while the Tinker's speech funnel made preparatory wheezes and whistles, and speech finally emerged. They were waiting now. The Pipe-Rilla, S'greela, was crouched next to Chan, nervously stroking her multi-jointed forelimbs along the side of her head. If her performance so far was a guide, when she had to confront the Simmie she would do nothing but chitter in terror and horror, then run away with great spring-legged leaps.

The Angel at least would not run away; it could not. It was too slow-moving. No matter how intelligent the crytalline Singer might be, it was bound within the vegetable body of the Chassel-rose, and suffered the plant's extreme slowness of movement. When the Angel wanted to move, the bulbous green body lifted the root-borers up close underneath it, and crept along on the down-pointing adventitious stems along the body base. Chan guessed that when it was in a hurry it could manage maybe a hundred paces an hour.

Which just left the Tinker, Shikari, as a potentially useful ally. And *its* reaction to danger, according to all accounts, was simple and immediate: it dispersed to its individual components, and they flew away. Chan looked around him at the three others and sighed. Great allies for a tough fight!

"We think that we have a satisfactory proposal to make," said Shikari at last. "The Simmie lacks circadian rhythms, and is indifferent to night or day. But we are not. We prefer to cluster, and Chan needs to become dormant. S'greela is partly nocturnal and can function well at night. And although the Chassel-rose will be almost immobile, the Angel has excellent night vision. So this is our suggestion. Angel and S'greela should perform a night survey, seeking the Simmie. Human and self will remain here and rest. If there is no success in the search, then in daylight we will reverse our roles."

The long blue-green fronds at the top of the Angel began to wave slowly in the air. Chan started to speak, then paused. He had seen that motion before—just before the Angel's computer communicator began its translation. Maybe even an Angel had some kind of body language!

"We agree," said the communicator's mechanical voice. "But we suggest one difference. We believe that we now know the location of the Morgan Simulacrum. Thus the mission for Angel and Pipe-Rilla should be one of confirmation, not search."

"But how can—?" began Chan, then stopped. The fernlike fronds were still waving.

"We have now completed the analysis of the imaging radar records obtained during the orbital survey," went on the Angel. "There are only two significant anomalies. One of them is almost certainly the Simulacrum." There was another brief pause. "We are now performing a confirming analysis. We have stored a copy of the ship's data record."

The Angel had answered Chan's half-uttered question—and another one, about the ship's radar records, that Chan had wondered about but not even begun to ask. Telepathy? Even as the thought came to him Chan rejected it. There were other more likely explanations. He remembered one comment from Kubo Flammarion during a briefing back on Ceres: "An Angel doesn't think like a human—but not because it *can't*. When an Angel wants to, it can put part of its brain in what we've started to call 'emulator mode.' That piece can think like a human, or a Tinker, or a Pipe-Rilla—and probably like anything else, or all three at once. And while that's going on, the Angel can still perform logical analyses in its own way. It doesn't lose the power for its own thinking—and *that* thinking we just don't understand at all." At that point Kubo Flammarion had looked puzzled by his own words, shook his head, and tugged at his uniform as though it had suddenly become too small for him.

Ignoring Chan's moments of introspection, the Pipe-Rilla had already unfolded its long, telescoping limbs and was reaching down to pick up the Angel. The Angel had objected the first time that S'greela had done it, protesting that an Angel was quite capable of independent locomotion. But a couple of minutes of the Chassel-rose's laborious movement had made the other three unanimous. Chan watched the Pipe-Rilla now as she casually picked up the Angel's solid bulk. He was more and more aware of the power in that thin, tubular body. S'greela was gentle, but if she chose she could swat him like a fly.

The Tinker did not speak again until S'greela and the Angel had left the camp in the aircar. It occurred to Chan that he was observing another data point. Unless they were speaking with him, the others were very economical of words. It seemed they added the human-style verbal padding just for his benefit. They had all realized that redundant words were part of human social interaction, as important to Chan as stroking to a Pipe-Rilla or clustering to a Tinker.

Chan forced himself to stand up and move across to sit by Shikari. After a few moments he felt the feathery touch of long, delicate antennae on his arms and legs. The Tinker Composite was quietly performing a partial rebuilding. Thumb-sized individual components were leaving the far side of the composite and re-attaching themselves close to Chan's body. Within five minutes Shikari was moulded solidly against Chan's left side, touching him all the way from breast to ankles. He turned his head and stared down at the purple-black vibrating mass. The contact was not at all unpleasant. In fact, that gentle thrumming touch against his skin began to feel surprisingly warm and reassuring. After a few more moments, free components who had not been part of the Tinker Composite when Chan sat down flew across and began to make additional connections. Soon Chan's whole body, feet to shoulders, was embedded in the purple swarm. He felt very relaxed, but not sleepy. The pressure surrounding him was just enough to be noticed. But it occurred to Chan that if the Tinker chose to swarm on something as a means of restraint, it would be very difficult to resist. Shikari had an effective way of neutralizing aggression.

He watched and waited as the final few components flew in to attach themselves. "Do you feel any different," he said, "when more units attach?"

There was an experimental whistle from the speaking funnel. "Of course," said Shikari at last.

Chan realized that the Tinker had given its full answer. "I don't mean more *intelligence*," he said. "I know that's true. What I mean is, do you feel that you are somehow a different individual when your size is greatly increased?"

The Tinker was silent for a longer period. "That is a difficult question," it said at last. "And we are not sure that it is a meaningful one. We are what we are, at this moment. We cannot feel what we were or will be. Every second, according to information that we have about humans, some of your own brain cells die. Do *you* feel different, when those units of intellect are removed from you?"

"It's not the same. In the case of a human, every brain cell has been there since childhood. We do not add units." (But Chan wondered at once if Shikari knew his own history—and how recently he had achieved full use of those same cells!) "We lose cells. But to constantly change, to recombine, and add or subtract units . . . it is hard for me to comprehend how you persist with the sense of a single identity during a time of major change."

The Tinker rippled against Chan's body, and a cascade of maybe five hundred units suddenly flew away to settle separately on the ground.

"Like that?" said Shikari. There was a breathy rattle from the voice-funnel—the Tinker was practicing a human laugh. "There is more than enough capacity for continous thought, even when no more than a hundred components are combined. Remember, each of the units that form a Tinker possesses nearly two million neurons."

"That sounds like very few."

"Compared with a human, or a complete Tinker

Composite, you are right. A full Composite may contain forty or fifty billion combined neurons. But compare one of our components with a honeybee that lives on Earth. That has no more than seven thousand neurons, and still it is capable of complex individual actions."

There was another whirr of tiny wings, and the units came flying back to rejoin the mass around Chan's body. The voice-funnel gave another and more successful attempt at a human laugh.

"We have a long distance to travel," said Shikari, "before we can really comprehend each other. When we first encountered humans we marvelled at your strange structure. How could intelligence be *delegated*, to reside in some special chosen group of cells within your bodies? In us, each component carries an equal amount of our intelligence. But how much of your brain lies here"—Chan felt an increased pressure on his midriff—"or *here*." The pressure moved to the calf of his left leg. "What intelligence lies in those parts? What are the thoughts of an arm, or a lung? We learned that a human could be reduced to less than half its size—no arms, no legs—and yet the intelligence would be unchanged! Who could believe such a thing?"

"It is quite true."

"We know—but who would believe if humans had not arrived on Mercantor to prove it to us?" There was another rustle of veined wings, and Shikari settled into a tighter mass. "Intelligence," said the whistling voice. "It is indeed a mystery. But this—closeness and warmth—is the *best* part of intelligence."

They both became silent. The pursuit team had set up their camp in a clearing, surrounded by the dusty blue-green vegetation of Barchan's pole. While Chan and Shikari had been talking full night had arrived, and the air temperature had rapidly dropped thirty degrees. Shikari was like a warm, soft blanket swaddling Chan to his chin. He lifted his head and looked up at the sky. Eta Cassiopeiae's brighter component had set, and the smaller sun of the binary had not yet risen. Chan could pick out S'kat'lan, the home planet of the Pipe-Rillas, as a bright point close to the horizon. Barchan's little moon, a shrunken irregular disk, sat above it in the sky.

Chan shivered in the warm night air. It was a tremor of apprehension. Three months ago he had lived in the quiet cocoon world of the Gallimaufries, happy, ignorant, and brainless, shielded by Leah from every danger and unpleasantness. Now he was wandering the surface of an alien planet, eighteen light years from home, not sure if he would see another sunset; and Leah was even farther away from Earth, and in greater danger. By now she might be landed on Travancore, pursuing not a Simulacrum but a real Morgan Construct.

Given a choice, would he go back? Back to the halcyon days of flowers and games? One man had been the agent for all those changes, and for the agony of the Tolkov Stimulator. If Chan closed his eyes he could see the face in front of him now. Esro Mondrian deserved the blame—or was it the credit? —for everything that had happened to him.

Chan stared up at Barchan's solitary misshapen moon, and wondered. About Shikari, about intelligence, about Esro Mondrian; and about himself.

By the time that the silvery spark of S'kat'lan was sinking into Barchan's dusty horizon, Chan had found a new truth. No matter what happened here, he would not want to go back to the old life in the Gallimaufries. Whatever it was, this mixed gift of intelligence and self-awareness, he wanted it.

With that knowledge the urge for revenge on Esro Mondrian acquired a softer focus. If Mondrian had earned Chan's hatred, perhaps he had also earned gratitude; for his action had dragged Chan, reluctant and screaming, into the world of responsibility. . . .

Chan drifted away into a strange mental state, remote and yet satisfying. His reverie was suddenly interrupted when the dark bulk of the Tinker stirred silently around him. He opened his eyes, and discovered to his amazement that there was already a hint of dawn in the sky.

"Listen," said Shikari's soft, whistling voice. "Do you hear? It is the sound of the aircar. The others are returning. We are sad. Our time of peace and closeness is ending."

## Chapter Nineteen

# THE VAULT OF HYPERION

Measured on any of the standard scales of human intelligence, Luther Brachis would score high in the top 0.1 percent. He always dismissed that fact as of trivial importance. Success in his job, he said, was not a function of intelligence; at least three other qualities were far more critical.

He called them the three P's: in order, persistence, paranoia, and persuasiveness. And when Lotos Sheldrake pointed out that persistence was no more than Luther's word for pigheadedness, and that paranoia and persuasiveness were contradictory impulses, he just laughed. According to Luther Brachis, the fourth important quality—not easily captured in one word—was the ability to know which one of the other three to apply in a given situation.

Brachis had taken the first moves to counter the strange legacy of the Margrave even before he was carried away from Adestis for medical treatment. It was immediately clear to him that he had been attacked by an Artefact, one that Fujitsu had chosen to make in his own image. He had killed it, but there could be dozens more. They might be stored anywhere in the solar system, and they might not look anything like the Margrave—it was not even certain that they would share any of his DNA. Which left a delicate and difficult problem: how could Brachis defend himself from future attacks?

He now acknowledged the truth of Fujitsu's claim; the other man's arm was indeed long, and it was reaching for Luther Brachis beyond the grave.

Earth was the easiest case to handle. Through the Quarantine service, Brachis had information on all individuals shipping up from Earth. It was easy to set tracers on every one of them, and make sure that none approached within a kilometer of him without triggering an alarm system.

But suppose an Artefact were stored elsewhere? The Margrave might have made other plans for revenge of his own death. Two off-Earth storage areas had to be checked: the Phoebe catacombs, and the Hyperion Deep Vault.

As soon as Brachis was released from the medical facility he set out to examine both possibilities. It was a task that he proposed to carry out personally. Godiva tried to get him to delegate it, arguing that he was still weak from his injury. Brachis shook his head.

"This one gets my personal attention. Fujitsu deserves no less. Come along with me, if you want to."

Godiva shivered and refused. "I'll travel with you, but I won't go down into the vaults. All those horrible frozen semi-corpses! They'd make me think about what could have happened to you if you hadn't come out of Adestis just in time. It's not for me, Luther."

The catacombs on Phoebe were relatively small and neatly organized. Luther Brachis was able to inspect them from end to end in one marathon session, and feel comfortable that there were no future surprises lurking there. But he knew that the Hyperion Vault would be another matter.

Early explorers of the middle system had more or less ignored Hyperion. The sixth major satellite of Saturn was a lumpy, uneven hunk of rock, whose dark and cratered exterior suggested that it was the oldest surface in the whole Saturnian system. Little water, few volatiles of any kind, and probably no interesting mineral deposits. It had been a no-hope old explorer, Raxon Yang, on his last trip out before his lungs rotted and caved, who first explored the Hyperion meteorite craters. He had discovered a peculiar structure at the bottom of one of them, a ragged-edged tunnel that zigzagged deep below the moon's battered surface.

Old Raxon Yang followed it, down and down, past the point of sanity and useful metal deposits. Seven kilometers below the surface, he found the upper face of the Yang Diamond.

He didn't know at the time what he had found. The tunnel at its end was only a meter and a half across, hardly enough to wield his instruments. He realized that it was diamond all right, as soon as his tools found it hard to cut and he made a first assay. Yang carved out a half-meter sample, as big as he could handle, and dragged it slowly back to the surface. On the way there he set up a claim marker and the usual array of booby-traps. The chance that anyone else would come along for years and years was slim indeed, but habits died hard.

Yang went back to Ceres. That was in the early days, when the reconstruction of the planetoid was a dream of the future. Ceres was still on the frontier, a sprawling and violent trade center for the system beyond the Belt.

Raxon Yang showed his sample to the assortment of crooks and villains who controlled the investment capital supply. They tried the usual techniques—stealing his samples, trying to trick him into revealing the location of his find, telling him that the diamond was inferior quality and hardly worth mining. Old Yang had heard it all before. He waited. And finally they came around, and gave him what he needed in exchange for a fifty percent interest in the claim. Yang performed the formal filing, bought equipment, hired his specialists, and set off on a secret trajectory to Hyperion to dig out his find.

And Yang *still* didn't know what he had found. The analysis had confirmed that it was diamond of the finest and purest water, perfectly transparent and free of all faults and discolorations. Yang had made the natural sales arguments to his backers: here was a carbonaceous body struck by a high-velocity planetoid impact generating great heat and tremendous pressure. The result: diamond.

But how much diamond? Yang had no idea. He hadn't put much stock in his own sales pitch—that was for the investors. He found out the truth on his second descent below the crater. The Yang Diamond had the overall shape of a fifty-legged octopus. The head, seven kilometers below the surface, proved to be almost spherical on top and a little less than fourteen kilometers across. The legs ran out and down, each major limb about half a kilometer wide and thirty or forty kilometers long.

Raxon Yang collapsed in the tunnel when the sonic probes revealed the extent of his find. He was dragged back to the ship, tied down on a bunk, and shipped back to Earth for the best medical treatment that the system could offer. The best, because he was now the solar system's richest citizen.

Two years later Yang was dead. He was murdered by the diamond cartel, for revenge rather than gain. He had unintentionally ruined every member. The Yang Diamond contained ten million times as much crystallized carbon as every other known source combined.

The mining began. Four centuries later it was at last finished. The Yang Diamond was gone, divided into a trillion separate fragments. And in its place sat the baffling labyrinth of the Hyperion Deep Vault.

Yang had never married—the old explorers never did. There were no children, and after his death the squabble over ownership and inheritance began. The lawyers feasted for eight years, and finally three hundred and eighty valid claimants were recognized. Each was assigned ownership of one region of the diamond, with separate responsibility and rights for mining it. Their descendants split the regions further. Over the generations and the centuries, owners proliferated: thousands, tens of thousands, millions of people. And once the diamond had been mined from a volume, that space was free for occupation.

Boundary planes were carefully drawn and ownership rights observed. The Deep Vault became a polyglot, polyfunctional melange of industries, the Hong Kong of the twenty-sixth century.

It no longer exported diamond—there was none to export. Instead it operated its own manufacturing industries from imported raw materials, and showed a degree of independence from central government that matched any civilization in the system. The storage vaults located in one of the major tentacles had a superb reputation. But they followed their own rules, and took little notice of any edicts from Ceres.

In another fine display of idiosyncrasy, the colonists of the Deep Vault had banned the use of the Mattin Link anywhere in their domain. Luther Brachis could link only as far as Titan, then was obliged to travel the rest of the way on a laden cargo vessel. It was transporting fish concentrates to the Vault residents. Despite the denials of its crew, it stank.

Brachis grumbled and cursed. Godiva took it all in her stride, wearing formal gowns for every dinner and dazzling the ship's crew with her ineffable beauty. Luther Brachis could not take his eyes away from her, and somehow he was not at all jealous of other men's looks.

"Are you sure you don't want to come with me?" he asked, on the last leg of the journey before the descent into the black depths of the Vault.

Godiva hesitated for a moment, then shook her head. "I don't want to—I told you that before we left Ceres. If you force me to, I will, but I don't *want* to—I'm afraid of what I might find there." She took his right hand in hers, inspecting it closely. The skin on the emerging fingers and thumb was soft and delicate, and there was now the first dark imprint of nails forming on the tips. "Please be careful, Luther. I don't want to hear that you've had another experience like the one that did this."

Brachis shrugged. He could tell Godiva Lomberd anything she wanted to hear, but in his own mind he could find no full reassurance. He had thought about the Margrave a great deal during his recent week in the hospital. That cunning and inventive mind demanded every respect, but no one could see *in detail* what lay beyond the grave. The Margrave had not known when he would die, or in what circumstances. It called for an unusual intellect to make *any* plans for vengeance from the tomb, but those plans could only operate in terms of probabilities—how, who, when, where? So all the advantage must lie with Luther Brachis. Unless he became careless.

The Margrave was a chess master; so was Brachis. They would both look many moves ahead. Luther had concluded that the Margrave's preferred haven for his other Artefacts had to be the Hyperion Vault.

The descent took them through many levels. Brachis looked around him carefully as they went down, noting safety points and shelters. Three blowouts in thirteen years had made the Vault inhabitants super-cautious. Each level had its own system of locks and deadman switches.

Below the seventeenth level the grey rock walls of Hyperion's silicon interior were left behind. To assure their own survival, the original miners had employed non-commercial impure diamond as supporting walls, buttresses, and columns. Now lit by the cold light of closed ecology bioluminescent spheres, the Deep Vault was a sinister grotto of light and color. The greenish-white glow of marine electrophores scattered from yellow and red diamond crystals, and broke into whole spectra from sharp columns and cornices.

Down forever, layer after layer, through the jumbled settlements. Brachis's guide was an emaciated woman with a bent back and drooping shoulders. She finally paused at a branch point and gestured to her feet. "Storage starts there. We'll be joined by a coldtank supervisor. How much do you want to see?"

"Everything."

"Just to look?"

"Maybe not."

She nodded. Other men had followed her through the coldtanks. She knew what they usually wanted. "Come on. Don't talk price with the supervisor. Wait until we're finished."

They began the slow drift through the stacks. Brachis wanted to see every chamber and examine each ID and each storage unit background.

It took two days. The tanks had not been laid out in a logical or time-sequenced order. Brachis, familiar with the wilderness of interior Ceres, felt

at times that the Deep Vault was even more an-
fractuous. It was amazing that even the supervi-
sors could navigate the dim-lit corridors and
tunnels. At the end, Brachis handed his companion a list of seven identifications. "These. What
will it take to put them into my full custody?"

She looked startled. "You mean—permanently?"

"Permanently, with no trace left in the Vault
records. Don't bother to tell me that it's impossible. Just give me the price."

She rubbed at her left eye, where the reddened
lid drooped to match her wilting shoulders. "Stay
here."

She was back in less than an hour. "We don't
need trade crystals here."

Brachis did not reply.

"But we do need volatiles and pre-biotics," she
went on, "and we're having trouble getting permits for them. If you could arrange a shipment in
from the Harvester—"

"How? You have no Link Exits here on Hyperion."

"Deliver to Iapetus. We'll arrange transfer. Ship
ten thousand tons, charges paid to Kondoport on
Iapetus."

"The price is high. I won't know if I have what I
want until they're out of cold storage."

"Makes no difference to us. Once they're warm
they're yours. But they'll rot unless you bring them
all the way to consciousness. You take them, and
you pay shipping charges."

Brachis paused for a moment, weighing his options. Even if six out of seven were false alarms, he
could not risk missing one. As for shipping charges,
he did not intend that anything taken from the
storage tanks would leave Hyperion. He would tell
Godiva that his search for Margrave Artefacts had
drawn a blank. "And if I get you the volatiles?" he
said at last.

"The seven will be yours." She smiled, a radiant, gap-toothed smile that made Brachis want to turn away from her. "All yours—to do just what you like with."

# Chapter Twenty

# DREAMSEA QUEST

The Team had come into official existence as soon as every member reached Barchan. It would be known as the Ruby Team—a name that Chan disliked as much as Leah had hated to be called Team Alpha. Like Leah, he had decided to change the name as soon as he had the chance.

The Ruby Team was now four days old. There had been three days of general survey and exploration of the planet, while Chan and the others went through their first attempts at cooperative effort—the "honeymoon," as Shikari had jokingly named it. But now, on the fourth morning, that easy period was over. Every team member knew it, and there was a reluctance to begin.

It was dawn on Barchan, a gorgeous sky-swirl of pinks and dark greys as the morning rays of Eta Cassiopeiae-A caught high-blown layers of dust and sand. The pursuit team members had dispersed during the night, to satisfy their individual needs for food or rest. Now at first light they were convened again within the aircar to hear the Angel's report.

The Angel was silent for a long time. At last it began a leisurely waving of upper fronds. "It is confirmed," said the communications unit attached to its central section. "At the 0.999 probability level, we now know the location of the Morgan Simulacrum."

"That is very good news" said Shikari, clumped in a bulging purple mound near the aircar's cabin wall. "Where is it, Angel? Not too near, we hope."

"Not near. The Simulacrum is far from here. It has a cave hideout, on the shore of Dreamsea."

There was a moment's silence. "And *that* is very bad news," said Shikari. "What do we do now?" In its agitation, the Tinker composite disassembled, so that the air in the car was filled with flying components.

Chan shook his head and turned to S'greela. "I can't do what Shikari just did, but I know how he feels. Do you have any suggestions?"

The pursuit team had discussed many alternative plans, for many situations; but this circumstance had never been considered. The Simulacrum could not have chosen a better hiding place.

The common impression of Barchan as a wholly desert world was not quite correct. There was one body of free water on its surface: Dreamsea. It was a round lake, forty kilometers across, lying in a depression about a thousand kilometers from the planet's south pole. The water in the lake was salty and bitter, and no Earth life-forms could survive there. The largest native life form was an amphibian, tolerating—and thriving on—Dreamsea's harsh salinity and caustic alkalines. It was one of those perplexing forms that had made the Stellar Group so careful in its policies. The Shellbacks looked like large, pale turtles, two meters across their flat backs. They employed no tools, knew no technology, had no recognizable language. And yet . . .

Most of the time the Shellbacks shared just two

obsessions: to be in water during Barchan's day, diving for clumps of water-weed; and to crawl ashore at night, so that they could crop the dull-colored, spiny vegetation close to Dreamsea's shores. Dull, grey animals, apparently living a dull, grey existence. The early human visitors to the Eta Cassiopeiae system had naturally concentrated their attention on S'kat'lan, the home of the intelligent Pipe-Rillas. No one had taken much notice of the Shellbacks of Barchan, until one day it was discovered that their flesh was a true delicacy; pink, fine-textured, of a unique and exquisite flavor. It became a luxury export from the Eta Cass system. The Shellback population dwindled. Without any special protection, it may have been headed for extinction.

It was a Martian xenologist, Elbert Tiggens, who saved the Shellbacks. His friends admitted that Tiggens had eccentric ideas. Other colleagues were less kind, and regarded as lunacy his scheme for a "universal taxonomy"—a general labeling system into which the organisms of every world would neatly fit by kingdom, phylum, class, order, family, genus, and species. Tiggens could not be dissuaded. For that purpose he was willing to endure a long stint on Barchan, studying the Dreamsea flora and fauna and patiently trying to force every organism into his classification scheme.

They wouldn't fit. Elbert Tiggens might have stayed there forever, putting square pegs into round holes; but after a few months he noticed an odd thing about the Shellbacks. He had been using them for food, and was very familiar with their habits and movements. Every morning they went down to the Dreamsea margin, and every night they came ashore. But they did not travel *directly* for food plants or for water. Instead, the animals followed peculiar and well-defined curves, different every morning and every evening. At certain points they would stop, turn around in a full circle, and leave a well-defined mark on the dusty ground. Tiggens photographed the tracks, wondered if they might be part of some kind of mating ritual, and went on with his attempted taxonomy.

After six months he had run out of a few staple supplies. He was also getting just a little tired of boiled, baked, fried, steamed, smoked and grilled Shellback meat. He hitched a ride with a Shellback harvester to Barchan's only space facility, intending to buy supplies and a meal there. Sitting near him was a Pipe-Rilla astronomer, about to leave Barchan to examine the Eta Cass ring system. Tiggens was starved for company, human or otherwise. He explained his reasons for being on Barchan, his notions on taxonomy, and his observations of the Shellbacks. The Pipe-Rilla listened in polite and bored silence, until finally Tiggens produced some of his pictures of the Shellback shoreline patterns of movement. The Pipe-Rilla looked, looked again. Finally she snatched them from Elbert's hands.

"Mating rituals?" said Tiggens.

The Pipe-Rilla shivered, stretched, telescoped her limbs, rose fourteen feet high, and shook her head. "Planetary orbits and positions! For the Eta Cass system!"

Suddenly the Shellbacks were no longer a food crop. Dreamsea was declared a protected area, and the Shellbacks a protected species. They had enough understanding of astronomy, mathematics, and celestial mechanics to know the position of the major planets of the Eta Cass system, regardless of their visibility or the time of year. They worked cooperatively, no Shellback duplicating the efforts of another. But—maddeningly—they refused to show other indications of intelligence.

The rules of the Stellar Group were explicit and rigorously enforced. The Shellbacks were a possibly intelligent species, even though the nature of that intelligence was not yet understood. Therefore, their protection was total. They could not be hunted—and their environment, which included the whole of Dreamsea and the land area around it, was totally off limits to anyone, including the Ruby Team. Which seemed to make the task of Chan and the others quite impossible.

After Shikari's initial consternation and disassembly, the Tinker slowly regrouped and re-formed its speaking funnel. The funnel turned toward Chan, gave a couple of preliminary whistles, and at last spoke. "Well?" said Shikari.

Chan looked at the Tinker, then turned to S'greela and the Angel. All three seemed to be looking at him expectantly—even the Angel had moved the arm-like branches on its lower section, to bring the microphone closer to Chan, and the Pipe-Rilla was leaning towards him.

"Well?" repeated S'greela.

"Well, what?"

"We are waiting?"

"Waiting for *what*?" Chan felt suddenly defensive.

"Waiting to hear your plan," said the dry tones of the Angel's computer voice. "How do you propose that we will capture and destroy the Morgan Simulacrum, when it is clear that we may not enter the protected area surrounding Dreamsea? To the rest of us, that seems like a totally impossible task."

Chan shook his head. "Don't look at me. I have no plan. Look, *you* were the ones who did the reconnaissance, who came up with the Simmie's location. You know the Dreamsea area, and you say you know just where it is hidden. Why look to *me* for a plan?"

Part of Shikari's lower grouping rippled out into a long extension of components that fluttered their way over to nestle around Chan's legs. He knew by now that it was the Tinker's way of showing its support and sympathy. "Because you are a human," said the whistling voice.

"Because you can do this, and we cannot," added S'greela humbly. "We always knew that it would come to this, if the Simulacrum were discovered. You alone have the gifts that will allow us to proceed."

"We have discussed this among ourselves, without you," went on Shikari. "Except in our largest composite form, we know that Tinkers do not have the intellectual power of Angels and Pipe-Rillas. But we are certain that all three forms have mental abilities that exceed those of humans—please, do not argue this point *now*. And yet we also know that logic, speed, creativity, memory, and accuracy are not everything. There is some other *dimension* to human thought that we three all lack. An unhappy dimension, for most purposes. But we cannot plan a *military* activity, organize a *war*, or *fight a battle*. Those very words are unique to human languages."

There was a long silence.

"Tell us your plan," said the metallic voice of the Angel.

"You don't understand. I *cannot*. I have no experience of war, no idea how it is conducted. Even though some humans are aggressive, I have never been involved in a battle—not even in an individual combat."

"Before a Pipe-Rilla mates," said S-greela slowly, "she cannot imagine how such a thing is possible. The very idea of joining bodies is grotesque, disquieting, and disgusting. But when the time and the need to mate arrives—she mates. Without thought. The action comes not from *experience*, it come from some somatic memory, stored within her brain and body."

"Make us a plan to destroy the Morgan Simulacrum," said Angel. "You are human. *You are large, you contain multitudes.* From within you, you can *create* that plan."

Chan felt anger rising fast within him. They were refusing individual responsibility! He glared around him at the others, at the impassive bulk of the Angel, the nervous stoop of the Pipe-Rilla, and the restless fluttering of the Tinker, with individual components constantly disconnecting and re-connecting. "When I was sent here to Barchan, I was told I would be part of a *team*. Every member would contribute, as an equal partner—not sit around and expect one member to give them orders. You command me to make a plan. What are you here for? What do you think *you* will be doing?"

"We will help to carry out the plan," said Shikari, "as much as we are able. Chan, human anger is a terrifying thing. We see it growing within you as we speak. But you are directing it at the wrong target. We ask you only to do what we *cannot* do. Sit. Think. Do not hurry. And then tell us where your thoughts have led you."

"But you still don't understand," began Chan. "I'm no more able to dream up what we need than *you* are. I've no experience, no way to—to—"

He stopped. It was pointless to go on talking. He shook his head and stared down at the floor of the aircar. He was just repeating himself, and it was getting them nowhere. Surely the Angel could do a better job than anything that Chan could conceive of? He had already seen astonishing proof of its intellectual powers. Or the Tinker—Shikari could add to its brain-power, just by adding more components, and increase its intellect to the point where Chan had trouble following the thought patterns. But as long as they all sat fretting here, the Simulacrum would sit safe in its hiding place.

Chan looked up. "You are not willing to invade the Dreamsea protected area?"

Shikari gave a high-pitched whistle of horror, and S'greela chittered in disapproval. She shook her broad head. "That is an unthinkable act. We would not even consider it."

"Not even for an observer only, if there was a guarantee that no Shellback would be touched?"

"Such a guarantee cannot be provided. If the Simulacrum observed and attacked you, you would insist on returning that attack."

Chan nodded. "You are probably right, if it were necessary for self-defense. But I was not thinking of me—of any one of us."

"Who, then?" The Pipe-Rilla waved her jointed arms. "We are the only undeniably intelligent species on this planet."

"I don't want intelligence. According to our briefings, the Simmie will be wary of any sign of intelligence." Chan turned to Shikari. "You told me that your individual components have two million neurons. They can eat, mate, drink, and cluster. But what about a small assembly? Could as few as six or ten components cluster?"

"Certainly. But why would we choose to do so?"

"I'm not sure. Could such a small group take direction from you?"

"Some direction—simple commands."

"Could the small group serve to collect information?"

"Undoubtedly." The surface of the Tinker bristled with motion, like a shrug running across the upper part. "But what good would that be? There would be no way that such a small group could integrate its information with anything else. We could not *combine* it."

"We have a superb integrator, right here." Chan jerked his thumb at the Angel. "Shikari, all you'd need to do would be to form a number of very small assemblies, and direct them to explore the region near the Simmie's hideout. Could you do that?"

"Certainly. But what then?"

"Once we know what it does, how it occupies its time, we can look for a way to lure it out—away from the protected area around Dreamsea where the Shellbacks live."

"But we have no idea what would attract a Simulacrum," protested S'greela. "We know its appearance and its structure, but we have no idea of its mental attitudes."

"Not yet—but we will." Chan turned to the silent Angel. "According to information I received before we came to Barchan, an Angel can operate its mind in an 'emulator mode' that mimics the thought pattern of other species. Is that true?"

"Given enough time, and enough information, what you suggest is *partially* true. We can often duplicate the thought patterns of another being in part of our own mental processes. But not always. For example, we have been completely unsuccessful in replicating any part of the human's aggressive processes."

"Forget humans. Could you duplicate the thought patterns of a Simmie?"

"No. That is impossible. We do not have enough information, and there has been no opportunity for interaction."

"Damn it, Angel, I'm not asking for *perfection*. All we need is a good working imitation—something that we can use to guess how a Simmie might react to a given specific situation."

There was a long silence. The Angel was considering a new concept. "An *imperfect* thought simulation?" it said at last. "Possibly. *Necessity is the mother of invention.* I have already within me a considerable factual data bank regarding the Simulacrum. A gross model of its mental processes may be achievable; perhaps enough to compare the *relative* probabilities of different courses of action, without assigning absolute values to any one. But the process would take me a long time to accomplish."

"How long?"

The Angel went into another brooding silence. "If we can be left undisturbed," it said at last, "perhaps three days? And during that same period of time I could develop within me the necessary mechanism to accept direct inputs from Tinker sub-assemblies. But to achieve that Shikari and I would have to be closely connected."

Chan turned to the Tinker. "Can you? Can you set up the close connection?"

"We will see. At the outset we predict no problems. It will be a new experience, and a pleasant and intriguing one." The Tinker began to drift slowly toward the Angel. When it passed in front of Chan it paused. "Should we begin now, Chan? Or do you first prefer to tell us the details of *the rest* of your plan?"

# Chapter Twenty-One

# DISASTER ON TRAVANCORE

The first experimenters with the Mattin Link transfer system had learned three facts very quickly:

• *Know your exit point.* Careless travellers had landed suitless in the airless interior of an extrasolar probe, or on the open surface of Mercury and Ganymede.

• *Close is not good enough.* Travellers who missed the long, coded sequence of Link settings by a single digit tended to arrive as thin pink pancakes, or long, braided ribbons of protoplasm.

• *Someone always pays.* The instantaneous transfer of messages and materials through the Mattin Link had opened the road to the stars; but it would never be cheap. A single interstellar trip between points of differing field potential could eat up the savings of a lifetime. Linkage of material from the Oort Cloud to the Inner System consumed the full energy of three kernels aboard the Oort Harvester.

To those three rules, Esro Mondrian had added a fourth of his own: *Access is power.* Certain Link coordinates and transfer sequences were held strictly secret, and knowledge of them was not permitted without lengthy checking of credentials and need-to-know. The coordinates for the ship orbiting Travancore were not even stored in the *Dominus* data bank. It was known to just three people in the system: Mondrian, Flammarion, and Luther Brachis. The latter two expected to use their information only if Mondrian himself was dead or unconscious.

The receiving point for information from Travancore was just as closely guarded. The Link Exit point was at Anabasis Headquarters, and nowhere else. The Solar ambassador had agreed to that grudgingly, after direct pressure on Dougal Macdougal from the other members of the Stellar Group.

What the Stellar Group had not approved—what no one outside the Anabasis had been told about—was Mondrian's other decision concerning Team Alpha. The Human team member had been equipped with a personal link communicator, to send back sound and vision through her headset for the entire period that she was on Travancore. Mondrian intended to monitor those signals personally, with help only from Flammarion and Brachis. Together they would provide round-the-clock coverage of Travancore operations. Leah Rainbow knew that the data were being sent to Team Alpha's orbiting ship; but she had no idea that they would be received in real-time at Anabasis Headquarters.

Dawn on Travancore; night on Ceres. Esro Mondrian tapped Flammarion on the shoulder to indicate his arrival, and sat down at the other side of the desk. Flammarion nodded, disconnected, and removed his Link generator. He placed it in his lap, rubbed his temples, and yawned. "Quiet night there. I heard a few peculiar noises outside the tent, and there was half an hour of heavy rain, and that was about all. The whole team is awake now."

Mondrian nodded and picked up his own Linkset. "I'm going to spend the whole day with them.

Don't interrupt me unless we have an emergency."
He fitted the set carefully over his head and turned
it on. After the first unpleasant moment of double
sensory input, he was linked across fifty-six lightyears. The Link connection was excellent. Suddenly he was seeing through Leah's eyes and hearing with her ears. Whatever she saw and did,
Mondrian would also experience as long as he
wore the generator.

She was standing now on the reinforced side lip of
their balloon tent gazing out across the vivid emerald
of Travancore's endless jungle. The growths below
the tent formed a tight lattice of stems and vines,
with ample space between them to permit the
morning light to penetrate. The early dazzle of
Talitha was scattered and diffused by the irregular
array of trunks and creepers, so that Leah could
see down for a couple of hundred feet. At that
depth a continuous layer of broad leaves hid everything beneath. She turned to squint up at the
sun. Even with Talitha's brilliance, the barrier of
leaves must be very effective. There could be
little photosynthesis deeper than the top few hundred meters. Which left a mystery: how did the
lower levels obtain their energy supply?

The Tinker team member, Ishmael, and S'glya,
the Pipe-Rilla, emerged from the tent to stand
next to her. After a few moments Ishmael flowed
and fluttered along the tent lip to form a living
blanket around Leah's legs.

"Cold," said S'glya as a greeting. She vibrated
her vestigial wing cases.

Leah turned to her and pointed over the edge.
"Is that a solid layer of leaves? I can't see a thing
below it."

"Correct. As I said last night, the vegetation of
this planet is structured in dense and continuous
layers. We are looking down at one of them."

"But that means the lower regions must be in
complete darkness."

"Certainly. Even our microwave signals were heavily damped in the first couple of kilometers. It will be dark."

"So where do you think that the lower layer of Travancore gets its energy supply?"

S'glya raised a thin forelimb and gestured around her. "From here. Where else?" She leaned far out over the edge, apparently oblivious to the chasm below her, and touched a half-meter shaft of bright yellow growth. "I suspect that we could follow this plant structure all the way down, another five kilometers, and find that its roots are set in the soil of Travancore. As for its width at the base . . ." The Pipe-Rilla wriggled her upper limb pairs. "Who knows? Many, many meters."

Behind them the Angel had come slowly creeping out onto the side-lip of the tent. When it finally stood in full sunlight, the Chassel-rose extended all its fronds and turned them to face Talitha's morning beams. "We have performed . . . confirming analysis," said the Angel's translation unit, after a couple of minutes of silent sun-bathing. "From the data of the orbital survey we now know the location of the Morgan Construct."

Ishmael gave a shimmering flutter of the whole composite, while the other two swung quickly to face the Angel.

"Where is it?" asked Leah.

"Approximately three thousand kilometers from here, roughly north-east. It is deep in the vegetation—perhaps on the surface itself."

"Good. We ought to be safe enough here for the moment."

"Safe," said Angel, "unless the Morgan Construct has chosen to move since the survey was performed. We judge that to be unlikely, at the 0.15 probability level. What do you propose for our actions now?"

"Should we seek out the Construct?" asked Ishmael.

Leah found that the other three were all looking at her and waiting expectantly. On every question of pursuit or capture, they deferred to her without hesitation.

She thought for a moment and shook her head. "No. Definitely not. We need to find out more about this planet. The Construct has been here for months. It has had nothing else to do but explore Travancore, and it is very intelligent. We've been here less than one day. There's no way I'll go seeking that Construct until we know our way around here."

*"Better safe than sorry,"* said the Angel. *"Look before you leap."*

Then the other three were silent, until S'glya, rubbing at her sides with her midlimbs, finally said: "But if we do not seek the Construct, what *should* we do?"

Leah turned again to the Angel. "Can you determine from the orbital survey data how far we are from the nearest spiral shaft into the vegetation?"

"Of course." There was a second's pause, followed by a series of clicking sounds from the translation unit. "We are less than two kilometers from a downward shaft."

"Excellent. That's where we go next. We ought to take a trip down that shaft, and find out what conditions are like on the lower levels of Travancore. We think of it as a vertical forest, but that's pure speculation."

"We should all go?" asked S'glya uncertainly.

Leah hesitated. Would it be wiser to leave one member of the team in the upper levels, for a possible rescue? But if so, who? S'glya would have to carry Angel, and Ishmael was easily the most mobile for exploring ahead in difficult areas.

*"There is safety in numbers,"* said the Angel slowly, while she was still thinking about it.

"All right. We all go." Leah paused, still unhappy with that decision.

"When?" asked Ishmael.

"I see no advantage in waiting. As soon as we
are all ready, let's get the exploration kit together
and head for the shaft. All right?"

"Yes."

"Yes."

*"Never do tomorrow what can be done today,"*
said the Angel.

The deep shafts noted during the first orbital
survey were far more than simple gaps in Travancore's dense vegetative cover. On closer inspection
they proved to be true tunnels, with well-defined
and continuous walls of ribbed leaves, plaited into
a tight fabric.

"Artificial," said S'glya, running a touch antenna
lightly over the leaves. "The sign of intelligence?"

"Not necessarily. We have insects on Earth that
build more complex systems than this, and we do
not believe that they are intelligent."

Overflow tubes to carry off heavy rain were set
into the tunnel walls every twenty meters. They
were very necessary. Leah had expected near-
vertical structures, plunging down towards Travancore's true surface. But the shafts were more
like spiral tunnels, curving down at a constant and
moderate angle. It was easy to walk along the
shallow gradient without supporting lines—and
heavy rain would impose a substantial load on the
tunnel's curving lower floor.

Leah took a last look around at the surface layer
of vegetation. They would have ten hours more of
light in Travancore's thirty-seven hour day. She
led the way into the tunnel, closely followed by
the continuously re-forming shape of Ishmael. The
Tinker was very nervous. Leah had long ago given
up on the question of how Ishmael preserved any

continuity of thought when it was constantly changing. (If it didn't worry Ishmael, she wasn't going to let it worry her.)

The Pipe-Rilla came last. S'glya carried the Angel tucked easily under her midlimbs. She sang softly to herself until Leah asked her to keep quiet. They did not want to attract attention—whether or not there was anything on Travancore, other than the Construct, to *be* attracted.

The light faded slowly. Two hundred meters down they were moving in a green twilight, floating along in the light gravity as though they were under water. An upward kink in the tunnel followed by a steeply plunging section took them below a thick layer of leaves. The light level dropped abruptly, and the temperature was noticeably higher. By the time they had descended four hundred meters they were shrouded in an intense emerald gloom.

Leah stopped and turned around to the others. "I can't see much now, and I don't want to use a light. S'glya, would you take over the lead? Angel can use a thermal band to tell you what's going on ahead of you."

They were still changing places when there was a sudden whistle from Ishmael. "Something moving ahead!" the Tinker said urgently. They all turned, in time to see a pearl-white glow in the tunnel below them. As they watched it moved beyond the spiral wall. A dozen Tinker components disconnected and flew away along the shaft. A few minutes later they returned, one by one, and rejoined the main body.

"Native life-form," said Ishmael after a few seconds. "And big. About ten meters long, snakelike form—no arms or legs. Bioluminescent. That glow we saw came from a row of lights along each side of it. And it seems afraid of us, because it went wriggling away from us at a good speed. We followed it as far as a branch point, about three hundred meters farther down the shaft."

"Is it safe to go on?" asked S'glya. They all
looked again at Leah.

"I don't know." She stared into the gloom ahead.
"But I think we have to keep going. If we turn
back every time we find evidence of a native life
form we may never get anywhere. I say we keep
going. S'glya, would you lead the way again?"

They continued a cautious descent. Soon they
were moving in total darkness. The last trace of
sunlight from Talitha had gone. At Leah's suggestion, S'glya shone a faint pencil beam to let them
see the tunnel for a few paces ahead. The Angel's
thermal sensors could see beyond that, and reported the curving tunnel clear ahead as far as
line-of-sight vision would permit.

The temperature had stabilized, at a level that
Leah found just bearable and that S'glya relished.
The pursuit team went on in silence for more than
two hours, winding steadily deeper and deeper.
The air was denser and more humid, and Leah
could smell a faint but pleasant aroma like new-
cut Earth grass. The tunnel at these depths was
less well-maintained, with ragged gaps here and
there in the sides and roof. When they were close
to one of the bigger gaps they could hear a soft,
rustling sound, like wind-blown dry leaves.

S'glya reached up to her full height and pulsed a
more powerful beam of light through a roof opening. It lit up the surroundings as brightly and
briefly as a lightning flash. Less than five meters
from the shaft they saw a small four-legged creature clinging to a thick branch. When the light hit
it there was a brief, alarmed quacking noise. S'glya
pulsed the beam again. The creature had turned to
face them. They had a glimpse of a brown eyeless
head, split by a broad mouth. A second, narrower
slit ran all the way across from temple to temple.
There was another sound, a high-pitched nervous

squeak, then the animal was scurrying agilely away from them around the side of the shaft.

"Intelligent?" said Leah.

The others did not reply. S'glya switched to a steady light-level and moved the beam slowly around the region outside the tunnel.

They saw the great boles of trees, each many meters across. The trunks were dark tan in color here, rather than the bright yellow of the upper levels. From them grew thousands of wilting finger-like excrescences, black and crimson and vivid orange. Legless slug-like creatures on each extrusion inched slowly away from S'glya's light. As they moved they left a faintly glowing trail on the tree fingers.

At this depth green had vanished completely from Travancore's bioforms. Photosynthesis was impossible. Everything depended for its existence on the slow fall of materials from higher levels, or on the transfer of nutrient juices pumping up and down the massive trunks.

The group moved on, ever downwards. In another hour the pleasant smell had been replaced by a nauseating odor of fleshy decay. Everything was coated with a misted layer of condensation, and dark droplets hung from the ribbed roof of the tunnel. Leah felt as though they had been descending for days. Finally the Angel waved its topmost fronds and gestured to S'glya. "Stop here. This tunnel ends in thirty paces."

Leah increased the illumination level of the light she was holding and came to stand by the Pipe-Rilla. "How does it end?"

"It simply terminates. We are less than forty meters above the true surface of Travancore. There is solid material beneath us, but descent past this point will be difficult for all of us except the Tinker components."

"Can you tell if we will be able to move over the surface itself, once we get there?"

"It should present no difficulty, once we are there." The Angel paused. "The descent would be easy enough, with the aid of a simple rope. But return might be complicated without more equipment."

"I'm not suggesting we should go down today." Leah turned to look back up the tunnel. "We have a long way to climb, even in this low gravity. I propose that we head back, and plan another trip with other equipment tomorrow. Now that we know what is here, the next descent ought to be much easier. But we have to be ready—" She stopped abruptly. Looking upwards, she had seen a movement in the faint scattered light from S'glya's pencil beam. It was far above them and indistinct, at the very limit of her vision.

"Angel," she began, "can you see if—" Her question became unnecessary. The object was approaching rapidly along the shaft, and it had a shape that was engraved deep in her memory.

Leah was looking at a rounded silver-blue diamond, four meters high and two across at its widest point. At the upper end was a blunt, neckless head, with well-defined compound eyes and a small speaking aperture. Latticed wing-panels shrouded the mid-part of the body. In their folded position they were compact and unobtrusive, no more than pencils of bright fabric. Extended, they could be shaped as needed to form solar panels, communication antennae, or protective shields. The base of the body ended in a tripod of supporting legs, each one capable of being totally withdrawn into the interior cavity. The mid-section contained a dozen dark openings. They held the weapons—the fusion devices, the lasers, the shearing cones.

Leah registered all those features in a split-second. She gasped, and stepped back along the tunnel.

Around her there was a sudden blizzard of Tinker components, as Ishmael dispersed instantly from the composite form. There was a high-pitched scream from S'glya.

Fifty-six lightyears away, Esro Mondrian was still watching and listening through Leah's monitor set. He had followed the group, all the way through their long descent. Now he felt a thrilling ripple of excitement and awe creeping along his spine.

The Angel's careful statement of probabilities when Team Alpha was still at their tent had been completely appropriate. The Morgan Construct had indeed moved its position since the time of the orbital survey.

The call came in midway through the sleep period on Ceres. A tiny communications unit implanted behind Luther Brachis's right ear provided a soft-voiced but insistent summons. He grunted in protest, lifted his head, and looked at the time. Then he swore, put his hands to his eyes, and slid quietly sideways to the edge of the mattress.

Godiva gave a sleepy questioning murmur. She slept like a child, deeply, peacefully, securely, snuggled against Brachis with one arm across his body. She usually fell asleep at once and said that she never had nightmares, or any unpleasant dreams that she could remember. Luther's departure from her side was one of the few things that would produce any reaction once she was soundly asleep.

He looked down at her as he pulled on his uniform. As always, Godiva slept unclothed. The skin of her naked body was so fine and fair that it seemed to glimmer like pink pearl in the faint light from the ceiling panels. He swore again, and hurried through to the living room. Once there he placed his unit into general message mode.

"Luther?" said a voice at once. It was Mondrian.

"Here. Bloody hell, Esro, this is a devil of a time to make a call." He was still straightening his uniform and reaching for his boots.

"I need you—at once." The dry voice had a tone in it that Brachis had never heard before. "Come to Anabasis Communications. Alone."

The unit went dead. Brachis cursed again. Alone! Of course he would come alone—what did Mondrian expect, that he'd lead in a brigade of bagpipers? (But Brachis headed for the door with his boots still unstrapped and his uniform half-fastened. Mondrian *never* gave instructions like that to someone he knew well.)

The door to the Anabasis Communications was locked when he arrived. That was significant, too. Brachis lifted his one good fist and banged hard on the door, taking some of his own irritation and edginess out on the metal panels. After a long delay there was a clicking of tumblers and the door slid open.

Esro Mondrian stood in the doorway. Brachis gave him a long, incredulous look. He had never seen such a rigid, horror-filled expression on the face of a living human. Mondrian stood as grey and lifeless as a freeze-dried corpse. He was like the things pulled out for identification after major airlock failures. He gestured Brachis to enter with one stiff movement, then locked the door behind them.

"Travancore?" asked Brachis.

Mondrian nodded.

"We lost Team Alpha?"

"That, and worse."

"*Worse*! For Shannon's sake, what happened? Did the Construct get loose?"

"And worse than that." Mondrian took the other man by the arm to lead him to the display unit. His fingers bit deep into Brachis's thick biceps. "I want you to see this, watch it through a couple of times with me. Then we're going to erase it. This is the only copy. And then we have to talk, just the two of us."

"Esro, I *told* you that Team Alpha wouldn't cut it when it came to blasting the Construct. They chickened out, didn't they? You know the 'Rillas and the Tinkers. I said that bunch of misfit aliens wouldn't have the guts to do a job properly. Why wouldn't you believe me?"

Mondrian paused in the middle of setting up the display sequence. "Who says I didn't believe you, Luther? But that's irrelevant now. We have to blockade."

"Blockade Travancore?"

"Not just the planet—the whole Talitha stellar system. Nothing can go in, nothing can get out." The screen began to flicker with the preliminary rainbow fringes of a Mattin Link recorded transmission. "And that's only the beginning. We can discuss what else we'll have to do."

Brachis banged on the desk with the flat of his hand. "Damnation! Esro, have you gone out of your mind? Do you realize what it takes to blockade a stellar system? How much it *costs*?"

"I know what it costs. And I know it won't be easy." Mondrian gave a tight-lipped little smile with no trace of humor in it. "Sit down, Luther. I don't want to argue with you now. You'll agree with me *completely*—as soon as you've had a look at this transmission from Travancore."

# Chapter Twenty-Two

# BARCHAN ENCOUNTER

The Simulacra used in pursuit team training were modeled on Livia Morgan's Constructs; but they had been designed and built by the Margrave of Fujitsu. Inevitably, he had woven into their mental make-up some of his own esthetic tastes. And certainly the habitat and lifestyle of the Simmie on Barchan suggested some of the Margrave's sensibilities and appreciation of beauty. The Simulacrum had chosen a relatively exposed position on the Dreamsea shore, one where it could obtain the best view of Barchan's long winter sunsets. Every evening Cassay shone golden-red through the dusty atmosphere, and the later setting of Cassby threw patterns of amber, garnet and jet across the dark basaltic sands.

According to the Tinker sub-assemblies who had flown sorties of the Dreamsea shore, the Simmie moved little from its preferred hiding place. It rested, half-hidden by a shallow ledge of rock that jutted out over Dreamsea's bitter waters, and looked out across the tideless shore.

The final attack plan would be Chan's. It had to be. He was skeptical of his abilities, but the others had given him no choice. They admitted the superior capability of humans in just one area: fighting.

On every other issue, each one was more than ready to give advice.

"Watchful, and suspicious, without question," said the Angel, while the others gathered round and listened closely. The Angel had been experimenting with trial runs of Simulacrum thought-processes, and was finally convinced that the emulation was as good as it could be without actual contact. "But its penchant for destruction is undetermined. The Simulacrum does not destroy every lifeform that it sees. It killed a few Shell-backs, when it first arrived on Barchan and was establishing itself here; but they seemed to be almost accidents. It has shown little curiosity or fear of small living things. Shikari's flights near its hideout stirred no action or apparent interest. It will not move from its safe position solely to make an unprovoked attack."

"For food, then?" asked S'greela. The Pipe-Rilla had folded and re-folded its flexible multi-jointed body to a compact mass. Now it looked like an isolated head, peering out from within a dark surrounding mound of Shikari's components.

"It will not move for food. There is ample sustenance close to where it is living."

"Are these things important?" said Shikari dreamily. The Tinker was almost dormant, with scarcely a movement of a component.

"We don't know," said Chan. "We don't know *what's* important yet. All I know is, we can't attack the Simmie where it is. So we have to find some method to lure it away from Dreamsea. Angel, so far you've given us nothing but negatives. What *does* interest or alarm it?"

"I do not know. If you will suggest alternatives, I can test them against the thought-process model.

But I have not been able to find anything that provides a strong stimulus."

There was a slow stirring of the Tinker's mass, and it slithered partly free of S'greela. The others waited. Shikari was close to maximum size, and by now they were becoming used to the Tinker's long integration time in that condition. They hardly noticed the sluggish response any more.

"We feel stupid to suggest this," said Shikari at last. "But perhaps one stimulus is astronomy? The Simulacrum watches the suns, the moon, and certain stars. Would it be willing to move for a better sight of those?"

Chan turned to the immobile figure of the Angel. "Can you run that?"

"One moment." There was another silence. This one lasted for almost twenty seconds, broken only by clucking sounds from the Angel's communicator. Chan had learned to associate those chirps and clicks with massive computational processes within the Singer's crystalline matrix.

"Shikari's suggestion is correct," said the Angel at last. "At the 0.98 probability level, the Simulacrum moves to respond to celestial events. No other stimulus has better than 0.35 correlation with observed movements." There was a shorter silence, then a wiggle of the Angel's lowest fronds and a very human-sounding sigh from the communicator. "Unfortunately, this information appears to be without value. I have checked the ephemeris for Barchan, and no heavenly events of unusual import are expected within thirty Barchan days."

"So what can we do?" said S'greela cheerfully. "Pray for a supernova?"

"Not quite," said Chan. "Heavenly events don't occur when you need them—unless you make them for yourself." He turned to S'greela. "You know the mechanics of the aircar better than the rest of us. Could it be made to hover with no one on board, under automatic control at a pre-determined height?"

"Certainly."

"And could it be made to move with the stars, so that it would seem to be far beyond Barchan's atmosphere?"

"Probably." There was a speculative buzz from the Pipe-Rilla. "It would need some careful programming of the onboard control to simulate a sidereal reference frame, but I think it can be done."

"And could it be *shielded*, or illuminated from within, in such a way that it would appear as a natural stellar or planetary phenomenon to the sensors of a Morgan Construct?"

"Possibly." The other three team members waited in polite but baffled silence. "But to what avail?" said S'greela at last.

"As a lure. We already know the terrain around the Simmie habitat, in detail. We know the topography—what would be visible over a particular route. If we plan the movement of the aircar, over several nights, so that a continued view of the car calls for a particular path to be followed, away from the shore of Dreamsea—"

"—a difficult inverse problem of computation," said the Angel. "Given the terrain, to define plausible aircar movements that would cause a preferred path to be followed *on the ground* to ensure visibility—"

"—but exactly the sort of thing you know how to do, Angel. We lure the Simmie away from its habitat, out in the open away from all the Shellbacks. And then we'll . . ." Chan looked around at the others. They were hanging on his words. "Then we'll—then we'll *subdue* the Simmie."

Chan suddenly found that he could not bring himself to say the word *destroy* to the other three.

\*     \*     \*

The "plan" was so simple-minded and fallible
that Chan had hesitated to propose it. Its instant
acceptance by the others gave him a new understanding of the whole Stellar Group. Even the Angel, with its great intellect and supposed ability to
"think like a human," found certain human thought
patterns quite beyond it. If Esro Mondrian's worst
fears ever came true and an aggressive race appeared from the Perimeter, the defensive plans of
the Stellar Group would depend on humans alone.
Intelligent as they were, the others would be only
cannon fodder. They simply could not think in the
necessary terms.

But with suitable human direction, they could
function outstandingly. Shikari and S'greela had
done an astonishing job on the aircar. Hovering
under automatic control high above Barchan, it
now looked like a brilliant celestial visitor, stream-
ing a cometary tail (how had the two of them ever
managed *that*?) halfway across the night sky. Each
evening the apparition became brighter and more
colorful. Each evening, moving consistent with a
possible cometary orbit, it appeared to retreat farther to the north. A good view of it from the
Dreamsea shore became impossible.

The Angel had calculated the Simmie's most
probable path away from the lakeside. Chan had
examined that path and the surrounding terrain,
and decided on the best ambush point and the
roles of each pursuit team member. The Angel, too
slow in physical response to be useful during the
final moments of confrontation, had been assigned
the job of observer. It would occupy an oversight
position, to warn the other three when the Simmie
left its hideout under the shelf of rock.

The form of that warning had been the subject
of heated argument. Worried by the Simmie's intelligence and the sophistication of its sensing ap-
paratus, Chan had finally vetoed any signal that

might be intercepted and decoded. When the Simmie moved from its hideout, the Angel would transmit a single, tightly-collimated flash of light to the others, and nothing more. Chan had worried then that such a short pulse might be missed, but Shikari had reassured him. With the many thousands of eyes available in the Tinker composite, some would always be focused on the Angel's secluded position.

And now, four days after the initiation of the plan, the time for action had arrived. Shikari whistled softly to the other two. Angel had given the sign, and the Simmie was on the way. It would soon be visible, skirting the underside of a broad lip of rock. The positions of the pursuit team members had been carefully chosen. If the Simmie followed close to the path predicted for it by the Angel, each of the pursuit team members would have a clean shot at it without endangering each other; and no matter what variation on the path the Simmie might adopt, at least *two* of the team would still have a clear target.

Chan, S'greela, and Shikari sat motionless and completely silent. They were roughly ninety degrees apart on the perimeter of a circle, with the Simmie's most probable emergence point at the center. When the Simulacrum came from cover they would be less than thirty meters away from it.

Twenty seconds more. Chan froze. The latticed wing-panels of the Simmie were peeping into view above the edge of the rock. In another ten seconds the silver-blue body should be revealed. At this range it should be impossible to miss. Chan already had his weapon lined up in the correct firing position.

He had a sudden worrying thought. Would S'greela and Shikari have had the sense to prepare their weapons ahead of time? Any warning noise would be a disaster.

The Simmie moved forward into full view.

The pursuit team had agreed, there would be no signal to fire. Each team member would shoot as soon as a complete target was visible.

Chan sighted along his gun. As he did so, the gigantic bounding figure of S'greela came flying across the field of view from Chan's left. At the same moment there was an intense whirring of wings from the right, and a frenzied cloud of Tinker components filled the scene. Before Chan could press the trigger, S'greela had pounced on top of the Simmie, and their struggling forms were buried at once beneath the swarming Tinker. Suddenly all that was visible in the sights of Chan's weapon was a blue-black, writhing mound.

Chan groaned aloud—no point in silence now— and ran forward, weapon still at the ready. It was no good. He could see no more than random glimpses of the Simmie. Any shot was just as likely to kill Shikari and S'greela. He skidded to a halt by the side of the wriggling mass. As he did so, the violent movement began to subside. The Tinker components were starting to separate, layer after sticky layer. Finally S'greela was revealed, eight jointed limbs locked tightly around the body of the Simmie. When the final fluttering components of the Tinker detached, S'greela stood up. She was clutching the immobilized form of the Simmie.

The Pipe-Rilla looked at Chan apologetically. "I am sorry. That was not a planned action. But as soon as I realized that I would not be able to discharge my weapon, I also realized that it was my full responsibility to incapacitate the Simulacrum. Fortunately, Angel and I had discussed a procedure for such an eventuality—but I did not expect to employ it."

"Nor did we," said Shikari hoarsely. The Tinker

was still in the process of re-assembly, and not quite ready for speech. "But we also found ourselves unable to fire. We thought that by swarming we could overcome the Simulacrum. We were probably wrong, but luckily S'greela had already accomplished the task for us."

"Not so!" The Pipe-Rilla shook her head, in a human gesture that she had learned from Chan. "I had *not* succeeded. Without the assistance of Shikari's swarm I could not have gained full control. But now"—to Chan's horror S'greela placed the Simmie gently on the ground, where it lay looking at them with luminous compound eyes—"now there is no danger. I have taken its weapons away." She held out an array of armaments, each one capable of atomizing the whole pursuit team. "Here they are. The Simulacrum is disarmed. Chan, what should we do now?"

Chan raised his gun and pointed it at the Simmie. A moment later he lowered it hopelessly. What he would have done readily to a dangerous enemy, he could never do to the helpless and unarmed creature on the ground in front of him. He felt ready to laugh hysterically. Shikari and S'greela had done just the opposite of what he had directed them to do—and now they calmly asked him what they ought to do next!

*What should we do now?* The perfect question. He turned to the Simmie, studying it more closely. Without the formidable arsenal of weapons, it looked delicate—almost fragile. One of the wing panels had been injured in the scuffle, and was trailing painfully along the ground. The glowing eyes stared at him steadily, intelligently, waiting docilely for Chan to decide its fate.

"Can you understand me?" Chan said abruptly.

The Simulacrum gave no answer. Chan turned helplessly to S'greela and Shikari. "It's supposed to have voice circuits, isn't it? Do you have any idea how to communicate with a Simmie?"

S'greela shook her head. "That is a situation that we never covered in any of the briefings."

"Well, *you* caught it. So *you* tell *me*, what are we going to do with it?"

"*Await our arrival.*" It was the voice of the Angel, unexpectedly breaking radio silence. "I am on the way now—and I am confident that I will be able to achieve some kind of communication."

Without consulting Chan, S'greela went bounding away across the rocky surface. Even at the Angel's best speed, they would otherwise wait half an hour for its appearance—for although the Angel would *accept* transportation assistance now, it would never ask for it. After a second, Shikari quickly dispersed and flew off after S'greela.

Chan was suddenly very much alone. He stared gloomily down at the Simulacrum. Without S'greela and Shikari, the Simmie looked a lot less harmless. If it suddenly decided the battle was not yet over, Chan wasn't at all sure what he would do.

In fact, he wasn't sure what came next in *any* circumstances.

*What in heaven's name were they going to do with this Simmie?* If they took it back to Pursuit Team Headquarters it might simply be re-cycled—put out as bait for one team after another, until one came along that was resolute or callous enough to kill it. That was a disquieting and distasteful thought. Studying the Simmie's quiet life on the Dreamsea shore for the past few days had given Chan a different perspective. The Simulacrum was no more than an Artefact, but even an Artefact might have its own joys and sorrows. Maybe it had *feelings*, dreams and desires all its own. And if *he*, a "war-mad" human, could think such thoughts, how must Shikari, S'greela, and Angel feel?

No wonder that the others could not kill the

Simmie; and no wonder that they had discussed ways to incapacitate it without harm.

Chan suddenly thought of Team Alpha. According to the pursuit team trainers, they had destroyed *their* Simulacrum. Was that true—or had they somehow found a way to let it continue its existence, in a way that no one would ever know about?

While he was still preoccupied with those disturbing thoughts, S'greela reappeared followed by the mobile cloud of Shikari. She was carrying the Angel lightly in her mid-limbs. The tall Pipe-Rilla stooped and placed her burden gently on the ground, right next to the Simulacrum. To Chan's surprise, every frond on the Angel's bulky body went at once into agitated motion. The communications unit on the Angel turned to face him.

"Before we attempt to converse with the Simulacrum," said the Angel, "we wish to congratulate you—and each other! S'greela, Shikari and I are in complete agreement. This is a wonderful day! Chan, we are a *team*."

"And what a team!" said S'greela. "Do you not agree, Chan? We have performed together *better than any of us ever dared to hope*."

"And we are still improving!" added Shikari. "We may become better yet."

"Better!" said Chan. "Do you realize that we'll have to explain all this? And do you realize—"

He stopped. The others were not listening to him.

"Yes, better," said the Angel cheerfully. *"Practice makes perfect!"*

# Chapter Twenty-Three

# ESRO MONDRIAN AND CHAN DALTON

Esro Mondrian's private briefing room was simply furnished. It contained one desk, one table, and nine chairs. Each wall was painted a subtly different color, the table was fixed in position, and every chair was precisely placed.

Chan Dalton had been brought to the room and left alone for five minutes. He was already seated when Mondrian entered. The Security Commander walked across to him and shook his hand briefly.

"Congratulations on a successful effort," he said. (*And what a change in a few weeks! Dalton grew up. He's in the boss seat, but he's tense, tight as a Linkline—better be careful.*)

The arrangement of seats and table was based on tens of thousands of psychological profiles. Visitors unsure of themselves usually took a seat near the darkest wall, or remained standing. Not Chan. He was sitting in what Mondrian thought of as the "controlling" seat, the chair from which comments and participation of others could best be emphasized or discouraged, and remarks made by someone at the desk most directly handled.

"Thank you." Chan shook hands firmly. "But your congratulations should go to our whole team.

It was a combined effort. I thank you on behalf of all four members." (*Mondrian can see right through me! And I think he knows about Barchan. But how can he?*)

Mondrian's face was white and weary, and his eyes unnaturally bright. His movements were careful and controlled as he went to sit behind the desk.

"Bad news," he said abruptly. "I'm afraid I have bad news for you." (*Dalton doesn't respond. I tell him I've got bad news, and a second later he seems relaxed again. So what is worrying him? Damn it, he's become unreadable. He's in full control of himself. And who does he remind me of? Not the features, the expression. Who?*)

Chan had stiffened for a split-second at the words "bad news," and his own thoughts had run wild. (*He knows! No, he wouldn't put it that way if he knew. Keep control. Remember what Tatty said—work with him, but never let him get an edge—or he'll own you.*)

Angel must be right, as usual. There was no way that anyone knew—*could* know—what they had done with the Simmie on Barchan. Certainly no member of the Ruby Team would talk; as Angel said, "Friendship binds, but shared guilt binds more strongly." (But Angel had never met Mondrian!)

"Bad news about our team?" asked Chan.

"No. Bad news from Travancore." (*And why did he jump to the conclusion that bad news must be news about the Ruby Team? Why not some other news completely?*)

"Travancore. What's happening on Travancore?" Chan's focus shifted at once, to a concern for Leah and her team. For the first time, Mondrian saw a chance to control the meeting.

"The planet is in total quarantine by the Anabasis. The Mattin Link access sequence for the ship in orbit around Travancore is now held only in the

Anabasis data bank." Mondrian hesitated. "I'm sorry, but there is no way of making this less painful to you. The Morgan Construct on Travancore is more dangerous than we realized. *Team Alpha has been destroyed.*"

Chan slowly straightened in his chair. "Leah?—"

Mondrian shook his head slowly. "Leah is dead. *All* the Team Alpha members are dead."

Chan shivered. He closed his eyes, leaned forward, and put his hands to his face. Mondrian had the control he needed.

"Tell me everything," Chan said softly.

Mondrian had batteries of recording equipment monitoring Chan's every word and movement; but their traces would not be available to him for hours. (*He had to review those records later—fatigue must be decreasing his own concentration, and Chan seemed to have other preoccupations. Meanwhile, he had to maintain the edge. How should he present recent events on Travancore?*)

"I will tell you what I have," he said at last. "It is not much. We obtained only limited information after Team Alpha descended to the planet. We know they decided to explore a set of shafts that lead down through the vegetation to the true surface. We also know that they encountered Nimrod— the code name given by Team Alpha to the Morgan Construct on Travancore. We *suspect* that the team then disobeyed instructions and attempted to establish communication with the Construct, rather than at once destroying it." (*Another reaction now. A definite tightening of Chan's facial expression, after the natural response of shock and horror. Look at that more closely, too, when the recordings of the session were available for analysis.*) "It was a fatal mistake for Team Alpha. The monitoring equipment in our orbital survey vessel obtained one brief sequence involving the Construct, then nothing. No video, no audio, no vital signs telemetry from any of the team members. And we are sure that the equipment was working correctly."

While Mondrian was talking, Chan's mind suddenly spun away on its own miserable journey. He was finally reacting fully to the shocking news. *Leah dead. Dead, dead, dead. Leah dead, Leah is dead* ... The words ran continuously through his brain, while other fragments of memory and new analysis flew past in a blizzard of disconnected thoughts ... *The happy time in the Gallimaufries, an endless succession of carefree hours and days.* (All the briefings had emphasized that each Tinker, Pipe-Rilla, and Angel was different, as different as individual human beings. So each pursuit team would also be unique in composition and behavior.) ... *The visit she had made to Horus, when he believed that she had come to take him away and save him from the dreaded Stimulator sessions ... he had cried for hours when she left.* (But despite that individuality, Team Alpha and the Ruby Team sounded closer in their response patterns than anyone had dreamed. Chan's other team members had found themselves unable to destroy their Simulacrum. It was still living happily by the Dreamsea, establishing its own complex relationship with the Shellbacks. Angel had even told the Simmie how to confuse survey sensors, so that a re-discovery would not occur.) ... *But the Morgan Construct was more dangerous than the Artefact. It had killed poor Leah, destroyed her, down some doomed tunnel below the vegetation surface of Travancore. Did she have time to think of Chan, to say any of her goodbyes? Had her end been painless and quick, or was it filled with agony and the knowledge of death?* (If Team Alpha had failed in the final moment of confrontation, surely his team would do no better. But Leah's failure and death would not relieve the Ruby Team of their responsibility. They would still be obliged to pursue a Morgan Construct and attempt to destroy it. Was that even *possible*? Maybe the Constructs were as Livia Morgan had imagined them, indestructible . . .)

Chan realized that Mondrian was staring at him intensely. The other man was swaying slowly from side to side as though he was about to topple over. Was he as exhausted as he looked? How long since Mondrian had received the news from Travancore, and how long since he had slept? But the look in his eyes was as fierce as ever.

"Did you hear me?" said Mondrian sharply. "Livia Morgan had plans to build other capabilities into some of her Constructs—including Nimrod. The evidence from Travancore suggests that she succeeded. Nimrod can generate an electrical field that disturbs the perceptions of wholly organic brains. The Construct itself is not affected by the field."

Mondrian paused. Before they went any farther, he had to be sure that Chan Dalton *believed* what he was being told. From his expression, Chan was again reasserting his independence. It was proving to be a difficult meeting. (*Maybe Luther Brachis had the right bull-headed approach. Forget the Morgan Construct, to hell with Travancore. Waste the whole planet, blame the Constructs for the act, and to hell with the Stellar Group's worries. But Brachis didn't give a damn about the Constructs. He didn't realize Mondrian's need. . . .*)

Mondrian forced his weary brain back into the present.

"—future plans?" Chan was asking. "What could the field do? Make us unable to move, or unable to think?"

"Not according to its original design." Mondrian switched to a less forceful tone, inviting Chan's understanding and cooperation. "The field was supposed to aid a Construct in escaping from danger. It would induce delusions in organic brains—make a creature see things that are not there, or imagine situations with no reality, while the Construct moved out of danger. But Nimrod could use it as an offensive weapon."

"And the defense against it?" (*The Ruby Team must be next in line for Travancore! Why else would Mondrian be talking this way. Go to Travancore, then, destroy Nimrod, and avenge Leah! Vengeance was purely a human concept—that's why Mondrian was so low-key now. He needed Chan's help to lead the others on the Ruby Team to destructive action. Well, as far as Nimrod was concerned, Mondrian didn't need to worry about that. Chan was ready.*)

Mondrian was shaking his head firmly. "There is no defense—except attack or flight. The field is a short-range effect. If events begin to make no sense to you, run. If you see things that could not possibly be on Travancore, destroy them without hesitation. And remember, *all* the Morgan Constructs are highly intelligent. Nimrod is no exception." (*And don't let me forget it, either.*)

"Flee, or fight." Chan nodded. "I hear you. What about the other team members?" (*He needs me. And he's badly scared of something. But what can it be? He has Nimrod already quarantined on Travancore; it can't possibly get away unless we bring it to space ourselves.*)

"I am relying on you to make these points to them." Mondrian rubbed his hand across his eyes. "So now, let's talk logistics. You will have twenty-four hours to prepare and rest, then your Link to the quarantine ship at Travancore will take place. The Ruby Team members will descend at once to the surface. There will be no return permitted until the Q-ship receives suitable signals and arranges for pick-up. Those signals will be very specific. We cannot risk a Q-ship's exposure to Nimrod."

"Who decides when the signal is safe for a planetary pick-up?"

Mondrian rose to his feet, came around the desk, and stood directly in front of Chan. "I do. I will be there personally, with a small selected group from the Anabasis. There can be no more important use of our time." He hesitated, then reached out and took Chan by the shoulders. "Remember your mission. If the destruction of Nimrod depends on your actions alone, do not hesitate. Do not wait for the approval of your companions. Shoot at once—and shoot to kill."

It had been a meeting typical of Esro Mondrian's conduct of business: short, and of few words. Less than twenty minutes had elapsed since Chan's arrival at Mondrian's office, and now he was outside again, mentally battered and drained. The real encounter had not been conducted verbally. It had occurred several levels deeper, in the relentless sparring and jockeying for psychological position.

Chan stood for a moment outside the door of Mondrian's briefing room, then staggered away along the corridor towards the Link Entrance. He was wrecked. He felt as though he had suffered an hour on the Tolkov Stimulator, then been kept sleepless for a week.

It would have cheered him considerably to know that Esro Mondrian was in no better shape.

# Chapter Twenty-Four

# TRAVANCORE

*Travancore from five thousand kilometers: a dream world; a soft-edged emerald ball, its colors muted by the deep atmosphere, its outlines touched with a misty impressionist palette. Peaceful. Beautiful. Relaxing.*

*Too* relaxing. Chan took a deep breath, stared gloomily down at the endless jungle, and wondered how he was going to shake the utopian calm of the rest of the team. With S'greela saying that Travancore reminded her of Pipe-Rilla abstract paintings, and Shikari babbling of misty mornings on Mercantor, how would Chan ever get through to ruffle their complacency? They sometimes referred to him as the junior member of the team— S'greela was ninety Earth-years old, and Angel much more than that—but in some ways *they* were the babies.

He turned to the other three. "How does it look to you now?"

They were preparing to enter the landing capsule, ready to leave the massive safety of the Q-ship and begin their spiralling descent to Travancore's surface.

"Magnificent!" S'greela spoke first, her voice bubbling enthusiasm. "A beautiful world. We are looking forward to seeing it more closely."

Chan felt ready to reach out and shake her. "Look, how many times do I have to say it? Don't judge by what you *see*. Team Alpha was destroyed down there. If we're not careful, the same thing could happen to us."

The other three exchanged looks—smug looks, Chan was sure of it. "Ah, but it won't happen to us," said Shikari confidently. "We are sure that Team Alpha was composed of beings of exceptional talent and intelligence—the selection process would assure it. But they could not have been a complete *team*, as we are a team."

There it was in a nutshell. Nothing that Chan said could make any difference to the others' opinions. They had gone in a few days from a general diffidence to an unshakable conviction that together they could face any situation—and win!

It was hard to dispute some of their logic. After the first awkward beginnings they had made steady progress, to the point where Chan could now read complicated messages from a single wave of Angel's side fronds, a ripple in Shikari's base, or one head movement from S'greela.

But that was only a small part of the story. The other three had not seen Leah's message to Chan. She too had spoken of the extraordinary level of communication enjoyed by Team Alpha. And that team had failed!

There were other problems, too, that Chan had so far not mentioned to the others. He had blackout periods, when he could not recall where he had been, what he had been doing, or what had been said. The attacks came without warning, and lasted anything from a few minutes to several hours. So far they had hit only in leisure spells, when he was relaxing with the other team members. But there was no guarantee they would not come at other more critical times—even during their coming clash with Nimrod. He had secretly asked Kubo Flammarion over a Link connection from the Q-ship, might there be after-effects of the Tolkov Stimulator treatments? He had received only a bemused shrug as answer. No one knew enough about the Stimulator to predict side-effects of a successful treatment.

Chan wondered if he ought to tell the others what was happening to him—at the very least it might knock a few holes in the solid wall of self-confidence they were displaying. Just look at them now! They were staring down at the approaching orb of Travancore with all the cheerful curiosity of vacationing visitors.

*One more try.*

"Look here, we must get one thing into our brains or we're all in real trouble. No matter what it looks like, *a Simmie is not a Morgan Construct.* A Simmie is less well armed and less murderous. I know we handled the Simulacrum on Barchan— but this job will be ten times harder."

"And we are far more of a unit than we were then," replied S'greela. (She sounded cheerful, of course—and she *was* cheerful; Chan could read her mood very well.) "Chan, it is normally the role of a Pipe-Rilla to be the principal worrier in a group. But I feel quite at ease. We are a *team*!"

And that was it. They would not budge.

They seemed to believe they were heading for some clean, rational confrontation down on Travancore. Even the destruction of Nimrod, if they thought of it at all, was imagined as brief and orderly. Maybe the actual video scene, where Team Alpha was blasted or burned to extinction, would have made them think differently. Chan hated the idea of viewing that murderous encounter, but it would drag the other team members to some understanding of what a meeting with Nimrod could really do to them.

Unfortunately, there was no record of that event. The final video in the Anabasis files showed Nimrod drifting peacefully down along the shaft towards the waiting Team Alpha. The Construct did not look belligerent, or particularly powerful. But it was. Suppose that the members of Team Alpha had lingered on, horribly wounded, for hours or days?

The Ruby Team had reviewed every transmission from Team Alpha to the Anabasis. Those complete sound and video records were now tucked away in the Angel's capacious memory, available for recall and analysis in a fraction of a second. Shikari had also performed a planet-wide microwave survey of Travancore from the Q-ship. The Angel had used that survey, plus the records from Team Alpha, to pinpoint a dozen areas on the planet where Nimrod might be located.

Chan looked at them excitedly. He thought that one site near Travancore's equator showed a slightly brighter point of light on the radar range. Might it be solid metal there? Nimrod ought to be the only metallic component on the planet's surface. But the signal was strongly damped by the planet's dense vegetation.

"What do you think, Angel? Isn't that point where we're most likely to find Nimrod?"

There was a slow and irritating wave of midfronds—the Angel's equivalent of skeptical laughter. "*It is a capital mistake to theorize before one has data,*" said Angel at last. And that was all the answer that Chan could get.

While Chan brooded over the microwave records, S'greela and Shikari had done their own analysis of Team Alpha's descent into the surface shafts. They had concluded that Travancore's light gravity would make the tunnels independently navigable by the Angel, provided a lift pack was strapped around its tubby mid-section. That would leave S'greela with better mobility.

Their finding was the only positive result that Chan could see from two whole days of analysis. He drew a reluctant conclusion. They could look at Travancore from high orbit *forever*, and never know significantly more about it than they knew now. Like it or not, they had to get on with it and go down to the surface.

Before they entered the landing capsule, Chan gave the others one more warning. "Make sure you have *everything* that you'll need on Travancore before we leave the quarantine ship. The Anabasis is terrified of Nimrod, even if you're not. They know the full powers of a Morgan Construct. We won't be allowed back on board the quarantine ship unless we can *prove* that we've destroyed Nimrod. And the burden of that proof will be on us. They won't even make drop-shipments to us from orbit, unless it's clear that the shipments couldn't be useful to Nimrod if things go wrong. Understand?"

The others gestured their assent. "We will return carrying our shields, or on them," said Angel cheerfully. Shikari gave his best human-style belly-laugh.

Chan gave up. He went to the communicator and initiated the Link sequence to Anabasis Headquarters on Ceres. Esro Mondrian and Kubo Flammarion were in the control room there.

"We're on our way," said Chan as soon as the Link connection had stabilized. "Do you have anything new to tell us?"

Mondrian nodded a greeting. "There's a slight change at our end, but it won't make any difference to what you'll be doing. The Stellar Group are insisting that the Mattin Link to the Q-ship be made *one-way* all the time that you're down on the surface of Travancore. Messages and materials from here can go to the Q-ship, but nothing can come back this way. The Stellar Group won't tolerate any chance at all that Nimrod might be able to Link out. So you won't be able to send any more messages back here—and of course no material objects can come here, either."

"That's no good! If we can't send you messages, how will you ever know we've done our job and are ready to be picked up?"

"We'll be shipping in a monitoring team of our own from here to the Q-ship. You'll be able to communicate with them." Mondrian smiled grimly. "I'll be on that team myself. So as long as Nimrod is still active, we'll be stuck in orbit around Travancore. Until you dispose of Nimrod, it's a one-way trip for all of us. We'll be with you and watching you every step of the way. Good luck, Chan."

Even across fifty-six lightyears, Chan could feel the force of Mondrian's determination. The other man was always careful to *say* that the policies were set by the Stellar Group, but Chan had no doubt who was really calling the shots. What did the rest of the Stellar Group understand about battles, quarantines, and blockades? Not a thing. Mondrian was manipulating them, defining all their actions, just as Chan was defining procedures for the Ruby Team. And Mondrian wanted to control Chan and the other team members when they were down on Travancore—why else would he come to the Q-ship?

Well, it wasn't going to happen the way that Mondrian wanted. Chan's annoyance with the other man was growing rapidly. If necessary, the team would break off every communication with the Q-ship once they were down on the surface. Mondrian wanted to face a Morgan Construct, did he? Fine. Let him do it for *himself*—the Ruby Team wouldn't be a puppet for anybody.

Chan did his best to mask his irritation; otherwise Mondrian would be certain to read it—and use it to his advantage. "We'll be on our way down within the hour," he said quietly. "Give us one Earth-week, and I hope we'll have some results."

"Take your time. *Festina lente.* And good luck."

Mondrian turned away. The display began to exhibit the rainbow fringes of a fading Link communication.

"*Festina lente?*" said Shikari.

"A piece of advice in an old Earth language. Mondrian adopted it as the motto for Boundary Security. It means *hasten slowly.*"

"I don't think that he needs to warn *us,*" said S'greela indignantly. "We will be in no hurry to get into trouble."

"*Fools rush in—*" said Angel, "Hmm. I think we are ready, Chan. Shall we begin the descent?"

Chan's analysis of the data transmitted by Team Alpha had led him to three main conclusions.

First, and worst: Team Alpha had made one big mistake: they had been careless in checking the Morgan Construct's location. Nimrod could obviously move about the planet at high speed. This time Chan would set up a system for continuous monitoring of the Construct's position.

Second, at least two life forms on Travancore might be useful to the team. They should be investigated. There was the long, legless form that lived in the shafts, and the nimble, nervous one that inhabited the deep jungle. If either one of them possessed intelligence and could be communicated with, the task of exploration might become much easier. Nimrod knew Travancore; the team did not. They desperately needed a quick guide to the features of the planet.

Third, Team Alpha had stayed together too much. No matter how well the four of them performed as a team, there were certain functions that called for individual actions.

That conclusion had produced strong protest from the other three. Shikari was particularly outraged. They were a team! They should work together! Despite all its interactions with other species, and despite the success of its own sub-assemblies on Barchan, the Tinker still found it hard to accept that *any* functions calling for intelligence might be better conducted by a group of individual units.

Chan had insisted. As long as he was in charge of finding and disposing of Nimrod, caution would predominate.

As a first part of that policy, the landing capsule did not stay with the team. It hovered briefly at one position on the planet's daylight side, while the team unloaded and inflated their balloon tent and fitted it into the upper layers of vegetation. As soon as the rest of the equipment was unloaded, the landing capsule took off again for low orbit. It would circle the planet under automatic control, monitoring the place finally picked out by the Angel as the near-certain site for Nimrod.

Once they were established in Travancore's upper jungle, S'greela was assigned a solo mission. The Pipe-Rilla was by far the strongest of the team members. She would descend the nearest shaft, seek a specimen of the long, snaky life-form, and try to bring it back to their base. According to the Angel, there should be considerable diurnal movement of Travancore's mobile life forms. Like ocean life on Earth, many forms would take advantage of daylight to feed and sun themselves in the upper levels. S'greela ought to have a good chance of finding one close to the surface.

S'greela set off, unarmed, on her mission. The others settled down for a long and nervous wait.

She returned at sunset, empty-handed and exasperated. The other three were sitting in the tent, the Angel next to Chan and Shikari spread like a thick cloak over both of them. S'greela joined them, and waited for the Tinker components to envelop her. She sighed.

"No luck?" asked Chan.

The Pipe-Rilla shook her head slowly. "It was a frustrating experience. *Many* times I saw several of the forms, but they crawled away through gaps in the walls of the shaft. Then I finally caught one—but I could not bring it here!"

"It was too strong for you?" asked Shikari. The voice funnel had formed down on the floor, by Chan's legs.

"Not exactly. I was stronger. But I was out-legged." S'greela held up three pairs of thin limbs. "It is not often that I meet a creature with more legs than I."

"But I thought that the animal you were after was *legless*!" said Chan.

"So did I," said S'greela. "Perhaps we need to re-define a leg. Each segment of its body had two gripping attachments—there were twenty-six in all. And when I took hold of the body, each one clung tight to the ribs on the tunnel wall. I could detach any of them easily enough, using two of my limbs. But I could not detach *all* of them—and I dared not use too much force for fear of harming it."

"Did it show any sign of being intelligent?" asked the Angel.

"That is what made it such a frustrating experience. All the time that I was holding the creature, it made sounds. They were very high-pitched, so although I could *hear* most of them easily enough, I had no way to *reproduce* them. I think they represent some kind of language. Finally I decided that I would release the creature and return here. It wriggled away unharmed. I suggest that tomorrow I return to the same place and Angel comes with me. Angel has the best language ability, and

the computer communicator can synthesize anything up to a hundred thousand cycles a second.
That ought to handle any signals we need." She
turned to Chan. "Do you agree? You are our leader
for these things."

Called on for a decision, Chan felt his mood
change. He had been following the conversation in
some perplexing way, understanding it almost without listening. Now he was somehow separated from
the group. He stood up, and at his feet the Tinker
stirred restlessly. Shikari also sensed the sudden
change in the group's relationship.

"I don't like that idea too well," said Chan after
a few seconds of thought. "If you want Angel to go
back down into the tunnel with you tomorrow, I
think I ought to go with you, too. I wanted you to
go on your own at first, because you are fast and
strong. But I don't want to split the team in two."

"Then you think that we should all go together?"

"I like that even less." Chan thought for another
moment. "Do you feel confident that there is no
trap—that the animals you found in the shafts are
nothing to do with Nimrod?"

"I'm sure they are not. But don't ask me to
prove it."

"Angel?"

"S'greela is almost certainly correct. I put the
probability of connection with the Morgan Construct at less than one in a hundred thousand."

"And the animal seemed harmless?"

S'greela nodded. "Despite its size, it is harmless.
All it seemed interested in doing was eating. Even
when I was trying to dislodge it from the tunnel
wall, it kept on chewing at the vegetation. It has
substantial mandibles, but it never tried to bite
me."

"Right." Chan sat down. "Tomorrow we will all
go—except Shikari."

"We do not wish to be left here alone!" The Tinker was outraged.

"I know. But listen to me for a moment. Shikari, *half* of you will go with us. Half remains here. We must leave *someone* in communication with the landing capsule, so that we can be warned if there is any action by Nimrod. And you know we can't send decent radio signals down through the vegetation—so we need some method of direct warning to the rest of the team. You're the only one who can provide that. You could send components from here, down through the shafts to join your other half, and alert the rest of us within a few minutes. I know you don't want to do it—but who else could do the job?"

Shikari did not speak, but there was a tremble through the whole mass of the composite and hundreds of components flew away to the sides of the tent. The voice funnel closed abruptly. The others could all read the signs. The Tinker was very upset.

"Come on, Shikari," said S'greela. "Chan is right. This is the only way we can explore and still be safe. Cheer up. It will be for only a little while."

*"Divide and conquer,"* said the Angel consolingly.

The voice funnel remained closed. But the components slowly came back to the assembly, and Shikari flattened to form a low and miserable heap around the other team members.

The Angel had used its mobility pack before, but only for a few minutes of limited practice. With the pack strapped now around its blue-green midsection, the Angel had made a few tentative back-and-forth movements. Then suddenly it was darting off on a complex three-dimensional pattern of zigzags, planing rapidly across the uneven uppermost layer of the vegetation.

"Stop playing around, Angel," said Chan through his communications pack. "We have to go."

More and more he felt like the disciplinarian of the group, the one who always had to say no and enforce the unpleasant rules. The others didn't seem to worry at all! Was that perhaps the general relationship of humans to the rest of the Stellar Group species? If so, Chan had certainly never heard it expressed that way before.

The Angel came skimming and diving back to the side of the tent, executing a final mid-air roll and loop before landing. The others were all ready and waiting. As they set out for the shaft, one part of Shikari bade a solemn farewell to the half who would stay behind. The Tinker explained to Chan that although there were seldom more than a quarter of the total number of components in the body of the composite at any one time, they were always *there*, available to attach whenever they were needed. The physical separation into two major pieces would be a unique and unpleasant event.

"Imagine going off on a trip without your legs," Shikari protested. "Or Angel being without the Chassel-rose! Well, it's like that for us, but it's much *worse*."

But once they were on their way, the Tinker soon seemed to be in excellent spirits. A steady two-way stream of individual components followed them as they descended the tunnel, providing a continuous link between the two main halves of the composite. Chan wondered how long a connected chain of single Tinker components would be. With, say, ten thousand components, each ten centimeters long—it would stretch for a kilometer! But the neuronal inter-connections would be minimal. Chan doubted that a Tinker would be able to actually *think* in such a mode.

The Angel had been leading the way, gliding silently along the curved tunnel. After about twenty minutes it halted and turned back to the others. "There is something moving ahead," the Angel said softly. "I think perhaps it is time for S'greela to lead the way."

As the two quietly exchanged positions, a handful of Tinker components flew off down the tunnel. They returned just a few seconds later and reconnected to the main body.

"It is the form S'greela described," said Shikari. "A very long body with no real legs, feeding at the tunnel wall."

S'greela bounded forward. The creature saw the light that she was holding, or sensed the rapid movement. It ceased cropping the vegetation and tried to wriggle away along the shaft. S'greela pounced. When the others arrived, she had it gripped around the middle, while it clung desperately to the wall of the tunnel.

Chan walked along the full length of the body. It was enormous, with a straw-colored, multi-segment body over a meter across and better than ten meters long. Despite its size, it made no effort to attack or even to defend itself. The head was eyeless and dark-red, and equipped with a mouth big enough to bite Chan's head off. It went on eating steadily, chomping on vegetation it clipped from sprouting sections of the tunnel walls. When Chan came close, the big head turned slowly from side to side. It emitted a shrill series of squeaks and whistles, almost completely off the human audible range. The sounds came from a second broad slit set a few inches above the mouth.

The Angel advanced to Chan's side and the communicator on its mid-section gave out an experimental series of squawks and squeaks.

"It is a language, I think," said Angel. "Perhaps a primitive one. It would be logical to assume that it modulates ultra-sonic navigation signals employed in the tunnels—a natural development for creatures living mostly in the dark. But before we

can be sure we must have more samples of the
sounds. Hold it tightly now, S'greela."

The Angel moved closer to the head, reached out
a lower frond, and poked the creature gently. The
monstrous caterpillar body struggled harder for a
moment, then the head turned to face the Angel.
There was another lengthy sequence of squeaks,
this time with a different emphasis and cadence.
Angel's communication box replied with a succession of very similar sounds, gradually ascending in
pitch until they became inaudible to human ears.
The body ceased to squirm in S'greela's grasp. She
and Shikari leaned closer to follow the interaction.

Chan knew that both Tinkers and Pipe-Rillas
could hear frequencies well outside his range. He
would have to be briefed when the initial communication attempt was over. He dropped back a
pace, and looked around him at the tunnel walls.

They were close to a branch point, where the
descending shaft divided to continue as a double
descent path. He had not seen that before, or heard
of it in any of the records left by Team Alpha. It
suggested a system of pathways through Travancore's jungles more complicated than they had
realized. Chan looked again at S'greela and Shikari. They were both still engrossed in the Angel's
efforts. He strolled slowly down along the sloping
tunnel and looked out along each branch in turn.

They were not identical. One continued steadily
down towards the surface of Travancore, five kilometers below them. The other was narrower and
less steep. It curved off slowly to the left with
hardly any gradient at all. If it went on that like the
narrow corridor would provide a horizontal road-
way through the high forest. Chan took just three or
four paces along it. He did not intend to lose sight
or sound of the other team members.

After three steps he paused, very confused. There
seemed to be something like a dark mist obscuring

the more distant parts of the corridor. He shone his light, and there was no answering reflection.

Chan hesitated for a moment, then started to move back up the tunnel. Whatever it was in front of him, he was not about to face it alone. He had weapons with him—but more than those he wanted S'greela's strength, Shikari's mobility, and Angel's cool reasoning powers.

As he turned, he heard a whisper behind him. "Chan!"

He looked back. Something had stepped forward from the middle of the dark mist and stood squarely in the middle of the pathway.

It looked like a human figure. Chan shone his light again along the tunnel. He froze.

It was Leah.

Even as Chan was about to call out to her, he remembered Mondrian's warning. *Leah was dead.* What he was seeing was an illusion, something created in his mind by Nimrod.

As though to confirm his thought, the figure of Leah drifted *upwards* like a pale ghost. It hung unsupported, a couple of feet above the floor of the tunnel. The shape raised one white arm. "Chan," it said again.

"Leah! Is it you—really you?" Chan fought back the sudden urge to run forward and embrace the hovering form in front of him.

It did not seem to have heard him. Chan saw the dark-haired head move slowly from side to side. "Not now, Chan," said Leah's voice. "It would be too dangerous now. Say goodbye—but love me, Chan. Love is the secret."

Ignoring all commonsense, Chan found that he had taken another step along the tunnel. He paused, dizzy and irresolute.

The figure held up both arms urgently. "Not now, Chan. Dangerous."

She waved. The slim form stepped sharply backwards, and was swallowed up at once in the dark cloud. The apparition was gone.

Chan stood motionless, too stunned to move. At last a sudden premonition of great danger conquered his inertia. He turned and began to stagger and stumble back towards the others.

A voice inside his head was screaming at him. *"NIMROD. Nimrod is active here. A Morgan Construct can produce delusions within an organic brain—it can change what you see and hear. Get back to the others—NOW!"*

He was suddenly back in the part of the tunnel where he had left the other team members. It was totally deserted.

They were gone! To his horror and dismay, there was no sign of the rest of them. *Where was the team?* Surely they would not have left him behind and gone back up the tunnel without him. Had they fallen victim to Nimrod?

Dizzy with fear, emotion, and unanswerable questions, Chan began to run back up the tunnel, back to the sunlight, back to the doubtful safety of the tent in the upper vegetation layers. As he did so, the face and form of Leah hovered shimmering before his eyes.

Chan burst back into the tent fearing every form of disaster. At the very least, the others would be buzzing with alarm at his absence. They would be terrified, full of fearful concern and organizing themselves to go off again and search for him in the tunnels.

There was certainly a tense atmosphere in the tent. But no one seemed to care what had happened to Chan. In fact, no one even seemed to have noticed his absence! He grabbed one of S'greela's forelimbs. She turned and gave him a little nod.

"It is just as well that you have returned. We are not sure what to do next. There has been a—a bad misunderstanding with the *Coromar*." She motioned towards the side of the tent, where the great caterpillar was stretched out along the flexible wall. "That seems to be the group name that these beings give to themselves."

The creature acted quite at home in the tent. It was free to move, but making no attempt to escape. Instead, the long mouth was chomping contentedly on a great bale of vegetation.

Chan looked confusedly around him. Everything seemed very peaceful. "A bad misunderstanding?" he said at last.

"I am afraid so. It is not very smart. As soon as Angel was able to communicate well, it agreed to come along with us, provided that we would feed it when we got here." The Pipe-Rilla shook her head testily. "Really, food seems to be the only thing it cares about. Well, naturally we agreed. We have ample provisions."

"So what's the problem?" said Chan. He looked again at the peaceful and slow-moving Coromar, happily browsing. "You gave it plenty of food, didn't you?"

"Yes, *now* we have given it all it wants. But when we first arrived here, the Coromar—its name is Vayvay—did not want to wait for me to give it food."

"You mean it tried to leave?"

"Worse than that. It tried to eat Angel."

Chan looked across at the Angel, sitting motionless at the other side of the tent. The side fronds were all lying limp against the barrel-like body, and the head fronds were tightly closed. He knew the signs by now. Angel was sulking.

"Well, didn't the rest of you try to stop—"

"Of course we stopped it. All that happened was that the Coromar took a bite at Angel's midsection—one little bite."

"And *that* was quite understandable," chimed in

Shikari. The Tinker, its parts now reunited, sounded in excellent spirits. It came rustling across to Chan's side. "After all, Angel cannot deny that the Chasselrose *is* a vegetable. And the real confusion was caused by the communicator that Angel wears. Vayvay apparently assumed that the *communicator* was the intelligent being—since it was the part that had done the talking. And so Vayvay thought that all the *rest* of Angel was just a sort of mobile food supply. Perfectly natural assumption. As Angel might put it, one man's meat is another man's mid-section."

There was an outraged crackle from the Angel's communicator. "We are not amused!" it said loudly. "This is no joking matter. If I had not moved quickly, it would have been more than just one bite—"

"All right, that's enough." Chan went across and sat down wearily by the Angel's side. "Cut out the bickering and the game-playing. We've got more important problems." He ignored the Angel's protest. "You three are supposed to be part of a *pursuit team*. Remember? You're tackling the most dangerous creature in the known Universe. Now, when you looked around in the tunnels and found I was gone, didn't it even occur to you that I might be in trouble? Didn't one of you think, wait a minute now, maybe we should take a look and see what happened to Chan? —instead of just heading along back here without me."

There was an embarrassed silence. "We were preoccupied with the Coromar," said Shikari at last. "The tunnel seemed quite safe, and the part of me that had remained here was reporting no threatening movements up near the surface. There seemed no cause for worry about you."

"And you *did* return unharmed," said S'greela. "So why are you so upset? Were you afraid?"

Chan sighed. "Not as much as I should have

been. Believe it or not, but I think I encountered Nimrod down there. I'm amazed that I'm still alive to tell you about it."

He summarized his experiences in the tunnel, carefully keeping his account as factual as possible. When he was finished, there was a polite and non-committal silence. Chan looked at each of the others. He could tell they were all skeptical. The silence ended when the Angel suddenly engaged in a long exchange of shrill squeaks with the Coromar, slowly waving its topknot fronds throughout.

"Vayvay has never heard of Nimrod," the Angel said at last. "And the Coromars exist planet-wide. But they are not very intelligent, and perhaps they do not usually travel far from their usual haunts." There was another brief squeak from the Coromar, and a grunt of satisfaction from the Angel. "Vayvay also says it is very sorry that it tried to eat me."

"You can communicate that well, so quickly?" asked Chan.

"It is not a complex language. About half the words seem to concern themselves with eating or looking for food."

"Can you ask what Vayvay knows about the other species—the agile one, down in the deep forest? If the Coromars won't be able to help us, maybe the others can. And maybe they know about Nimrod."

Chan waited impatiently through another long exchange. The Angel seemed less sure this time, and several strings of sounds had to be repeated before the answer finally came: "According to Vayvay, we will obtain no help from the other creatures. They are named the *Maricore*. Vayvay was very confused by our questions, because it seems that both animals are the *same species*. The Coromar are the feeding, intelligent—keep quiet, S'greela!—stage of the life cycle. They live about twelve earth years, then encyst and undergo a complete metamorphosis. Before the change, a Coromar is apparently either asexual, or at least has no sex drives. After metamorphosis, a Coromar becomes a Maricore.

"In this stage they mate. They live only one year, they eat very little, and during their lives they actually shrink in size. According to Vayvay, they exhibit no sign of intelligence. They also have poor survival skills, so for safety they are denizens of the deep forest and never come close to the upper layers. It is one duty of the younger Coromars to descend, guard the mature Maricores, and assure their survival until they can give birth to a litter of Coromars. Without that aid, most Maricores would not even live long enough to breed." The Angel paused. "An interesting inversion of a familiar theme. *The child is father to the man,*'—but in this case that concept is almost literally true."

"What about other life-forms on Travancore?" Chan didn't want to hear Angel philosophizing. He was feeling absolutely exhausted, with a return of the dizzy feeling he had experienced in the tunnels. With Shikari warm around him, what he wanted now was sleep. "Does Vayvay know of anything else that might help us?" he said at last.

"I already asked that question. The answer is unfortunately a definite negative." The Angel had slowly extended its adventitious base stems and was beginning to creep towards the Chassel-rose's preferred rooting spot near the exit to the tent. Shikari and S'greela had already become silent, and the only noise was Vayvay's steady chewing. The fronds on top of the Angel were slowly tightening in on themselves.

"The Coromars may help a little bit, Chan," said Angel at last. "Vayvay is certainly willing to stay with us and go anywhere in exchange for food. But I am afraid that everything is really up to us. If we fail, no one else can do our work." The roots of the

Chassel-rose began to settle into the patch of dark earth that had been brought all the way from the home planet of Sellora. The Angel sighed with pleasure. "Chan, I do not know if you met Nimrod or your own mental illusion in the tunnel. But I do know this: we are as good a team as the Stellar Group will ever find. Together, we will defeat the Morgan Construct . . . or no one will."

# Chapter Twenty-Five

# EARTH

At the moment when Chan was staring incredulously at the apparition of Leah Rainbow in Travancore's abyssal tunnel, Esro Mondrian stood in a corridor in the Earth warrens. He was at the door of Tatty Snipes' apartment. Twice he had lifted his hand to insert his I.D. key, and twice he had hesitated and pulled back.

Tatty was watching him through her own hidden screen. She was puzzled. What was wrong with Mondrian? He was often thoughtful and preoccupied, but never indecisive.

At the third attempt he completed the sequence. The door opened. Mondrian stepped inside and looked thoughtfully around him. Less than a year ago this had been his favorite haven. He knew he could come here, shut out the whole solar system, and do his deepest thinking and planning. Tatty had respected his need for privacy. She knew when he was really working, when he needed relaxation. She never intruded. She had been taking Paradox shots, but even there he never saw it happen. Tatty was always infinitely discreet.

And now?

So much had changed in the past few months.

The apartment was no longer a place of peace and sanctuary. Tatty had become more independent. She had broken the Paradox habit (Shannon knows how much agony that had cost her!) and the array of little purple ampules no longer sat in each room of the apartment. She had lived through Chan's transformation in the Tolkov Stimulator. Although she would not talk about it, that experience had affected her deeply. Worst of all, Tatty had become *unpredictable*. Mondrian was no longer sure how she would react to his words, what she would say or do.

He knew the correct action; knew it instinctively. *What cannot be controlled or destroyed must be banished.* He must make a complete break with Tatty. And he could not do it.

"I have them," said Tatty, as the door closed behind him. "Shall we begin?"

Mondrian nodded. "Let's get on with it, Princess." (*That was the change in her. No words of affection or greeting. No tenderness, or loving touch. But this was not the time for his own self-indulgent feelings of nostalgia or disappointment—what came next was too important.*)

She had sensed his depressed mood. "It won't be all that bad, Esro. Think of it just as Earth sight-seeing."

"Most of it will be. But if Skrynol is right, one of those scenes may jump up and murder me."

"How will it affect you?"

"The Fr'opper doesn't know, and I certainly don't." Mondrian gestured to the phial of anesthetic spray that Tatty had prepared. "Keep that close to you, but don't let me get my hands on it. I hope that I won't even try. But Skrynol says the experience we are after is very deep—I may be willing to kill, or to die myself, before I'll let it up to the surface." He sat down on the reclining chair and leaned back in it. He nodded. "Go ahead. Any time."

Tatty taped his wrists to the chair's arm-rests. She attached the electrodes and microphones to wrists, palms, fingertips, throat, temples, and genitals. Finally she sat down where she could see both the displays and Mondrian's face.

The equipment and the recordings were all ready. Since Mondrian had given her no preferred order for the list of sites, she had made her own. She had visited the scenes of his early childhood systematically, linking around the planet in a zig-zag pattern that spanned Earth from pole to pole. At each location, as the fancy struck her she had made her own voice-over on the 3-D recordings, and added local sounds and smells.

She began with an area that sat firmly at the center of her own nightmares—maybe Mondrian shared her horror of it. The Virgin lay in what had once been the American West. It was a dumb-bell of total devastation a thousand miles long and three hundred wide. The Virgin's Breasts were at Two Strikes, in the north. Twin ten-mile craters of ground zero defined each nipple. The broad hips in the south were formed by the fused circular plain of Malcolm's Mistake. Tatty had set them down midway between the two. "The Virgin's Navel," said her quiet voice-over commentary. Then everything was silence. The Navel was the most scarred and desolate spot on Earth's surface.

In the first few years after the fusion glows began to fade, experts had made their measurements and predicted that Earth's life-forms would not return to the Virgin in less than a millennium. They had been wrong—outrageously wrong. The first seeds had germinated and were fighting the radiation in less than a generation.

And yet in some ways the experts had been vindicated. Today the Virgin teemed with its own plants and animals. But no birds sang, no bees buzzed, no coyotes howled. Life at the Virgin's Navel was abundant; but it was totally silent, and somehow it was *alien*.

The display scanned steadily across the landscape. Mondrian looked on silently while Tatty shuddered again at the scene she had recorded, at plants stunted or overblown, at misshapen animals that parodied the rest of nature.

"Did you know you can still see the outline of the Virgin from the Moon?" he said at last. "I don't think it's the color of the ground. It must be the vegetation."

His voice was calm. Tatty quietly cut short the presentation. Otherwise Mondrian would be using the anesthetic on *her*. They moved to another one of her own private hates. Mondrian recalled being taken to the Antarctic when he was a tiny child. He had unpleasant memories of it. So had Tatty. The travel guides spoke only of the bursting polar summer, with the new hybrid grains running their full course from germination to harvest in thirty days of twenty-four-hour light. Tatty had come away with different memories. Of savage winds, age-old ice, and the cruel black water lapping at the edge of the ice cap.

Her images caught the desperate haste of the short summer to perfection. Nature was racing to fill a complete cycle in a few short weeks of continuous sun. The rate of plant growth created the illusion of time-lapse photography.

Mondrian watched while the view scanned across a great flock of emperor penguins standing at the water's edge. He seemed relaxed. "If you don't like it there *now*," he said—he had seen the expression on Tatty's face—"you should have gone there in winter. Imagine the life of one of those birds. They mate when it's a hundred below. And they stand there right through the blizzards, balancing their eggs on their feet."

Tatty gave him an angry glare, and cut short the scene. Mondrian seemed almost to be enjoying himself. She moved on to Patagonia.

When Mondrian first told her what he needed, it had sounded like an impossible job—hundreds of millions of square kilometers to be surveyed. He had—as usual—persuaded her that she was wrong. She could do it easily. Although the centuries-long exodus from Earth had provided a safety-valve on population growth, it had never been quite enough. And as most of the planet gradually became more densely peopled, it became more homogeneous. It was not necessary for Tatty to make recordings of BigSyd or Ree-o-dee—in all essentials they were identical to Bosny and Delmarva Town. Mondrian's memories would not be hiding there.

The only real candidates left were the equatorial and the Antarctic reservations, plus those few other areas of Earth that were still almost uninhabited. The Kingdom of the Winds in Patagonia, where Tatty had gone next, was a good example. People *could* live there, in the bleak shadow of the Andes— but few wanted to. The west winds that blew with incessant gale force from the mountain peaks created a *psychological* vacuum. Every generation the area was settled, and a few years later abandoned.

It was not the source of Mondrian's trauma. He looked at the bleak landscape without enjoyment, but also without terror. Tatty studied his blank face, and moved the display forward again.

She had little hope for the next location. She had never visited the great African game preserve before, but what she had seen on her recent trip had captivated her completely.

This had been mankind's first home. Earth's remaining large herbivores and carnivores still lived here in their natural conditions, grazing and prowl-

ing as they had for millions of years. Tatty had
wandered on foot for many hours, savoring and
recording the sights, sounds and smells of the open
plain. She loved to watch the herds break and
wheel across the dusty ground, responding to real
or imagined danger. This was lightyears away from
life in the Gallimaufries—farther from her experience than even the confinement center on Horus.

Mondrian did not seem to share her pleasure.
He looked bored now, lolling back in his chair.
Tatty suspected that he was thinking as usual of
Travancore and the ongoing hunt for the Morgan
Constructs. He appeared half asleep as the images
roamed back and forth over the rolling ground.
Tatty was ready to move on to another region. But
she recalled that one of her own favorite memories
was captured in a shot that would come in just a
few seconds time.

"Look at this," she said. "Ngorongoro Crater—
isn't it spectacular!" The display moved to show a
majestic volcanic peak, with the evening sun behind it. The broad, red face of Sol was already on
the horizon, sinking rapidly to an equatorial sunset. The great plain of Serengeti and the reservation lay beyond, purple and tan in the fading light.

"Beautiful!" said Tatty. She turned to Mondrian
for the first time. He was stretched rigid in the
chair, limbs trembling. She saw the protruding
eyes and the straining, purple-veined countenance,
and grabbed for the anesthetic.

It was not necessary. Before she could pick up
the phial, Esro Mondrian had uttered a low, hopeless groan. While she watched, the spasm ended.
He gave a great sigh, and sank low into the chair's
supporting folds. His eyes slowly closed; he slept.

Tatty stood alone within the little circle of light,
wondering what she was getting herself into. Her
heart was racing. She was perspiring profusely. At

this depth in the basement warrens, the circulators and coolers could do no more than make the air marginally breathable.

She held the light higher and stared around her. This should be the correct place—*had* to be the right place. But she was nowhere. She was standing halfway down a long, deserted corridor, with no side branches visible in front or behind her.

Tatty bent her head to check the Tracker reading again. It was showing exactly zero, and the little red trace arrow had disappeared. Useless! And just a couple of hours ago she had imagined that she was being so cunning!

Mondrian had taken a full half-hour to emerge from his trance—half an hour during which his pulse had slowed almost to zero and she had been forced to inject adrenalin and heart-stimulants. Then, as soon as he was fully conscious, he would not wait to recuperate. He had grabbed the final recording she had made and struggled to the apartment door. He looked like a corpse. He would not say where he was going—not even when she unprecedentedly lost her temper and shouted and stormed at him. He would say only that he had to leave at once. And it was so obvious where he was going! He was heading for another meeting with Skrynol, to see if the Fr'opper could finally exorcise Mondrian's hidden compulsion.

And then, in the middle of their argument, Tatty had thought of the Tracker. It was still in Mondrian's light travel bag, the only luggage he ever carried down to Earth with him. She quietly removed it while he was re-setting his I.D. key, and stuck it away out of sight. If Mondrian wouldn't ask her help with the Fr'opper, he might get it anyway! Wherever he chose to go, she would be able to track him down.

But now she felt like a complete fool. When he left the apartment, she had followed, careful always to keep a long, long way behind. As soon as the Tracker's moving arrow stopped, she stopped also and fixed its setting. The Tracker showed that Mondrian stayed in one place for over an hour, then began to retrace his steps. Tatty hid well out of the way until he had gone past her, then started forward again towards his first destination.

Forward—to nowhere!

Or was there some trick to using the Tracker, some technique that she had failed to understand?

She peered around her again at the walls of the corridor. It was high and narrow, no more than a couple of meters across, and lined with tremendous air-pipes. According to Luther Brachis, a Tracker was accurate to better than twenty feet— which was simply impossible. The tunnel extended monotonously away in both directions for ten times that.

She looked down again at the Tracker, bringing the hand lamp that she was carrying closer to the instrument. As she did so, that light was suddenly plucked *upwards* from her hand, and instantly extinguished.

Tatty screamed. She had been plunged into absolute darkness. She moved backwards, until she struck the hard wall of the tunnel. She grabbed at the warm padded air-pipes, the only familiar thing she could find. As she did so, something caught her around her waist. She was lifted easily off her feet, up and backwards *over* the pipes, and placed down again gently on a soft surface. Thick bindings snapped firmly into place around her wrists and ankles.

"Don't bother to scream again or struggle," said a cheerful voice high above her. "Both those actions would be quite pointless, and you are in no danger."

Tatty drew in a deep breath, ready to scream anyway. Uselessness was not the point! Before she could begin a dim red glow filled the air and gave her the first faint view of her surroundings. Instead of screaming, she gasped, and gawked around her. She was in a Thiefhole!

The secret rooms were almost a legend, mysterious places scattered all through the deepest part of the basement warrens. They were supposed to be the Scavvies' sanctuary, the final hiding places for hunted criminals and contract-breakers. Their locations were passed on only by word of mouth, from one generation to the next. The Earth authorities denied their very existence.

Tatty had never been in one before, but she recognized it from the descriptions. This one had been tucked away behind the main airpipes. The room was ten meters long and five meters high, but less than two across. There was a crude tap to the basement power lines in one corner, feeding the glowing red fluorescents that threw their murky light across the long room. Another tap to the airpipes provided just enough circulation for breathable air. On the far wall stood an ancient food synthesizer, not apparently in current use. Next to it was a long painted screen of dull silver, hiding part of the room from her.

"You know where you are?" said the same gentle voice.

"Yes. In a Thiefhole."

"Exactly. With your permission, now." The light suddenly snapped off again, and a few seconds later Tatty felt chilly metal electrodes attach to her body. She shivered.

"This is for my convenience, not for your discomfort," said the voice cheerfully. "You will not notice them after a few moments. And do not worry, the lights will return shortly."

"Who are you?"

There was a high-pitched laugh. "Now, Tatty

Snipes, you know very well who I am—otherwise you would not be here."

"You are Skrynol—the Fr'opper who has been treating Esro Mondrian."

"Of course I am."

"Well, you may call it treatment if you want to." The lights had come on again, and there was no sign of Skrynol. Tatty's courage was returning, and with it her anger. "But you've been making him *worse*—far worse." Her voice was bitter. "God, how I wish I had never even mentioned your name to him."

"Even if you had not, someone else would have brought him to me." Skrynol sounded calm behind the silver screen, unmoved by Tatty's anger. "It was absolutely necessary that I should meet him, and treat him. Tatty Snipes, how well do you know Esro Mondrian?"

"As well as anyone!" And then some tone in Skrynol's voice made Tatty sit back, and think about that question objectively, for the first time in her life. "He is the most intelligent and hard-working man I have ever met," she said at last. "But often I wonder if I know him at all. Sometimes he seems like a monster, somebody who cares for no one and will use anyone and anything for his own purposes."

"And yet you have been his lover—and you still work for him."

"I know." Tatty laughed harshly. "You don't need to tell me what a fool I am. I sometimes think that Esro Mondrian can persuade anyone to do anything if he tries hard enough."

"You know him very well," said Skrynol softly. "But there is perhaps one thing that you do not realize. Esro Mondrian is in some ways the most valuable person in the solar system, yes. *But he is also the most dangerous human in the Stellar Group.*

Mondrian is the reason—the single reason—that I am here, on Earth."

Tatty saw a monstrous shadow cast from behind the screen. Then the worse reality appeared, a gigantic stooped body shuffling forward on multiple jointed legs. She shrank back, as the Pipe-Rilla came slowly toward her and squatted down at her side.

"I have decided that I will gain nothing by concealing the truth from you." Skrynol's voice was gentle and comforting. "I know that you are afraid, but there is no reason for that fear. I will not harm you. Come, Tatty, you know that we are a peaceful species. We need your help."

Tatty shuddered. "I can't possibly help you," she said faintly.

"I think you can." The tall body stretched upwards, almost to the ceiling of the room. "Let me at least tell you the problem. The Stellar Group has been studying the human species for centuries— just as intensively as humans have been studying the other Group members. In each generation, we identify humans whom we believe have unique powers for good or evil. Those people are of course closely monitored. Our record of behavior prediction on this is excellent—but occasionally we find an anomaly, a human being who is a total enigma. Such an individual must be watched even more closely, so that the potential for harm is not realized. In the case of Esro Mondrian, we have the extreme—a human of exceptional abilities, whose own compulsions are so strong that they might lead to the destruction of the whole Stellar Group."

"No." Tatty shook her head. "I don't understand him fully, but I know this much about Esro: he *likes* aliens."

"That makes no difference. Mondrian is not a simple man, like Luther Brachis, who hates all aliens in a direct and predictable way. Mondrian actually likes all the Stellar Group species. But in some ways he cannot *tolerate* us, because at a deep level he cannot stand the threat that the whole Stellar Group represents to him. Brachis we can handle; Mondrian is a mystery. In such a situation, the human reaction might be to destroy both those individuals. But that avenue is not open to our kind. We realized that we must *help* Mondrian. We must find the source of his destructive drive, and banish it. And you can assist us."

"No." Tatty was shaking her head blindly. "You don't understand. I've tried to help Esro—God knows how I've tried. But I can't do it. I can never *reach* him, never really get through to him."

"If it makes you feel any better, nor can I—and my whole life and training has been for just such a purpose. But in my sessions with Mondrian I have discovered at least one thing. He is torn apart by conflicting drives. The capacity to love is drowned by fear. He is obsessed with the Morgan Constructs. Do you know why?"

"They must be destroyed. He has been working night and day on plans for the Anabasis."

"True. But did you know that Mondrian himself *originated* the whole program for the Morgan Constructs? It began at his initiative. When the project went out of control, the Constructs became a terrible danger to everything in the Stellar Group— the worst danger since the Group came into existence. The ambassadors reluctantly reached a decision that the Constructs were too dangerous. They had to be destroyed. I cannot argue with that decision. But I know that the decision to leave Esro Mondrian in charge of that operation was a terrible mistake. He *needs* the Morgan Constructs."

"But he's trying to destroy them!"

"Are you sure? Suppose that he has been choosing the pursuit teams so that they will try to control the Constructs rather than killing them. I can assure you, Mondrian will never allow the Constructs to disappear if there is any way at all to save them. He needs them in some terribly urgent way, far below the rational levels of his brain. And *that* need stems from the early experience that we have been probing. Thanks to you, we know now that it happened in Africa. But it is so deep-rooted that I despair of ever reaching it. The *nature* of his torment is still hidden within him, and I am still unable to pry it loose. So the compulsion continues— unless you can help me to bring its cause to light."

"I already told you I can do nothing with Esro."

"Perhaps. But permit me one more question. Mondrian has used you, over and over. You are a logical person, with a considerable intellect. Why do you continue to help him whenever he asks for help, knowing that he will probably use you again?"

Tatty found that she was crying. Salt tears and sweat were trickling down her cheeks and nose onto her upper lip. "*I don't know.* I suppose it's because—because I have no one else. Without Esro, I have nothing, no one. He is all that I have."

"Possibly." Skrynol's voice was still gentle and rational. A soft forelimb came forward to gently stroke her hair and dab delicately at the tears on Tatty's cheeks. "But there is another explanation. Suppose that you stay because you realize that *you* are all that *he* has? If not you, to whom would he turn for comfort and aid? You know that in some ways you still love him. Ask yourself, do you want to see Mondrian destroyed?"

"I don't know." Tatty tried to sit up, but the bindings still restrained her. "Many times I've cursed him and wished he were dead."

"But you have always relented. If you really want to help Mondrian—and it may be impossible, or already too late—then you should do the one thing that might make his treatment more effective: *Remove your support for him.* Tell him that it is all over, that he cannot come back to you and expect to be forgiven. Tell him that he has *no one!*"

Skrynol reached forward and unclasped the soft bindings that were holding Tatty. She sat up, and leaned forward to put her face wearily to her open hands. "And suppose I did that? What good would it do him?"

"Perhaps nothing. But perhaps it would give us that little window, the chink of vulnerability that I need to treat him successfully. I am looking for any sort of lever that might make him more open to me. Emotional dependency might be that lever."

Skrynol helped Tatty to her feet, and she stood there leaning weakly against the giant figure. "Do you think that it will succeed?"

"No. I believe that it will almost certainly fail." The Pipe-Rilla gave a human shrug of her narrow body. "But I have no choice. It is the only course left to me, and so—it must be attempted." Skrynol reached down with a soft and fleshy appendage, and took Tatty's hand. "Come. Let me lead you away from here. If you are to have a confrontation with Mondrian, you must do it before he prepares to leave Earth again."

Tatty took a last look around the Thiefhole, before she was led away into stygian darkness. "Suppose I were to tell someone else of this meeting? Would it destroy your plans?"

"Tell anyone you like," said Skrynol cheerfully. She chuckled. "Tatty Snipes, who would ever believe you?"

# Chapter Twenty-Six

# TROUBLE WITH MINISIMS

It was late when Luther Brachis and Godiva Lomberd returned to their living quarters on the ninety-fourth level of Ceres. They had been on a much-postponed trip to the outer shell. Luther had guided them on a sight-seeing tour there, pausing at the high-mag viewing ports so that he could point out to Godiva the many worlds of the system and the scattered stars of the Stellar Group, far beyond.

Brachis had known them all since early childhood. It was a shock to find that Godiva, raised in the dark runs of the Gallimaufries, had only the vaguest idea of planets, moons, and stars. She had never heard of Oberon Station. She seemed to think that all the asteroids were as developed and as cosmopolitan as Ceres. And she had absolutely no idea of distances—to Godiva, the Oort Harvester was as near (or as far) as the remote Angel's world of Sellora.

She had laughed at Brachis's protests. "What does it *matter*, Luther, how far away they are? You can get to all of them in nothing flat using the Mattin Link."

"Yes, you can. But the *distance* ..." Brachis

stopped. Godiva was uniquely Godiva. Time and space meant nothing to her. She had quietly taken his hand and led him on, drifting and dreaming through the endless outer corridors of the planetoid.

A one-hour tour had turned into a lazy day and evening. The corridor was deserted when Brachis paused at the apartment door and made a thorough inspection of the settings. All the seals were unbroken. There had been no callers. He carefully slid back the door and they went through into the hallway.

The advent of Godiva into Luther Brachis's life had changed it completely. When she came up from Earth, he had abandoned his barracks-style one-room living area in favor of a luxury apartment. The main living-room, dining area and kitchen were off the hall to the left, the bedroom, bathrooms and study to the right.

"Hungry?" asked Luther.

Godiva shook her head. She yawned, stretched, and slipped off her light wrap. She gave Brachis a smile of sleepy suggestion, dropped her bag on the hall table, and went quietly through the bedroom to the bathroom.

Luther Brachis slipped off his uniform, then sat on the broad bed and pulled off his boots. Naked, he walked thoughtfully through into the study, and sat down at the communication terminal. He switched the system on to make his usual evening check for messages.

There was a sudden high-pitched hissing sound, then a sting of intense pain like a hornet's sting on his left cheek. Brachis saw a little puff of vaporized blood blossom below his left eye. He shouted at the pain and jerked upright. As he did so there was a second sting by his right nostril, and another puff of bright red.

He jumped to his feet. The hiss that went with each blow seemed to come from the top of the display unit. Brachis looked that way, at the same time as three more jolts hit him, one on the chin and the other two above his right eyebrow. He saw four miniature figures crouched behind the front lip of the display. Each mannikin was no more than an inch and a half high—the maximum height permitted for an Adestis simulacrum. Each carried a long weapon trained on Brachis's face.

They were after his eyes! Brachis covered his face with his left forearm, just in time to block three more shots. He started to sweep his right arm across the top of the display, but before he could complete the action a hail of shots from the rear made him shudder with pain and spin around. On the desk at the far side of the room, hiding behind a jumble of data cubes, he saw another group of small figures. At the same time a new rattle of shots sounded from his left, and explosive projectiles riddled his left cheek, arm, and hip with thumbnail-sized craters.

Brachis roared with pain, and ran across the room. He used both arms to shield his eyes. If they blinded him he was finished. Halfway to the door he felt another hail of shots in his groin and belly. They had switched their target to his genitals.

Brachis stopped and spun around again. The attack was obviously well-organized and orchestrated. They would have allowed for his natural urge to run for the only door. While he hesitated another half dozen hits stung his neck and face. They were flaying him, systematically denuding his body of flesh with a hail of tiny shells.

He had to find time to think. Brachis dived to his left, rolled across the floor, and came to his feet close to the wall. He smashed his hand at the lighting panel. The door through to the hall was closed, and the study plunged at once into total darkness. The spatter of shots went on, but the miniature simulacra no longer had a target. Brachis had dropped to the floor again. He was shuffling on hands and knees to the other side of the room. He could track the minisims by the uvarovite-garnet glint of their crystalline green eyes, and he saw them moving about in confusion. But he knew it was a temporary respite. The attackers must have allowed for darkness, too. It would be only a few seconds before they used some other light source.

He felt his way back to the display and slapped the Emergency switch on the communications panel. It would bring help—but far too late. Another half minute of those explosions and he would be a sightless, skinless eunuch. He was filled with a new terror. Suppose that Godiva came out of the bathroom and wandered into the study? A shout to keep her out now might have exactly the opposite effect.

A moment after he hit the Emergency switch there was a bright point of orange light on the other side of the room. It was a flare, ignited near the door. That was where the maximum cross-fire would have hit him if he had tried to escape that way. There was another crackle from the miniature weapons, and another hail of blows across his body. He dived, rolled again, and came up near the desk. Before the attackers there could focus on their new target, he hit a sunken wall panel with the palm of his left hand.

The fire system activated in a fraction of a second. Jets of high-pressure water and emulsifier criss-crossed the room from walls and ceiling, and the loud warning tones of a gong sounded through the apartment. Emergency low-power wall lights filled the study with a sickly green glow.

The spray filled the room. All the shots were instantly silenced.

Luther Brachis hurtled across the study, a soaking, bloodied figure. He ran first for the place where the shots had been most dense. Water hit him from all sides, stinging his wounds. He welcomed it.

Brachis headed for the major emplacement of minisims. They were struggling to stand amid the bombardment of water droplets and foam. Ignoring the pain in his hands, Brachis smashed them flat and crushed them between finger and thumb, one after another.

The study door slid open and Godiva suddenly appeared. She was naked except for a pair of gauzy briefs. "Luther!" she screamed.

He ignored her and ran back across the room, a scarlet Nemesis that left bloody, puddled footprints behind him. The first group to attack had been swept by the deluge from the top of the display to the study floor. They were there now, hurrying for cover through a quarter-inch flood of water. Brachis stamped them under his naked feet, wincing as the hard figures cut into his soft soles.

He moved on, smashing and devastating with bare hands and feet.

By the time that help arrived the battle was over. The sprinkler system was off. The room was cleared of simulacra. Godiva had taken Luther through to the bedroom to apply antiseptics, healing creams, and surrogate skin. He lay naked on the bed, his face and belly an eroded mass of raw wounds connected by shreds of loose hanging skin. He swore continuously as Godiva began to smooth on the yellow synthetic flesh. The emergency service began to clean up the mess, suctioning the apartment clean and dry. They were still in the middle of it when Esro Mondrian arrived.

Godiva had finished the left side of Brachis and was telling him to turn over. He was ignoring her, talking furiously on a handset.

"They don't know one damned thing," he said to Mondrian by way of greeting. "Adestis Headquarters is closed for the night. Until tomorrow morning they can't even tell me if any simulacra are missing, never mind how many." He winced as Godiva began to patch skin onto the ball of his thumb.

"Does it matter how many?" Mondrian held up one of the flattened simulacra. "No one but Adestis has anything like this. In fact, I didn't know they had anything so big. What are they for?"

"The biggest game—scorpions, crustaceans. They'll operate under water, but lucky for me they were never designed to handle a rainstorm."

"What about the headsets? The real question isn't the Adestis minisims—it's who was handling them."

"They have no idea of that, either." Brachis touched his fingers tenderly to his face, feeling a one-centimeter crater on his cheek. "But I know the answer. It's that bastard's Artefacts again—it has to be."

Mondrian was studying Brachis's pitted and furrowed skin closely. "I'm sure you're right." He smiled grimly. "Someday, Luther, you'll have to tell me just what you did to earn such undying enmity from Fujitsu that he'd try to give you more craters than the surface of Callisto."

"I underestimated him," said Brachis gruffly. "And for that, I deserve what I've been getting."

"I told you to get everything locked up tight. What went wrong?"

"I did my best. But it proves a point. I tell every Trainee for Survey Basic Training—it's the things you *don't* expect that always get you. I'd set up the apartment so that nothing at all could get in through the door, or burrow through the walls, floors, or ceilings. I'd checked that the sniffer systems would automatically blow the whistle if anything poisonous or radioactive was blown in as gas or particles through the air ducts. What I *didn't* expect was that something smart and dangerous could actually *march* in through the air ducts. The openings are only a couple of centimeters wide."

"Perfect size." Mondrian looked again at the simulacrum he was holding, and then at Brachis's battered body. "I'm surprised to see how much firepower one of these things can carry. You don't need to hit *that* hard even for scorpions."

"They were carrying the absolute top of the weapons line—it took two minisims to handle a few of the guns. It's the sort of thing that Adestis normally gives only to a group that's inexperienced and scared shitless. One shell might not actually *stop* a scorpion, but it would slow it down long enough for everyone to get the hell out."

"Last time we met, you told me you thought you had located every Artefact left by the Margrave. It's obvious that you were too optimistic." Mondrian nodded his head towards the door. "But if you thought you were safe, why all that security system?"

"At her insistence." Brachis jerked his thumb at Godiva. "*I* thought I'd caught every one, out on Hyperion. Now I'll have to start over."

Godiva had been totally absorbed in her work on Luther Brachis, too busy to worry about clothes in the first few frantic minutes. She had carefully patched skin onto every one of his wounds. Now, directly introduced into the conversation for the first time, she seemed to become aware of her own near-nude condition. She gave Mondrian a worried smile, kissed Brachis quickly on the lips, and headed back to the bathroom. "Ten minutes," she said. "To dry my hair and put on a robe. Please don't let him get into any more trouble while I'm gone, Esro."

Her departure created a sudden silence in their conversation. Mention of the Margrave's Artefacts carried Brachis's mind back to the silent surface of

Hyperion. After he had arranged for payment of the volatiles, seven items had been delivered to him from storage. The crew who brought them had gone back at once to the Deep Vault. They had no idea—or perhaps they suspected only too well— what Brachis intended to do with his purchase. They did not look back.

The logical thing to do was to flashfire the seven containers at once and leave the airless surface of Saturn's moon with minimal delay. Some dreadful driving streak of curiosity had forced Brachis to open and thaw them.

The first four varied in appearance, but they were recognizably in the image of the Margrave. Two more looked younger, clean-shaven, and fatter, but the DNA match was far too good for coincidence. They were Artefacts derived directly from Fujitsu. When the eight-million-degree flame passed over them, they were all gone in a eyeblink flash of purple light.

It was the seventh and final box, where the identification had been poorest, that lingered on in Luther Brachis's memory. The box held a young girl in her early teens. Naked, clear-skinned and fair, she was barely past puberty. And she was beautiful. When those young breasts and slender hips matured into full womanhood, she would be like a younger Godiva Lomberd.

The container gave her complete identification and DNA sequence. It differed from the Fujitsu line in every significant detail. She was the oldest daughter of a *bend sinister* royal line on Earth, now long extinct. Whoever had committed her to the Deep Vault of Hyperion had purchased a perpetual endowment. For four hundred years she had lain there in frozen silence, dreaming of whatever phantom shadows might flee through a brain held at the temperature of liquid helium. Left to herself now on the surface, she would waken and die on the barren, airless wilderness of Hyperion.

Brachis had made no contingent plans for his purchase from the Deep Vault. Even if he were desperate to do so, it was impossible to save her. He groaned, cursed, and looked hopelessly around him at the black-shadowed plain. At last he shuddered in his suit, breathed deeply, and raised the torch. Subnuclear fire reached out to caress the pale young body. As it consumed her bare breast, Brachis fancied that she opened dark-blue eyes and stared up at his face. . . .

"Luther!" Mondrian was snapping his fingers in front of him. "Here, break out of it. I think we have to let the medics take a good look at you. Just how much blood did you lose tonight? The water could have sluiced a couple of liters down the drain."

Brachis shook his head slowly. "I'll be all right, Esro. But I'm wondering where I go from here. Do you realize what would have happened if Godiva had come through with me to the study instead of heading for the bathroom? She doesn't have our training in survival. I don't know if I could have saved her."

"Do you want to send her back to Earth for a while, until we can handle the Fujitsu Artefacts?"

"She wouldn't go. And I don't think Earth would be safe, either." Brachis rubbed at the thickened synthetic skin on the back of his hands. It was beginning to itch furiously as the chemical bonding became complete. "Anyway, we made a lifetime contract. I promised Godiva that we'd stay together if she wanted it. But I can't *protect* her. The next hit could come from anywhere. Poisoned food, assassins, sabotaged transport equipment, faulty airlocks—anything."

"You found yourself a genius, Luther. Fujitsu

has been two steps ahead of us all the time. But I
have a suggestion for you."

Mondrian's voice was casual. Luther Brachis had
known him far too long to be deceived by that.
"No hidden agendas today, Esro," he said wearily,
as Godiva appeared again from the bathroom. "I'm
too battered to argue."

She had dried her blond hair and re-styled it in
an ancient form, so that it hung over her forehead
and partly hid one eye. She drifted across to
Brachis, looked closely at his wounds, and finally
nodded. Without speaking she sat down at his side.
A short tunic left her legs and arms bare, and her
skin glowed rosy from a vigorous toweling.

Mondrian was studying the two of them closely.
"We all have hidden agendas, Luther," he said at
last. "But in this case I think you and I share one."

"Persuade me."

Mondrian smiled. Luther Brachis was quoting
one of Mondrian's own favorite lines. "I'll try. Luther, where's the safest place in the Universe for
you and Godiva? Not here, that's for sure. And
certainly not down on Earth. Fujitsu's Artefacts
could be anywhere. But there's one place that even
the Margrave won't be able to get to: the Q-ship.
The Mattin Link coordinates to the quarantine ship
orbiting Travancore are only known to three people in the Universe: you, me, and Kubo."

"It's a safe place, I'll buy that." Brachis was
frowning. "But you already told me it's a one-way
trip until the pursuit team is finished. Suppose
they take years to do their job? Anybody who goes
to Travancore will be stuck on the Q-ship until
they die of boredom."

"There are worse things." Mondrian surveyed
the other man's battered body. "Stay here, and it's
certainly not boredom you'll die of. Anyway, if you
go to Travancore I don't think we have to worry
about being there too long. The crisis I told you

about is on the way—for good or bad, I can't tell. Within a couple of days we must be out there, ready for action. My original idea was to take Kubo with me, and leave you in charge here. But it makes sense to switch that—Kubo's a rock, but you're a devil of a lot better in a crisis. He can stay here, give information out to nobody, and send us anything we need through the Link."

"What about Godiva?"

"She'd be safe here. Once you're out of the way she's in no danger."

"No. Definitely not." Godiva looked up and stared calmly at Mondrian. "If Luther goes, I go."

"All right." Mondrian shrugged. "That's not a big issue. And if you both want to go, I can't stop it."

"I won't go without her." Brachis tried to smile, and produced only a pained grimace as the skin on his face stretched. "And you're right, you can't stop us. You don't outrank me on that."

"I know." Mondrian looked again at Brachis, noting the new pallor around the eyes. "Luther, you look terrible. We have to get you to a doctor. And then you can tell me what you promised Lotos Sheldrake, to fix it so you'd have equal rank with me in the Anabasis. No, don't try to talk now. You look ready to fall over."

"I'll manage." Brachis stood up with difficulty. He shook his head when Godiva tried to help him, and hobbled away to the bathroom. She sighed.

"Stubborn!" She sat down opposite Mondrian, studying his face and the set of his body. "And so are you. What's happened to you, Esro? You look nearly as bad as Luther."

"I'm fine."

"You're not." She stared into his eyes. "Are you taking Tatty with you to Travancore?"

"No," he said shortly. Then his control failed, and he had to ask the question. "Godiva, what for

Shannon's sake made you suddenly ask about *Tatty*? I didn't even mention her name."

She gave him a satisfied smile. "I know. You didn't need to. Esro, if I understand anything at all in this world, I understand men's emotions. You're *radiating* your misery. Have you two been fighting?"

He shook his head. "Nothing that dignified." He smiled, but it did not reach his eyes. They remained bleak and haunted. "There was no fight. Tatty dumped me, that's all. We were down in her apartment on Earth. I wanted her to come back here to Ceres with me. She refused. She says she'll never see me again."

Godiva took Mondrian's hands in both of hers. He felt a subcutaneous tingle of electricity all along his forearms—what Tatty had once dubbed "The Godiva Effect."

"I'm sorry, Esro." She seemed ready to say more, then checked herself. "Let me find out what's keeping Luther. Maybe he needs help."

She stood up and went across to the bathroom. She avoided looking again at Mondrian. Decency demanded that such pain and desperation be permitted privacy.

# Chapter Twenty-Seven

# SEEKING THE MORGAN CONSTRUCT

Pulling useful information out of Vayvay was almost impossible. The Coromar seemed to have only two interests in life: finding food, and eating it. Chan had sat through three weary hours of the Angel's painstaking questioning and re-questioning, then given up. He lacked the Angel's infinite patience. He wandered out to the lip of the tent, where S'greela and Shikari were basking in the mid-morning sunlight.

"How can Angel *stand* it?" he said. "Every question repeated ten times, and nothing to show at the end."

"Talking to Vayvay?" The Pipe-Rilla nudged Shikari with one hind-limb. As usual, the Tinker was trying to creep up into a lumpy heap around their legs. "I admit, Vayvay is not easily mistaken for a genius. In fact, I myself asked Angel that same question: how was he able to be so patient with such an idiot?"

"But he didn't answer you."

"Certainly he did. Angel indicated that communication with human beings had provided a sufficient base of prior experience."

Chan glared, and decided not to react. He had

noticed an odd phenomenon. S'greela, and even the Angel, seemed to be picking up the Tinker's sense of humor. In fact, they were all beginning to sound like each other! It was harder all the time to tell who made a remark simply from its content, or the way in which it was phrased. Was *he* starting to sound like the rest of them, too?

Chan thought not. In some ways, he now felt like the outsider of the group. When he had rushed back yesterday to tell what had happened to him in the tunnels, the others had listened patiently enough; but he knew they had rejected what he said, almost without considering it.

That idea was full of disturbing possibilities. The Angel insisted that the Morgan Construct had not moved. It was still sitting in the same location, far from them. And Mondrian had told him that Nimrod's mental disturbance field was *short-range*. Close contact would be needed for it to have any effect. So if his bewildering encounter had *not* been with Nimrod, there was one other clear possibility: Chan was going crazy.

There was other evidence for that. After Chan arrived back at the camp the previous night he had almost no memory of the rest of the evening. He recalled sitting in a close, compact group, listening to Angel talk to the Coromar. And that was *all* he remembered ... until he had awakened today under the outspread mantle of the Tinker Composite.

Suppose that his fears and confusion were affecting his judgment? He had to discover the source of his delusions, before the others were put in danger by them. And that urgency made him want to proceed too fast with a continued exploration and hunt for Nimrod. *Festina lente*—hasten slowly. It was hard to do. When the others were in favor of rapid action, it was more than he could manage to slow them down.

And the rest were absolutely raring to go. The Angel was sure he could simplify the task of stalking Nimrod through Travancore's vertical forests. "There is a grid of horizontal tunnels," Angel said, "down close to the true surface of the planet. It is not so well maintained as the tunnels higher up—the Coromar look after those much better, because they are their primary feeding grounds—but it is adequate for our needs. We can move close to Nimrod, and minimize the chance of our detection."

"Better than coming down from above?" asked S'greela.

"Safer," said Chan. "Nimrod will sense our presence easily if we try to move straight down through the vegetation, but the surface of a planet helps to confuse the signal return for a Construct's sensors. We'll use the horizontal tunnels. Will Vayvay lead us himself?"

"I don't know." The Angel turned again to the Coromar. A few seconds of squeaks produced a shake of the Angel's top fronds and a sigh. "Why did I ask? I could have predicted the answer. Vayvay will take us to a safe distance from Nimrod—provided that we guarantee plenty of food as payment. Vayvay asks us, how close to Nimrod do we wish to approach?"

Chan thought for a moment. The others patiently waited, as they always did for anything to do with tactics. Finally he shook his head. "I've no idea. For all I know—and my experience yesterday supports it—Nimrod could be aware of us all the time. How else do you explain what happened to me down in the shaft?"

There was another noncommittal silence. Chan began to feel annoyed all over again. The other three were being diplomatic—but they still didn't believe him! When he had filed his report on the incident and sent it back to the Q-ship, the other three had been annoyingly passive. They did not comment on or add to what he had sent—and *that* was unusual for such an opinionated group.

"All right," he said at last. "Let's approach the problem from the opposite end. How close is Vayvay *willing* to approach Nimrod?"

There was another sequence of bat-squeaks from Angel's communicator, dipping and weaving in and out of Chan's audible range. Then a reply from the Coromar, and finally a longer exchange.

The Angel turned back to face Chan. "I am sorry. The answer was quickly given, but it was not in terms that are easily translated to human notation. Truly, there is no fixed reply. There is only a complicated balance of food offered against risks taken. And the distance unit itself is not a constant—it is measured in *browsing-distance-days*, and it is location-dependent. But in oversimplified terms, Vayvay will go as close as we want—provided we will guarantee sufficient amounts of food."

"Can you negotiate something specific?"

"It is already done. Primitive as he is, Vayvay seems to understand the barter principle perfectly. For three thousand kilos of synthesized high-protein vegetable matter, he will take us to within two kilometers of Nimrod's most likely current position—which I now assign a probability of 0.98 of being correct."

The Angel was still leaving the most difficult decision to Chan. How close to Nimrod dare they go, before they descended to the solid surface of Travancore? Traveling above the vegetation could be done in the aircar, but surface travel would be on foot.

Chan decided they would go down a shaft that was one full day's march from the location of the Morgan Construct. Say, twenty kilometers. The Angel at once read out an appropriate set of coordinates for shaft entry. Chan confirmed them. And having made his decision, he at once felt very uncomfortable with it. He no longer had any faith in his own judgment. Since the previous night he had been feeling strange—light-headed and feverish. Was he actually getting *sick*? His immune system had been boosted at the beginning of pursuit team training, supposedly enough to handle any micro-organisms on Barchan or Travancore. But that could be an optimistic assumption. Maybe yesterday's hallucinations were the result of some definite physical ailment, nothing to do with either Nimrod or madness. It was a comforting thought.

With a decision made on where to descend, every member of the team wanted to go ahead without more delay. The aircar was recalled from its hovering orbit. It took all their efforts to lift Vayvay aboard, then they set off around the great bulge of Travancore. The car skimmed fast over the billowing waves of vegetation rising and falling below them like an endless turbulent sea. Before they entered the chosen black tunnel, S'greela sent the capsule again into orbit. If they returned safely it would be easy enough to use it to take them back to the Q-ship. If not . . .

Still no problem, said S'greela. The capsule's parking orbit was low. Atmospheric drag would bring it to re-entry and burn-up within a couple of weeks. Whatever happened, Nimrod would not gain access to the Q-ship and the Mattin Link.

Everyone except Vayvay was subdued when they entered the shaft. Chan felt particularly low. As they gradually lost the sunlight, his mood sank to match the shadowed green gloom of Travancore's lower forests. The spiraling path went on forever, down and down and down. It took much longer than Chan expected, because Vayvay always wanted to stop and browse. The Coromar could be persuaded to keep going only by constant bribes from the supplies they were carrying. The final ten-meter drop from the end of the shaft to the surface took place in a close and dripping darkness. It felt like an irreversible step.

Chan was claustrophobic, filled with unnamed dreads. The surface of Travancore would be a terrible place to die; lightless, silent, stifling. He could not get Leah out of his mind. Had her fatal encounter with Nimrod taken place close to here—perhaps only a few kilometers from where he stood?

He could not remember. Somehow he did not want to ask the Angel to check the official records.

The floor of the vertical jungle was flat, spongy, and damp. Nothing grew here except the immense boles of the megatrees, scores of meters across at their base. Long trailers of creeper hung down between the trunks. Faintly phosphorescent, their intertwined filaments hindered the path of any traveler moving on the natural surface. After a few seconds of squeaking and searching, Vayvay set off determinedly across the forest floor, burrowing his way through the resistant creepers. Within five minutes they were walking into an arched structure and shining their lights around them on the yellow-brown walls of a primitive roofed chamber.

"Home of the Maricore," said the Angel. "Apparently they do a poor job of maintenance. Vayvay says we should not expect to see any Maricore. They'll keep well out of our way."

They set off along one of four tunnels that ran out from the chamber. It was only just wide enough for Vayvay, who led the way. The Coromar kept stopping for some reason. S'greela had to prod hard at his rear end to start him going again. Chan was last in the group. He was still in a black mood. When they met Nimrod, they had to act at once to disable or destroy the Construct. There could be none of the do-as-I-choose behavior that had occurred on Barchan. It had worked then, but only by blind luck. But how could he be sure that

Shikari and the others would follow his instructions this time, when the critical moment came?

It was a time for fears, memories, and introspection. No one spoke. Chan, hot and sweating, observed their surroundings with the floating, feverish intensity of his worst nightmares. After another interminable hour Vayvay halted again at a branch point in the surface network. No amount of prodding by S'greela would move him. Angel moved forward, and determined that the Coromar would now go no farther. They were within two kilometers of Nimrod's presumed location. They would meet the Morgan Construct if they continued along the broader branch ahead of them, ignoring any side branches.

"Vayvay asks, do we want him to wait here with the supplies?" said Angel. "He is willing to do so."

"Tell him to wait here for one day," said Chan. "If we're not back by then, everything is his."

They paused for a final check of equipment. Each team member carried weapons, but after their experience on Barchan Chan was convinced that for the Angel and Shikari it was a waste of time. It took forever for either of them to aim and fire. Chan wondered again about the way the pursuit teams were being used by the Anabasis. Now that he had met Brachis and Mondrian, it seemed more in keeping with their mentality to lob a bomb in from orbit. They might blow away a few cubic miles of Travancore along with the Morgan Construct, but there would be no risk to them. Maybe they had already proposed it—and been vetoed at once by the Stellar Group.

Chan had run out of time for speculation. Conscious that this was the time of greatest danger, he moved to lead the group. S'greela came next, holding a pencil light high above Chan to cast a narrow, bobbing beam along the roofed corridor. Vayvay gave a squeak of farewell, returned by the

Angel, and then everything was silent. The loudest sound in the tunnel was the whispering flutter of the Tinker's many wings.

Less than a kilometer to go. Chan found he was staring hard at the darkness, trying somehow to see beyond the point illuminated by S'greela's ghostly light-beam. There was nothing but the silent yellow-brown tunnel, stretching out forever in front of them.

And suddenly, that tunnel was ending. The walls simply stopped, and the group was moving out to an open area of the jungle floor. As Chan paused to decide what to do next, three things happened. There was an insane burst of metallic clicking from Angel's communicator, rising to a supersonic scream of activity. Shikari seemed to burst apart, instantly filling the air around Chan with the whirling swarm of components. At the same moment, the light held by S'greela jerked high into the air, and then abruptly went out.

Chan froze. The darkness around him was absolute. He turned to go back towards the others. Before he could move he was gripped tightly around the waist and whipped off his feet. Something immensely strong spun him dizzily end-over-end, then violently *threw* him, outwards and upwards.

He was flying. Chan curled into a ball and protected his skull with his arms. At any moment he expected to smash into one of the huge and solid tree trunks. At the speed he was moving the impact would be fatal.

The collision never came. Instead his wild flight was ended by a soft material that stretched indefinitely as it absorbed his momentum. Within a fraction of a second he was slowed to a halt, then dropped. He prepared for impact with the spongy jungle surface, but that too never came. Instead he found himself suspended in mid-air, wriggling against the restraint of a rubbery, fine-meshed net.

Chan had never felt so helpless. He had lost his weapon. The net offered no resistance, nothing to struggle against. And even if he could get out of it, he was still in total darkness. He would have no idea where to go or what to do next. While he was reaching that conclusion, the problem was solved. The whole net was suddenly moving, carried along at high speed in a horizontal direction. Something big was moving in front of him. He could hear the rustling sound of its rapid passage through the soft, hanging creepers.

It was another short trip. Within half a minute they stopped, and Chan was lowered gently to the ground. The net loosened and rolled him out of it. He came to rest face-down on the fibrous, damp floor of the forest. He sat up, but he was still dizzy and still in darkness. After a few moments he clambered slowly to his feet and took a couple of hesitant steps forward, holding his arms out in front of him. His groping fingers met the furry bole of one of the giant megatrees. He moved forward gratefully to rest against it. Then he turned, sat down, and leaned his back on the trunk, staring out into the darkness.

There was another faint whisper of movement in front of him. Something there, drifting towards him, almost silent on the spongy surface. Chan felt a new horror. A warm, dry grip closed on his outstretched hands and secured his wrists. He struggled, and tried to stand up. It was impossible. More fastenings curled around his ankles and waist. He was moved, gently but irresistibly, until he was lying flat on his back on the soft jungle floor. Thick and velvety bonds pinioned him there, holding him securely at wrist and ankles.

He waited. And finally came the event that told him he was doomed. Either Nimrod had taken him, or he had crossed the border between sanity and total madness.

"Chan," said a musical voice, whispering no more than a couple of feet away from his face. "Ah, Chan."

It was a voice he had known forever, a voice he had always loved. It was the voice of Leah Rainbow.

# Chapter Twenty-Eight

# NIMROD

Night in the Gallimaufries had been dark, but there were always at least a few lights. And there had always been plenty of noise—usually too much. Nothing in Chan's experience had prepared him for the close, silent, and enveloping darkness of Travancore's abyssal forest. One second after Leah's voice had spoken, it had gone forever. Its reality had drained away into anechoic blackness. Chan longed desperately for another sound, for a single spark of light.

Finally the gentle voice came again, near enough to reach out and touch. "Chan?"

"Who are you—*what* are you?" Chan's own voice sounded thin and remote, not generated within his own body.

"Relax. Lie quiet. There is something that cannot be explained. It can only be experienced. Do not struggle."

There was a steady rustling, just inches away. Something touched his arm, then moved along to his chest. He tensed, and tried to writhe away from it.

"Don't be afraid." The words were breathed close to his face. He felt the warmth on his cheek and

347

his neck. Something—surely it was a human hand—was placed on his stomach. His clothing was being loosened, opened to expose his unprotected body.

Chan struggled against his bonds. He could cry out—but what good would that do? If any of the other team members had been able to help him, they would already be calling to him, asking him where he was. The forest around him was as still as the grave.

His body was now totally bare and defenseless. The same soft touch came again on his chest, then moved lower. There was a curious little laugh in the darkness above him.

"And how many times did I dream of doing this? But never quite like this."

Chan's chest was being touched by soft lips. Fingers drifted gently across his midriff, then wandered slowly down his abdomen. He felt chilled with fear, and feverish to the bone. The caresses became more intimate. It seemed impossible to Chan that in his present circumstances he could become physically aroused, no matter what the stimulus. But it was happening.

In total darkness the succubus above him slid its body close. Chan felt naked flesh pressed close against him. He could not move, either to resist or encourage the embrace. There was a faint, pleasant fragrance in the air, filling his nostrils. As he became more aroused he felt an urgent breath along his neck, and an increased warmth in the body moving above him.

"Relax," said Leah's voice. "This is right, Chan. Don't resist it."

Beyond any conscious control, his own body was responding urgently. His silent partner was moving more strongly above him, lifting him and drawing him irresistibly towards a climax. The breathing was harsher and deeper. Chan shivered and shuddered, straining upwards against the unseen pressure.

The critical moment came. His partner groaned, flexed powerfully against him, and cried out. "NOW!"

There was a roar in the darkness, and a whirr of invisible wings. Chan, in the very moment of most intense ecstasy, was inundated by a pressing clutch of tiny bodies. They covered his eyes and ears. They blocked his mouth completely. Chan, still straining upwards in climax, could not breathe.

*He was strangling.*

He writhed and groaned, feeling the agony of asphyxiation deep in his chest. He shuddered to draw a last breath. *Dying. Dying on Travancore.*

And then, quite suddenly, he could breathe again—even though his nose and mouth were still covered.

He could see. But not through his own eyes.

He could hear. But not with his ears.

Chan had left his body, sucked away into a no-man's-land of non-identity. With one set of ears he listened to the ultrasonic song of jungle creatures, sending their calls at frequencies far beyond human senses. With one set of eyes he studied the thermal infra-red emissions from the forest floor, tracing the faint darker swaths that told of water beneath the surface. He could see there also the bright thermal outline of two coupled humans, the smaller one kneeling astride the other. He was filled with multiple sensations . . . the soft forest floor on his back, the exciting touch of a body (*Chan's* body) against him. Closeness. Warmth of touching.

"YOU ARE WITH US NOW," said a voice inside him. "NOW YOU WILL UNDERSTAND. DO NOT *LISTEN*—FEEL FOR US."

For a few moments there was an intolerable level of input. Chan was drowning in the torrent of emotions and memories. Then the data stream steadied, and the pattern cleared. He was swimming in the middle of a single consciousness, but at the same time he could sense individual presences within it. There was an Angel, coolly observing and smiling at him with its mind (and it was not the Angel that Chan had known). There was a Tinker, the master-linkage, pressing all around and urgently serving as central conduit for the whole group. It was not Shikari. The great, gentle form of a Pipe-Rilla crouched close to his head. He could feel the love and kindness glowing out from it. But it was not S'greela.

And there was Leah.

It *was* Leah. No matter what illusions a Morgan Construct might be able to create within a human mind, he was sure it could not do this. The mind that he was touching was filled with memories that only he and Leah shared. He could see her, still sitting astride his body, smiling down at him. She was naked—and he was seeing her through the Angel's infra-red sensors.

Tinker components were fluttering at his bonds, loosening them. Leah squatted back on her haunches, then took Chan's hands and helped him to sit up. She was smiling lovingly at him. As she moved close and kissed him on the mouth he felt a new stirring of multiple pleasures—from himself, from her, from all the other members of the group.

She put her arm around him, and they hugged each other close.

"I thought you were dead," he whispered. "They said you met the Construct, and it destroyed you. I thought Nimrod had killed all of you. I should have had more faith in you."

"NIMROD?" There was a feeling in Chan's body like an intense electric shock, and then a burst of incredulous laughter, directly in his mind. "CHAN, DON'T YOU UNDERSTAND YET? NIMROD COULD NOT KILL US—*WE ARE NIMROD*!"

No more words came to Chan, but there was an intense and mind-stretching torrent of emotions, images, and information. Everything rushed in at once, an explosion of parallel input data.

*Image.*

. . . The Alpha Team, frozen in position. Above them, floating down with all weapons ports open, the Morgan Construct. Too late to flee. This was the moment for Ishmael to fall apart into independent components, for Angel to stand useless and immobilized, for S'glya to seek futile escape in the terrified bounding leaps of a Pipe-Rilla.

Instead, the group coalesced.

*Fusion.*

Every component of Ishmael flew to a new position, embedding Leah, S'glya and the Angel within the Tinker's extended body. There was a split-second of total chaos, and then everything fused. Instead of a pursuit team of individual members, there was a single mentality.

*Image.*

The Morgan Construct was set to obliterate everything. Weapons ports were glowing with impending energy release, and the air shimmered with electromagnetic field defenses. Ionization surrounded the broad head and latticed wings with a violet-blue nimbus.

*Evaluation.*

The Mentality calmly formulated and reviewed a score of options. It held within it the whole logical structure of the Morgan Construct, together with the separate and combined capabilities of the pursuit team.

*Selection and application.*

The preferred option was chosen. A loud, pure tone emerged from the communications box on the Angel's midsection. At the same time a second note, precisely placed in pitch, phase, and volume, came as an octaves-higher scream from S'glya. In a fraction of a second the wing panels on the Morgan Construct began to vibrate.

*Commentary.*

("RESONANCES IN INORGANIC CONTROL CIRCUITS. DESIGN DEFICIENCY. VULNERABILITY TO ACOUSTIC/ELECTROMAGNETIC COUPLING EFFECTS. NO SAFETY LEVEL SHORT OF OVERLOAD AND TEMPORARY SHUTDOWN.")

*Image.*

The whole Construct started to shake. A crackling sound emerged from the body cavity, followed by a violent series of random jerks. There was an agonized twisting of the latticed wings. "TEMPORARY OVERLOAD," said the accompanying voice. With a final shudder the Construct's frame locked into one distorted position. It floated silently down to the forest floor. A dozen Tinker components at once flew across and entered the Construct body cavity.

*Commentary.*

("NO PERMANENT DAMAGE. NOW IS THE TIME TO IMMOBILIZE FOR MORE SYSTEMATIC ANALYSIS OF CONSTRUCT MENTAL PROCESSES.")

*Image.*

The crisis was over. Beside the quiet form of the Morgan Construct, the pursuit team members huddled closer together. Every external sensory input was damped to lowest levels. It was a time of wonder, time for the Mentality to look inward and learn more of its own nature and function. The group lay motionless on the forest floor.

*Commentary.*

("WE BECAME NIMROD. IT WAS OUR CHOSEN NAME, WE *ARE* NIMROD. THAT IS ALL THAT CAN BE GIVEN SAFELY, TO ONE WHO IS NOT A UNION. BREAKPOINT.")

It was over. Chan felt awareness of his surroundings slowly bleed back into his mind. The information transfer had been as intense as a bolt of lightning, and as short-lived. He and Leah were still holding each other close, her lips touching his cheek. He took in a long, shivering breath, and looked around him. Nothing. The forest was still dark. A trace of remembered after-image seen through the Angel's sensors told him where the other members had been. There was a brief whirring of tiny wings, then he was once more in the darkness, holding Leah alone.

Chan sighed. He lay back on the damp floor, Leah at his side. His brain felt jellied and contused, with all the familiar agony of a bad session on the Tolkov Stimulator. For a few minutes he lay there in silence, content to feel but not to think.

"Chan." It was Leah's voice again, whispering in his ear. She had turned, so that they touched each other from breast to thighs. "I know it was terrifying for you. But you would not have merged willingly. The only way we knew was to take you when emotion ran strongest. I want you to know that I am sorry it had to happen that way."

Chan sighed, and did not speak.

"I'm sorry, Chan," said Leah again, after another few moments of silence. "If you feel betrayed, I promise you that I will never again use lovemaking in that way. Please don't feel that you were *used*—we only wanted to pull you quickly to partial union."

"Who are you?" asked Chan huskily.

"Me?" The voice in the darkness sounded puzzled. "I am Leah."

"Not any more. You are Nimrod. What happened to the Leah that I knew?"

"Ah." There was an indrawn breath of comprehension. "Nimrod, yes. But truly, Chan, I am Leah. I am no less Leah than I ever was. I am *more*. Now I am part of Nimrod, too."

"*My* Leah has gone."

"Rubbish!" Leah's voice lost a good part of her patient concern. "What are you talking about, gone?

I'm *me*—the same Leah as always." She slapped her hand down flat on his chest, and he jerked at the unexpected blow.

"Gone, have I?" she went on, leaning over him. "You think I'm some sort of illusion? Just part of something else? Well, you're dead wrong. You seem to imagine I'm just like a cell in your body, with no separate existence of its own. I'm not. I still think, I still breathe, I still laugh, and I still love. Get that into your thick skull, Chan Dalton. When I first touched you today, that was *me*—not Nimrod." She banged his chest again. "You've got rocks in your head. Did you feel any less, when you were merged?"

Chan shook his head slowly in the darkness. It was Leah next to him, no doubt about that. Beating him up just like the old days. "Not less. Different."

"Different, and *more*." She left his side, and moved to a standing position. "Remember this, Chan. I love you, and I'm still all that I ever was. You have to know one other thing. We humans are the most difficult element. We're the pacing factor for everything. So when it happens, *relax*. You're halfway there now, thanks to what happened here."

"Halfway where?"

"You'll see. It was all necessary." There was a final soft kiss on his cheek. "And it was fun, too. As good as I'd dreamed it would be."

Chan heard the pad of footsteps moving away across the soft forest carpet. Before he could do more than sit up, a faint light came bobbing towards him, weaving through the creepers. It was S'greela. The Pipe-Rilla was moving rapidly, with the tubby form of Angel tucked under two arms. The dark nimbus of Shikari breezed along close behind.

"You are safe?" said the Pipe-Rilla.

Chan was about to reply—apparently the fact

that he was scraped by creepers, wet, wild-eyed, and nearly naked was a matter of indifference to the others. But then he became aware of something new; an instruction that Nimrod had slipped into his mind, along with that high-pressure information flow. The instruction was there now, a time bomb ready to explode. And it was the needed piece. He knew just what to do.

He lay back and waited, while Shikari swarmed in to cover and connect them. Chan felt his way inwards, seeking the first stir of interaction. There it was. The others were all ready—had been ready for a long time. Leah was right. Humans were the most difficult element. At the right moment, Chan closed his eyes. And opened his mind.

*Contact*—powerful and immediate. Chan felt the surge like an electric current through every cell of his body. He went drifting off on a tide of pleasure and satisfaction. It was the feeling he had sometimes experienced when the pursuit team sat together at night, amplified a million times.

His mind re-oriented, meshed with the other three, and settled into full group mentality mode. First contact was complete.

Data transfer did not take long. The contents of the primary, secondary, and tertiary files that had passed from Nimrod to Chan occupied the new mentality for less than twenty seconds. At the end of that time the Mentality knew as much as Nimrod did of its own origin and nature.

The quaternary data stream was the smallest in volume. It had been flagged by Nimrod for special attention. The mentality stored it in the Angel's data banks and began review. The data stream was a complete record of the first hours following Nimrod's own formation. Complete with Nimrod's situation analysis, it was perceived by the new mentality as a multi-channel flow, a meld of facts, conjectures, and conclusions.

*SITUATION.*

*Team Alpha, full of excitement and awe at the miracle of creation. There was first a naming of names: Nimrod, the fusion of will, information, desire, and understanding. Then the Morgan Construct was prepared for long-term stasis, until the source and cause of its insanity could be understood and remedied. Finally Nimrod took the most difficult step: dissolution back to the individual team members. Leah, S'glya, Ishmael, and the Angel stood for a silent moment, looking at each other. At last they made their separate ways back to the upper levels of the Travancore forest. Like the components of a Tinker Composite, each part of the Mentality looked after its own needs for food, rest, and movement.*

*ACTION.*

*Nimrod re-assembled back in the living tent, high in the jungle. A complex and complete message was generated for transmission through the Link to Anabasis Headquarters. Its tone was perhaps a little self-congratulatory, and it assumed that news of Nimrod's existence would be received with Nimrod's own enthusiasm for that event. Nimrod requested shipment up to the Q-ship for itself, and for the now-harmless Morgan Construct.*

*RESPONSE.*

*A long delay. Mondrian's inscrutable face. Nimrod made allowance for the inadequacy of single-species thought. The mentality waited. The Anabasis reply came at last: Leave the Morgan Construct in stasis on Travancore, and move up at once to the quarantine ship.*

*Nimrod possessed the empathy of a Pipe-Rilla, the quirky logic of a Tinker, the analytical capability of an Angel—and the irrational suspicions of a true human. The message clashed with Nimrod's perception of a plausible response. Nimrod flew the capsule* upwards, back to rendezvous with the high-orbiting Q-ship. When the capsule was within forty kilometers, it was vaporized by a maximum-intensity salvo.

But Nimrod was still in the tent in Travancore's upper atmosphere, watching. The capsule had been flying under remote control. Nimrod was stranded on the surface of Travancore. And now there was plenty to occupy the full powers of the Mentality's intellect.

QUERY. (The data stream transferred from Nimrod to Chan added a modifier field, to indicate the change from factual reporting to probabilistic analysis.)

The Anabasis did not want to capture Nimrod, only to destroy it. Why not achieve that effect by simply removing the Q-ship from orbit around Travancore, and abolishing all Link coordinates from the central files?

CONJECTURE.

Travancore was still of interest to the Anabasis. And since Nimrod and the pursuit team were not the source of that interest, it must derive from the Morgan Construct. The Anabasis is interested in the continued existence of the Morgan Construct.

CONTRADICTION.

The pursuit team had supposedly been sent to Travancore to destroy the Morgan Construct.

FACT.

On Barchan, Team Alpha had not destroyed their Simulacrum. Like Chan's team, they had subdued it and tried to hide the evidence.

QUERY.

Had the attempt to hide the Simulacrum succeeded?

CONJECTURE.

The Anabasis knew that Team Alpha had not destroyed the Simulacrum. It believed, at better than 0.83 probability level, that Team Alpha would also prove incapable of destroying the Morgan Construct.

ALTERNATIVES PERCEIVED BY THE ANABASIS.

*Team Alpha had been sent to Travancore by the Anabasis in anticipation of only three possible outcomes:*

*(1) The Construct would destroy Team Alpha.*
*(2) Team Alpha would destroy the Construct.*
*(3) Team Alpha would subdue the Construct, but would not destroy it.*
*SITUATION ANALYSIS ASCRIBED TO THE ANABASIS.*

*In case (1) a second pursuit team could be sent to Travancore to try again. No danger to the Anabasis.*

*In case (2) Team Alpha would return to the Q-ship unharmed. A different and less ferocious pursuit team could be tried when the next Morgan Construct was discovered. No danger to the Anabasis.*

*In case (3), Team Alpha and a now-controlled Morgan Construct would return to the Q-ship. The prime intent of the Anabasis would have been achieved.*
*NIMROD'S CONCLUSION.*

*The Anabasis had not been threatened by any predicted outcome of operations on Travancore. But the creation of Nimrod had introduced a new variable. Nimrod was perceived by the Anabasis as a threat— enough of a threat that Nimrod had to be destroyed. Saving the disabled Morgan Construct was only of secondary importance.*
*ANABASIS ANTICIPATED ACTIONS.*

*A second pursuit team would be employed on Travancore, with explicit instructions to destroy Nimrod on sight.*
*NIMROD'S ACTION.*

*Since Nimrod had no way of escaping from the planetary surface, it must await the arrival of the second team.*
*END OF DATA FILE.*

The review occupied the mentality for a full minute. It drew these corollary conclusions: If the Anabasis learned that both pursuit teams had coalesced to form group minds, it would make new plans. The disabled Morgan Construct would be abandoned, and the weapons of the Q-ship would be unleashed against Travancore. Both Nimrod and the new mentality would be equally vulnerable to attack.

It was a time for change. The mentality clung tighter for a moment, vibrating in a sympathy of feeling. Then the union ended. Dissolution began. Chan found himself sitting on the forest floor, half-naked and exhausted. He was surprised to be there. The images from Nimrod had such clarity and depth of detail that he felt he had been with them in their tent, high in Travancore's jungle.

The other three waited in a dreamy silence while Chan fastened his clothing and slowly stood up. With S'greela leading the way they drifted slowly back up the spiral tunnels. After their intense and total bonding, speech seemed inadequate. Only Shikari spoke as they ascended to the highest layers of vegetation. The Tinker was unusually chatty, talking enough trivia for everyone.

*Naturally*, thought Chan wearily. *Merging units is no big deal for a Tinker. Does it all day, every day. Shikari probably wonders why we're making such a fuss about it.*

They finally reached their tent as the last rays of sunlight were cutting across the billowing forest. Amazingly, they had been gone for less than a single day. They each settled into their preferred resting places. Chan had no appetite, but he forced himself to nibble at a block of curd—and suddenly he was ravenous. He watched with detached surprise as he wolfed down masses of protein-rich synthetics and drank two liters of sweetened liquid. The energy drain of the merged state must be formidable.

"I finally sympathize with Vayvay," said S'greela suddenly. The Pipe-Rilla had been eating with a total and concentrated attention. "I think he feels starvation like this all the time. We must go back to him."

"Tomorrow," said the Angel. "He has plenty of food. He will be happy to wait for us."

There was another long silence.

"And we must decide on our own name," said Shikari finally, as Chan was drifting off towards exhausted sleep.

"That is simple," said the Angel. "We were supposed to hunt the Constructs. If they are *Nimrod*, we will be *Bahram*—another great hunter of Earth's early days. Let me tell you his story . . ."

*Earth's history.* Angel was the Universe's most boring speaker about Earth history. Chan ought to learn more of it . . . but not today. The Angel was still talking, but Chan did not hear him. He heard nothing. He had fallen into the profoundest sleep of his life, too deep for dreams. His last thought was of the Q-ship, somewhere far overhead. Tomorrow they also had to decide what they would do about that . . . or they would spend the rest of their lives on Travancore . . .

Chan was awakened a few hours before Travancore's slow dawn. A warm body had slid under the sheet that covered him, and snuggled close to his side. He awoke in tingling terror to the gentle pressure of fingers on his lips.

"Sshhh," breathed a voice in his ear. "It's only me, Leah. I couldn't sleep. It was wonderful meeting you when I was part of Nimrod, but I had to reassure you. You won't lose enjoyment of your own life when your team forms a union."

"I know. It has already happened." Chan was still half-asleep. He looked at Leah, but the darkness was near-total and he could see nothing but a pale blur. He sighed, and put his arms around her. "All this time I've waited to see your face—and still you're invisible."

She laughed. "I haven't changed a bit. You'll see

me in daylight tomorrow. The two mentalities will have their first full meeting. We have already moved close to this tent." She settled in comfortably, fitting her body to his. "That union will come soon enough. But now, this union is just for us."

Their embrace was slow and gentle, lacking any urgency. It was the quiet culmination of twenty years of love and affection. Afterwards Leah fell asleep quickly, nestled close to Chan's chest. He remained awake for a long time, convinced that he would not sleep again before dawn.

A new worry began to push at his mind. Ever since Horus he had puzzled over the question of his identity. Who was he, what was he? Now, despite Leah's reassurances, he wondered if Chan Dalton, the individual, would vanish before he ever discovered the answers.

*Am I going to be nothing more than one piece of a union—like one of Shikari's components? That's a frightening idea. I want to be me, I don't want to disappear. Maybe I should write my obituary tonight, while I still exist.* His thoughts were drifting out in long, lazy lines. *Obituary. What would it say? Chan Dalton, dead at twenty years. Or did he really only live three months? Mental life-span, or physical? Hard questions.*

His brain was running in circles. He would lie awake *forever.*

And with that thought, Chan slept.

Twenty thousand kilometers above his head, the brooding hulk of the quarantine ship maintained its vigil. Power had been damped to a minimum for best instrument response. Now the sensors were trained on the nightside of Travancore and all weapons systems were primed.

Within the Q-ship's central control room sat Esro Mondrian and Luther Brachis. They were busy in a curious late-night ritual. Each of them held a recording block, and each was quietly entering a sequence of digits into it. When they had finished, they exchanged the blocks and inspected the other's notation.

"Looks all right to me," said Brachis. "Anything else? If not, I'm going to call it a day."

Mondrian nodded. "We agree on all digits." He picked up both blocks and looked at them again. "We're going to carry this sequence in our heads for the rest of our lives, Luther. But we'll keep doing it, just to be sure. I don't want to spend my life here any more than you do."

"You still don't want to tell Godiva the sequence? As a safety precaution?"

Mondrian shook his head. "You, me, and Kubo. No one else. And nothing in any data bank. We play it safe until we're absolutely sure that what's down there"—he nodded towards Travancore's dark disk—"is under full control."

"The reports from Chan Dalton's team look good."

"So far. I think the team will dispose of Nimrod for us. But I'm not sure of it. And Nimrod is too dangerous to take risks with. It's an alien lifeform we've never had to worry about before."

"So why do it now?" Brachis followed Mondrian's look at Travancore. "We think we know where Nimrod is down there. Why not turn up the firepower here, roast Nimrod to hell, and get it over with?"

"No." Mondrian's tone was firm. "That won't do. I will not risk the Morgan Construct. We've never tracked down another one, and it's my bet we never will. I will not chance destroying the only one we've got. We will go slow, and assume we can win."

Brachis started to protest; then he shrugged and went out without speaking. Godiva was waiting for him. He didn't want to waste time arguing.

Mondrian made a final check for incoming messages. Nothing from Kubo Flammarion, except the usual complaint by Dougal Macdougal about the energy expenditure needed to keep the Anabasis-Travancore Link open. Mondrian ignored that. Macdougal couldn't do anything but grumble. He was more than fifty lightyears away, and he was not about to ship one-way to Travancore.

After a moment's hesitation Mondrian erased the recording block in his hand. The Link sequence vanished.

*In the folded, multiply-connected mapping provided by the Mattin Link, space-time lacks affine connections and metric. There is only a point-to-point Link transformation, with its own discontinuous topology. As long as the Link is maintained between two locations, they will remain neighbors in Link-space. The Q-ship around Travancore and the control room at Anabasis Headquarters are close now, an infinitesimal distance apart. The Link will provide just the minute (but high-energy) nudge needed to move matter across the gap.*

*The Mattin Link seems like magic, but it is an unforgiving magic. Transfer locations must be specified correct to within a Planck Length—ten to the minus thirty-third centimeters. Fifty-three decimal digits are needed to specify each spatial coordinate within the hundred lightyear sphere of the Perimeter; one hundred and fifty-nine decimal digits to store a position in the data bank—or to be remembered, if all stored forms but that of human memory are rejected.*

*Night and morning, Luther Brachis and Esro Mondrian repeat to each other the 159-digit Mattin Link sequence. It is their life-line back to the rest of the universe. Without it, they will be marooned for the rest of their lives in orbit around Travancore.*

# Chapter Twenty-Nine

# THE FUSION

Chan woke late, to find himself alone in the tent. When he rubbed the sleep from his eyes and went outside, he learned that during the night all the other team members had arrived.

The group was unusually subdued. Everyone seemed to be waiting for some signal. The two Angels had night-rooted out on the tent side-lip and sat there now in companionable silence, spread fronds absorbing Talitha's morning light. S'glya and S'greela had wandered away together on a food hunt, climbing easily through the thin branches at the very top of the forest until they were out of sight. And Ishmael and Shikari had both disassembled. The whole tent area was filled with their motionless purple-black components, covering every free surface.

Chan reached out and picked one from its roost on the tent wall. The creature spread veined, leathery wings and made a feeble attempt to fly away. A ring of tiny green eyes peered at him with no sign of understanding. He released the component, and at once it flew up to the vegetation canopy. Chan watched it hanging there and wondered. How did the two Tinker Composites retain their separate identities? What rule told a single component where to go?

Well, what told a human cell that it was part of his liver, and not part of a lung? Chan dropped that question at once. He and Leah had their own preoccupations; breakfast, and conversation—apparently in that order, judging from Leah's behavior.

She had tied her dark hair back with a scarlet turban, providing the brightest splash of color on Travancore. Now she was sitting cross-legged on the tent floor, eating food as fast as Chan could get it heated. He couldn't believe how much she was packing away.

"No more," she said finally. She leaned back against the flexible wall, patted her belly, and sighed. "You've paid me back right there for half the thousand meals I've cooked for you. Take my advice and stoke up now for yourself. You'll need all the energy and calories you can get." She gave a grunt of satisfaction and closed her eyes.

*Too casual.* They were *all* too casual. Chan seemed to be the only one pessimistic about their chances of getting away from Travancore.

He remembered Mondrian's face, knowing and resolute. It was easy to feel omnipotent when the mentality was in the merged state, but it would not take Mondrian long to learn their limitations. A few minutes of union had left Chan exhausted for hours. And during union the group was immobilized. A mentality could not move as a unit, and if it dissolved in order to move, the union would be destroyed. Leah believed that the mentalities were the next evolutionary step for all the Stellar Group members. *Maybe.* But unless they could gain access to the Q-ship and defeat the Anabasis, it was an evolutionary blind end.

The return of the two Pipe-Rillas put a sudden end to his worrying. They dropped together through a leaf layer and crouched down next to the Angels. As though they had been waiting for that as a signal, every Tinker component lifted from its roosting position. They flew around the tent with dizzying speed and precision and suddenly swarmed over each team member. As the individuals coalesced, the mentalities awoke. A thick cable of living Tinker components provided direct mental connection.

WELCOME. Q-SHIP BEHAVIOR UNPREDICTABLE . . . TIME SHORT . . . NEED FOR MENTALITY ACTION . . . (The split-second of greeting from Nimrod to Bahram came across a broad channel of communication that carried a hundred parallel side-messages. Assessment began at once. Parallel analyses provided the conditional probabilities and options for mentality action.)

OPTION 1. NO MOVEMENT OF CAPSULE TO Q-SHIP, NO TEAM COMMUNICATION WITH Q-SHIP.

PROBABLE OUTCOME: DESTRUCTION OF NIMROD AND BAHRAM AT P = 0.58 LEVEL WITHIN TWO TRAVANCORE DAYS; AT P = 0.71 LEVEL IN THREE DAYS; AT P = 0.93 LEVEL IN FOUR DAYS.

(Chan was *within* the Bahram group mind; but this time, for the first time, he retained some elements of individual consciousness. Thought streams between Nimrod and Bahram left echoes in his mind, weak eddy patterns from the strong main current . . . Ideas from other team members came swirling in, alien yet accessible . . . Sometimes they translated to sounds, to images, to transient illusions of physical touch. Chan felt the cross-fertilization of minds. Those came to him as pictures, vivid patterns and designs. The transfers of new ideas and speculation were like blazing fireships, moving to ignite convoys of logic in every member of the group . . .

From the Angel component, a five-fold statistical conclusion blazed in on Chan as a crimson starfish of analysis . . .)

---

*Personnel believed present on Q-ship.*
Esro Mondrian, 0.99 probability
Luther Brachis, 0.84 probability
Kubo Flammarion, 0.77 probability
Tatiana Snipes, 0.41 probability
Godiva Lomberd, 0.28 probability
All others, less than 0.20 probability

---

OPTION 2. CAPSULE APPROACH TO Q-SHIP WITHOUT ANY PRIOR COMMUNICATION.

PROBABLE OUTCOME: DESTRUCTION OF CAPSULE AT P = 0.97 LEVEL.

(The Pipe-Rilla thoughts were sinuous and delicate, full of *feelings* rather than logic. They rippled across the mentality, drawing shimmering silver ropes of inference. Chan grasped at the gossamer strands. In his mind he felt them condense and turn to solid numerical form. His attention seized their conclusions . . .)

---

*Preferred human contacts for mentality on Q-ship, if present:*
Tatiana Snipes, 0.32 probability
Godiva Lomberd, 0.26 probability
Kubo Flammarion, 0.21 probability
Esro Mondrian/Luther Brachis, less than 0.01 probability

---

OPTION 3: APPROACH OF CAPSULE TO Q-SHIP. COMMUNICATION TO Q-SHIP INDICATING THAT RUBY TEAM SURVIVED, BUT DOES NOT HAVE MORGAN CONSTRUCT.

PROBABLE OUTCOME: DESTRUCTION OF CAPSULE AT P = 0.87 LEVEL.

(Angel thoughts were a passacaglia and fugue in three dimensions, too complex for Chan to assimilate. He *sensed* the rock-solid logic behind the patterns. He *saw* that logic as coral monoliths, reaching up from a crystal sea . . .)

---

*Q-ship specifications*

Three main entry ports; all monitored by defense system

Sustained energy output level, 94 gigawatts

Burst output energy legel, 144 terawatts

Defensive systems: radiation, particle beam, projectile

Back-up: jamming fields, shearing cones, fission/fusion, E/M shield

Offensive systems: sterilizing, subnucleon reaction, fusion

---

(Chan knew he was seeing the Angel data banks, screened through the group minds. *Too bright*, said an urgent internal voice. It switched to show a dark-glass image of a naked star. Chan groped inward for the message, finally found it. He could not look into that data bank directly. The storage complexity of the Angels was too great for a human mind. He must settle for this pale reflection . . .)

OPTION 4: APPROACH OF CAPSULE TO Q-SHIP, COMMUNICATION TO INDICATE THAT RUBY TEAM HAS MORGAN CONSTRUCT, NO MESSAGE REGARDING ALPHA TEAM.

PROBABLE OUTCOME:DESTRUCTION OF CAPSULE AT P = 0.62 LEVEL.

(Now there came a bewildering jumble of sensation, a light that pulsed and flickered and was never still. Chan struggled, resisted, struck back against it. Finally he managed to relax and let it dictate its own pattern of meaning. He was at once in a world where steady states were banished. There were only averages of continuous fluctuations, as though classical theory had given way to quantum mechanics. At last he understood. He was seeing the thoughts of a Tinker Composite. When individual components were added and subtracted, all minor fluctuations must be ignored. It was cerebration as a *statistical* process, the *grand canonical ensemble* of mental function. He learned to watch only the average state. And now he saw gleeful kaleidoscopes of Tinker ideas burst with firecracker exuberance through the web of the group minds . . .)

---

*Assessment.*
Probability that location of Morgan Construct on Travancore is accurately known to Q-ship is estimated at 0.34 or less

---

OPTION 5: APPROACH OF CAPSULE TO Q-SHIP. PRECEDED BY COMMUNICATION TO Q-SHIP INDICATING THAT RUBY TEAM SURVIVED AND HAS MORGAN CONSTRUCT, AND THAT ALPHA TEAM HAS BEEN DESTROYED.

PROBABLE OUTCOME: DESTRUCTION OF CAPSULE BEFORE REACHING Q-SHIP IS UNLIKELY (LESS THAN 0.17 PROBABILITY LEVEL).

(Underlying every function of the mentalities was a cruel driving energy, propelling the groups toward decision and action. Chan sensed its presence as an imminent force-field. It was always there, permanent and irresistible as gravity. He groped for its origin. At last he found it. His mind recoiled in surprise. The group driving force originated in Chan and Leah . . .)

*Summary*.
Option 5 probability of capsule reaching Q-ship is acceptable
Probability of defeating Q-ship still unacceptably low
Additional information needed on Q-ship personnel

ANALYSIS/CONCLUSIONS. Q-SHIP WILL INITIATE AGGRESSIVE ACTION WITHIN TWO DAYS UNLESS CONTACTED . . . BAHRAM MUST THEREFORE FLY CAPSULE TO Q-SHIP . . . PRESENCE OF NIMROD ON CAPSULE MUST BE CONCEALED . . . MORGAN CONSTRUCT WILL BE LEFT BEHIND ON TRAVANCORE AS INSURANCE FOR BAHRAM'S SAFETY . . . SURVIVAL PROBABILITY MAXIMIZED BY PROMPT ACTION . . .

(The mental activity was reaching a great crescendo. Chan was helpless, adrift on a tidal wave of thought. He felt individual control weaken, shiver, and vanish into total group mind absorption. The climax was nearing . . .)

DECISION: THERE MUST BE AN IMMEDIATE CAPSULE ASCENT BY NIMROD AND BAHRAM TO THE Q-SHIP. ASSESSMENT: OVERALL MISSION SURVIVAL PROBABILITY: 0.16.

The two group minds slowly loosened their links. The connecting chain of Tinker components broke, and fluttered to rest on the jungle creepers and branches. The orgasm of joint thought was dying. It faded now to a waking dream . . .

Chan, still dizzy from the surge of mental energy that had flooded through him, stood up slowly and went inside the tent. Leah was already there, entering the control sequence that would bring the hovering capsule down for their use. She looked at him without speaking. *Only a sixteen-percent chance we'll make it,* said her expression.

Chan nodded. *Bad odds.* We've got to find something to change them.

# Chapter Thirty

# ABOARD THE Q-SHIP

The ascent to the Q-ship was anything but comforting. Chan stared at the enormous ellipsoidal mass filling the sky in front of him, then looked around at their capsule.

*Disturbing contrast.*

A Q-ship was designed to bottle up the inhabitants of full-sized space colonies, even of whole planets—populations with their own weapons, who as often as not didn't want to cooperate. Each quarantine ship was shielded, armored, and bristled with defensive and offensive weapons. Even ignoring the mass of their power kernels they were million-ton behemoths. In the extreme case, a Q-ship might be called upon to purge or permanently blockade an entire planet. The extreme had never yet been necessary—but there had been scares. The discovery that it was an organism, a native brain-burrowing *gnathostome*, that was affecting all the inhabitants of Pentecost and causing their planet-wide blood-lust, had been made only at the eleventh hour. A Q-ship had already been in position, ready to carry out planetary sterilization.

And the capsule? Chan grimaced. It was nothing

more than a flimsy, thin-walled shell, vulnerable even to a mild stellar flare. The Q-ship could vaporize it with an accidental puff from its secondary exhaust.

They crept closer, on an unpowered approach trajectory. The Q-ship crew were taking no chances. Their designated entry port was protected by a gleaming array of projectile and radiation weapons. After docking, the Ruby Team members had been instructed to enter the Q-ship one by one. Chan would go first. The others would not leave the capsule until they had permission to do so. And even within the docking area, Mondrian could order the instant destruction of the capsule and its contents—including Nimrod, who was hidden away in the capsule's primitive cargo compartment.

(The journey to the Q-ship was a one-way trip, for more than one reason. With Nimrod aboard, all spare supplies and fuel had been left behind on Travancore to avoid a mass anomaly. The Q-ship would detect any discrepancy when the capsule was caught for docking—and it would take violent action.)

As they neared the ship Chan heard a whisper in his ear. Nimrod's analysis was passing from the cargo hold through a single-link chain of Tinker components, then converted by the Angel to a form that Chan could recognize.

"... twelve hundred meters to docking," said the Angel. "*Excellent.* If the Q-ship intended to destroy us before we docked, the best time to do so has already passed. Current probability estimate for success of mission is 0.255, *up* from the last estimate of 0.23 ... Nimrod now believes that Tatty Snipes is not on the Q-ship. If so, the probability of finding a sympathetic contact who can be worked with goes *down*, by 0.13. And in that case, the overall probability estimate will unfortunately be *reduced* by 0.04 ..."

Chan groaned to himself. The Angel was perfectly happy puttering around with the data and passing on the odds; but Chan found no comfort at all in endless statistics. He wished that he could enjoy Bahram's comforting closeness and togetherness. Unfortunately, the capsule cabin was certainly under Q-ship surveillance. Merging now might be suicide.

"Ready for docking," he said to the blank communications screen. So far they had received no visual signals from the Q-ship. The port was less than two hundred meters ahead.

"Proceed," said a metallic voice from the capsule communications set.

". . . still computer controlled," whispered the Angel. The bulk of the Chassel-rose was hanging upside-down over Chan's head, in the free fall of their ballistic approach. "If they were to shoot at us now, there would be some minor damage to the Q-ship. *Onward and upward!* Nimrod feels sure that we will be permitted to complete the docking."

"Get down off the ceiling," said Chan. "They'll be grabbing us in a second or two and we'll feel acceleration. Go and lie next to Shikari. I don't want you wrapped around my neck when we dock."

As he spoke there was a jolt on the hull. The Angel sailed backwards and bounced on the cabin wall behind Chan. There were a few seconds of vibration and then a clang from outside

"Docking complete," said the communicator.

Chan moved slowly towards the capsule door, while the other team members remained in the cabin.

*Careful now. This is one moment of maximum danger.* Had he heard those words, or was he saying them to himself? He paused at the door and waited.

The capsule had been tucked neatly into a berth in the contoured fourth deck. Chan heard the outer port seals clang into position, and the creak of the car's hull as external air pressure increased from vacuum levels. He watched until the meters showed internal and external equality, then opened the capsule.

A narrow pier alongside the hull led to an airlock on the interior wall. Chan pulled himself across to it, reflecting that even after this he would not be in the ship's real interior. According to the Angel's reconstruction of Q-ship geometry, there would be another lock to pass through with its own checking system for interlopers. If anyone failed a test, the whole entry port could be blown free into space. The Q-ship would still operate at close to its full potential.

The lock slid open, and Chan stepped through. Decontaminant sprays blew over him from head to foot. The personnel handling system wafted him gently along a white-walled corridor, to another lock. Chan watched everything closely, and wished there were some way he could send back information to Nimrod. The mentality needed more data to gain unobserved entry to the Q-ship.

The next door slid open to an area that was not in free-fall. They must be within a few meters of the shielded kernel that powered everything on the Q-ship. Chan thought of the nearby singularity, and imagined he could feel tidal gravitational forces. He swayed for a moment to make sure of his balance, then walked around the curved floor to the chamber's other door. After a second's hesitation he went through it.

He was in a primary quarantine area: a large, hexagonal room, thirty meters across. It was divided into seven parts. The central area where Chan had entered was surrounded by six individual vaults, each with its own triple-layer transparent glassite walls and inert-metal door. The whole room was visible from every chamber—but a kiloton fusion explosion could take place in any one of them and be totally confined there.

Two men were waiting for Chan at the far end of the central area.

*Mondrian and Brachis.* Chan recalled the prediction of the mentalities. These were the two individuals he was most likely to meet on the Q-ship—and the ones least likely to be controllable!

Esro Mondrian was unarmed. Luther Brachis carried a Class-one beam weapon, aimed at Chan's midriff.

Mondrian alone nodded a greeting. He was pale and haggard, his eyes sunk deep in their sockets. "Welcome back, Chan. According to our records, you're the first human ever to return from the surface of Travancore. The original surveys were all done with inorganics. Sorry we don't have the red carpet out for you." He managed a smile at those last words, despite the obvious tension that filled the room. "We are glad to see you, but we've got a lot on our minds. Sit down."

Three straight-backed chairs formed the only furniture, diagonally placed so that each provided a view of the wall-sized display screen. Chan sat on one, Mondrian on the other. Luther Brachis remained standing, his weapon still unholstered.

Chan looked at it, then turned to Mondrian. "We never asked for a red carpet. But I did expect better treatment than this. You send us to do a job. We perform it for you. And then you point guns at us."

By intention, Chan's tone was bitter and confused. The mentalities had advised him how he should begin the meeting on the Q-ship. But they had warned that they could not predict beyond the first few exchanges. Chan would have to use his own judgment as the encounter proceeded.

"You did not complete your mission," said Mondrian quietly. "You were to destroy a Morgan

Construct. According to your message, it is still alive."

"We did *more* than we were asked. Thanks to the Ruby Team, you will have available to you a live, functioning Morgan Construct in a safe environment."

*Live, functioning, safe.* Chan carefully stressed those words. He thought he saw a positive reaction from Mondrian. Brachis showed no emotion at all. (*Another problem? Brachis now seemed softer, less dynamic. Had something happened to him since Chan left Ceres?*) Chan wished that S'glya or S'greela were present. The Pipe-Rillas were far better than humans at reading emotional states.

"You can study the reasons why the Construct went insane," Chan continued. "Maybe you can even cure it. And whatever happens you will have advice to give the pursuit teams that hunt down other Constructs."

"Perhaps." Mondrian's eyes were gleaming, but still cautious and calculating. "However, you have not explained why you failed to follow orders. Why did you not destroy the Construct as directed?"

Chan had to gamble on his answer. He was at a branch point in the group mind analysis of the situation.

"It was not necessary," replied Chan. "We could— and did—neutralize all its offensive powers. It is now in stasis, safely immobilized on the jungle floor of Travancore."

"Undamaged?" Mondrian's voice had a slight tremor in it.

"Completely so. But the capsule isn't big enough for us and the Construct. Do you want to go down and collect it?"

*A principal branch point.* If Mondrian agreed, Chan's chance of survival increased enormously.

Mondrian was shaking his head and fiddling with

the star opal at his collar. "Not yet. Tell me, Chan, what do you see as the future of the Ruby Team?"

"I didn't think the team *had* a future. We came together to do a job, and we did it. I suppose I expected that we'd be rewarded, and all go home. I'd like to go back to Earth, at least for a while. Is that a problem?"

"I don't think so." Mondrian took his fingers away from the star opal, and Luther Brachis lowered his weapon. "Any need to have your whole team there when we pick up the Morgan Construct?"

"I don't see why. It's perfectly safe now, and I could do it on my own."

"Good." Mondrian stood up. "We'll bring them into the ship. I'd like to thank them—individually. Then they can be Linked to their home planets."

"Immediately?"

"Why not?"

*He suspects*, thought Chan. He can't know we coalesced to a group mind, but he's not taking any chances. "I thought we'd all get together here— maybe even have a celebration. We expected to go our separate ways, but not this suddenly."

"When we have the Construct, the work on Travancore is over." Now there was undisguised triumph in Mondrian's eyes. "And we must get back to Ceres. But first, if you please, there are other things to attend to here."

Brachis walked to the door leading to one of the left-hand room compartments and opened it. He gestured to Chan with his gun. "In here."

"Just for a few minutes," said Mondrian. Chan protested and was ignored. Brachis guided him through, and the heavy door closed.

Mondrian stepped to the communications panel and pressed a sequence there. "And now for your companions. It is time for them to leave the capsule."

The communications equipment still allowed

Chan to hear and see events in the central chamber. A few seconds later a display screen there revealed the bulky figure of the Angel, leaving the capsule and slowly floating towards the lock. After a few minutes the Angel itself appeared in front of Luther Brachis. This time there was no discussion. The Angel was at once confined in a second chamber.

No one spoke as S'greela and finally Shikari were brought from the capsule. The Tinker was handled with special care. Luther Brachis set his weapon to a broad-beam setting, capable of throwing a fan of destructive energy from floor to ceiling. If necessary, he could kill a whole swarm of components in mid-air.

It was not necessary. S'greela and Shikari quietly allowed themselves to be shepherded into separate sealed chambers. When all the pursuit team members were present, Mondrian went again to the control panel. He pressed a new command sequence.

"Destroying the capsule," he said casually. He looked hard at Chan. "We don't want to risk a dangerous life-form taking a free ride up from Travancore, do we?"

Chan nodded, and kept his face impassive. He watched, as the capsule flared into blue incandescence on the screen. The possibility of such an action had been considered by Nimrod and Bahram when they were still on Travancore. But no counteraction had been devised. Either Nimrod had now found a way to move from the capsule to the safety of the ship, or Leah and the others were dead. Chan wished that he had an Angel's inborn ability to assess the odds.

"There is one other important question to be answered," went on Mondrian. "Then you can lead us down to collect the Construct, and we can talk of celebration." He paused. "I am curious to learn one thing. In your later efforts on Travancore, were you again troubled by illusions or a distorted perception of reality?"

Chan hesitated. Mondrian probably knew of Chan's first and incomplete encounter with Nimrod—Chan had reported seeing Leah, and it must still be in the data files. But what was the right answer now? Was it better to report that there had been a subsequent meeting—or should he say he had fired immediately on the next contact, before there could be any exchange?

While he tried to decide on an answer, Brachis raised his gun again and took a step towards the door of the chamber where Chan was standing. "Damn it, Esro, he's taking far too long. Can't you see he's stalling?"

Mondrian gestured him to silence. "Keep calm, Luther. Chan, we're both nervous. I *need* that Morgan Construct. But there are some risks that we— and the human race—can't afford to take. I *have* to know what happened on Travancore. Did you see signs of Team Alpha?"

As Mondrian was speaking, the door to the central chamber was silently opening. Chan held his breath as a figure slowly stepped through into the quarantine chamber. Then he gasped in disappointment. It was Godiva Lomberd, dressed in a loose-fitting white dress. She had a bewildered expression on her face.

"Luther," she said. "I have to talk to you. It's tremendously important."

Brachis had swung round, weapon raised and finger tight on the trigger as the voice came from behind him. Now he exhaled hard, and lowered his gun.

"Goddy, don't ever do that again." His voice was soft and urgent. "Do you realize I almost fired at you? We're busy here. Go back to our rooms, I can't talk to you now."

"It *has* to be now." Godiva took a couple of steps forward. She spoke with a strange and remote intensity. "Now, Luther. Please. For your own sake."

"Go with her." Chan was surprised to hear his own voice. In spite of the mentalities' probability analysis, he had not really expected to find Godiva on board the Q-ship. But she had been identified as one of the people most likely to help. "Godiva is right, Brachis. Go with her—now."

"What the hell is all this?" Brachis swung to face Chan, but Mondrian was moving quickly to the control board.

"*It's on board,*" he said. "God knows how, and God knows where. But it's here—and it's taken over Godiva. Look at her face."

"Goddy!" Brachis gave a cry of horror.

"Esro's wrong, Luther." She moved to stand in front of him. "I'm all right. There is someone new on board, and we did talk. But I can't be taken over—ever." She smiled at him dreamily. "Luther, Nimrod can help you. Nimrod can take away all the violence, and all the hatred. Don't you understand that I would never have come here if I thought it might hurt you? Luther, please come with me."

She touched his arm, and looked up into his face. He stared back at her, mesmerized. "Go with you and be changed, you mean—make me into a *thing*, a part of some alien life form. Goddy, how did they get you?"

She gripped his shoulders. "Nimrod *didn't* take me and change me—Nimrod only *talked* to me. It can't change me, ever. But it can help *you*—if you'll just let it!"

As she spoke, the door behind her opened further. Mondrian and Brachis had a new view of the corridor beyond. Both men took a sudden and involuntary step backwards.

Nimrod was in the doorway. For the first time, Chan had a view of a mentality without being a

part of it. It was a terrifying sight. The forms of
Leah, S'glya, and Angel stirred feebly within a
swarming, choking mass of Ishmael's components.
Long purple-black tentacles, chains of Tinker elements, writhed away from the main body. They
extended now into the room, reaching out towards
the locks of the closed vaults. As Chan watched,
the whole mass gave a convulsive jerk and moved
sluggishly nearer. The door between him and the
central room slid open.

"Godiva is right, Luther." Leah's voice spoke
suddenly from the depths of the vibrating mass.
"You and Mondrian can be helped . . . if you will
let us work with you and learn your minds. And
you both need help. We saw into Godiva's mind
. . . but we did not enter it. *We could not.* She gave
us permission to tell you why. Luther, you must
accept a new shock. *Godiva Lomberd is not human.*"

"What the hell—" Brachis raised his weapon,
pointing it at the central mass of Nimrod.

Godiva moved in front of him, forcing him to
lower the gun. "They are right, Luther," she said
quietly. "I am not human. My coding did not permit me to tell you, and I wondered if you would
ever know. But now I am glad. Luther, my love,
don't you see it yet—what I am, where I came
from?" She stretched up to kiss him. "Let them
help, and then we will really belong to each other."

"Luther, get back!" Mondrian was looking at
Godiva with sudden comprehension. "Don't touch
her any more. Godiva, *what are you?*"

"Why do you ask? You know the answer, Esro. I
am an Artefact."

Brachis had ignored Mondrian's warning. He
stood frozen, with Godiva's arms holding him in a
soft embrace around his neck. Now he gave her an
uncertain smile, denying her words. "Godiva, don't
say that. Don't *ever* say anything like that."

"But it is true. I am an Artefact—and the Margrave of Fujitsu made me." Her incredible body moved close to him.

"That *can't* be true. You were with me when Fujitsu's Artefacts were trying to kill me." His face was white, and the hand that held the gun was shaking. "Goddy, you helped to *save* me, over and over, when the Artefacts were attacking me. You didn't try to kill me. You can't be—can't be one of *his*—"

She pulled him closer and kissed him passionately on the mouth. "I love you, Luther. I would never want to hurt you, you should know that. Fujitsu made me, in the vats of his own Needler lab. But I was made for love, not death."

Godiva's beautiful face showed her torment. Instead of returning her kiss, Brachis was leaning back, pulling hard away from her.

"Don't you understand yet, Luther Brachis?" It was Leah's voice again, emerging from the middle of the Tinker swarm. "You should feel *pity* for Godiva, not anger or revulsion. She was Fujitsu's weapon, but it was not from choice. When the Margrave was alive, her only program was to love you, watch you, and stay with you. *When he died, that program was not cancelled.* It remained as strong as ever. But she also became a tool for your destruction, the master source of information for all the Margrave's Artefacts. How do you think the Artefacts were able to follow you and know your actions? Feel her misery, Luther Brachis, as we feel it. All her nature tells her to love you, but she could not help providing information that would harm you. When you came to Travancore, she rejoiced—for she knew the other Artefacts could not follow you here and try to kill you."

Tears were trickling down the flawless skin of Godiva's cheeks. She was nodding slowly, still clutching at Brachis. "Listen to them, Luther. I love you, Luther."

Brachis leaned away as she rose up on tiptoe to kiss him again. "Love? Making money for Fujitsu, is that your idea of love?"

She rested her head on his chest. "Commercial love, if you want to call it that. I was made for it—but it is still love to me, all the love that I have ever known. Even after he was dead, I could never *harm* anyone. My instructions were to stay with you, and when he was gone there could be no change to that part of my programming. And I did not *want* a change—only to make you more happy. I love you. I want to stay with you forever." Her face mirrored mixed emotions; love, misery, contrition, compulsion. She pulled him again towards her. "Come, Luther. Let us help you to drive out hatred."

He stood rigid, looking out across the top of her blond head, out across time and lightyears. Then he was straining back again in revulsion from Godiva's touch. "Damn your soul, Fujitsu." His voice rose to a shout. "Damn you, wherever you are. You win. You demanded your dues, but you never said they included this. You win, Fujitsu."

He looked down at Godiva. *"Don't touch me. Get away from me."*

She shook her head, but she slowly released her hold. Her hands went to her throat, and she ripped open her loose-fitting dress from neck to thighs. "I cannot use words, Luther. All I can give you is myself. It is all I have. This belongs to you. It will always belong to you."

Luther Brachis glared at the opulent body. Godiva moved closer, looking up lovingly into his face.

"Stop him." S'greela spoke suddenly from within her closed chamber. "Stop him, or he will—"

Before anyone could move, Brachis had raised his gun to point it at Godiva's head. She looked at the weapon and smiled, a dreamy and loving smile, and put her hand up to touch his cheek. He fired.

There was the sickening, dull explosion of human flesh superheated to twenty thousand degrees. Her head vanished in a bloody vaporized mist. The perfect body stood for a moment, arms still raised in supplication. Then she fell backwards. Even in death, there was a strange grace to her fall. Luther Brachis drew in a long, sobbing breath.

Mondrian was the only one who foresaw the next act.

"Luther! For God's sake, no!" He jumped forward and grabbed at Brachis's arm. The other man looked at him, then almost casually began to turn his wrist. Mondrian pulled as hard as he could, but Brachis's arm movement did not slow. He turned the weapon steadily to face his own head, then looked down for a long moment at Godiva's tumbled body.

"I loved you, Godiva," he said softly. "I still love you." He fired the gun into his own open mouth. His headless corpse fell backwards, pulling Mondrian with it.

The body was still twitching when Mondrian scrambled to his feet and headed back towards the control panel.

"Stop him!" said Leah's voice. "He is now the only one who knows the Link sequence back to Sol."

Chan ran through into the main room, S'greela bounding to join him. They were too slow. Mondrian was already at the panel, flipping switches. Chan grabbed his arm, pulling it away.

"S'greela, help me! That's the Q-ship destruct pattern."

As Chan spoke there was a sudden blizzard of Tinker components around his head, moving in to surround all three of them. Before S'greela could reply, the group mind awakened. Chan flowed in with Bahram towards the man he was holding, and felt the shock of conflict run back to him.

"CAN YOU REACH HIM?" That was Nimrod, connecting in through the Ishmael/Shikari link.

It was a new experience, to feel through into a resisting mind. There was a long moment of introspection from Bahram.

"NO. WE CANNOT." Surprise and alarm from Bahram. Chan felt Mondrian's mind rising powerfully against them. There was more strength there than he would have believed possible. Bahram was recoiling from the intensity of emotion it encountered.

"WE CANNOT BRING HIM TO CONTACT. THERE IS A BLOCK THERE . . . IMMOVABLE . . . PERMANENT . . . DEEP-SEATED."

"CAN YOU BYPASS IT?" Nimrod was adding all its mental resources to the struggle.

"NO. IT WOULD DESTROY HIM TOTALLY. IT IS BURIED BELOW ALL ACCESSIBLE LEVELS."

S'greela and Chan were holding Mondrian tightly. He was not resisting physically, but his mind boiled and burned, rejecting all contact with the group minds. Bahram tried again, feeling along a new path. Chan felt the repugnance, as it reached the seething undercurrent of Mondrian's mind.

"SEEK THE ABORT PATTERN FOR Q-SHIP DESTRUCTION." That was Nimrod.

"IT CANNOT BE REACHED," said Bahram. "THE Q-SHIP DESTRUCT IS CLOSE NOW."

"Should we destroy Mondrian?" Chan's mind had partially disengaged and added that thought, unbidden, as an individual input to both group minds. "It may yield the abort pattern."

"NO . . . NO . . . NO." Chan's suggestion produced a mental gale of disapproval. He felt the shocked reaction from the Pipe-Rillas at the same moment as he pulled further back from the group mind. Channeling the group mind strength, Chan used it to reach deeper, burrowing his way into a matrix of thoughts that struggled and fought furiously against him. He seemed to make no progress at all. *Mondrian would not yield.*

Chan forced himself on, and finally reached the memory block. It was a dark, confined presence, sealed off from everything around it. Using the full power of Nimrod and Bahram, Chan pushed deeper, turning an obsidian edge of hidden memory to pierce the naked, delicate fiber of Mondrian's conscious mind. The darkness resisted for another long moment, then swung suddenly under massive pressure.

The block was gone. As Bahram reached past him to pick the abort command and Mattin Link sequence from Mondrian's mind, Chan was caught in the mental explosion when Mondrian faced the horror from his own distant past. There was a scream of pain and pure mental anguish, blowing Chan out of the dying brain and far away into his own sea of fading consciousness. Mondrian's intellect flickered and faded, a quenched ember of mind that sank rapidly too nothing.

The group minds caught Chan, cradled him. "Safe? Are we safe?" he asked. But he did not hear an answer.

"Death. Death," said the only echo. Then he was swirling into bottomless terror, knowing it was only a faint shadow of what he had found inside Esro Mondrian.

At last he let go, and sank all the way into the maelstrom.

# Chapter Thirty-One

# IN THE GALLIMAUFRIES

The transition came at the hundred-and-twentieth level of the Gallimaufries. It was sudden. Above this point were the signs of success: fashionable apartments, bright lights, high rents, and easy access to the surface. Below the hundred-and-twentieth a traveller found dark hell-holes, fugitives, and failures.

Chan approached the apartment cautiously, pushing a trolley in front of him. In the trash-filled corridor he stood thoughtful for a while, then left his burden—the one thing that would not be stolen, even here!—by the grimy wall and moved to the apartment door. He put his hand on the ID unit and pressed hard. The light glowed. He was allowed through to the inner foyer. He stood there, patiently waiting.

It took a long time. The woman who finally opened the inner door was tall and stooped, with long, unkempt hair. She peered out into the dimlit foyer. After another pause she pushed a greasy lock away from her forehead with a skeletally thin hand. Tired, bleary eyes stared at him. There was a sigh. "Chan?" she said uncertainly.

He nodded. "It's me, Tatty. May I come in?"

She did not speak, but turned and shuffled slowly back into the apartment. Following her, Chan saw the vivid purple of Paradox shots down both of her upper arms. They went through into a small living-room. Uninvited, Chan sat down in an armchair and looked around him. The place was a clutter of papers, dishes, and clothes, the result of many weeks of too-casual living with no attempt to clean.

She had sat down opposite him on a ragged hassock and was staring hard at his face. At last she nodded slowly. "It's you, Chan. It's really you. You've changed, just like they said."

"We've all changed." He sat stiffly, hands on knees. "What did you expect, Tatty?"

"I heard the rumors. The Gallimaufries are full of stories. How you and Leah went out to the stars, with Esro Mondrian and Luther Brachis, and the aliens. How you were changed, and caught a super-being. They say it will make everything different, out there and back here too. A super-being ..." She rubbed at her eyes.

"Maybe *it* caught *us*. Don't believe all the rumors, Tatty. We didn't catch anything. But we did have terrible casualties. Did you hear about ... all of those?"

"You mean about Esro." Her eyes had a glazed look. She was coming off a Paradox high. "Yes, I heard. And about Luther, and poor Godiva."

"You heard ... the other thing about her?"

"Ah, yes." For the first time Tatty showed a sign of real emotion. She leaned forward. "You know, if I'd had my brain working—back in the days when I had a brain—I'd have guessed it. She came from nowhere, and she was too good to be true. The perfect woman, the perfect partner. Poor, doomed Godiva. Lord, what a genius Fujitsu was. How did you ever find out she was an Artefact?"

"She couldn't be linked into the group mind. Controlled, yes—but not merged with it. That was one of the few good things to come out of the whole damned business—it got rid of some of my worries." He wriggled in the chair at an intolerable memory. "You know, I thought for a long time that I might be an Artefact myself. I was a twenty-year-old moron with an undamaged brain. That never made sense. I wondered if I was human."

She looked at him in surprise. "You mean—Esro Mondrian never told you?"

"Told me what?"

"He wanted to know where you came from. When I first came back to Earth, he asked me to find out anything I could about your background. And I thought he passed what I learned on to you." She hesitated. "I guess he didn't. Do you really want to know?"

"Of course I do. Even a moron wants to know why he is one."

"You're not a moron, Chan, and you never will be. But you *were* an experiment—a failed one. One of the Needler labs— *not* the Margrave, he would never have tolerated such incompetence—was trying to make a superman, a physically and mentally perfect specimen. They failed. They didn't realize you needed a final set of mental stimuli. They dumped the result down in the basement warrens." She smiled sadly. "Welcome to the outcasts' club. But you're all human. Isn't it a rotten group to belong to?"

She leaned back on the hassock and closed her eyes. Her face was grey and bony. To Chan, she seemed no more than the aging specter of the woman he had known back on Horus.

"Do you want to know what happened to Mondrian?" he asked at last.

The dark-shadowed eyes slowly opened. "Should I want to know? Esro Mondrian, the man who used me, and then threw me away when there was

nothing left for me to do for him? I don't think
there is anything to tell me."

"I was inside Esro Mondrian's mind, in the last
few moments. He didn't throw you away. He believed you had rejected *him*. You left him alone, to
face what he couldn't face. He was never at peace.
He was a driven man."

"I know that better than you will ever know it."
Tatty had closed her eyes again, and tears rolled
out from under her dark lids. "He could never tell
me what it was—never tell anyone."

"He could not. But he didn't need to. I—"

Chan halted. He found that he could not speak
of what he had seen in Mondrian's mind. Even at
second hand, the terror was too all-encompassing.
He felt the impact of that hidden memory, taking
him again, as it had taken him every day since . . .

*The grass is three times as high as his head. It
grows all the way around, like the walls of a big
circular room. The blue sky above is a domed ceiling,
holding in the heat. It is much too hot, and he is
sweating. He bends down, staring curiously at the
little bugs running fast and squiggly among the stems
of the grey-green plants.*

*"Come on, keep up. We don't have time for you to
dawdle."*

*He straightens at the shouted words and hurries
along after the others. Mummy is still walking next
to Uncle Darren, holding his hand and not lookig
back. He comes up behind them and impulsively
reaches out to clutch her around the knees. He can
smell her sweat, and see it glistening on her legs.*

*Is she still mad at him?*

*"Mummy, hold me." He looks up uncertainly, hop-
ing for a hug and fearing a blow. It is a long time
since she held him without being asked. "Cuddle
me."*

*She does not look down at him. "We've no time for*

*that now. Can't you see we're in a hurry.*" The angry voice again.

The man laughs, but it is not like a real laugh. "*Too right, we're in a hurry. But this ought to do as well as anywhere. Come on, let's get on with it.*"

Mummy looks down at him now, and it is her cold face. "*Uncle Darren and I are going to be very busy for a little while. I want you to sit right down here, and wait quietly until we come back.*"

"*I want to go with you, Mummy.*" He holds tighter to her legs. "*I don't want to stay here.*"

"*We can't do it that way, Big-boy.*" Uncle Darren crouches down until his face is on the same level. He is smiling. "*Look, you just wait here for me and your Mummy, just for a minute. And if you're good I'll let you have this to play with while we're gone. See?*"

Uncle Darren is holding the little electric lamp, the one they had played with in the camp last night. It had been a fun time, with the three of them all safe and cosy in the tent, and Mummy laughing a lot. She wouldn't let him crawl in with them, but she had sounded happy, and Uncle Darren had told him a bedtime story.

He reaches out his hand, drawn by the little lamp. "*Look, watch me do it.*" Uncle Darren works the control. "*Switch on—switch off. Think you can do it for yourself?*"

He nods, takes the lamp, and sits down to put it onto the hard earth.

"*That's my Big-boy.*" Uncle Darren stands up and begins to walk away. "*Come on, Lucy, he's all right now.*"

He looks after them, watching as they move into the long grass. They have their heads together, and they are talking quietly again, the way they did in the tent last night. He bends down to the lamp, wanting to please Mummy and do whatever she wants to make her happy with him. He stoically begins to turn the little lamp on and off. It seems brighter than it did when Uncle Darren first worked it. The sky is a darker blue, and when he looks up he can see stars creeping out, one by one. They look like little lamps themselves, but they do not give any light.

He feels a sudden urge to run after Mummy, but he knows what that will do. Mummy will be very angry, and he will get another beating from her or Uncle Darren. He looks around him, wishing that the tent were here to crawl inside. Last night in the tent it was wonderful. The light had been turned very low, but he could hear them whispering together in the dark. It made him feel warm and comforted.

"Are you absolutely sure?" That was Mummy. Her voice was funny, with the words all warm and slurry. "We have to be sure."

"Of course I am. Look, I checked it with the game park authorities—I pretended to be scared. The animal control beacons make us perfectly safe. Nothing will come near us. But if we didn't have them, or if we turned them off, we'd be in trouble. You know what's out there, Lucy? Lions, leopards, rhinos"—he listened harder; he has seen pictures of the animals— "and jackals and hyenas and vultures. Make a loud noise when it's dark, or go running around outside at night, and there'd be nothing left in the morning to collect and take back. Why all the questions now? I thought we had it all agreed."

"I want to be sure it will work. If it doesn't, we'd have done a lot better with a straight sale. There's good money to be had for a healthy one, back in Delmarva Town."

"Not a hundredth as much as we'll get here. They'll pay, just to keep us quiet." He laughed, and there was again a gurgling sound of drinking from a bottle. "They'll pay. What sort of publicity would it give the game reserve if we wanted to play it for news? Left for a few moments—strayed away on his own—little boy lost, frantic mother ready for breakdown. That would be news."

"Shhh. Watch what you're saying. Could still be awake."

"So what? For Christ's sake, he's hardly three."

"He's very smart. He could be listening, and he remembers everything he hears."

"Naw, he's asleep." Another laugh. "Very smart, is he? How'd he ever get you for a mother?"

"My mistake, that's how." Her voice changed from slurred to bitter. "The biggest mistake of my life. Never again. And don't you pretend to be so smart. How did you get hooked into your idiot marriage contract, you and the bitch? Answer that, if we're asking questions."

"Aw, come on, Lucy. That's all over, so don't let's start it again. I don't even think about her any more. Look, once we get some money it'll just be you and me. We can forget the false starts. All right? It'll just be us."

There was a rustling noise, and a different sound from Mummy like a soft groan. Then the light from the little lamp went out, and all the light disappeared.

Now the light is disappearing again. Over beyond the grass he can see the big hill, still as far away as ever. It always seems to be the same distance, and when it gets dark he can see the smoke on top. It is there now, with the red sun behind it. He steps a little way in that direction, then comes back. The grass is too tall there, too frightening.

The sun seems to be sinking down into the warm ground, melting into it. All of a sudden he cannot see the long grass. The sky is black, with stars scattered bright across it.

"Mummy." He shouts as loud as he can into the swallowing dark, and begins to run in the direction where they went. Then he thinks of the lamp, left behind on the ground. He hurries back for it and turns it on. It throws a bright circle all around him, except behind his back. When he turns his head to look there, he sees a wedge of darkness, the shadow *cast by his body. He moves backward, and the darkness follows.*

The light circle has become the whole world. Out beyond its edge he begins to hear night noises. There are mutterings and growls in the darkness. He stares out, trying to see detail at the shadowy perimeter. ("... lions, leopards, rhinos ... jackals and hyenas and vultures." Uncle Darren's words echo back to him, terrifying now. "Make a loud noise when it's dark ... there'd be nothing left in the morning to collect and take back ...")

He shouldn't have shouted out into the dark. He mustn't shout. Where is Mummy?

He has begun to weep; slow, silent tears that trickle down his cheeks. He wants to scream for Mummy, but he knows he must not. Behind him he hears a slithering noise, and the soft rustle of moving grass ("... lions, leopards, rhinos ... jackals and hyenas and vultures"). He holds the lamp tightly and starts forward across the clearing. The edge of darkness follows. New noises begin in front.

He stops and crouches close to the ground. The lamp in his hand is beginning to weaken, the boundary of the safe circle to shrink. He bites hard on his fingers, and stares out into the night. He thinks he can see eyes appearing there, flashing glints of green and yellow. The lamp is almost done. The eyes stare in from all around. He pushes with his hands at the dark boundary, willing it to go back.

The fear runs all through him. He cannot stand it any longer. He drops to the ground, flattening his body and scrabbling at the hardened dirt. Far away on the horizon, the top of the big hill is glowing with its own smoky red light. He fixes his eyes on it, too afraid to look again at the narrowing circle.

"Mummy, Mummy, Mummy, Mummy." He says the incantation over and over, beneath his breath. "Mummy, Mummy, Mummy ..." She is the only

*thing he has left to hold onto in the whole world. But
he dare not call out to her, dare not even whimper.*

*He lies on the ground and shivers. He must not
cry. He will not cry. Mummy will come back soon
... she will come back ... she will come back ...*

*Esro Mondrian does not know it, but dawn and
rescue are more than ten hours away. The sale in the
basement warrens of the Gallimaufries will take place
a few days later.*

Chan was shivering, too. He knew that Tatty
was speaking to him, but he couldn't understand
her words. She came forward and gripped him by
the shoulders.

"Chan! What's wrong? You're crying."

"I can cry. I can." He took a deep breath and
shook his head. "I'll be all right."

"What happened to you?"

"Memories. Now I understand why Esro Mondrian found it impossible to trust anything in the
Universe. I know why he needed the Constructs so
badly."

She released his shoulders and went back to the
hassock. "I've known that for a long time. They
were supposed to be his protection—from everything that sat out on the Perimeter. That's why he
had them built."

"And instead, they led to his destruction."

"That's only fair." Tatty's voice was bitter. "He
was willing to destroy everybody else in the universe to keep them. It's only right that he would
destroy himself as well. Damn him."

"You hate him that much? I'm sorry."

She rubbed at her eyes with a too-thin hand. "I
have a right to hate him—every right. If *anyone*
has earned the right to hate Esro Mondrian, I
have."

Chan stood up. "I can't argue with you, Tatty.
And I guess that tells me all I need to know. I'll go
now."

She glared up at him, her brown eyes gleaming. "You mean you don't want anything from me?" She laughed harshly. "My God, that's a first. Nobody comes all the way down here to see me unless they want something. Nobody except poor old Kubo. He's the only friend I've got left. He comes and we take our Paradox shots, and we sit here grinning at each other." Her voice broke. "I think of us, and I think of what I was. I was a *Princess.* And then I think of what I've become—what Esro Mondrian *made* me . . ."

"I did want something from you. But I see I'm not going to get it." Chan put out his hand, and gently touched Tatty's untidy hair. "I'm sorry, Tatty. I'll come here again, and it will be just to see you." He stepped back. "I suppose Kubo already mentioned to you that Mondrian's body is still alive?"

She jerked as though hot wires had been run through her breast. "Alive? What are you talking about—he's *dead.*"

"Yes—but also no. Wait here, Tatty. I'm going to show you something." Before she could protest, he was out through the door and into the corridor. He returned a few minutes later pushing the wheeled trolley in front of him. He brought it to where Tatty was still sitting wide-eyed on the hassock, then went back and closed inner and outer doors. Finally he returned to take Tatty by her thin shoulders and lift her to her feet.

"Look," he said quietly.

She stared for a long time. "That is not Esro Mondrian," she said at last.

The body on the trolley looked tiny and shrunken, lying on its back with eyes closed. The face was calm and unlined, a blank tablet. Every line of concentration and resolve was gone, smoothed away to nothing.

"Look again, Tatty," said Chan. "It is Mondrian. He's sleeping now."

She stared, and shivered. Her teeth began to chatter together, and she groaned. "Please." She turned away from the trolley. "Please, take him away, I can't stand—"

She ran for the bathroom and slammed the door. Chan heard the sound of violent retching, then running water. He sat down on the hassock, staring at Mondrian's unmoving body. After a few minutes Tatty came out and stood in the bathroom doorway.

"What did they—what did you *do* to him? It *was* you, wasn't it?"

"I suppose it was. I had to do it. He would have destroyed the ship, or kept everyone there until we all died. We had to find the information to prevent that. He wouldn't allow it. I had to reach in, way down, and erase whatever was blocking the group mind access. It went a long way back, all the way to the time when he was a little child. Everything from that time forward has gone. Wiped out." He nodded down towards the body in front of them. "I don't know if this is Esro Mondrian or not. That's a three-year-old child, with a three-year-old's brain and memories. But maybe the intellect—"

"No!" She screamed at him, and reached out her hands like claws. "I know why you came here. I know what you're trying to do."

"I only wanted to—"

"Don't lie to me. You're a monster—worse than Esro Mondrian. You think that I could endure that *again*. It was as bad for me as it was for you— think about that, Chan Dalton. Think about it, and get him out of here. Take him away!"

Chan sighed. "Wait a moment. Let me open the doors again, and we'll go."

He went slowly to open both doors, and came dejectedly back to the living-room. Tatty was still standing, hunched over the sleeping body. She did not look up.

"What are you going to do next?" she asked. "Are you going back to Ceres?"

"Ceres, then farther out. Leah and I have to go back to Travancore. We have a Morgan Construct there, still held in stasis. We have to go in with Nimrod and Bahram and try to make it sane."

"Nimrod and Bahram—they're the super-beings?"

"Don't call them that. They're surprisingly unsuper when it comes to difficult actions."

She nodded her head down at the body on the trolley. "And— this?"

"I don't know. Take him back up, I suppose."

"Can you wait for a few minutes? I'm overdue for a trip to the surface myself. I'll help you to move him."

She retreated to the bathroom. Chan was left alone, wondering what was happening to Leah and the others. He was itching to be back up there with them.

Tatty was gone for a long time. When she returned her hair was washed and brushed until it shone, she was wearing a clean white dress, and carefully-applied makeup hid the Paradox stigmata and the dark rings around her eyes. She was raddled and pathetically emaciated; but her back was straight.

Chan began to offer a compliment. The words stuck in his throat. "Come on, Tatty," he said at last. "You need to put on some weight. Let's go, and I'll buy you dinner on the upper levels."

She shook her head. "I changed my mind. I'm not going. When will you be leaving Earth?"

"The sooner, the better. But not for a couple of days. I have to visit Skrynol. She promised to show me Mondrian's 'humanity expansion plans,' and I have to tell her exactly what happened to him. They had a strong mental bond, and I know she'll be very upset. It will take me quite a while."

"Could you do that today, before you go up to the surface?" Tatty sat down again by the trolley. "I'd like you to leave him here with me overnight, and come back in the morning."

Chan started to speak, changed his mind, nodded, and turned to go. At the inner door he paused. "Tatty, I don't want to mislead you. It couldn't be here, you know. It would have to be on Horus, with the Stimulator. There would be no Paradox supplies, and it would be—"

"I know." She was looking at him and through him, with the glowing brown eyes that he remembered from the time when he was a small and tormented child-mind, dreading the daily horror of the Stimulator.

"And it will be no easier than last time." He had to say it all. "Kubo says it may be *worse* for the person who works the Stimulator."

"Kubo doesn't know about torture. But *we* know torture, don't we, Chan? You and I, we know it well. We can count the ways." Tatty's face was like a death mask. "No more talk. Come back tomorrow. I'll tell you my decision."

Chan nodded. He gently pushed the door almost closed, then looked back into the room. Tatty had ignored his departure. She stood by the trolley, where Mondrian was stirring in his sleep. Perhaps he was dreaming, for there was the hint of a smile on his face.

And perhaps Tatty was smiling, too. She hovered over Esro Mondrian, waiting the re-awakening.

| ISBN # | Title # Author | Publ. List Price |
|--------|----------------|------------------|
| 55979-6 | ACT OF GOD, Kotani and Roberts | 2.95 |
| 55945-1 | ACTIVE MEASURES, David Drake & Janet Morris | 3.95 |
| 55970-2 | THE ADOLESCENCE OF P-1, Thomas J. Ryan | 2.95 |
| 55998-2 | AFTER THE FLAMES, Silverberg & Spinrad | 2.95 |
| 55967-2 | AFTER WAR, Janet Morris | 2.95 |
| 55934-6 | ALIEN STARS, C.J. Cherryh, Joe Haldeman & Timothy Zahn, edited by Elizabeth Mitchell | 2.95 |
| 55978-8 | AT ANY PRICE, David Drake | 3.50 |
| 65565-5 | THE BABYLON GATE, Edward A. Byers | 2.95 |
| 65586-8 | THE BEST OF ROBERT SILVERBERG, Robert Silverberg | 2.95 |
| 55977-X | BETWEEN THE STROKES OF NIGHT, Charles Sheffield | 3.50 |
| 55984-2 | BEYOND THE VEIL, Janet Morris | 15.95 |
| 65544-2 | BEYOND WIZARDWALL, Janet Morris | 15.95 |
| 55973-7 | BORROWED TIME, Alan Hruska | 2.95 |
| 65563-9 | A CHOICE OF DESTINIES, Melissa Scott | 2.95 |
| 55960-5 | COBRA, Timothy Zahn | 2.95 |
| 65551-5 | COBRA STRIKE!, Timothy Zahn | 3.50 |
| 65578-7 | A COMING OF AGE, Timothy Zahn | 3.50 |
| 55969-9 | THE CONTINENT OF LIES, James Morrow | 2.95 |
| 55917-6 | CUGEL'S SAGA, Jack Vance | 3.50 |
| 65552-3 | DEATHWISH WORLD, Reynolds and Ing | 3.50 |
| 55995-8 | THE DEVIL'S GAME, Poul Anderson | 2.95 |
| 55974-5 | DIASPORAH, W. R. Yates | 2.95 |
| 65581-7 | DINOSAUR BEACH, Keith Laumer | 2.95 |
| 65579-5 | THE DOOMSDAY EFFECT, Thomas Wren | 2.95 |
| 65557-4 | THE DREAM PALACE, Brynne Stephens | 2.95 |
| 65564-7 | THE DYING EARTH, Jack Vance | 2.95 |
| 55988-5 | FANGLITH, John Dalmas | 2.95 |
| 55947-8 | THE FALL OF WINTER, Jack C. Haldeman II | 2.95 |
| 55975-3 | FAR FRONTIERS, Volume III | 2.95 |
| 65548-5 | FAR FRONTIERS, Volume IV | 2.95 |
| 65572-8 | FAR FRONTIERS, Volume V | 2.95 |
| 55900-1 | FIRE TIME, Poul Anderson | 2.95 |
| 65567-1 | THE FIRST FAMILY, Patrick Tilley | 3.50 |
| 55952-4 | FIVE-TWELFTHS OF HEAVEN, Melissa Scott | 2.95 |
| 55937-0 | FLIGHT OF THE DRAGONFLY, Robert L. Forward | 3.50 |
| 55986-9 | THE FORTY-MINUTE WAR, Janet Morris | 3.50 |
| 55971-0 | FORWARD, Gordon R. Dickson | 2.95 |
| 65550-7 | THE FRANKENSTEIN PAPERS, Fred Saberhagen | 3.50 |
| 55899-4 | FRONTERA, Lewis Shiner | 2.95 |
| 55918-4 | THE GAME BEYOND, Melissa Scott | 2.95 |
| 55959-1 | THE GAME OF EMPIRE, Poul Anderson | 3.50 |
| 65561-2 | THE GATES OF HELL, Janet Morris | 14.95 |
| 65566-3 | GLADIATOR-AT-LAW, Pohl and Kornbluth | 2.95 |
| 55904-4 | THE GOLDEN PEOPLE, Fred Saberhagen | 3.50 |
| 65555-8 | HEROES IN HELL, Janet Morris | 3.50 |
| 65571-X | HIGH JUSTICE, Jerry Pournelle | 2.95 |

| ISBN # | Title # Author | Publ. List Price |
|---|---|---|
| 55930-3 | HOTHOUSE, Brian Aldiss | 2.95 |
| 55905-2 | HOUR OF THE HORDE, Gordon R. Dickson | 2.95 |
| 65547-7 | THE IDENTITY MATRIX, Jack Chalker | 2.95 |
| 65569-8 | I, MARTHA ADAMS, Pauline Glen Winslow | 3.95 |
| 55994-X | INVADERS, Gordon R. Dickson | 2.95 |
| 55993-1 | IN THE FACE OF MY ENEMY, Joe Delaney | 2.95 |
| 65570-1 | JOE MAUSER, MERCENARY, Reynolds and Banks | 2.95 |
| 55931-1 | KILLER, David Drake & Karl Edward Wagner | 2.95 |
| 55996-6 | KILLER STATION, Martin Caidin | 3.50 |
| 65559-0 | THE LAST DREAM, Gordon R. Dickson | 2.95 |
| 55981-8 | THE LIFESHIP, Dickson and Harrison | 2.95 |
| 55980-X | THE LONG FORGETTING, Edward A. Byers | 2.95 |
| 55992-3 | THE LONG MYND, Edward Hughes | 2.95 |
| 55997-4 | MASTER OF SPACE AND TIME, Rudy Rucker | 2.95 |
| 65573-6 | MEDUSA, Janet and Chris Morris | 3.50 |
| 65562-0 | THE MESSIAH STONE, Martin Caidin | 3.95 |
| 65580-9 | MINDSPAN, Gordon R. Dickson | 2.95 |
| 65553-1 | THE ODYSSEUS SOLUTION, Banks and Lambe | 2.95 |
| 55926-5 | THE OTHER TIME, Mack Reynolds with Dean Ing | 2.95 |
| 55965-6 | THE PEACE WAR, Vernor Vinge | 3.50 |
| 55982-6 | PLAGUE OF DEMONS, Keith Laumer | 2.75 |
| 55966-4 | A PRINCESS OF CHAMELN, Cherry Wilder | 2.95 |
| 65568-X | RANKS OF BRONZE, David Drake | 3.50 |
| 65577-9 | REBELS IN HELL, Janet Morris, et. al. | 3.50 |
| 55990-7 | RETIEF OF THE CDT, Keith Laumer | 2.95 |
| 65556-6 | RETIEF AND THE PANGALACTIC PAGEANT OF PULCHRITUDE, Keith Laumer | 2.95 |
| 65575-2 | RETIEF AND THE WARLORDS, Keith Laumer | 2.95 |
| 55902-8 | THE RETURN OF RETIEF, Keith Laumer | 2.95 |
| 55991-5 | RHIALTO THE MARVELLOUS, Jack Vance | 3.50 |
| 65545-0 | ROGUE BOLO, Keith Laumer | 2.95 |
| 65554-X | SANDKINGS, George R.R. Martin | 2.95 |
| 65546-9 | SATURNALIA, Grant Callin | 2.95 |
| 55989-3 | SEARCH THE SKY, Pohl and Kornbluth | 2.95 |
| 55914-1 | SEVEN CONQUESTS, Poul Anderson | 2.95 |
| 65574-4 | SHARDS OF HONOR, Lois McMaster Bujold | 2.95 |
| 55951-6 | THE SHATTERED WORLD, Michael Reaves | 3.50 |
| | THE SILISTRA SERIES | |
| 55915-X | RETURNING CREATION, Janet Morris | 2.95 |
| 55919-2 | THE GOLDEN SWORD, Janet Morris | 2.95 |
| 55932-X | WIND FROM THE ABYSS, Janet Morris | 2.95 |
| 55936-2 | THE CARNELIAN THRONE, Janet Morris | 2.95 |
| 65549-3 | THE SINFUL ONES, Fritz Leiber | 2.95 |
| 65558-2 | THE STARCHILD TRILOGY, Pohl and Williamson | 3.95 |
| 55999-0 | STARSWARM, Brian Aldiss | 2.95 |
| 55927-3 | SURVIVAL!, Gordon R. Dickson | 2.75 |
| 55938-9 | THE TORCH OF HONOR, Roger Macbride Allen | 2.95 |

## SCIENCE FICTION AND FANTASY (continued)

| ISBN # | Title # Author | Publ. List Price |
|---|---|---|
| 55942-7 | TROJAN ORBIT, Mack Reynolds with Dean Ing | 2.95 |
| 55985-0 | TUF VOYAGING, George R.R. Martin | 15.95 |
| 55916-8 | VALENTINA, Joseph H. Delaney & Marc Steigler | 3.50 |
| 55898-6 | WEB OF DARKENSS, Marion Zimmer Bradley | 3.50 |
| 55925-7 | WITH MERCY TOWARD NONE, Glen Cook | 2.95 |
| 65576-0 | WOLFBANE, Pohl and Kornbluth | 2.95 |
| 55962-1 | WOLFLING, Gordon R. Dickson | 2.95 |
| 55987-7 | YORATH THE WOLF, Cherry Wilder | 2.95 |
| 55906-0 | THE ZANZIBAR CAT, Joanna Russ | 3.50 |

## COMPUTER BOOKS AND GENERAL INTEREST NONFICTION

| ISBN # | Title # Author | Publ. List Price |
|---|---|---|
| 55968-0 | ADVENTURES IN MICROLAND, Jerry Pournelle | 9.95 |
| 55933-8 | AI: HOW MACHINES THINK, F. David Peat | 8.95 |
| 55922-2 | THE ESSENTIAL USER'S GUIDE TO THE IBM PC, XT, AND PCjr., Dian Girard | 6.95 |
| 55940-0 | EUREKA FOR THE IBM PC AND PCjr, Tim Knight | 7.95 |
| 55941-9 | THE FUTURE OF FLIGHT, Leik Myrabo with Dean Ing | 7.95 |
| 55955-9 | THE GUIDEBOOK FOR WINNING ADVENTURERS, David & Sandy Small | 8.95 |
| 55923-0 | MUTUAL ASSURED SURVIVAL, Jerry Pournelle and Dean Ing | 6.95 |
| 55929-X | PROGRAMMING LANGUAGES: FEATURING THE IBM PC, Marc Stiegler & Bob Hansen | 9.95 |
| 55963-X | THE SERIOUS ASSEMBLER, Charles Crayne & Dian Girard Crayne | 8.95 |
| 55907-9 | THE SMALL BUSINESS COMPUTER TODAY AND TOMORROW, William E. Grieb, Jr. | 6.95 |
| 55921-4 | THE USER'S GUIDE TO CP/M SYSTEMS, Tony Bove & Cheryl Rhodes | 8.95 |
| 55948-6 | THE USER'S GUIDE TO FREE SOFTWARE, Tony Bove & Cheryl Rhodes | 9.95 |
| 55908-7 | THE USER'S GUIDE TO SMALL COMPUTERS, Jerry Pournelle | 9.95 |

*Here is an excerpt from* Between the Strokes of Night *by Charles Sheffield, coming in July 1985 from Baen Books:*

## Pentecost—A.D. 27698

The last shivering swimmer had emerged from the underground river, and now it would be possible to assemble the final results. Peron Turco pulled the warm cape closer about his shoulders and looked back and forth along the line.

There they stood. Four months of preliminary selection had winnowed them down to a bare hundred, from the many thousands who had entered the original trials. And in the next twenty minutes it would be reduced again, to a jubilant twenty-five.

Everyone was muddied, grimy, and bone-weary. The final trial had been murderous, pushing minds and bodies to the limit. The four-mile underwater swim in total darkness, fighting chilling currents through a labyrinth of connecting caves, had been physically demanding. But the mental pressure, knowing that the oxygen supply would last only for five hours, had been much worse. Most of the contestants were slumped now on the stone flags, warming themselves in the bright sunlight, rubbing sore muscles and sipping sugar drinks. It would be a little while before the scores could be tallied, but already their attention was turning from the noisy crowds to the huge display that formed one outer wall in the coliseum.

Peron shielded his eyes against Cassay's morning brilliance and studied each face in turn along the long line. By now he knew where the real competition lay, and from their expressions he sought to gauge his own chances. Lum was at the far end, squatting cross-legged. He was eating fruit, but he looked bored and sweaty.

Ten days ago Peron had met him and dismissed Lum as soft and overweight, a crudely-built and oafish youth who had reached the final hundred contestants by a freakish accident. Now he knew better. Peron had revised his assessment three times, each one upwards. Now he felt sure that Lum would be somewhere high in the final twenty-five.

And so would the girl Elissa, three positions to the left. Peron had marked her early as formidable competition. She had started ten minutes ahead of him in the first trial, when they made the night journey through the middle of Villasylvia, the most difficult and dangerous forest on the surface of Pentecost.

Now Elissa turned to look at him while he was still staring along the line at her. She grinned, and he quickly averted his eyes. If Elissa didn't finish among the winners that would be bad news for Peron, too, because he was convinced that wherever they placed she would rank somewhere above him.

He looked back at the board. The markers were going up on the great display, showing the names of the remaining contestants. Peron counted them as they were posted. Only seventy-two. The last round of trials had been fiercely difficult, enough to eliminate over a quarter of the finalists completely.

Peron wished he could feel more confidence. He was sure (wasn't he?) that he was in the top thirty. He *hoped* he was in the top twenty, and in his dreams he saw himself as high as fourth or fifth. But with contestants drawn from the whole planet, and the competition of such high caliber . . .

The crowd roared. At last! The scores were finally appearing. The displays were assembled slowly and painstakingly. The judges conferred in great secrecy, knowing that the results would be propagated instantly over the entire planet, and that a mistake would ruin their reputations. Everything was checked and rechecked before it went onto the board.

Peron had watched recordings of recent Planetfests, over and over, but this one was different and more elaborate. Trials were held every four years. Usually the prizes were high positions in the government of Pentecost, and maybe a chance to see the Fifty Worlds. But the twenty-year games, like this one, had a whole new level of significance. There were still the usual prizes, certainly. But they were not the real reward. There was that rumored bigger prize: a possible opportunity to meet and work with the Immortals.

And what did *that* mean? No one could say. No one Peron knew had ever seen one, ever met one. They were the ultimate mystery figures, the ones who lived forever, the ones who came back every generation to bring knowledge from the stars. Stars that they were said to reach in a few days—in conflict with everything that the scientists of Pentecost believed about the laws of the Universe.

Peron was still musing on that when the roar of the crowd, separated from the contestants by a substantial barricade of rows of armed guards, brought him to full attention. The first winner, in twenty-fifth place, had just been announced. It was a girl, Rosanne. Peron remembered her from the Long Walk across Talimantor Desert, when the two of them had formed a temporary alliance to search for underground water. She was a cheerful tireless girl, just over the minimum age limit of sixteen, and now she was holding her hand to her chest, pretending to stagger and faint with relief because she had just made the cutoff.

All the other contestants now looked at the board with a new intensity. The method of announcement was well established by custom, but there was not a trial participant who did not wish it could be done differently. From the crowd's point of view, it was very satisfying to announce the winners in ascending order, so that the name of the final top contestant was given last of all. But during the trials, every competitor formed a rough idea of his or her chances by direct comparison with the opposition. It was easy to be wrong by five places, but errors larger than that were unlikely. Deep inside, a competitor knew if he was down in ninetieth place. Even so, hope always remained. But as the names gradually were announced, and twenty-fourth, twenty-third, and twenty-second position was taken, most contestants were filled with an increasing gloom, panic, or wild surmise. Could they possibly have placed so high? Or, more likely, were they already eliminated?

## For Science Fiction with Science In It, and Fantasy That Touches The Heart of The Human Soul . . .

Baen Books bring you Poul Anderson, Marion Zimmer Bradley, C.J. Cherryh, Gordon R. Dickson, David Drake, Robert L. Forward, Janet Morris, Jerry Pournelle, Fred Saberhagen, Michael Reaves, Jack Vance . . . all top names in science fiction and fantasy, plus new writers destined to reach the top of their fields. For a free catalog of all Baen Books, send three 22-cent stamps, plus your name and address, to

*Baen Books*
*260 Fifth Avenue, Suite 3S*
*New York, N.Y. 10001*